D1826574

Protecting *Paige*

SERVE AND PROTECT 3

NORAH WILSON

Protecting Paige

Copyright © 2010 Norah Wilson

Published by Norah Wilson

Cover by Kim Killion, Hot Damn Designs

Book design by Michael Hale, Hale Author Services

ISBN: 978-0-9878037-4-0

Protecting
Paige

Prologue

DEREK WEAVER RAN A hand across his shaved head as he waited for the weekly call. His hand came away wet.

His eyes darted to the clock on the wall of his Union Street apartment — the nicest address he'd managed since being released from prison two years ago — then back to the silent satellite phone lying on the coffee table. He wished he could spark up another doobie, but the Big Guy would hear it in his voice. Bastard knew everything.

Cursing, he wiped away a fresh sheen of sweat before it could trickle down his face.

The phone rang. He lunged for it.

"Hello."

"Good evening, Mr. Weaver. I trust you have a promising report for me?"

The Big Guy was always polite. Formal, even. But Derek was no fool. He'd never met his boss, but he recognized the ruthlessness which underlay those soft, foreign-accented tones.

Derek closed his eyes. "I lost him."

A chilling pause.

"I think perhaps you'd better explain."

"He won't do it."

"Ah, but that's where you are wrong, my young friend."

"But he's a straight arrow, sir. I'm not making a lotta headway with the usual tools." Again, Derek cursed his luck. Trust him to run up against the only 18-year-old in the western world who wasn't eager to be seduced with mega-doses of sex, drugs and rock-n-roll.

"Of course he's of sterling character. If just anyone could do the job, I'd simply have you do it."

1

"But I can't cross the border. Even if I could hide my convictions, they'd take one look at me and tear my car apart —"

"Precisely. Which is why you'll have to bring our young man around to our way of thinking."

"But I tole you, he ain't having no part of it."

"Then you'll just have to adopt new tactics, won't you?"

"New tactics?" Distaste, the kind he'd thought he was long past feeling, rose in his throat like bile. "What kind of tactics?"

"Why, whatever tactics are required, of course. We have just three weeks left and no time to recruit a new candidate of such impeccable quality. There must be no — how do you say? — foul-ups. Are we clear, Mr. Weaver?"

Derek dug the fingers of his free hand into his knee. Hard. "Perfectly, sir."

The line went dead. Derek closed the phone and hurled it to the other end of the sofa. Goddamn raghead! Piece-of-shit camel-jockey. By the time he exhausted his considerable lexicon of derogatory insults, his rage had passed and fear seeped in to take its place.

Shit. How'd he get himself into this mess?

He should run, dammit, and to hell with the mysterious boss he'd never laid eyes on.

But what would he do if he gave up this gig? All he knew was crime, and with his record, if he made one more appearance before Her Majesty, the judge would lock him up for a good long stretch. And Derek had good reason to want to avoid prison. Several of them, in fact. He'd gotten on the bus, sold out some cell-mates to shorten and sweeten his own stint. If he got sent up again, he just might find himself bunking down with a roommate who'd stick him with the sharpened point of a toothbrush first chance he got.

No, he couldn't give this job up. It was his ticket out of here. All he had to do was stick to it long enough to see the big payday, then he could clear the hell out of town. Get right out of the country.

But how was he going to secure the kid's cooperation?

He reached for the fattest of the joints lined up like little soldiers on the table's glass surface. The answer would come to him. And if it didn't, at least he'd be too stoned to be as scared as he knew he should be.

Chapter 1

CONSTABLE TOMMY GODSOE'S BLOOD sang.

His breath rasped harshly in his ears as he pelted along the concrete sidewalk, but he wasn't winded. Not yet. Not even close. Max, the four-year-old Belgian Malinois straining at the business end of the thirty-foot lead, lent Tommy extra speed. Even now, backup was falling further and further behind, but Tommy couldn't check Max's momentum or the dog would think he was being corrected.

Suddenly, at the mouth of an alleyway, Max slowed. Without conscious thought, Tommy took up the slack in the lead even as he studied the dog nosing the asphalt. The dog wheeled in a tight semi-circle, then turned away from the alley and shot off again down the sidewalk. Tommy fixed the location in his mind. Max had eliminated the alleyway as a direction of travel. Always had to remember the last negative sign. If they lost the trail further on up ahead, they could come back to this spot, so Max could pick up the scent again.

At the next alleyway, Max did the same check, but this time he bounded off down the narrow passageway. Tommy raced after him, his heart rate kicking up another notch.

Fence!

Max cleared it in one leap, and Tommy vaulted over it right behind him. Over the sound of his own breathing, he heard backup in the mouth of the alley now. Good. No need to radio his location. He could save his breath for —

Ding-*dong*.

What the hell?

Tommy jerked awake, struggling up into a sitting position. The sheets, cool with sweat, pooled in his lap, and his heart pounded against his ribs as though he'd run a marathon.

Ah, Jesus wept. A dream. It was just a dream. He wasn't a cop anymore. He wasn't a dog handler. Bitterness, familiar as the pain in his hip, curdled his stomach.

A light tapping at his door.

"All right, all right, keep your shirt on."

Throwing off the sheet, he swung his legs gingerly over the edge of the bed. He thought about scooping up the blue sweat pants from the floor and hauling them on over his boxers, but another peal of the doorbell dissuaded him. Grabbing his cane, he lurched to his feet and hobbled toward the living room, grimacing with every step.

Ding-*dong*.

Cripes, that's what his doorbell sounded like? Something from a '50s Avon commercial? He'd lived here four years and couldn't remember ever hearing his own doorbell. No doubt the 'Beware of Dog' sign had something to do with that. He and Max never stayed indoors when they could be outside, and they sure as hell never waited around for life to come to them.

Until now.

The doorbell sounded again, and he wished he still had his service weapon. He'd happily put a round into that little speaker by the front door.

Reaching the door at last, he tore it open. *"What?"*

❧

Paige Harmer took an instinctive step backward.

When she'd moved into this duplex last month, the other side had been vacant. The landlady'd said its occupant was in hospital recovering from surgery. But even after her neighbor had come home nearly two weeks ago, the unit next door had been unnaturally quiet. No visitors came or went, and no music thrummed through those walls. If it weren't for the small bag of garbage that materialized at the curb beside hers every Tuesday morning, and the occasional muted sound of a television deep in the night, she'd have sworn the other apartment was deserted. Now, her neighbor stood framed in the doorway, wearing a pair of white boxers and a thunderous expression.

And oh, Christmas, he was most gorgeous thing she'd clapped eyes on in years, outside of a Calvin Klein ad.

Despite their current storminess, his eyes were blue as the July sky. Black hair, a startling contrast to his pale complexion, stood up in all directions, all the sexier for its dishevelment. Thick, black eyebrows slanted over those killer eyes. More dark hair crowned his chest in a liberal thatch, tapering to a thin line that arrowed out of sight beneath his boxers.

Runner, she thought. *Endurance athlete.* Just a hair over average height, with a leanness that shaded toward too thin. Yet the conformation of arms and chest disclosed enough wiry muscle to give the impression of power.

"Can I help you?"

Mister, if you can't, there's no help for me.

The thought barely had a chance to form before her internal censor roared to life. He was way too young for her to be ogling, for goodness sake. *Hardly much older than Dillon, by the look of him.*

There, that did it. Though he was clearly nowhere near as young as her son, the mental association was enough to clamp a firm leash on her imagination.

Unfortunately, the extra seconds it took to channel her thoughts in more pure directions didn't go unnoticed. One thick eyebrow arched inquiringly, reminding her she hadn't yet stated her purpose.

She felt a flush begin to climb her neck. No chance he'd miss that, either. Her skin was almost translucent, at least the stuff between the freckles. She lifted the foil-wrapped plate she held. "I thought you might like some dinner."

He looked at the plate. "Thanks, but I'm not a big eater."

"I can see that," she said, injecting her tone with the same censorious note she might use with her son when he ignored his body's nutritional needs. He shifted, and she finally noticed the cane, which he appeared to be leaning on pretty heavily. "Don't worry. It'll freeze nicely if you can't handle it all right now."

"Look, lady, that's real nice of you, but —"

"I'll just put it in the refrigerator for you, shall I?"

She angled sideways and slipped right past him before he could finish brushing her off. No way was she going back to her lonely unit to worry about Dillon. Not tonight.

"That way, I presume?" She indicated the direction the kitchen must be, if the place were laid out in the mirror image of hers.

"Uh … yeah."

Seconds later, Paige stood in front of a white dinosaur of a refrigerator, a twin to the one that rattled and hummed in her own kitchen, right beside the commercial refrigeration unit she'd installed for her business. That's where the similarity ended, she discovered, as she opened the refrigerator's door.

Five bottles of beer, domestic. Some Chinese takeout cartons that bulged ominously as though approaching an explosive state. A drying chunk of cheddar cheese, circa 2008. A few bottles of condiments. No eggs, no dairy, no vegetables, no fruit.

Hearing him arrive at the kitchen door — the thumping of the cane on the linoleum-covered floor announced his progress — she glanced over at him.

"Is this the part where you tell me you're really one of the undead and have no need of sustenance beyond human blood?"

He didn't smile. If anything, he scowled more fiercely. "I've been meaning to get to the grocery store."

"It must be hard."

He followed the drift of her gaze. She could tell by the way his hand tightened on the cane's handle.

His jaw hardened even further, if possible. "I manage."

"Are you hungry? The food's still hot." She waggled the foil-wrapped plate temptingly. "Stuffed pork chops with mashed pota-toes, glazed carrots and gingered parsnips."

"It's okay," he said, after a split-second hesitation. "You can just put it in the fridge."

Fat chance. She'd caught the fleeting look of indecision in his eye as she'd described what was under the foil. He was hungry, all right. "Aw, come on, sit down and eat. I need the distraction."

Those cigar-thick eyebrows soared. "You want to stay and watch me *eat*?"

"Relax, fella. Nothing kinky. I just don't want to go back over there yet. I've done two loads of laundry, vacuumed the carpet within an inch of its life, baked three cheese cakes and seven pies. I have nowhere to put any more baking and nothing left to clean. So if I go home now, I've got nothing left to do but worry about Dillon."

"Who's Dillon?"

Ah! A question. And she hadn't even dragged it out of him. That was an improvement. "My son."

"Where is he?"

She blew out her breath, lifting a strand of auburn hair off her face. "If I knew that, I wouldn't be worried, would I? Or maybe I would, at that," she amended, thinking about the hard-looking young man Dillon had been hanging with lately.

"He's missing?"

The sharpness of his tone drew her glance to his face. His eyebrows were drawn together again in a frown.

She shrugged. "He's seventeen, almost eighteen. I can hardly describe him as missing every time he slams out of the house in a foul mood."

That surprised him. She could see him doing the mental arithmetic, calculating her minimum age. *That's right, son. Old enough to be your mother, even if I don't look it.*

Okay, that was an exaggeration. A huge exaggeration. But older than him by quite a few years, she'd wager.

"Sit." She pulled a tea towel off the oven door handle where it had been hung to dry after its last use and flopped it on the table as an impromptu place mat, then plunked the plate down on it. "I nuked the ceramic plate before dishing up the food so it would stay nice and warm."

"I don't even know your name."

Way to go, Paige. Barge in and take over the man's life without an introduction.

"Sorry." She wiped her right hand on her jeans and extended it. "Paige Harmer. Your new neighbor."

She regretted her gesture immediately, as he had to lurch forward to grasp her hand. He didn't grimace, but she could feel the tension in his grip. Pain.

"Tom Godsoe."

"I know." At his enquiring look, she hastened to add, "Mrs. Graham mentioned your name."

Paige had been impressed at how close-mouthed her landlady had been about her tenant's private life. As a prospective new tenant, all Paige had needed to know was that her neighbor wasn't a creepazoid. She'd found her landlady's discretion commendable at the time, but now she couldn't help but wish the other woman had been a little less discreet. For instance, what did Tom Godsoe do for a living? How had he sustained the injury that made crossing a room the grueling ordeal it appeared to be?

"Okay," he said at last, "if I'm going to have an audience, I think I'd better get dressed."

Not on my account.

Before something like that escaped her mouth, she averted her eyes from those square shoulders and lightly-muscled expanse of chest. "Take your time. I think I spotted some coffee beans and a grinder. I'll just brew us a pot of java."

"Be my guest," he drawled, then turned and thumped away.

A smile tugging at her lips, Paige reached for the gourmet coffee beans.

⁂

A film of perspiration slicked Tommy's brow before he'd made it halfway to his bedroom. Damned useless leg. He paused by the couch and leaned on the back of the hulking piece of furniture for a few seconds. Gritting his teeth against the white-hot shards of pain he knew would explode in his hip and lower back with each step, he resumed the trek to the bedroom.

Why hadn't he given that crazy, wild-haired woman the boot? He wasn't *that* hungry. He still had waffles in the freezer, and dry Fruit Loops were a perfectly adequate source of nutrition.

Yeah, right. The hospital food he'd subsisted on for so long was better than anything he had left in the cupboards. A pork chop and actual vegetables sounded like heaven. He only hoped the price of dinner wouldn't be too high. She had the look of a hard customer to move along, if she wasn't of a mind to go.

Of course, she'd never experienced Tommy's post-injury brand of hospitality. He'd managed to chase off friends and fellow officers — no, make that ex-fellow officers — even before he'd checked out early from the rehab center. Getting rid of one slip of a woman shouldn't be too hard.

When he reached his bedroom, he sank down on the edge of the bed and cursed his trembling leg. Weak as a damn baby. It took another few minutes to drag the sweat pants on. By the time he'd located a t-shirt and pulled it over his head, his whole body was slicked with sweat. Pitiful. Completely done in by a twenty-foot walk.

He grabbed the pill bottle off the night stand, dumped two tablets into his palm and dry-swallowed them. His hip was gonna kill him tonight, for all this activity. Already, he pictured himself lying on the mattress in the dead of night, going quietly crazy while the pain radiated down to the soles of his feet.

Kitchen, he reminded himself. If he was going to sell his soul, or at least his privacy, for a home-cooked meal, he'd better get there before the food fossilized on the plate.

By the time he made it back to the kitchen, the crazy woman — Paige? — not only had a pot of coffee brewed, but she'd cleaned out his refrigerator as evidenced by the armload of inedible stuff she was dumping in the garbage can when he hobbled in.

She glanced up at him. "I hope you weren't too attached to any of that stuff."

"You cleaned my refrigerator?"

She grinned. "Couple more days, that stuff would have walked off on its own, anyway."

As he lowered himself onto a chair, a laborious proposition in itself, she washed her hands under the tap and dried them on a clean towel she must have found in a drawer. Then she zoomed in on him again, removed the foil covering from his meal and rotated the plate so the meat was within easy reach. The delicious aroma that rose up from the hot meal was almost enough to take the edge off his irritation at her hovering solicitousness.

Almost.

"I swear to God, if you pick up those utensils to cut my meat for me, I won't be responsible for my actions."

She started at his tone, and although she didn't evacuate the physical space she occupied by his left shoulder, he felt her take a mental step backward. And she looked at him, really looked, which she'd managed not to do since she'd inventoried him in the doorway earlier. He met her gaze, keeping his expression flat. Best way to discourage sympathy, he'd found.

"I'm sorry," she said.

He picked up his fork. "If I detect the merest whiff of pity from you, you'll be taking that coffee to go, good deeds notwithstanding. Understood?"

"Pity?"

She blinked at him in what appeared to be genuine disbelief. Her eyes were green, he noticed. Not the improbable green of those tinted contacts women wore, but a soft, mossy green.

"Mr. Godsoe, I assure you it hadn't occurred to me to pity you. It was just the mother in me coming out."

He stabbed a parsnip. "I don't need a mother."

"That's going around, I guess. Neither does Dillon."

She turned away to grab a mug, but not before he caught a glimpse of the worry lines creasing her forehead.

He went back to eating as she fixed her coffee. By the time she plunked down opposite him at the small pedestal table, her brow was smooth once more. He'd also devoured half the pork chop.

"This is wonderful," he said around his food. "Where'd you learn to cook like this?"

"My fourth and final foster home. I finally figured out you had to bring value-added if you wanted to stay put."

His question had been rhetorical; he certainly hadn't expected an answer, let alone one like that. With her wide, inviting face, freckled complexion and burnished hair, she looked like apple pie and picket fences, not the product of an underfunded and overburdened child protection system.

Dammit. It was no concern of his who she was and where she came from. He had more than enough of his own problems to worry about. Instead of uttering one of the half-dozen questions that sprang to mind, he nodded and went back to his meal.

"Actually, I make my living cooking," she said. "Desserts, specifically, for some of the nicer restaurants around town. Cheesecakes, pies, flans, tarts, you name it. Speaking of which, would you like a piece of lemon meringue pie? I could run home and get you one."

Homemade lemon pie sounded great, but he wouldn't send her out for it. "No, this is good."

"Coffee?"

He felt her gaze on him as he used the last morsel of meat to mop up any lingering traces of juice from his plate.

"Please." God, it felt good to have a hot meal inside him. He could almost forget the insistent throb of pain that was his constant companion.

Once again, *almost.*

She put a mug of steaming black coffee before him, along with a half-pint of cream and the bowl of lumpy sugar she must have found in his cupboard.

He shot her a look. "Where'd the cream come from?"

"I ran home and got it while you were changing. Eggs, too, and whole-wheat bread. Some dry cereal. A couple of bananas. Wish I'd thought of the pie."

It was his turn to blink in disbelief. Until twenty minutes ago, he'd never laid eyes on her. Since then, she'd pushed her way into his home, fed him, cleaned his kitchen and done her level best to restock his cupboards.

"Okay, this must be the part where you smile disarmingly and tell me you're some kind of *Pacific Heights*-type psycho and I'm never gonna get you to leave."

A smile lifted the corner of her lips, making a dimple flash on the right side of her mouth. "I guess this wouldn't be the time to confess that I really loved Michael Keaton's tenant-from-hell character in that movie?"

Irritated with himself for noticing her mouth, he grated, "Dammit, I told you, I don't want your pity, or your groceries. I let you in the door, and now you're making yourself at home, digging through my cupboards—"

"Look, Tom—can I call you Tom? Tommy?" Without bothering to wait for a reply, she forged on. "I can see you don't get around very well, whereas I do. Your cupboards were bare. Mine aren't. No biggie. Heck, you can replace the groceries, if you feel that strongly about it."

He scowled at her reasonable tone. "I just don't want anyone feeling sorry for me. I'm doing fine, dammit."

"I didn't mean to imply you weren't." Her green eyes narrowed. "Do you have some tragic story I should know about?"

"Hardly." He said it without hesitation, and just to prove how tragedy-free he was feeling, he lifted his coffee cup to his lips and took a sip.

"Good, because now wouldn't be a good time to talk about it. It'd just ruin your digestion. Let's talk about me instead."

He choked on his coffee.

She turned those big eyes on him. "What? I thought we'd established you don't want to talk about your accident or your surgery or whatever, so why not me? Or my suddenly difficult son."

Why talk at all? He could plead a bone-deep agony in his hip and leg, which would be no lie. The pain pills hadn't kicked in yet. Then he remembered the look on her face when she'd first mentioned her son.

"Dillon, right?"

She brightened. "Yes, Dillon."

"What's his problem?"

She shrugged, but it wasn't the same nonchalant gesture she'd displayed before. This shrug spoke of helplessness.

"I wish I knew. We used to be really close, but now … his moods are so … changeable."

"He's eighteen."

"Not for another couple of weeks."

"My point is, being surly and uncommunicative is par for the course."

"I know. But he's always been such a sweet kid."

He watched her absently stroke her coffee mug. "Boys grow up."

She shook her head. "That's part of it, for sure. Maybe even the biggest part of it," she allowed. "But he really didn't want to make this move, or at least not as fast as we did. Consciously or not, he's punishing me for disrupting our lives." She chewed the inside of her lip a moment. "Maybe I should have postponed the move. But I'd already held off until he finished high school, and he'd have had to move *somewhere* in the fall anyway, for university, so I figured why not here, right?"

He realized she was looking at him as though she expected some kind of reaction. "UNB's a good school. He'll like it."

She looked down into the depths of her coffee mug again. "Besides, I'd won a major contract that pretty much required me to relocate here. Not that he had to pick *this* university just because I was coming here. He'd been accepted by three different schools, and we could have stretched the budget to pay for residence, but this one really does have the best computer science program."

What was he supposed to say? "I've heard very good things about it."

"I know it was a wrench to leave his friends so soon after graduation, but I figured he could use the time to get to know the city, make a few friends here."

Man, she'd obviously been over this ground a few times, rationalizing, regretting, second-guessing. He knew all about that. "His father around?"

Another shake of the head. "Not since Dillon was little."

"Maybe he needs to connect with his dad."

As soon as the words were out of his mouth, he recognized that he'd slipped into problem-solving mode. Dammit, he wasn't a cop anymore. And he sure as hell wasn't a social worker.

"That's not in the cards."

He pushed back his own too-raw emotions. She clearly needed to talk to someone, and he'd been elected. What had she said? Oh, yeah. The kid's dad was out of the picture. "Dead? Dillon's father, I mean."

"Dead*beat*," she corrected, lifting her gaze from her mug.

"What about Big Brothers?" He found himself looking away. "It's a good program. A lot of kids from single-parent families benefit from the influence of a male role —"

She held up a hand to stop him. "You're preaching to the converted, here. We were in the program for four years, until Dillon's Big Brother moved to Halifax. Now, he thinks he's too old for that kind of stuff."

Tommy gingerly shifted in his chair. "Again, he's nearly eighteen. It's natural for him to look to his peers rather than an adult."

"I think he found something else to fill the void."

Of course. "Girl, eh?"

She grimaced. "I wish."

Whoops. "I see."

"Oh, no! It's not like that. Dillon dates girls. There's just no one special."

"You know, a lot of mothers might be glad there was no one special. I seem to remember my mother getting uneasy when I was that age and stuck on a girl."

That drew a weak smile from her.

"Afraid one of those sweet young things was going to whisk her son off to the altar, was she?"

Shotgun marriage? There'd never been much chance of that. Not that an accidental pregnancy had been out of the question. He'd just been far too immature and self-involved for marriage, as had the girls he'd run with. His father would have just pulled out his checkbook. Of course, his father also would have given him a hearty thump on the back as though he'd finally done something praiseworthy. *Well, at least this proves you're not a queer.*

"Something like that," he muttered, taking a sip of his coffee. Lord, even her coffee was incredible. "So, if it's not a girl, he must be hanging with a bad crowd."

Her hand tightened on the handle of her mug. "Bingo."

"It's probably not that bad," he offered. "Kids that age talk a good line of trash, but they're not nearly as bad as they'd have the world believe. I've seen 'em fold pretty quick when —" Damn. Talking like a cop again. "What I mean is, it's usually just posturing. He'll grow out of it."

She slanted him a look. "You don't have kids, do you?"

"No, I don't."

"Adults." She sighed and pushed back in her chair.

"Huh?"

"He's hanging around with adults. I only got a good look at one of them. He was relatively young, I suppose, but still a lot older than Dillon. Mid-twenties, probably, and way, way harder than my son, from the look of him."

Tommy frowned. That kind of age differential usually spelled bad news. He could too easily picture unscrupulous adults feeding a troubled kid's ego and thirst for attention until the kid was ripe for exploitation. Drug-dealing, auto theft, pornography, prostitution .... All the ugly possibilities flashed through his mind.

"And you think they're up to ... what?"

"No good," she said darkly. "Although since I haven't had an actual conversation with any of these men, I have to admit I'm basing that judgment entirely on prejudice and stereotypes. Which makes me feel like a total hypocrite, since it's exactly the kind of thing I've tried to teach Dillon not to do."

"Let me guess — shaved heads, baggy pants, shirts buttoned at the neck and open at the bottom, tattoos?"

"Not to mention the cold eyes. Oh, yes, and the chopped pick-up with the tinted windows, and the kind of stereo that sets off minor earthquakes with the bass notes when it drives by."

The cynic in him said she'd probably nailed the demographic accurately, but he stayed silent.

"So?" She looked at him expectantly.

"So, what?" He shifted again, just a few millimeters, to ease the ache in his leg. The relief was exquisite. Unfortunately, it lasted about a tenth of a second, then started throbbing again.

"So, are you going to pat me on the head and tell me I'm being a paranoid, over-protective mother?"

"No," he said. "No, I won't do that."

She sagged. "Damn. I was hoping you would. Hoping even harder that you could make me believe it."

"Sorry."

Their gazes locked for a few seconds, and Tommy felt an unexpected surge of sexual awareness rocket through him.

His first reaction was relief; he'd begun to think of his libido as KIA. Then the inappropriateness struck him. This was a distraught woman, a worried mother. A mother whose son, technically speaking, was old enough to make her a *grandmother.*

She jumped up and carried her cup to the sink, where she rinsed it and set it on the draining board. "Look," she said, turning back to him. "I can see you're in pain. You probably need to lie down or something. I'll get out of your hair."

"The leg's gonna hurt no matter what. You don't have to rush off, if you don't want to."

Christ, was that him talking? Had he just invited the original Velcro woman to stay?

Her green gaze caught and held his again. "Really?"

"Really," he heard himself say. Oh, Lord, he must have taken too many of those pain pills.

"That's very generous of you, especially after I pushed my way in here."

"You *did* feed me."

She tilted her head in an attitude of listening. "Looks like you're off the hook. That must be Dillon now."

He heard it too, the sound of a car's engine. At the end of this cul-de-sac, just barely inside the city limits, they didn't get much drive-by traffic. Good. The kid was home where he belonged, and now he could have his solitude back.

"Thanks for holding my hand," she said, turning to pick up her plate. "No offense, but I hope it'll be the last time."

The latter was delivered with a wide smile, but he could see the tension and worry beneath it.

"Look, do you want me to talk to him or something?"

Oh, hell, where had *that* come from? She looked just as stunned by the offer as he was about making it.

"Thanks, but I don't think so. I know my son. If I just spring you on him, it'll be worse than if I just leave it alone."

"Well, if you change your mind … ."

She smiled at him again, and he was struck once more by a pang of desire, this one even stronger than the last.

"Thanks, Tommy."

She let herself out, and the sound of the door closing echoed behind her. For a split second, her absence felt like a hollowness, in his house and in his chest.

Damned lust. Now that the relief had passed, he almost wished he'd stayed dead that way. Didn't he have enough aches without adding another?

Pulling himself to his feet, mainly by dint of his upper-body strength, he picked up his cane and clumped toward the bedroom. He'd almost reached his customary resting spot by the sofa when he heard the scream, shrill, female and clearly terrified.

Paige.

Adrenaline ripped through his system like a shot of juice from a live electrical wire. He covered the distance to the door in a flash, with no sensation of pain. Endorphins. He'd pay for it later. Tearing the door open, he lurched out onto the step.

"Paige?"

⚜

A hand still clamped to her mouth to stifle the scream she'd been unable to suppress, she swiveled her head toward Tommy's voice. He stood on the steps outside his unit, looking like he was ready, willing and able to use his cane as a weapon, if need be.

"What it is? What's the matter?"

She pointed to her doorstep.

"Jesus. What's *that*?"

"I don't know." Her stomach did a sick little flip, but her voice was surprisingly steady. "But it's dead and it seems to be minus its fur."

He swore, then hobbled a few feet closer. "I take it that the car we heard wasn't Dillon coming home?"

"Dillon's car's not home," she replied, choosing her words carefully. These days, she couldn't rule out anything where her son was concerned, even his participation in something as ugly as this. He'd closed himself off so completely from her. Not that she thought he'd *lead* something as gruesome as this, but he might go along for the ride, especially if he didn't know in advance what the plan was.

"You're welcome to call it in from my place," he said, gesturing toward his unit. "Phone's on the wall just inside the kitchen."

Call the police? Without talking to Dillon?

"Ah, that's okay." She took a step backward, closer to her own doorstep. "Thanks for the offer, but I think I'll just deal with this myself."

"You're making a mistake, Paige."

His tone was quiet, without any detectable inflection, but it arrested her retreat in a way a forceful command might not have.

"What do you mean?"

"By not reporting this. You think you're protecting your son, but if his new friends did this, with or without his involvement, you'd do better to tackle it head on. He needs to know that his choices have repercussions."

He was right and she knew it, but it wasn't that simple. Dillon was her *son*. He was all she had, and getting further away from her every day. She didn't know how to guide him toward a better path without driving him to worse rebellion. Her frustration boiled up into anger.

"Who said I thought this has anything to do with Dillon?"

"So, you think it was what? Random sicko? Or maybe a customer who didn't like your Tiramisu?"

She glared at him. "There's no need for sarcasm."

He sighed. "Okay, let's say it has nothing to do with your son. All the more reason to call the cops right now. They might be able to get impressions from the car's tires. Presuming somebody carried it to your doorstep, there could be footprint evidence. But that stuff is transitory. You have to act fast."

She snorted. "You sound like a cop."

"That's because I am."

Oh, shit.

Chapter 2

A COP? WHY HADN'T he said something? The whole evening, she'd been all but handing Dillon over on a platter.

"Relax. I should say, I *was* a cop, past tense. Now I just take up space on the couch watching late-night TV talk shows."

For a second, his eyes went bleaker than anything she'd ever seen. Then the flat, slightly bored expression was back.

"I figured Mrs. Graham would have told you," he said.

"She said you were in hospital recovering from surgery and she didn't know when you'd be back." Paige knew she shouldn't ask, but she couldn't curb her curiosity. "What happened?"

"I got shot."

Just like that. No change to his expression or tone.

"I'm sorry."

"Me, too. Now about this skinned offering, you really should call the police, and you should do it now."

"I need to talk to Dillon first."

He sighed, and seemed to lean more heavily on his cane. "Okay, I get it. You're not gonna report this in case it comes back on your son, somehow. But at least let's have a look at the carcass before you dispose of it. If somebody's trying to send you a message, you might as well try to hear it."

He lurched forward, and she realized he intended to inspect it himself.

"You don't have to go all the way out there. I'll bring it to you," she hastened to say, although the thought of picking up that mass of bloody tissue made her stomach flip over again.

"Paige." His voice held a note of warning.

"But the steps . . . ."

"I can handle them. And I want to look the ... situation over before you disturb it."

Crime scene was the word he'd been going to use. She shivered. "Okay. Let's go."

"Just a sec. I should get my camera."

Camera? This was starting to sound pretty official. "Oh, I don't think that's necessary."

"Relax, it's a Polaroid. No negatives, and you can keep the prints yourself."

God, was he a mind reader? He seemed to know where she was going almost before she could decode her own gut reactions.

"I'm not out to build a case against your son or anyone else," he continued. "I'm not fit for duty, in case you didn't notice. The doctors concur I'll never be, so you don't need to worry about that. But just in case this turns out to be more than a nasty prank, you'll be glad you documented it."

He was right again, and once again, she knew it. "Okay, tough guy, you convinced me. Let's go get your camera and we'll do the CSI thing." She started toward his place, thinking to retrieve the camera for him and save him the steps.

"Stay there," he commanded. "I'll get it."

She had to bite her lip as she watched him hobble back into his side of the duplex. God, that had to hurt.

For the first time, it struck her as odd that he would use a cane instead of a crutch. A crutch conveyed much more machismo than a cane. Then she recalled his words — the doctors agreed he would never be fit for active duty. Crutches were for people who were recuperating. Intuitively, she knew the cane would be his version of the hair shirt, a constant reminder of the event that ended his career. A mortification and a penance.

He reappeared a moment later, camera in hand. His injury must be to his hip, she decided, as she watched his awkward descent of the steps. His facial expression remained unchanged, hard and set, but she could see the beads of sweat materializing on his brow and dampening his shirt. Every step cost him dearly, but she knew better than to remark on it.

When he reached level ground at last, she let him lead the way to her stoop. Not anxious to look on the bloodied carcass again, she focused on Tommy's face as he surveyed the scene. Once again, there was no appreciable change in his expression. Even his voice sounded flat when he spoke.

"Rabbit."

A rabbit? Could have fooled her. "Really? How can you tell?"

He flicked her a glance. "Skinned a few in my day."

Her horror must have shown.

"Don't worry, princess. That was back in my bloodthirsty youth." Lifting the Polaroid to his face, he snapped a shot, then pulled the photo from the camera, waving it briefly while it finished developing.

"Hold this," he instructed.

She took the photo from him, unable to keep from looking at it. Dear God, that bloody mass was a rabbit? And what was she doing talking to a man who knew what a skinned rabbit looked like? She abhorred hunting. Of course, it could be worse. It could be the neighbor's cat. She shivered. "You know, I was half afraid it might be a cat."

"Definitely not a cat."

"Skinned lots of those, too, have you?"

He slanted her a reproving look, but made no comment. Leaning heavily on his cane, he moved closer to the animal for a tighter camera shot. Before snapping this one, he took off his watch and laid it beside the animal.

"You're concerned about recording the time? Couldn't you just write that on the photo?"

"It's for perspective," he said. "It's hard to know how big or small an object is without a frame of reference, especially with a close shot."

He took the picture, then another from a different angle.

"What now?" she asked, when it appeared he was satisfied.

"I thought I heard a vehicle drive past just before you said your son must be home. I'm thinking that was your culprit. He must have cruised by, turned at the dead end and come back, so he'd be pointed down the hill for a quick getaway."

"So?"

"So, the road's not paved at the very end. There could be tire tracks." He handed her the camera. "Capture anything that looks fresh."

"You want *me* to look for tracks?"

"It's too far for me tonight."

Again, his bleak cast of mind was all the more palpable for the lack of inflection in his tone. And again, she felt a pang for dragging him into this in the first place. "I really don't think we need —"

"Humor me, all right? There's rain on the way. I can smell it. Any tracks that might be there could be erased by morning."

Okay, so he had a point. They'd get just one crack at this. "Just —"

He cut her off with an impatient sound. "Look, Mrs. Harmer, this might not be my doorstep exactly, but it's pretty damn close, and I'm not too thrilled about the fact we're not calling the cops, which anyone with a functioning brain would do, so if you don't —"

"Easy, there." She held up the Polaroid, waggling it in front of him. "I was merely going to ask if I just point and shoot this thing."

"Sorry," he clipped. "I was anticipating some resistance." Except he didn't *sound* very sorry. He sounded downright crabby. "As for the camera, that about sums it up. Point, shoot, wait for the picture to eject. That's it."

What was his problem? Despite having gained her compliance on the photography point, the tension in his jaw hadn't eased one iota. Sheesh. And Dillon thought *she* was uptight.

"All right, then. I'll be back in a flash." She started toward the street, moving briskly in the hope of discharging some of her annoyance, but he called her name. She turned back, cocking an eyebrow at him.

"Be careful."

The lightbulb went on. *Well, duh.* That's why he looked like he might crack a molar. He hated sending her out to do something he figured he should do himself. Something warm stirred in her breast.

"Hey, I'm a single parent. Careful is my religion."

Whether it was her dead-serious tone or the truth resonating in the statement, she saw a definite ebbing of tension in his face. Then, as though recalling himself, his expression tightened again.

"Be quick about it," he growled. "The rain won't hold off forever."

Any warm, fuzzy feelings she may have been experiencing evaporated at his tone. Because she appreciated his not over-riding her wishes and calling the cops himself, she restrained the impulse to march back and hand him back his camera.

"Ten minutes," she said, whirling away.

It took her closer to fifteen minutes, and not because of the petty desire she felt to reward his poor manners by keeping him waiting. The truth was she found it spooky out here, the woods around her unnaturally quiet. It would have suited her nicely to find there were no tracks so she could beat a hasty retreat. Unfortunately, there were several sets of tracks, and they looked fresh.

She bent to examine them. Wide, deep, and new enough that they hadn't begun to fill in with organic debris. Glancing around nervously, she lifted the Polaroid and took the first shot. The photo seemed to take forever to eject. As did the next and the next. By the time she figured she'd captured enough to satisfy Tommy Godsoe, the hairs on the back of her neck were standing up. Which was totally stupid. It was just kids pulling a nasty prank. Kids who were long gone. Still, she didn't dawdle.

She came back to find Tommy sitting on her top step scrubbing the concrete with a wire brush. At her arrival, he levered himself up awkwardly.

"There. If you just throw a bucket of clean water across the step, you'll be good as new."

How had he managed to get a bucket of water out here?

Not without a terrible physical toll, came the answer.

Her irritation with him, which she'd been nursing as a defense against the ridiculous and unwarranted fear she'd felt out by the woods, vanished.

"You didn't have to do that."

"I'm not completely useless."

She blinked. "I don't think I ever suggested you were. Socially challenged, maybe. Surly, definitely. Unable to accept help, let alone ask for it, not to mention too self-absorbed —"

"Yeah, I'm all that and more," he interrupted. "Now, unless you want to freeze that for posterity, or unless you have a way to incinerate it," he gestured toward the carcass which he had bagged, "you probably should take it out and bury it."

He looked dead on his feet, she realized suddenly. And his face was positively grey. And here she was, dressing him down for his attitude. Talk about self-absorbed.

She grimaced. "I'm sorry, don't mind me. I'm letting the weirdness of this whole episode get to me. Thank you for taking care of the dirty work."

"You're welcome."

His primly polite tone drew her gaze back to his. Even with the pain etching deep lines in his face, she saw a spark of humor light his eyes.

She grinned. "Very good."

Amazingly, he returned her grin. Paige caught her breath. Oh, Christmas, he looked like a Hollywood agent's dream when he smiled.

In that instant, the shared humor was gone, replaced by something that made her blood surge and swell. In her mind's eye, she saw him again as she'd seen him when he first opened his door to her. Then she saw new images. Breath-stealing images. Powerful runner's legs tangling with hers. Wide, hair-roughened chest abrading hers . . . .

The sound of a vehicle accelerating up the hill broke the spell. She swung away, her movements jerky. "That's Dillon."

He cleared his throat, stepped back. "I'll get out of your hair."

Paige stood there, torn. Part of her wanted Tommy to go, the part that demanded she shield her son from all things unpleasant, even the consequences of his own behavior. The other part wanted Tommy to stay. How long had it been since someone — a *male* someone — had stood behind her while she dealt with her child?

Never. Steve had left when Dillon was a baby, long before that developmental stage when children could be reasoned with.

But, oh, how seductive the idea was . . . .

And how dangerous.

She was Dillon's sole parent, first, last and always. No one else could be counted on to do the job.

"Thank you very much for your help," she said, hating how lame that sounded, hating even more the relief she glimpsed in his eyes.

"No problem."

Tommy reached for his bucket, but before he could make his escape, Dillon pulled into the driveway in his battered old Toyota and killed the engine.

"What's goin' on?" The words were out of her son's mouth practically before his feet hit the driveway. There was no mistaking the anxiety in his voice, or in the brown eyes that were the mirror image of his dad's.

"Somebody left a calling card on our doorstep," she said.

Dillon eyed the scrub bucket and the wet concrete. "What kind of calling card?"

"A grisly one." Paige handed him one of the photos of the skinned carcass.

"Jesus."

"Dillon!"

"Sorry." He cast another look at Tommy, then turned his attention back to her. "Did you see who did it?"

"No." Was that relief in her son's eyes?

"But you called the cops?"

"No, I did not."

"Then what's *he* doing here?" said Dillon, indicating Tommy with a tilt of his head.

Paige blushed at her son's tone. And how had he pegged Tommy as a cop so fast? Surely they didn't know each other in a . . . professional . . . context?

"Officer Godsoe is our neighbor," she said, watching her son's face. No, he didn't know Tommy personally, she decided, relaxing a little. "He's just home from the hospital, recovering from an injury."

"Hi, Dillon."

Tommy, leaning heavily on his cane, made no offer to extend his hand, thank God. Dillon didn't interact with enough men to respond confidently in a handshake situation.

Dillon made a gruff, mumbled acknowledgment, and Paige's face burned again. He'd get an earful about his manners later.

"So, where'd you get to tonight?" she asked, trying to keep it easy. "Did you hook up with your friends?"

A pause. "Nah, I just ran into town for a while, to the arcade. A little therapy, you know?"

"Hmm." Frankly, she didn't know whether those games relieved the anger that seemed to ride him since the move, or whether they made it worse.

"Hey, is that the dead rabbit from the photo?" Dillon gestured to the plastic bag beside the steps.

Paige permitted the change of topic. "Yeah, that's it."

"Good call," Tommy interjected softly. "You know your carcasses."

Dillon's face darkened. "Well, of course, it's a rabbit. What else could it be?"

God, that had slipped right past her. How *had* he known it was a rabbit? He shared her aversion to hunting, and she was sure he'd never dissected such a large mammal in biology.

She gave him her narrow-eyed, truth-serum look. "You wouldn't happen to know anything about this, would you, Dillon?"

"Great. Wonderful."

His eyes glittered with fresh anger. Or were they unshed tears?

"Something bad happens, you automatically assume I'm to blame."

"I merely asked —"

"You *always* do this. Ever since we moved here, you think I turned into this delinquent jerk."

Her grip on her temper slipped. "I think your new friends are delinquent jerks," she snapped.

"You don't know my friends. How can you say something like that?"

"That's exactly right," she retorted. "I *don't* know your friends. Why is that, exactly?"

"Okay, you know what? Forget it. You don't hear anything I say anyway, so I'll just shut up."

He started up the steps.

"Dillon!"

He stopped, back tensed, muscles quivering.

"I'd like you to take that animal out into the woods and bury it. You'll find a shovel in the shed out back."

She watched him open and close his fists a couple of times, but when he turned back to her a few seconds later, he'd mastered his emotions.

"Yes, ma'am."

He descended the steps, grabbed the bag and strode around to the back yard. Sighing, she massaged her aching temple.

He was lying. Her son was *lying* to her. The knowledge dropped like a weight in the center of her chest. Why couldn't he talk to her anymore? Why couldn't he trust her? Was she really that horrible a parent?

"I think he's lying."

Tommy's softly-voiced echo of her own conclusion scraped across her exposed nerves. The tangle of her emotions — the sick sense of parental failure, the disappointment in Dillon, the after-effects of that stupid attack of fear as she'd searched for tire tracks in the shadow of the woods — all came together, coalescing into fury.

"Oh, yeah? You know my son so well after a three-minute encounter that you can pronounce on his *credibility*?" She heard her own voice rising, getting shriller by the second. "You think you can pass judgment on his character, just like that?"

"Actually, it was more of a comment on his body language and physical presentation." Tommy's tone was normal, but his eyes had turned into chips of blue ice.

Her fury just kept growing. She felt it smashing down barriers, rolling through her on a fierce wave that left her skin taut and tingling.

"Body language? Physical presentation?" She made an effort to control her breathing, but her words still emerged jerky and breathless. "My son may have been rude. He may have been obnoxious.

But there was nothing *furtive* about his demeanor. So you can go to hell with that body language crap."

His eyes hardened still further. "Happy to oblige." Once more, he picked up his scrub tools and started to limp away.

At the sight of his gait, her anger died away, leaving her mortified at the words she'd flung at him. He'd gone out of his way to help her, at considerable sacrifice to his leg, and here she was flaying him for speaking an obvious truth.

"Tommy, wait."

He turned back, his expression unreadable. "When you asked him if he'd hooked up with his friends, he glanced to the right, and paused a few seconds before answering. Usually, when people are retrieving memories, which are mostly visual, they glance up and to the left. The glance to the right is more consistent with auditory function. Since you weren't asking him to recall the latest Eminem lyrics, there's a good chance he was test-driving his answer, listening to it in his mind, trying to gauge how it would sound."

She blinked. "You figured out that he was lying from his *eye movements*?"

"That, and the blood on his right hand and shirt sleeve."

"Blood?"

"I'm guessing he didn't get those scraped knuckles from toggling a video game."

Her stomach churned. Dillon's blood or someone else's? Or, omigod, rabbit's blood?

"Goodbye, Mrs. Harmer."

She came out of her daze in time to realize he'd started off again, crossing the small patch of grass to his own walkway.

"Tommy ... ."

This time, he didn't turn. "Good luck with your son."

Paige watched him climb the steps to his own unit, open the door and disappear inside without a backward glance.

Damn, damn, damn.

Chapter 3

DILLON DUG WITH COMPLETE disregard for his injured right hand. If he just ignored the pain, maybe it would go away. Except that philosophy was just about as effective with his bloodied hand as it was on every other front. Jesus, how had his life disintegrated into this?

He paused to swipe the sweat out of his eyes with his good hand, then went back to digging. Three minutes later, he figured the hole was deep enough. Dropping the spade, he picked up the plastic bag containing the rabbit carcass.

His stomach gave a lurch. Ten to one, this was Brandy, the little doe Derek kept in his apartment, mainly to amuse his friends when he fed it dope. For a moment, guilt weighed heavy. This animal, this innocent little bunny, had died because he, Dillon, had refused Derek's request. And maybe because Dillon had landed a solid — and totally flukey — right uppercut to Derek's face outside the arcade earlier tonight.

No.

Dillon's mouth hardened. The rabbit's death was on Derek and nobody else. And if the poor rabbit could think at all, it would probably count its death a blessing after those months with Derek.

Bending, he gently placed the bag in the cool, dark pit he'd dug. "Sorry, Brandy. You didn't deserve any of this. Rest in peace, girl."

He stood. Looking down at the rabbit's body, he wondered if he should say some kind of prayer. But all that came to him was the thought, *Rachel's right — Derek is a total dickhead.*

Rachel. His grip on the shovel's handle tightened. Man, what he'd give to have her here right now.

He caught the drift of his thoughts and smiled. *Yeah, right, Harmer. You're scared shitless of her.* And not because she looked strong enough to take him in a fight, which she no doubt could.

No, he was scared because she could see straight through his tough-guy act, right from the first minute she turned those liquid green-brown, all-seeing eyes on him.

Tough guy? Christ, it was like he didn't even have a *skin* when he was around her. Everything was just out there, exposed and vulnerable, as easily crushed as a bug on a sidewalk. If he had two clues to rub together, he'd steer clear of her.

Unfortunately, he hadn't done anything lately to prove he had even half a clue. He looked down at the pitifully small carcass and felt his throat tighten.

Yeah, he'd made some mistakes lately. And he had nobody to blame but himself. On second thought, it was a damned lucky thing Rachel *wasn't* here right now. She'd take one look at his face and see his guilt flashing as plainly as a neon sign.

Man, what a loser he was turning into.

Swallowing around the marble-sized lump in his throat, he began shoveling dark soil back into the hole.

⚜

Tommy watched the digital display on the clock by his bed change once more. Two fifty-eight. The pain was rapidly becoming the focal point of his existence, driving him quietly mad. He couldn't even describe it as localized to his hip anymore, since it was now referred to the groin, the buttock, the back of his thigh. Which would be tolerable, if it were the usual dull ache, but it was sharp, now. Hot. Stabbing.

Dammit, there he went again, gauging it, dwelling on it. Pain, he knew, was quite literally in the head, even if right now it felt like it was in his sorry, bony ass.

Mind over matter, Godsoe. Think of something else.

Paige Harmer's face immediately formed in his mind. He'd pushed her image away a dozen times already, just as firmly as she'd pushed him away earlier this evening, but this time he didn't fight it. Anything was better than thinking about the grinding agony.

He closed his eyes and let the picture slowly form. There. He had it. Her face was a little too flat for beauty, her mouth too wide and full, but she managed to be striking just the same. It was the eyes. Huge, green, fathoms deep. They invited a man to drown in them. But beyond their exotic beauty, they were a fascinating paradox, at once boldly outgoing and quietly cautious. He supposed the former was a necessary attribute in anyone who was self-employed, while the latter would be second nature for a single mother.

Those strange eyes had also held frank sexual interest. So frank, he suspected she had no idea how transparent she'd been. Almost as transparent as her pale, lightly freckled skin . . . .

Again, he felt desire stir.

And again, he marveled at his reaction. After all, he was well used to women looking at him with interest, or at least he had been before he'd walked into a hail of lead. He didn't usually react so strongly. Why should this be any different?

Maybe because she'd stifled it so quickly, cultivated caution overruling natural curiosity.

Of course, she'd also looked at him with pity when she finally noticed that his leg was damaged, then proceeded to treat him like an invalid.

His eyes sprang open as a possibility occurred to him. Is that why he'd gone out there, why he'd overtaxed his leg? Not out of concern for her and her son, but to prove he wasn't as useless as he looked?

Dammit, this was what was wrong with this gimp gig. Too much time on his hands, too much quiet. He'd managed to get through twenty-nine years without examining his life too closely, and he damn well didn't want to start now, particularly as he didn't much like what he was finding. Only trouble was, there was no way to outrun his thoughts.

Run. Sweet Jesus, if only he could.

He closed his eyes again, and this time the image he saw was of himself running. *Breathe in, breathe out, dig deeper, run faster.* He could hear his police windbreaker chafing with the rhythmic swinging of his arms, see Max ahead of him, off the lead and running for the pure joy of it.

He was fully prepared for it, expected it, and yet when the wave of yearning swept over him, it nearly swamped him. Gritting his teeth, he fought back.

You can't have it. You can't have any of it. Not the job, not the dog, not the girl. What the hell was he doing lying here lusting after things he could never have again?

He grasped for the physical pain again, sinking gratefully into it.

Hot knives, that's what it felt like. A virtual girdle of stabbing, hot knives . . . .

✻

Tommy didn't waken until the sun beating through the window raised the temperature in his bedroom beyond the comfort point. Amazed that he'd slept at all, let alone until mid-morning, he shifted experimentally. Yep. His hip was still on fire, but it was localized again. Excruciating but livable.

Half an hour later, after a breakfast of cereal which he didn't have to eat dry thanks to the carton of milk Paige had left, he collapsed on the couch. Much as it aggravated him to admit it, he was grateful she'd left those few staples. He wasn't up to a trip to the grocery store. Maybe tomorrow, or the next day. Today, he was going to ... what?

Nothing. Today, he would do nothing, just as he'd done for the last twenty-eight consecutive days. The thought threatened to overwhelm him. Dammit, he was used to moving, running, training. This inactivity was going to drive him around the bend! Hell, he'd almost welcome the crazy neighbor lady.

As if on cue, the doorbell rang. He looked skyward. "Oh, God, I didn't mean it. I take it back."

The doorbell pealed again, twice in quick succession. God, the woman had no patience. Groaning, he pushed himself to his feet, picked up his cane and hobbled to the door. With a thanks-but-no-thanks expression pasted to his face, he opened the door, ready to send her on her way. But it wasn't Paige who stood on his steps. It was her son, and he held an armful of very dirty yellow-furred dog.

"This your dog?"

Tommy gripped the door handle harder. "No. No dogs here."

Dillon looked surprised. "I just thought … I mean, there's a kennel in the back yard."

He felt a tic start up beside his left eye. "I used to have a dog. I don't now."

"Oh."

Tommy looked closer at the dog, a Lab cross of some kind, under the mud, matted fur and burrs. And not very old. Still a puppy, really, despite its size. It was shivering almost rhythmically, but wasn't struggling. Probably too weak to put up much resistance. "Where'd you get it?"

"Found it out by the road. I heard him crying in the ditch, but when I tried to round him up, he kept trying to run away, but he was tied to a cement block."

Jesus. "A cinder block?"

"Yeah, that's it. Plus there's something wrong with one of his back legs."

"Her," Tommy corrected automatically. "She's a female." The little dog shivered again, hard. Poor emaciated little thing. Neglected, abused, and dumped. Maybe even struck by a car. Or possibly tossed out of a moving car with that goddamn cinder block attached.

"Call the SPCA," he advised. "They'll take care of it."

The kid blanched. "Take care of it? What do you mean, *take care of it*?"

"They'll clean her up, evaluate her, see if she's adoptable."

Dillon's arms tightened around the puppy. "Why wouldn't she be adoptable?"

"She hasn't had a good start," Tommy said softly. "That leg, for instance. Looks like she's got a gash high on her hip, there. Could be she needs surgery, which would make her an expensive proposition." He stretched a finger out to stroke the trembling animal's matted coat, feeling the creature's ribs easily. "Nutritional deficit, inadequate socialization, exposure to stress at a critical age … ." He shrugged. "These things shape her personality. Even if she's cleaned up and treated, she might not make a good pet."

"No." Dillon backed away as he spoke. "Un-unh. I'm not turning her over to the SPCA. I'll take care of her myself."

Great. "Better check with your mother, don't you think?"

"She won't mind."

Yeah, right. Tommy cast a glance over Dillon's shoulder to see the van Paige usually drove was gone. "Where is she?"

"Making deliveries, shopping, the usual stuff. She won't be home for a while yet."

Tommy exhaled slowly. If she came home and saw the dirty, blood-smeared bundle, she'd probably think it was another ghoulish offering in the style of last night's.

"Bring her in," he said, and stepped back from the door. "We can clean her up and check that leg out, at least."

⚜

Paige carted the plastic crates she used to transport her desserts up the steps. They weren't especially heavy, but they were damned awkward. Of course, it would be too much to hope that Dillon would be home and ready to help her carry her stuff in. Sighing, she juggled the crates, dug her keys out of her slacks pocket, slid the house key home and twisted her wrist.

Nothing. It wouldn't move. Grasping the knob, she turned it experimentally. It yielded under her hand, swinging open.

Unlocked. Dillon must be home after all. Probably crashed on his bed, listening to Korn or Slipknot or some other vile metal band, with his headphones set at industrial-hearing-loss volume. Too bad. She'd put him to work carting groceries.

She did a quick tour of the house. No Dillon. Which meant he'd left without locking up behind himself. Her mouth thinned. Wonderful. Another thing she'd have to talk to him about, which would lead inevitably to another one of those I-can't-seem-to-do-anything-right-in-your-eyes-anymore arguments.

So be it. She couldn't put up with the house being left unlocked when they were out. He might have no fear, but she had plenty for both of them.

Putting it out of her mind for the moment, she proceeded to carry in her supplies. It took two trips, then another ten minutes to put everything away.

Well, almost everything.

Her gaze fell on the one bag she'd left on the table. On impulse, she'd picked some things up for Tommy, wanting to do something to thank him for his help last night. Chances were that his hip would hurt after yesterday's exertions. Having ready, nutritious food within easy reach might be appreciated. The trouble was, now she had to walk over there and ring his doorbell, and she knew he wouldn't welcome the intrusion. His goodbye and good luck as he'd left her last night had rung with finality.

Too bad.

She picked up the bag and marched out.

❧

The doorbell rang just as they were toweling off the dog. Dammit, who was it this time? Probably Ray Morgan, or maybe John Quigley. Unlike the rest of the guys, they didn't seem to be getting the message that he didn't want to see anyone, especially other cops.

"Would you get that, kid? And tell them I'm indisposed. Indefinitely."

Dillon's eyes widened. "What if it's your boss or something?"

Tommy thought about his sergeant's intense discomfort in the hospital room, the naked fear in the man's eyes as he'd looked at Tommy and seen his own vulnerability. No, his boss wasn't likely to drop by.

"I'm indisposed," he repeated.

Dillon nodded once, then went to open the door.

"Dillon? What are you doing here?"

Great. The crazy neighbor lady.

"I needed some help with the dog."

"With the dog?" she repeated, sounding as though she'd stumbled into an episode of the *Twilight Zone*.

"I found a dog. Someone dumped it in the ditch and it was hurt and dirty and hungry and I couldn't just leave it there."

Beneath Tommy's hands, the puppy in question trembled, probably at the sound of a new voice.

"Where is it?"

"It's a she, and she's in the kitchen. Come on, I'll show you."

"Some threshold guardian," Tommy muttered to the dog, who trembled again.

Seconds later, Dillon and his mother entered the kitchen.

"Good job," Tommy said.

Dillon colored. "It was my mom."

"So I see."

"Hi," she said, holding up a grocery bag. "I brought you some fresh fruit and a little trail mix. I figured your leg might bother you today, after all you did for me last night."

"Thanks, but the leg is fine."

She held his gaze long enough to communicate she knew he was full of shit, then glanced down at the puppy cowering on his lap.

"Oh, my gosh, it looks terrified."

"For good reason. I'd say she's had a tough life so far."

"Can we keep her, Mom?"

She looked up at her son, who wore an anxious look.

"She must have an owner . . . ."

"Not one who deserves to get her back."

Tommy had to agree with Dillon's assessment, but he kept his mouth shut. Paige reached out to stroke the dog, and it shrank back, giving a yelp.

She snatched her hand back. "What's wrong? I didn't even touch her."

"She's got a bad leg right now, but it's hard to say what's wrong with it, other than that she's got a pretty deep wound on her hip."

"But that can be stitched up. And the leg's probably not broken," Dillon said, turning to Tommy. "That's what you said, right?"

"Yeah, but I'm not a vet, kid. I just know a little first aid."

"First aid for dogs?" Paige arched an eyebrow.

"He's a dog master," Dillon explained.

"Was," Tommy corrected. "I was a police K9 handler."

"Of course. The kennel in the back yard . . . ."

"So, can we keep her, Mom?"

"Keep her?" She turned back to her son. "A dog is such a big responsibility. You know I wouldn't have time to walk it morning and night."

"I'll do it," he volunteered.

"That's well and good. It's summer vacation for you. What about when you start university? Whose going to walk her then?"

"I'll get up earlier. Please, Mom?"

"She'd need companionship . . . ."

"I'd stay home more, spend time with her. Honest."

Congratulations, son, you just acquired a dog, Tommy thought. To his surprise, his mother didn't concede immediately. Rather, she turned to him and asked, "What do you think, Tommy? You must know dogs. Is this a good idea?"

Tommy dropped his gaze to the dog's too-thin face. "You want a good pet, go to a reputable breeder and get a seven- or eight-week-old puppy with a clean bill of health and a stable personality. This one's probably going to be a bundle of phobias, not to mention you know nothing of her health status." Even as he said the words, his arms tightened around the shivering bundle.

"I don't want another dog. I want *this* one," Dillon said. "Somebody just dumped her. Come on, Mom, they *threw her away*. She deserves better than that. She deserves a good home."

Paige had turned to face her son, so Tommy couldn't see her expression, but he heard her voice quaver a bit when she said, "Okay, you've got yourself a dog."

"Thanks, Ma." Dillon slung his arm around his mother's neck. For a minute he looked about twelve years old despite his six feet of height, and Paige looked like she might burst into tears.

Tommy cleared his throat. "Here, kid, you better take her."

He obliged, carefully accepting the delicate creature into his arms. "What about her leg?"

"I'd take her to get it checked out as soon as you can. They might want to x-ray it. She'll also need her shots. I'd say it's a safe bet she hasn't had any to date."

"I'll call the vet," Paige said. "If I can get in, I'll take her right away."

"No, Dillon should."

"What?"

"Dillon should be the one to take her. If she's going to be his dog, he has to do everything for her. He has to feed and water her and see to whatever she needs. Otherwise, she'll be your dog. Once she makes her decision who she's going to bond with, there'll be no reversing it. It's important he become her world right now, and that world has to be stable, reliable and predictable." He turned to Dillon, fixing him with a hard, measuring look. "If she's going to have a chance to develop into a reasonably well-adjusted dog, she needs that kind of commitment. Can you give her that, kid?"

Dillon seemed to stand taller, "Yeah, I can do it."

"Good." Tommy did his best to ignore the gratitude Paige was telegraphing with those luminous green eyes. "Now get out of my kitchen. My leg is killing me, and I need to lie down for a while."

⊰❦⊱

Four hours later, Paige stood outside Tommy's door and rang the bell again.

"Come in," he called from his seat on the La-Z-Boy. "It's open."

Open? She tried the knob, and sure enough, the door swung inward on its hinges.

Paige walked through to the living room, where she found him sprawled on the recliner, wearing loose-fitting black jeans and a close-fitting black t-shirt. With his black hair and attire accentuating his natural pallor, he looked more like a slightly debauched movie star nursing a hangover than a cop with a serious injury. *Don't stare, don't stare.* The last thing she needed was him thinking she had the hots for his body.

Even if she did.

She flicked her gaze away, noting the bag of trail mix that sat on the occasional table beside his chair. Well, at least that had come in handy. "Did you have company this afternoon?"

His eyebrows drew together. "No. Why do you ask?"

"I could have sworn I locked that door on the way out."

"You did," he said dryly. "I unlocked it before I sat down. Saves wear and tear on this pitiful old body."

His body, she thought, was neither old nor pitiful.

Rats, there she went again.

"How'd you make out with the dog?"

The dog. Right. That's what she'd come here to tell him about. "Cleo."

"Huh?"

"Dillon christened her. He thought she looked like a Cleo."

"Okay, how's Cleo?"

"She's fine, now, but you won't believe what happened." She plunked herself down on the couch a comfortable distance from his recliner. "Dr. Simon found a foreign object in the dog's wound."

"You mean, like dirt or debris?"

"I mean, like a key," she said.

His eyebrows drew together in a fierce frown. "A *key*?"

"Yes, you heard right. A small metal key, probably to a padlock."

He swore. "It must have been in there deep. I looked that wound over pretty closely when we cleaned her up."

"It was very deeply imbedded. You couldn't possibly have seen it." Oh, God, she felt sick all over again just thinking about it. "Even the vet said he wouldn't have found it if he hadn't done that x-ray. He might have sutured it right in there. Can you imagine? How painful would that be? And would it have tried to work its way out, caused inflammation, infection?"

"I'm still trying to get my head around the fact that it was a key. A broken-off knife blade or something like that ... I mean, lousy as that is to think about, you could at least understand how it got there. But a key ... ."

"Had to have been embedded there purposely," she said, finishing his thought. "That's exactly what Dr. Simon said. And the wound was made with a knife, a deliberate incision. The key was jammed in there afterward."

He swore, the words emerging in an even, conversational tone, in stark contrast to the black fury on his face. Gone was the image of the indolent male model. Suddenly, he looked like the angel of death, ready to wreak bloody, violent vengeance. She couldn't have torn her gaze away to save her life.

Even more amazing was how quickly he reined in his emotions. Just as quickly as it had come, the avenging angel was gone and the cool GAP-ad guy was back.

"Musta upset your son."

So fascinated was she with watching the lightning change of expressions, she was caught off guard by his question. She blinked.

"That's a bit of an understatement. He was *wild*. I thought he was going to self-combust there for a minute."

He was watching her now with a speculative look creeping into those hooded, sleepy eyes.

"What?"

"Do you suppose he knows something about this?"

"God, no!"

Tommy said nothing.

Her lips thinned. "Mister, I think you've been a cop *way* too long. My son's response was perfectly natural, perfectly under-standable."

"You said his reaction was off the charts . . . ."

"So was the sadistic nature of this act!" A strand of hair fell forward, and she raked it back. "Dillon's not overly sheltered, but neither has he witnessed senseless brutality like this before."

"Of course not." He shifted in the recliner with difficulty. "You know your son better than anybody."

"Yes, I do." She stood, her thoughts churning. Was it possible? Could Dillon know more about this than he was letting on? "Look, I'd better head back. With all the time I lost this afternoon, I'll have to bake all night." She glanced around. "Is there anything I can do for you before I go?"

"No, I'm good. Thanks for letting me know about Cleo."

Back home, Paige found Dillon in the kitchen, putting down kibble and water for his new pet.

"Hey, not in my kitchen. This is a commercial food-preparation area, kiddo. You'll have to teach her it's off limits. I can't be losing my food premises license over a stray dog."

"Where, then?"

"How about the end of the hall, by your bedroom. You can put her dishes on one of my serving trays so her supper doesn't wind up all over the carpet."

Dillon obliged, placing the filled casserole dishes onto a plastic serving tray and carrying it to the end of the hall. Paige followed.

"Wow, look at her go after that food," he said, hunkering down on the floor to watch.

"Remember what the vet said. Not too much."

"I remember everything." Dillon's gaze remained fixed on the dog. "I measured it, just like he said."

She watched the two of them for a moment, the dog bolting her food quickly as though fearing it might be taken from her, and Dillon watching in a sort of tender fascination.

Had he always wanted a dog? And why hadn't she known that? Had he been so imprinted with the precariousness of their financial situation in the early days that he dared not ask?

Dammit, why did this get harder all the time instead of easier? She knew she'd done the right thing in removing Dillon from the cruel capriciousness of his father's careless affection, even though it meant foregoing any financial support, however sporadic. She couldn't, wouldn't, second guess herself now.

"I have to get to work," she said. "Keep her occupied, okay?"

"Okay."

Back in the kitchen, she'd started to pull out the ingredients for a batch of pie crust when she noticed the note on her counter top. She picked it up.

"Dillon? Do you know anything about this?

A few seconds later, he popped his head in through the kitchen door. She held up the note.

"Oh, yeah. It was stuck on our door. Something about someone bein' here while we were out. Thought you'd wanna see it."

"A physiotherapist, to be precise. This must have been intended for Tommy, and she got the address wrong."

"Want me run it over?"

"No, I'll take it," she said quickly, not wanting to risk Tommy grilling Dillon right now. It had been a hard afternoon for all of them.

Dillon shrugged and went back to his dog.

Note in hand, she marched next door again. Having no time to waste, she knocked briefly to announce her arrival, turned the unlocked doorknob and stepped inside. "Tommy?"

A muffled sound of exasperation coming from the living room.

"Tommy?" she called again.

"I thought you went home."

She walked through to the living room, bracing for the sensual impact of the sight of his lounging length. He was still sitting in the La-Z-Boy, but this time, he looked like hell. His hair was damp with sweat, and his face looked haggard with pain.

"Omigod, what happened?"

⋘⋙

"What happened?" Damned woman. Why did she have to come back? "What happened is I'm a goddamn cripple and I can't get out of this chair."

Her lips thinned, and a spark of temper lit her eyes. Good. At least that look of horrified pity was gone. She moved over to stand by his chair, towering over him. He was acutely conscious of her wholeness, her easiness within her own body.

"It usually works better if you collapse the footrest," she observed. "Until you do that, you'll never get it out of reclining position."

"Thanks, but I've had this thing for eight years. I think I know how it works by now."

More green sparks. Good. He felt like a fight.

"Then what's the problem?"

He gestured to the side of the chair, where the lever for the footrest had broken off. Her gaze darted off to the left, locking onto the smooth and totally useless piece of wood laying on the hardwood floor where he'd hurled it in frustration.

"That was there earlier when I was here." Her voice held astonishment. "You were stuck in that chair all the time, yet you didn't ask me for help."

"I hadn't tried very hard to get up at that point."

"And now you have."

"Now I have." He managed to keep his voice calm, though his heart banged against his ribs.

"And what would you have done if I hadn't come back?"

Her voice was calm and quiet, too, but her eyes still glittered with a slow-burning anger.

Here's your chance. You can get rid of her right now, for good.

"Not come back?" He laughed, low and insulting. "Like *that* was gonna happen."

For a fraction of a second, the fire leapt higher, but then she tamped it out. She knew what he was trying to do, he realized. She knew and forgave him. *Goddammit.*

"Yes, you're right. I would have come back. Because you do need help, and because you've clearly driven all your friends away with that incredible charm of yours."

Easy for her to say, standing there, whole and healthy of limb. Vital. Alive. Beautiful. "Okay, dammit, I need help. So help me. Get me out of this chair, already."

"No."

He blinked at her. "No?"

"I think you should get out of it yourself."

"Hello? Did you just parachute into this scene? If I could get out of the damned chair, we wouldn't be having this conversation."

"Stay there," she instructed, then left. He heard the door slam shut and knew he was alone in the house again.

Stay there? *Stay there?* Where was he going to go? And did she mean to make him wait, payback for his rudeness?

He didn't have to wonder long. A few minutes later, he heard the door open and close, and she came into the room carrying a red metal toolbox. Placing it on the floor, she opened the lid and rummaged around a moment before extracting a very big, very heavy set of vise-grips.

He eyed the tool warily. "What do you propose to do with that? Teach me some manners?"

"Tempting, but no." She approached his chair, vise-grips in hand. "I'm going to talk real slow, because it's important that you get this. You're stuck in that chair because of a failure of the chair, not because of your failure," she said. "I'm going to fix the chair like so . . . ." She clamped the vise-grips onto what remained of the broken lever and tightened the grip until he heard the unmistakable sound of wood being compressed. "And voila," she said, stepping back. "You can get up now."

He found the makeshift lever with his right hand and shoved it forward. The footrest retracted obediently and he was able to bring the recliner to an upright position. Using his upper body, he levered himself out of the chair.

"See? It was just a matter of —"

He gripped her by the shoulders, and whatever words she'd planned to say died on her lips.

"I'm gonna say this real slow, because it's important that you get this." He ground the words out slowly. "I'm a *man*, dammit! I am *not* a child."

He saw awareness leap in her eyes. He saw a kind of fluttering panic flare there, too. Both gave him a sense of satisfaction. Then he closed his eyes and covered her maddening mouth with his.

Her lips parted on a shocked gasp, and he took full advantage, sweeping into her mouth. She tasted of surprise and cinnamon and an unexpected innocence, which took the edge off his anger, but did nothing to dull the keenness of his intent. He grasped her face, tilting it for better access to her mouth, and proceeded to kiss her with deliberate, frank eroticism. No gentle request, no teasing enticement, no sweet cling of lips. Just pure, driving sexual demand.

She tried to pull back, but he held her fast, determined that the lesson stick. For a moment, she stood there, her mouth slack under his, accepting his intimate invasion with a kind of shocked passivity.

Then something changed. The hands on his chest no longer pushed; they splayed, tested, clung. Reflexively, he deepened the kiss, sinking into the sweet, erotic mystery of her. Suddenly, her mouth was making demands of its own, even as one arm snaked around his neck.

It was supposed to be a punishment, a correction, an exercise in instruction. He hadn't girded himself against the possibility that she'd respond on a sexual level. Now, with the warm solidity of her body pressed eagerly against him and the taste of her fogging his brain, desire rocketed through him.

Skin. Paige's translucent skin, the very stuff he'd been fantasizing about. He had to touch it. Sliding a hand under her t-shirt, he skimmed his palm up her back. Smooth, warm, silky. Was it as enticingly freckle-dusted as her delicate collar bone? He let his fingertips glide over her flesh as though he might discern any tiny pigmentations by touch alone. That skimming caress drew a sigh from her throat, a sound that was pure sex. His loins grew heavier, harder.

Breaking the kiss, she tipped her head back and arched into him in clear invitation. Lord, she was hot. Liquid, luscious, her flesh swelling, yearning.

He swept her t-shirt up to close his hand around a small, perfectly formed breast. This time, the sound she made was a cry of delight. Needing no instruction, he stroked her taut flesh through the seamless cup of her bra, letting his fingers draw closer and closer to the thrust of her nipple.

Her breathing grew more ragged until finally, finally, he brushed her tightly drawn nipple. A sob broke from her lips. He covered her mouth again in a heated, hungry kiss. Without warning, she sagged against him, committing herself into his hands.

Oh, goddammit!

He didn't even have a chance to utter a warning. Down he went, like a derelict tenement house under a wrecking ball. Or rather, he would have if she hadn't grabbed at him. As it was, she guided his fall. Instead of hitting the floor, he landed right back where he'd started on the recliner, though heavily enough to drag a curse out of him.

"Oh, shit. Tommy, are you all right?"

Pain screamed along his nerve endings, clawing clear through him, then radiating out. "I'm fine."

She caught her lower lip, reddened and full, between her teeth. "I'm so sorry."

Just goddamn great. Way to show her what a man you are. The minute she leans on you, you literally crumple. "It's okay. Forget it."

"It's my fault."

"Dammit, Paige, don't make it any worse." Gritting his teeth, he pulled himself up again. The wave of dizziness that washed over him passed quickly, but the nausea that came with it remained.

She leapt up to retrieve his cane from where he'd left it propped against the coffee table. "I'm sorry," she said, offering him the cane. "I just wasn't thinking."

He wished he could refuse it, wished he could just walk away. But, dammit, he couldn't. Taking the hated thing from her, he started to hobble toward the kitchen.

"Where are you going?"

He unclenched his teeth to say, "To take a pain pill."

"I'll get it for you."

He stopped, looked up at the ceiling. *Please God, take me now.* Unfortunately, no bolt of lightning materialized from on high to strike him down. "I can get it myself."

Leaning heavily on the cane, he trudged on.

Of course, she beat him to the kitchen, quickly taking a glass from the cupboard and filling it from the tap. By the time he made it to a chair and picked up his pills, she was there with a full tumbler of water. He shook two pills into his palm, tossed them back and dry-swallowed them. Recapping the bottle, he put it back on the table.

"Better wash those down properly," she said, pushing the tumbler toward him. "They can ulcerate your esophagus if they get stuck on the way down."

He fixed her with a baleful look. "Okay, I'll admit, I'm not much of a man anymore, as you just saw. But that doesn't make me a goddamn infant."

"No?" She pulled back, those kiss-swollen lips thinning. "Tell you what — I'll stop treating you like a child when you stop acting like one. How about that for an idea?"

"How about you leave so I can get some rest?"

She looked at him for a long moment. "You're upset because I saw you fall."

He bit back a savage oath. When he spoke, his voice was controlled, cold. "Go away, Paige."

"You are. You're upset because you were helpless in that chair, then you lost your balance —"

This time, he didn't censor his reply, but she merely smiled and handed him a slip of paper.

"In that case, you might be interested in this."

He unfolded the note and scanned it. It was from his physiotherapist. Or rather, the woman who was intent on becoming his physiotherapist. He hadn't kept any of the appointments they'd made for him. "Where'd you get this?"

"It was left on my doorstep. She must have had the wrong unit number in her file."

"I'm sorry they bothered you."

She shrugged. "No bother." Then, after a pause, "So, are you going to call them?"

"No."

"Why not?"

"Why would I be interested in physio?" He balled the paper up in his fist and tossed it onto the table. "They've already told me no amount of therapy will put me back where I was. I'll always limp. I'll certainly never go back to being a dog master, or any kind of active duty."

He watched her digest that information, waited for the pity. It didn't come.

"So what?"

So what? Had he heard her correctly?

Before he could stammer a reply, she was talking again.

"Okay, so maybe you'll never run the Boston Marathon. But maybe, with a little work, you'll be able to keep your feet when a woman throws herself at you." She arched an eyebrow. "That would come in handy, wouldn't it? I imagine it happens pretty frequently."

Yeah, like there was much risk of that happening these days. The type of women he usually gravitated to wouldn't have much use for him now. And even if they did, he no longer had the easy out when the sex was done. He couldn't leap out of bed to ostensibly answer the call of duty anymore, since he no longer had a job, or even a dog to tend to. The very thought made him feel trapped, claustrophobic. He shook the thought off. "You hardly *threw* yourself at me."

"Oh, I think I did," she said, and her gently self-mocking tone went some distance to easing the knot in his gut.

"Not before I jumped on you." He ran a hand around the back of his neck. "Sorry. You were right. I was smarting about being stuck in the damned chair and needing help."

"And I was being a wise-ass."

"That's no excuse for me losing my temper. I shouldn't have."

She laughed. "Hey, don't apologize. Old girls like me, it's not every day we get kissed by handsome young men like—"

"Why do you do that all the time?"

Her smile faded. "Do what?"

"Exaggerate the age difference between us. If you're not making me out to be an infant, you're making yourself out to be a grandmother."

Her eyes cooled. "Technically, Dillon has been old enough to make me a grandmother for a few years now."

The thought gave him pause, but he'd be damned if he'd let her see it. Instead, he borrowed a phrase from her. "So what? Technically, I could be a grandfather myself by now, but I'm not." He shifted in his chair in an attempt to ease the pain in his hip. "How old *are* you, anyway?"

"I should go." She brushed her hair back with a nervous hand.

"Thirty-nine? Forty?" He deliberately guessed high.

She drew her breath in on a hiss. "I'm thirty-four!" Then, after a pause, "You think I look forty?"

He grinned. "Relax, you don't look a day over twenty-five, especially in that t-shirt. I just wanted an honest answer."

She lifted her chin. "And how old are you?"

"Old enough."

"Twenty-two? Twenty-three?"

His smile disappeared. Holy hell. She couldn't really think him that young, could she? "Twenty-nine."

She chewed her lip a moment, as though considering what to say next. He wished she'd just out with it. His leg was killing him.

"Look, Tommy, I'm not looking to have an affair with you."

Whoa, now there was a big leap! He'd met her what ... ? Twenty-four hours ago?

On the other hand, maybe not so big a leap, he thought, recalling the kiss. But somehow it stung that she was rejecting him, never mind that he had no intention of making a pass at her. "That's a relief. I don't think the body's up to it yet."

Her eyes sparked again. "That's got nothing to do with it. Even if you were perfectly fit .... I just don't have affairs. I have Dillon to think about, and my business. It's a small town, and single mothers ... my image is vulnerable."

"Whoa, whoa. No need to pull out the full-body armor." That strange anger burned in his belly even as he tossed her that answer in his best amused tone. "I have no intention of storming the citadel."

"Well, good." She smiled brightly. "That's settled, then."

Ah, so, his quick dismissal had struck a nerve, he thought, noting the artificial wattage of her smile. Not so uninterested after all. He couldn't deny the spurt of satisfaction, even though he wasn't interested in starting anything.

"It's settled," he agreed.

Halfway to the door, she hesitated.

He cocked an eyebrow. "Something else?"

"Yes, actually. Dillon has about a million questions about training his puppy. He's already talking about picking your brain. Is that okay?"

Something inside him clenched. Was it okay? To have a dog around again, reminding him of everything he'd lost?

It would hurt like hell, and then some.

Which perhaps was no less than he deserved.

"Tell him to come over in the morning. Door'll be open."

Chapter 4

PAIGE AWOKE THE NEXT morning with a dull, persistent throbbing at her temples. She'd slept lightly, waking often with Tommy Godsoe's blazing blue eyes and full, sensuous lips on her mind, and a heavy, sweet ache in her breasts. Her dreams were hot, incredibly erotic, and they left her feeling restless and edgy.

It had been hard enough to keep him out of her dreams when she'd thought such fantasies branded her a depraved old lady. Now, she knew he wasn't as young as she'd imagined. She also now knew exactly how he tasted, remembered perfectly the feel of his hands on her body. Rusty as the old sex drive was, it had been well and truly reawakened.

Of course, he was still too young for her. Not that she was going to get involved with him. She had enough on her plate without complicating her life with a man, let alone a younger one who looked like he'd fallen out of a Calvin Klein ad. Still, it was a relief to know she needn't feel like a total lech for secretly lusting after him.

She found Dillon in the dining room, working on a bowl of cereal while Cleo sat watching him with soulful eyes. She blinked, rubbed her eyes, but the apparition didn't vanish. Her son was actually up and around. "What happened to you? Dog drag you out of bed?"

He lifted one shoulder in an elegant shrug, a gesture that never ceased to remind her of his father. "I just figured she'd need to go out for a whiz."

Ah, the responsible Dillon. Her heart lifted. *Welcome back, kid. Stay as long as you like.* Of course, it wouldn't do to make a fuss, so she walked through to the kitchen and took the coffee canister down from the shelf. "How's her leg?" she called.

As her son gave her a health status report on the dog, she started the coffee. Once the brew had started to drip, she headed back to the dining room, where Cleo continued to gaze adoringly at Dillon, notwithstanding the fact that his breakfast was gone.

"So she's getting around better already. That's good." Paige pushed her hair back from her face. "I still can't believe someone did that to her. To take a foreign object and purposely jam it —"

"Oh, geez, can we not talk about that? It makes me want to hurl." Dillon bent to stroke the little dog. "You're safe, now, Cleo, girl," he crooned. "No one'll hurt you ever again."

Yes, this was her Dillon. Kind, compassionate, empathetic. Not the surly, taciturn stranger who'd taken up residence in his stead. To hide the sheen in her eyes, she popped up off her chair and went back into the kitchen to pour herself a coffee.

"I'm gonna go over to Tommy's now, okay?"

She glanced up from adding cream to her coffee. *Tommy's?* Since when had he graduated from *that cop* to Tommy?

Since he'd helped him with the dog, she supposed.

She angled her head to check the clock on the wall. It was barely seven o'clock. She put the cream carton back in the refrigerator. "Isn't it a little early? Maybe you'd better wait a while."

"Nah, he's been up for ages. I heard him movin' around."

"He might be up, but maybe he's not at his best at this hour."

Dillon snorted. "I'm thinking he's never at his best, so it probably doesn't matter when I barge in on him."

"Dillon!"

"S'okay, ma." He rolled his eyes. "It's not like I'd say that to *him*." He grabbed a banana from a bowl on the dining room table, peeled it, and devoured it in a couple of bites. "And if he doesn't want to talk to me right now, I'll go back whenever he says. I don't even care if he's his usually sunny self, long as he shows me how to train Cleo. The vet said she'd probably need lots of work." He walked over to the compost container in the corner of the kitchen and disposed of the banana peel. "This is just about full," he remarked, frowning down at it. "Remind me when I get back, and I'll dump it for you."

Yes, her Dillon was definitely back. She smiled and sipped her coffee.

Dillon summoned Cleo, clipped a leash to her collar and started to lead her away. At the first tug, the dog cringed, planting her feet. Dillon increased the tension on the lead and her collar slipped right off over her head, hitting the floor with a jangle of tags. "Okay, so we have a little work to do."

Coming back to where the young dog cowered, he knelt down, scooped her up gently and carried her outside.

Dillon didn't come right back, so Paige assumed Tommy must have been at least marginally receptive. Putting it out of her mind, she hit the shower, dressed, and pulled her hair back into a tight ponytail. Then she loaded the CD player with five of her favorites and put it on random play. And because Dillon and her neighbor were already up, she cranked the volume a little higher than she normally would. Then she went to work.

Four hours later, her face flushed from her exertions and the heat of her kitchen, she packed the van to make her deliveries. Dillon still hadn't returned, but when she killed the music, she could hear his muted voice next door, interspersed with Tommy's deeper, chesty baritone.

Briefly, she wondered if she should be worried that Dillon was spending so much time over there, then she caught herself. He could be killing the hours with that cold-eyed young man who looked like his heaviest thinking involved deciding which body part to pierce next. She shuddered. Thank God Dillon had found something else to get enthused about. And thank God Tommy was prepared to share his knowledge of dogs with her son.

Blinking back tears yet again, she decided she would cook a thank-you dinner for her neighbor, and this time, she'd do a proper job of it.

It took her a little longer than usual to make her deliveries. Tomaso, the chef at a downtown dining room and one of her best customers, wanted to brainstorm ideas for new desserts to tempt diners in the summer heat. They'd settled on strawberry zabaglione and a gorgeous raspberry and ricotta semifreddo.

Another stop at the supermarket to buy fresh fruit, ricotta, superfine sugar and the makings for tonight's meal. A third stop at the liquor store for rum and Grand Marnier for a couple of her more exotic desserts. While she was at it, she put a nice Muscadet in her shopping basket. The wine would be just weighty enough to wash down the delicate fish entree she planned to make for dinner.

As she was leaving the mall, a lingerie shop caught her eye. She paused to admire the mannequin in the shop's display window. God, what she'd give to look half as curvaceous as that! Though Tommy hadn't seemed to mind her slightness in that department. Her skin tingled at the memory. Still, maybe it wouldn't hurt to own at least one undergarment that tried to make the best of her scanty —

When a passerby bumped her elbow and muttered a quick apology, Paige jerked out of her daze and glanced around. Dear Lord, she'd been obstructing traffic. Worse, she'd been coveting those bits of satin and lace, or rather their impossible promise of engineering feats that would make her look like the mannequin in the window who wore them. And all because of a pair of blazing blue eyes that wouldn't let her be, even in her dreams.

She hurried out of the mall.

In the parking lot, she stopped ten feet from the van. *Dammit.* The rear driver's side had been tagged by a hit-and-run graffiti artist. The last thing she could afford was another paint job. She'd just had the van professionally painted two months ago. She scratched the white substance, which came away easily on her fingernail. Lifting her fingers, she sniffed the substance. Soap. Thank goodness! It would come off with a little elbow grease.

Kids these days, she fumed as she lifted the hatchback and shoved the grocery bags inside. They were like animals, traveling in packs, marking territory as visibly and frequently as possible. And her vehicle made a great target, with her corporate logo painted on the doors. Closing the door, she studied the signature a moment. It looked like a Z with a long tail on the end, and a strike through the diagonal bar. It didn't mean anything to her, but she'd make a mental note to look out for it.

Dillon was there to open the door for her when she got home. He even helped her put the stuff away.

"Thought you got groceries yesterday," he said, as he unpacked the first bag.

"I did, but one of my clients wants to try some new desserts. Cooler stuff, for the hot weather."

Dillon pulled an item out of the last bag. "And you're going to make these cool desserts with —" he paused to examine it a little closer, "a big, ugly fish?"

She took the fresh sea trout from him and put it in the refrigerator. "That's for supper. I thought I'd invite Tommy over, as a thank-you for helping you with Cleo." Paige glanced around. "Speaking of which, where is she?"

Grinning, Dillon indicated the dining room with a nod of his head. "She's showing off *stay.*"

Paige turned to see the little yellow dog sitting just outside the room. Her thin body seemed to vibrate with the desire to enter the kitchen, but she held her position. Paige turned back to her son. "She learned that today?"

He lifted something and made a few quick clicking sounds. "Along with *sit, down,* and *come.* Although *stay* only works for maybe a minute, if I'm lucky."

On cue, Cleo broke and rushed into the kitchen. Dillon instructed her to sit. After several repetitions of the command, she complied, whereupon he praised her lavishly.

"That's incredible. But what was that clicking sound you were making before?"

"A clicker." He opened his palm so she could see the small device. "Tommy says it's a good idea to teach her to equate the clicking with positive reinforcement."

"Why don't you just tell her she's a good dog?"

"I do." He bent and gave the dog a treat, which she crunched noisily. After praising her again, he stood, giving Cleo a command to lie down. She obeyed, her gaze fixed on Dillon. *Click, click.* "But if I were running and wanted to tell her she did good, I could save my breath and use the clicker. Or someone else could use the clicker, and she'd think I was reinforcing her."

She smiled. Her son was completely hooked, whether he knew it or not. "Fascinating. How's her leg?"

"Pretty good. Tommy said it's good to keep her moving around a bit, as long as she doesn't overdo it."

Tommy could take that advice himself. "What are your plans? Are you going to hang around for supper, or were you planning to go out?"

"I'll hang around. In fact, I'll probably be under foot a lot more. You know, for Cleo."

Paige had to blink rapidly again. "Having you under foot more often would suit me fine."

"Guess I said I'd dump the compost, didn't I?" he said gruffly, moving off to do just that.

As soon as Dillon and Cleo disappeared out the back door, Paige went out the front and over to Tommy's. She rapped on the door once, then opened it. "Hello?"

"In here," he called from the kitchen.

She found him standing by the cupboards, contemplating a pile of stuff at his feet. Dog paraphernalia, she saw. Stainless steel dishes, dog treats, toys.

"I was digging some things out for Dillon," he said.

Paige's heart contracted as it struck her for the first time how truly hard it must be for him. Not only had he lost a job he loved, he'd also lost his dog. "You must really miss your dog."

"Wasn't mine." He didn't look up. "City property."

"I'm sure neither of you made that distinction when you were together."

No reply.

"Well, I know Dillon will appreciate it. Cleo is currently eating out of a very sissified French white casserole dish."

He bent to gather up the things. Paige rushed to help him, and they almost knocked heads.

"I got it," he growled.

She backed off, watched him flinch as he stood up again.

"I can't believe how much Cleo learned today," she said.

"Don't get too excited. She'll have to learn it all over again tomorrow and the next day, and the next, and get it reinforced about a million times. But she's pretty smart, and anxious to please."

"Thank you for taking the time with Dillon."

"No problem." He shifted his weight. "Well, are you going to take this off my hands or not?"

She shot him a grin. "I thought I'd better wait until I was invited. Didn't want to risk getting my head bit off again."

"Smartass, just like that kid of yours."

Her smile died. "He didn't give you any trouble, did he?"

"Nothing like that. But he does have a pretty dry wit."

Dillon and Tommy must have had a very good visit for Dillon to loosen up that much. She stepped forward to take the dog supplies from him. "He does, doesn't he? You know, most adults never notice that about him."

Relieved of his burden, he leaned on the cupboard and shifted his weight. "Most adults don't notice much."

But Tommy did. Whether by training or nature, he noticed plenty. Remembering his observations about Dillon's body language the night the rabbit carcass turned up, she shivered. What was he noticing about her right now?

"I came over to invite you to join Dillon and me for supper, as a thank-you for everything you've done."

"That's not necessary."

"It wasn't necessary for you to coach Dillon either, but you did it, and I'm grateful. Besides, what am I going to do with a whole sea trout if you don't come over and help us eat it?"

"Sea trout?"

She laughed at the unmistakable interest in his tone and the hungry gleam in his eye. "Hah! I knew you'd be a fish eater. You ectomorphs have to have your protein."

"Ectomorphs?"

"Body type," she answered. "Fast metabolism. You could eat six meals a day and stay lean without doing a lick of cardio, am I right?"

"Pretty much."

"Lucky," she said with genuine envy. "I'm a meso-endo. I have to be more careful."

He looked a little bemused. "I'll take your word for it."

Oh, hell, she was babbling. About body types, for heaven's sake. Time to make her exit. "Six o'clock. Don't be late; there's nothing worse than overdone fish. My door will *not* be unlocked, so please ring the bell." She whirled and left, giving him no chance to decline.

⁂

Tommy eyed his reflection in the dresser mirror critically. The casual slacks he'd pulled on rode lower on his hips than they should. Even the severely tailored shirt he wore, the only thing he owned that didn't make him look like a hastily dressed scarecrow, left more room than the designer had intended.

Paige was right; at the best of times, he had a hard time gaining weight. Every ounce of muscle he owned was hard-won through rigorous weight training and careful attention to diet. While the enforced inactivity of the past weeks would have spelled unwanted weight gain for most people, Tommy could see he'd lost weight. Lots of it. Muscle, too.

What would his father say if he could see his scrawny son now? Probably nothing, but he'd get that tight look around his mouth. Just as well the old man was in his grave. No more disappointments.

Thomas Godsoe, Sr. had been a career soldier, an avid hunter, an equally avid womanizer, and a fierce lover of boxing. He'd wanted a son with whom he could share those passions, but had wound up with a pale slip of a kid, a sensitive soul who more closely resembled his mother than his father. A kid who'd puked after being forced to kill, then skin, his first rabbit.

Tommy cursed and turned away from the mirror. His father's opinions had long since ceased to matter. It was a mark of just how weak he was that he'd let the old bastard into his head again, even for a minute.

Checking his watch, he saw it was ten to six. Better get moving. Something told him he wouldn't want to face Paige Harmer if he were responsible for ruining her fish. A minute later, he stood on Paige's doorstep, waiting for her to answer the bell. Despite himself, he felt his pulse kick up a notch. Anticipation of a good meal, he told himself.

The door opened, but it was Dillon on the other side, not Paige, and he was holding Cleo by her collar.

"Come in."

Tommy stepped across the threshold.

"Mom's changing. Said she didn't want to sit down to dinner smelling like a fish."

Tommy inhaled appreciatively. "Smells pretty good to me," he said, then turned to look at Cleo. Immediately, she squatted and piddled on the floor.

"Cleo!"

"Ignore that," Tommy said quickly, before the kid could punish the dog.

"Ignore it? She just *peed* on my mother's hardwood floor."

"Remember what we talked about. With a dog like this, you have to ignore unwanted behavior, and heavily reward the kind of behavior you want to encourage."

"So we just let her whiz on the floor whenever she feels like it?"

"She'll stop doing it as she gains some confidence. Right now, she's nervous and excited and scared. Try giving her something to do that you can reward her for."

Dillon commanded Cleo to sit, and the undersized lab settled on her haunches immediately. "Good girl," Dillon said, slipping her a biscuit.

"Perfect. Now, I'm going to do what all your guests should be instructed to do, and that's ignore her for at least a minute before I greet her. We need her excitement level to abate a little."

"So, she peed because she's excited?"

"Some dogs do. But with her, it's more likely that she's scared. If I were to zoom in on her, bend at the waist and pat her on the head the way most people are inclined to do when they're introduced to a dog, she'd see that as very aggressive. Since adult dogs won't usually hurt a puppy, she's trying to protect herself by emulating a small puppy."

"Of course! She's making herself look smaller by crouching down, and by urinating."

"Exactly."

"So, how do we get by that?"

"Easy. Have your guests ignore her for a minute, then when she levels off a bit, they can crouch right down, like this." Awkwardly, he lowered himself, feeling his lower back, hip and thigh scream in protest. "They should come at her from underneath, pat her chest, her neck, then maybe work their way up to her head, if she doesn't mind." He demonstrated the right approach, and though Cleo trembled once, she didn't shy away. With considerably more difficulty, Tommy stood again, grimacing. "Once she gains some confidence, she'll probably come to tolerate a head-patting as well as the next dog. They all flinch a little."

"Thanks." Dillon's voice was gruff. "I'da handled that all wrong."

"You'd have figured it out after a while. You're very intuitive. You just have to resist —"

"Anthropomorphizing." The kid completed Tommy's sentence with only the mildest of eye-rolls. "I know, I know. She's a dog, not a person, and we can't attribute human thoughts or feelings to her."

"It sounds hard-hearted, I know, but the biggest kindness you can do for her is to quite literally treat her like a dog. If you treat her like a person, you'll only confuse her. You can't let her be alpha dog sometimes, then expect her to be beta dog the rest of the time. She needs to know her place in the pack in no uncertain terms. And you have to be top dog, all the time, or this training will be a waste of time."

"Got it. Now, I think I'd better clean up this mess before Ma comes down and finds it. Why don't you wander out to the deck? That's where we're gonna eat."

Paige stood on the last step of the carpeted stairs, listening to the exchange between her neighbor and her son. She hadn't meant to eavesdrop, but the sound of Tommy's voice had arrested her. Out of nowhere, she was swamped with a longing so sharp and unexpected, she didn't know how to contain it. Needing a moment to compose herself, she sagged against the wall that concealed her from view, took a few deep breaths and willed her heart rate to slow. Then she'd tuned into the gist of the conversation.

This was precisely what her son needed. A positive male influence, someone who could teach him about being a man. A firm, confident hand that was still capable of tenderness.

So why did it hurt so much? Where did this pain come from, so swift and piercing, it stole her breath away?

"Oh, there you are."

Dillon's voice nearly made her jump. Instead, she descended the last step to stand beside him. "Yeah, here I am."

"Tommy's here," he announced. "I just sent him outside so he could take a load off. Oh, and Cleo had a little accident on the floor. I'm just gonna clean it up, then I'll wash up and join you."

"Great."

Fortunately, Dillon carried on without noticing anything amiss. Paige hurried to the kitchen to rescue her fish. Removing the baking pan from the oven, she placed it on the counter. Creole seasoning wafted up as she examined the fish. Thank goodness! It was all right. Better than all right.

Quickly, she sautéed the new potatoes that she'd cooked and diced earlier. In another pan, she sautéed asparagus, and in yet another, snow peas. Finally, she stirred the vegetables together and heaped them onto a serving tray. Then she carefully transferred the fish, it's skin intact, onto the nest of vegetables. Perfect.

Dillon glided into the kitchen. "Anything I can do?"

"Yes, you can get the patio door for me."

He complied, following her out onto the deck.

She kept her focus on the patio table. In the periphery of her vision, she saw Tommy lurch to his feet as she approached. By now, she knew better than to tell him the gesture wasn't necessary. It would only aggravate him. Since the whole point was to make nice and express her appreciation for what he was doing for Dillon, she held her tongue.

"That smells wonderful," he said.

She placed the platter in the middle of the cloth-draped table, then turned to smile a welcome at him. Her breath died in her throat.

Oh. My. God.

He wore a startlingly blue shirt, bluer than his eyes, and it followed the lines of his torso faithfully. The shirt's cuffs were shot back casually, and its tail, cut square, hung down past the waistband of loose-fitting khakis. His hair, still damp from the shower, glistened with health. His lean cheeks were clean-shaven, the deep grooves on either side of his mouth drawing attention to generous lips. Lips she'd tasted . . . .

Knowing there was no point trying to hide her reaction now, she grinned. "Wow, you look great."

His gaze dropped to the tobacco brown silk tank she wore, tucked into her best casual trousers. "You clean up pretty good yourself."

She felt her cheeks firing. "Thanks."

"Geez, can we eat, already?" grumbled Dillon.

Paige started. She'd forgotten her audience. "Of course. Sorry."

Before she could pull out her chair, Tommy did it for her. Flustered, she accepted the unfamiliar assistance. She darted a glance at Dillon, anticipating a flash of derision for Tommy's old-fashioned courtesy, but her son seemed to be watching thoughtfully. She found herself wondering if Tommy was modeling for Dillon's benefit, or if the gesture was ingrained.

Tommy took his seat again. He didn't wince as he lowered himself into the low-slung patio chair, but Paige did it for him. Dammit, she should have thought of that. Her dining room chairs would have been much easier for him to manage.

"Did I mention that smells incredibly good?" he said.

She laughed. "Then pass your plate and let me dish some up for you."

He passed her his plate. As she carved him a piece of the perfectly done trout, she nodded toward the bottle of wine at his elbow, now dewed with moisture in the warm evening air. "Why don't you open that and pour us a glass?"

He accepted the task, opening the bottle smoothly, but with a slow deliberateness. As he poured just the right amount of golden liquid into two wine glasses, she felt certain he was giving Dillon a silent lesson. A quick glance at her son told her he wasn't missing a beat.

"Dillon, your plate?"

He handed it to her, and she performed the same service for him as she'd done for Tommy, before putting a generous portion on her own plate. Taking his lead from Tommy, Dillon didn't dive into his meal as he normally would, but rather waited for her.

The whole meal passed that way. Paige was frankly grateful for the odd dynamic which had defused the electrical awareness she'd felt initially. All the while, Cleo lay a short distance from Dillon, watching gravely but with no real expectation of a windfall.

"Can I give Cleo my leftovers?" Dillon asked when they were finished.

Paige glanced at Tommy, inviting his opinion with a raised eyebrow.

"A few table scraps won't hurt, as long as it's balanced. No fat or gristle or bone, and nothing too spicy. Just make sure she continues to mind her manners when you're eating and waits her turn."

"Great." Dillon jumped up and headed for the patio door.

"Not from the plate!" she called after him. "Scrape it into her dish. And please bring out that dessert when you come back."

"Sure."

She smiled as boy and dog disappeared into the house. "I still can't believe we have a dog. We never had a pet before, other than hamsters when Dillon was little."

Tommy picked up his wine and leaned back in his chair. He held the glass properly, she noticed, by the stem so as not to warm the chilled contents with his hands. She shivered.

"Never had a pet yourself when you were a kid?"

"No." Her smile faded. "One place I stayed had a Rottweiler, but I wouldn't say he was a pet. I don't even know why they kept it.

It was tied to its dog house all the time. It was half crazy, I think, and I was petrified of it."

Tommy cursed under his breath. "Poor devil probably was half crazy. Banishment from the pack is about as bad as it gets for a dog. Unfortunately, animal protection legislation is pretty toothless when it comes to that kind of emotional abuse. As long as the owner provides food, water and shelter and isn't actively abusing it in a physical way, there's not much the authorities can do."

She leaned back in her own chair, trying to reconcile his outrage with the image he'd painted of himself as a hunter, a man who engaged in blood sports. She was about to ask him about the contradiction when Dillon yanked the patio door open and burst onto the deck. He strode over to the table and thrust her notepad under her nose.

"What's this?"

Chapter 5

DILLON'S HAND TREMBLED. A tendril of alarm unfurled in her belly. Ignoring it, she peered at the words scrawled on the yellow ruled sheet. "It's a partial list for my next market run, obviously."

"Not that." He pointed to the doodles she'd made on the corner of the pad. "*That.*"

She leaned closer. It was the symbol the graffiti artist had left on her vehicle, the long-tailed Z with the slash through the diagonal. She must have drawn it while she'd waited on hold as the accounts payable people at her largest customer checked into an unpaid invoice.

She leaned back in her chair, relieved. "Maybe *you* can tell *me* what it is. It's all over my delivery van."

He blanched. "Omigod, somebody tagged your van with this?"

"It's okay. It wasn't paint. Just soap. It'll wash off."

"Damn right it will! Right now." Dillon wheeled, notepad still in hand, and headed for the door.

"Whoa, son. Before you tear off, let's have a look."

Tommy's tone stopped Dillon in his tracks. Tommy extended a hand for the note pad. Dillon looked like he wanted to refuse Tommy's quiet authority, but after the merest pause, he handed the pad over.

Tommy examined it. "Gang signature."

Paige sighed. "I figured as much. Do you know it?"

"No, I'm not familiar with this one," he said, handing the pad back to Dillon. "Don't suppose you know it, Dillon?"

He shrugged. "Not really. I mean, I've seen it around, I guess."

He was lying. Again. Or at least, not telling the complete truth. Paige swallowed a lump of disappointment. "You seem pretty upset about it."

"Of course, I was upset," came his indignant reply. "I thought someone spray-painted the van. I was thinking we'd have to pay a bundle to get it repainted and I'd be S.O.L. when I have to replace my goalie pads this winter."

Good improv. He was his father's son when it came to rationalizing away his behavior. The lump in her throat grew. "Of course." She smiled brightly. "Now, how about bringing that dessert?"

"Sorry," he mumbled. "Be right back with it."

As Dillon closed the patio door behind him, the silence rang in Paige's ears. She closed her eyes. "Don't say it. I know he knows more than he's letting on, but I don't want to get into it with him right now."

"Makes sense."

At his agreement, her eyes sprang open. She must have looked pretty startled, because he grinned at her expression.

"Judging from his reaction, I'd say he definitely knows more than he's saying. In fact, my guess is that he's had some up close and personal experience with this particular gang. But he seems to have found another focus now, with Cleo's arrival. This might be one of those situations where you'd do better to ignore the missteps he's made and reward the positive steps."

Despite the lump of anxiety sitting on top of her supper, she had to smile at that. "Treat him like a dog, you mean?"

To her surprise, his expression stiffened. "Hey, I don't claim to know anything about kids. Lord knows my father wouldn't have taken that approach."

Surprised by the vehemence of his tone, she asked the obvious question: "What would your father have done?"

"I don't know." He picked up his wine glass, drained it and placed it back on the table. "Conducted his own version of a court-martial, I expect."

She grimaced. "Military?"

"Career soldier." He relaxed back into his chair, but she had the idea it took conscious effort. "A real man's man, my Dad."

"Your father was a soldier?" This from Dillon, who'd returned with a tray bearing the desserts, Cleo trailing after him.

"Yessir. And big on the outdoors. By the time I was your age, I could have survived a week in the woods in mid-winter, with nothing but a hatchet, a knife, some matches, and wire for snares."

Dillon's eyes widened. "You're kidding!"

"Not a word of a lie."

Tommy's tone was dryly amused, but his words sent a chill through Paige. Suddenly, and with utter certainty, she knew that he *had* survived a week in the woods under the do-or-die circumstances he'd described.

"Wow, that's so cool. Could you teach me that stuff?"

He shrugged. "I could, but only an idiot would be caught in the woods under those circumstances, without emergency rations. Short of falling out of the sky in an airplane crash, you should never find yourself in that situation. It's infinitely easier to stay safe through proper planning."

"That'd be cool, too," Dillon conceded. "But maybe you could show me some of the worst case scenario stuff? Just so I could impress the guys."

"The guys?"

Tommy's tone had turned teasing, and his posture looked more naturally relaxed. Paige let her pent-up breath escape.

"Okay, the girls," confessed Dillon.

"Yeah, yeah, break it up," she groused. "Enough guy talk. It's time for dessert."

Tommy turned his attention to the zabaglione-topped strawberries, served up in her best balloon glasses. "Oh, my Lord, that looks good."

Paige smiled, thinking how closely the sentiment echoed her reaction when she'd walked out here earlier and seen him in that shirt. "Strawberry zabaglione," she said. "My first attempt, and I need critical feedback."

He picked up his dessert spoon and tried it. Closing his eyes, he emitted a groan, a slow, nasal exhalation as his mouth savored the explosion of flavor and texture.

"Told you it was good," said Dillon, who'd sampled it earlier.

"Yeah, but you'd say that about a peanut-butter-and-jelly sandwich."

"So? Peanut butter and jelly is classic."

"It's fantastic." Tommy seemed to have found his voice again.

"Good, because the rest of it's going home with you when you leave."

He laughed. "So you're not tempted to eat it yourself, you mean?"

"There is that. Plus it'll only keep for about six hours in the refrigerator, and only because I put whipped cream in it to make it commercially viable. The straight stuff is only good for an hour or so." She picked up her own and tried it. "Damn, it is good, isn't it?"

Minutes later, Dillon excused himself to go wash the van. Tommy helped her clear the table, and again, she didn't protest, though she could see he'd grown stiff from sitting. She poured coffee for them, suggesting they take it inside at the dining room table. If he realized she was trying to spare him getting in and out of the low patio chair again, he didn't mention it.

"This was nice." He sipped the rich Columbian brew appreciatively. "You're a helluva fine cook, Paige Harmer."

Feeding him, watching him relish every mouthful, had been reward enough for her homemaker's heart, but hearing the words made her feel positively smug.

"Glad you enjoyed it, because I'm hoping I can use those skills to buy your services."

Tommy choked, nearly spewing his coffee. Christ, hadn't she said she wasn't interested, mere hours ago? Hadn't he said he wasn't up to it? Coughing, he plunked his coffee down on the table and pushed his chair back. The burn of coffee gone down the wrong way brought tears to his eyes.

"Not *those* services!" Paige's face flamed as brightly as his probably did after that coughing jag. "I meant, helping Dillon. He likes you. You both love dogs, and there's so much you can teach him. It's given him a whole new focus, a *healthy* focus."

He scowled. "You don't have to bribe me for that. If the kid wants to talk dogs, he can come over any time."

"It's more than dogs." Her brows drew together in a frown. "He could go to the library to learn what you can teach him about training a dog, if he wanted to. What he needs is a male role model."

If the idea of playing gigolo had dismayed him, the prospect of serving as a role model for an impressionable teenager scared the living hell out of him. "I don't think I'm the man for that job, Paige."

"Sure you are. You're a natural. I saw what you did tonight. You modeled appropriate behavior at the dinner table, and Dillon lapped it up."

He shoved a hand through his hair. "That's Dining 101. That's nothing. I'm not qualified to model anything else."

"Sure, you are."

He glared at her. "Right. What would you have me follow with? Safe sex? Time-tested cures for a hangover?"

She lifted her chin, green eyes sparking. "Why not? Whether I like it or not, those are things a young man has to learn."

"How about the Tommy Godsoe catch-and-release approach to dating? No? You don't like that one? How about landing your buddy in an IAD shit-storm out of sheer carelessness?" He could hear his voice gather volume with every word, but he couldn't seem to stop it. "Oh, I know! How about, how to screw up on the job, jeopardize your dog, get shot, and almost get your backup killed?"

Her eyes hardened. "Tommy Godsoe, if you're trying to persuade me you're an unfit specimen, then you really haven't been paying attention."

She pushed to her feet and Tommy leaned back in his chair reflexively.

"Dillon has been hanging around with bona fide *thugs*," she continued, hands on hips. "Genuinely scary men who think the height of fashion is branding their own skin. I don't even want to think about what their approach to 'dating' entails, but I'm afraid it might incorporate GHB, or alternatively, the exchange of money."

"But —"

"But what, Tommy? You think I imagined you were Ward Cleaver?"

Dammit, she just didn't get it. "I'm not role model material. To begin with, I don't know anything about kids."

"You were a kid once," she pointed out.

"Don't even go there."

"Why not?"

"Let's just say, my father wasn't Ward Cleaver, either."

"Did your mother know?"

He shook his head, as though her question would make more sense if he could just clear his brain. "Did my mother know what? That my father wasn't Ward Cleaver?"

"Did she know your father left you in the woods for a week in the middle of the winter to fend for yourself?"

"Jesus Christ!" He lurched to his feet, catching the chair by its back just in time to prevent it from crashing to the floor. How the devil did she know that?

"So, did she?"

"Of course, she didn't know. She thought we were winter camping together."

"You didn't tell her any different?"

"Christ, no. I never told *anybody*. How the hell did you figure it out?"

She shrugged. "You learned to catch rabbits in snares and build shelters; I learned to fill in the space between what people say and what they mean."

The way she said it, with no trace of self-pity or sentiment, caught at his heart. Obviously, she'd learned some basic survival skills herself. Not so different from him, maybe. But somehow she'd found a better equilibrium, not feeling the need to hide her difficult past, yet not wearing it on her sleeve, either.

She tilted her head. "So what do you say? Will you teach Dillon?"

Lord, she was like a dog with a bone. "You're not going to make this easy for me, are you?"

"I'll make it very easy if you say yes." A dimple flashed on the right side of her cheek. "Come on, Tommy. All you have to do is spend a little time with him on the dog training thing. Then come over for supper in the evening, hang around a while like you did tonight, then go home. That's not such a bad deal, is it?"

He shook his head. "You are one determined broad."

This time, she smiled widely. "Yes, but I'm a helluva cook."

Six days later, Tommy leaned back in the very same chair at Paige Harmer's dining room table and rubbed his full stomach. He'd downed a juicy burger done on a charcoal grill, accompanied by cold salads and two ears of corn so fresh that they had to have been picked that very day.

She was right; as deals went, this one wasn't half bad. A couple of hours with the kid and the dog in the mornings, the afternoon to rest and recuperate, and an exquisite meal in the evening. He suspected he might even have gained a pound or two, thanks to Paige's cooking, and the fact that his cupboards were no longer bare. Dillon had driven him to the supermarket, then zipped around getting everything Tommy needed while Tommy leaned on the shopping cart for support. The kid had humped it all into the house, too, and helped put it away. And he wasn't that annoying to have around. Didn't talk nearly as much as his mother, for one thing. Plus he had a good way with Cleo, a real aptitude for dogs.

Yeah, this wasn't half bad.

Not that he'd gone into it without reservations. If Paige had brought up the subject of his late, unlamented father even once, he'd have been out of there like a round fired from the Sig he used to carry. He wasn't interested in talking about ancient history.

Well, at least not *his* ancient history. Oddly, he'd found himself wondering about *hers* from time to time. Life couldn't have been a bed of roses for her, moving from one foster home to another, not to mention a teen pregnancy and the whole single mom/no child support deal. Unfortunately, she didn't seem inclined to bring it up, and he sure as hell wasn't going to ask in case she demanded *quid pro quo*.

"Dessert." With that announcement, Paige swept back into the dining room and plunked down in front of him a small cut-glass bowl filled with ice cream. She deposited a second one on her own woven-reed place mat, then went back to the kitchen and returned with their coffee.

She settled on her chair, one leg tucked up under her. "Weird not having Dillon here, isn't it?"

Dillon had gone to the lake with some friends — safe friends from their old neighborhood in St. Stephen, Paige had stressed — and had taken Cleo with him.

"Yeah," he agreed, "but what's weirder is you serve fancy desserts all week when he was here, then drag out ice cream, the universal kid pleaser, when he's gone."

"Ice cream?" Paige shot him a horrified look. "I'll have you know that's a raspberry ricotta semifreddo."

He regarded the stuff in his dish. "Uh ... right."

She laughed. "Okay, so it's glorified ice cream. But it's way better."

He tried it. It was. "You *made* this?"

"Darned right I did —" She turned her head at the sound of a car pulling into the driveway. Two car doors slammed, one right after the other. "Dillon already?"

"Not unless his car's had a major tune-up, and not unless he brought back company."

From the empty unit next door, the doorbell pealed.

"They're here for you." She popped up off her chair. "I'll just go let them know you're over here."

"No!"

She stopped with her hand on the doorknob, then turned back. "No?"

"Black Pathfinder?"

She peered out the rectangle of glass flanking her front door. "Black SUV of some kind."

"Don't call them over."

She stood a moment longer with her hand on the doorknob, looking like she badly wanted to turn it, but at last she dropped her hand. Tommy relaxed his grip on his spoon, which he belatedly realized he'd been bending. Next door, the doorbell sounded again.

"They'll go away in a minute when there's no answer."

She arched an eyebrow at him. "Dodging your physiotherapist again?"

"No." She'd given up calling, thank goodness.

"Your bookie?"

"Hardly."

She gave him a hard look. "Bill collectors?"

He snorted. Bill collectors. Razor and Quigg'd love that. "No bad debts." At least not that kind. "Cops," he said, before she could make an even wilder guess. "Detective Ray Morgan, and unless I miss my guess, his passenger would be his sergeant, John Quigley."

Her eyes widened. "I don't believe this. You're turning your friends away?"

"Look, I'm doing them a favor. They're making the obligatory visit, but they don't really want to see me." He pushed away from the table, his gut churning.

"How can you say—"

"Look, Paige, none of the guys want to see me. You know why? Because when they look at me, they can't avoid thinking about what might happen to them on their next shift, if they're careless, or just plain unlucky. Or if somebody else screws up, like I did."

She held his gaze, and her chin took on that stubborn angle. "Don't you think they should be allowed to make that decision for themselves?"

"You think I dreamed this up?" A pulse had begun to throb in his temple. "You don't think see I saw the fear in the eyes of every man who came to visit me in hospital? The relief on their faces when they could finally make their getaway? You don't think I noticed when the visits dwindled away? They just want to forget about me."

"How can you say that?"

"Hey, I don't blame them. It's nothing personal. I really do understand. And the thing is, it shouldn't have been such a surprise to me. Talk to any cop who's been knocked out of the game like this, and they'll tell you the same story." He felt a grim smile twist his lips. "Except I never heard that particular story, 'cuz like everyone else, I'd go out of my way to avoid those guys."

The doorbell pealed again, long and continuous.

She bit her lip, clearly tortured by the unanswered summons. "This pair are pretty persistent. Maybe you should give them the benefit of a doubt. Maybe they're bigger than that."

"Oh, I know they are. They'd suck it up and be frequent visitors, but I won't have it."

Outside, doors slammed again and Ray Morgan's truck roared to life. Paige turned to watch as the vehicle reversed out of the driveway and headed back down the hill. When she turned back to him, she wore the same expression she did when Dillon disappointed her.

His temple still throbbing, Tommy turned back to his melting semi-whatever-she-called-it. She joined him a moment later, picked up her spoon and tasted her own handiwork. For what seemed like forever, she pushed the mixture around, apparently completely absorbed with the texture and color of the softening dessert.

"You know," she said finally, lifting her gaze to look at him across the table, "if you took the physical therapy and improved your mobility, maybe the guys wouldn't have such a drastic reaction —"

He dropped his spoon into the delicate dish with a clatter. "Physio would undoubtedly improve my mobility some," he conceded. "But it wont — *can't* — restore me sufficiently for active duty. The doctor was very clear about that."

She blinked, then put her own spoon down. "You're not going back, are you? Ever."

Once again, her acuity rattled him. She'd known him for what — a week? ten days? — and she'd somehow learned to see right into the darkest corners of his mind. He'd lay odds most of his friends of ten years and longer didn't even begin to suspect what darkness lurked there.

"That's right," he said evenly. "The only way I could possibly go back is as a desk jockey, and that's not gonna happen. Right now, I'm this … I don't know … this shadowy worry that can be pushed to the back of their minds. If I went back, I'd be a concrete, ever-present reminder. I'd be the station's very own personal albatross."

"You really believe that, don't you?"

The sadness in her eyes made his throat tighten. "Not because I want to, dammit. I believe it because it's the truth."

She picked up her spoon again, toyed with her dessert. "Then you need to make a new plan, I'd say."

Following her example, he picked up his spoon and ate another bite of the raspberry stuff. It might as well have been soggy newspaper.

"I do have a plan," he said, neglecting to mention this plan of his involved laying around until his injuries healed sufficiently, then using the considerable inheritance his mother had left him to buy a sailboat, which he would sail south to warmer climes and moor in some lazy marina. There, he would lie around some more and let the hot, semi-tropical sun leach the thoughts from his head and the pain from his bones.

He felt her gaze on him, but kept his attention on the dessert, as he scraped the dish clean. Then the phone rang. She went to answer it, and he carried his empty dish to the kitchen and put it in the dishwasher. Mentally, he started preparing his excuses to make an earlier than usual exit. After all, Dillon wasn't here to absorb —

"Tommy."

He turned to see Paige standing in the kitchen doorway, her hand pressed to her mouth, eyes stricken.

"What is it? Dillon? Has something happened?"

"No, not Dillon. That was one of my clients, a major hotel. My cheesecake … a diner damaged a tooth … ." She stared directly at him, but Tommy knew she wasn't seeing him. "Omigod, what am I going to do?"

"How could someone hurt a tooth on a *cheesecake*?"

"On a foreign object hidden in the cheesecake. Someone sabotaged my product."

Her eyes had regained their focus, he noted. "What kind of foreign object?"

"A key. A little padlock key."

Jesus. Just like the one the vet had found embedded in the dog's hip. His pulse kicked into high gear. She was talking again. He had to force himself to concentrate on her words.

"The hotel staff, they checked the rest of it, and there were five more. Six of them, all told."

His mind raced. "Have they called the cops?"

"No. I was their first call. They thought the problem originated here. But I would never … I mean, there's no way a foreign object could make its way into one of my desserts. It's just not possible, even if I had handfuls of keys lying around, which I don't. And the hotel is the first stop on my delivery route. The product is never out of my sight."

"It could have happened at the other end, after delivery."

"Of course!" She brightened momentarily, then sagged again. "But no matter where the tampering happened, the problem originated here, didn't it?" She paused, and he saw her throat bob, as though she were swallowing with difficulty. "Because it wasn't contaminated with shards of glass or bits of ceramic. It was riddled with keys, tiny ones, just like the one that showed up on Cleo's x-ray."

The throbbing in his temple had graduated to a full-fledged headache. "Can you think of anyone who might want to harm your business? A competitor? An enemy?"

She dragged her breath in on a harsh gasp, hardly seeming to hear him. "This is about me, isn't it, this whole thing? God, I was so worried about Dillon, so focused on him and his friends, I didn't stop to think … ."

Personally, Tommy wasn't ready to rule anything out, and certainly not Dillon's unsavory friends. The whole key thing was just too creepy.

"I guess I should have taken your advice and called the cops that night the rabbit carcass appeared," she said. Her eyes had taken on that unfocused look again.

Yeah, she should have, but she didn't need to hear 'I told you so' now. "Easy to say in hindsight, but you had your reasons."

She blinked rapidly at his concession. "Dillon swore he didn't have anything to do with that carcass turning up, and I believed him, yet there was this little grain of doubt … ."

"Understandable. There was the little matter of the blood on his shirt."

"He explained that. He was at the arcade, just like he said, but he had an altercation with someone there." She ploughed a hand through her hair. "It checks out. I called mall security. Turns out they actually trespassed him, a little detail he neglected to mention when he told me. He can't go back there for a year."

That would explain the blood and the kid's belligerent attitude that night. Somehow, however, that new information didn't make Tommy feel any better. Because if these bizarre events weren't tied to Dillon and his erstwhile friends, maybe Paige was right. Maybe this was about her.

"What am I going to do?"

Tommy massaged his temple. "You're going to run next door and get the business card Detective Morgan will have left wedged into the doorframe and bring it back here. It'll have his cell phone number on it."

Her eyes widened. "You're going to call them back here?"

"Looks like it."

Chapter 6

LESS THAN FIFTEEN MINUTES later, Paige opened her door to two men who couldn't have looked more different from each other. Or from Tommy.

"Mrs. Harmer?" said the younger one. He was casually dressed, yet managed to look like he'd be right at home in one of those magazine ads she so often pictured Tommy in. But this guy was *Gentleman's Quarterly* to Tommy's *Rolling Stone*. Still, Paige imagined he got good cooperation from the ladies.

"Detective Ray Morgan," he said, then nodded to the man standing behind him. "This is my sergeant, John Quigley."

"Ma'am."

She shifted her attention to the second man, who was the antithesis of elegant. *Classic mesomorph.* The phrase flashed through her brain as she took in the wide set of his shoulders and deep, powerful chest. That kind of physicality would burn away any veneer of sophistication he tried to drape it with.

She stepped back, opening the door wide. "Come in. Tommy's in the dining room."

"No, Tommy's right here."

At the sound of Tommy's voice, Paige turned to find him several feet behind her, leaning on his cane.

"Thanks for coming," he said.

"No problem. We were actually here not fifteen minutes ago. We must have just missed you." This from Sergeant Quigley.

"Yeah." Tommy cleared his throat, then turned to Paige. "Can we do this in the living room? Maybe with some of that coffee of yours?"

As distracted as she was by the upsetting phone call from her customer, she couldn't help but wonder why Tommy hadn't opted to go back to the dining room table. The tall, hard chairs were so much easier for him to manage. Did he want to prove something to his buddies? Or was it just the opposite? Was he intent on show-casing his disability?

Or did he just want to get rid of her for a few moments?

Realizing they were all waiting for a response from her, she gave herself a mental shake. "Coffee? Sure. Make yourselves at home, gentlemen."

She might have been dispatched to the kitchen, but as she pre-pared the coffee, she had no difficulty hearing the exchange taking place in the living room.

"You look like hell, Godsoe." That voice had to be the younger man's. Ray.

A short, unexpected laugh from Tommy. "Bite me, Morgan."

"Hah! That looks more like your department." Ray Morgan said. "We'll just call you Lestat. When was the last time you saw the sun, anyway?"

"Gee, I was sorta aiming for the dissolute look, but I guess the walking dead is close enough."

"Ignore him." The deeper voice had to be the Sergeant's. "You're getting around a lot better than the last time we saw you. How's the hip?"

"Great." Tommy's voice was downright jovial. "I'm thinking about joining a Can-Can troupe next week."

Another bark of laughter, this time from Ray Morgan. "Oh, man, spare us the visual!"

This rapid-fire, three-way exchange continued as she assembled mugs, spoons, cream and sugar, but fell off when she returned with the tray. She seated herself beside Tommy on the sofa, conscious that she'd changed the dynamic.

"Okay, Paige, the floor's yours," Tommy said, after everyone had fixed their coffees.

Suddenly, she felt very much center stage. "Where do I start?"

"The beginning is usually a good place," offered Ray.

"I'm not sure where the beginning is." She looked to Tommy for guidance. "We don't even know if the skinned rabbit carcass is connected."

"Ah, dead, mutilated critter. Sounds like something we should hear about." Ray leaned forward, his steaming mug having disappeared in his cupped hands. "Just take it from there, and we'll worry later about if or how it relates to the sabotage of your product."

She put her mug down and stood. "Let me get the photos."

"Wow. You've got photos?"

She sent a glance toward Tommy, and felt her face flushing. "Tommy wanted me to call the police right away, but my son — he's seventeen, nearly eighteen, and I'm a single mother .... Anyway, he was going through a bit of a hard time. It's not that I thought he was involved, exactly, but I was afraid it might somehow come back to bite him if I reported it. He was hanging around with some pretty rough characters at the time."

"Still think your son might be involved? Indirectly, of course."

Very slick. "No, he was definitely, verifiably elsewhere that night." Getting trespassed for an altercation at the arcade, in fact, but she saw no reason why these strangers needed to know that. She crossed the room, took a file from a drawer in her entertainment unit, and returned with it. Ray Morgan extended his hand, and she passed the file to him. "When I chose not to call the police, Tommy insisted we document it."

"Good thinking," Ray said.

Tommy lifted his mug in mock salute. "Yeah, well, every once in a while, I manage not to screw up."

There was an awkward little silence, and Paige rushed to fill it. "That was nine days ago, on July 8."

"Oh, very nice." Ray passed the Polaroids to his sergeant. "A rabbit, you say? Hope it wasn't somebody's pet."

"It definitely was," Tommy said. "It was plump and healthy, whereas a wild rabbit would be a lot leaner. Also, it appeared to have had its neck snapped."

"Couldn't that have been done post-mortem, when they skinned it?"

"Absolutely, but if it was a wild rabbit, I'd have expected to find snare injuries or gunshot wounds, neither of which were present. They could have used a live trap, of course, but that just brings me back to how over-plump it was. Had to be domesticated."

"Okay, we're dealing with a pet rabbit. Any ideas about who put it there?"

Paige turned toward the speaker, John Quigley, and shook her head. "I was over at Tommy's place at the time—I'd taken him some supper. We heard a car, but I didn't get up to look because I thought it was my son coming home. A few minutes later, I came back here and found it on the doorstep."

Ray held up the photos of the tire impressions. "Where are these from? You're driveway's paved."

"Tommy thought the car might have turned at the dead end before dropping the carcass to ensure a quick getaway after the deed, so I went up there right away and photographed all the tire tracks I could find."

Ray nodded. "More good thinking."

"Again, Tommy's idea. I would never have thought to do that."

"Okay, then what?"

"Then a stray dog turned up. That was the next day, wasn't it?" She turned to Tommy for confirmation.

"Yes. The 9th."

"Dead, like the rabbit?"

"No, alive, but with a leg injury. My son and I took it to the vet for medical attention. They x-rayed her lame leg, and found something pretty bizarre buried in her wound."

"Yeah?"

She went back to the TV cabinet and returned with the pill bottle in which Dr. Simon had deposited the recovered key. "Yeah," she said, handing Ray the canister. "See for yourself."

"A key? Holy hell." Ray tilted the transparent bottle to get a better look at the object inside, then passed it to his sergeant. "How does a freaking key get inside a dog's leg?"

"Some malicious sonofabitch takes a knife and makes an incision, clean and neat as you please, then jams the damned key in there, deep as it'll go, probably with a pair of needle-nosed pliers."

Paige glanced at Tommy, whose face was set in hard lines, then back at the other men, who both looked seriously disturbed. She cleared her throat. "The vet said he probably wouldn't have found it if he hadn't ordered the x-ray."

"So, where's this dog now? SPCA, I suppose?"

"We've actually adopted her ourselves. Dillon — my son, that is — wouldn't hear of packing her off to the pound." She wrapped both hands around her coffee mug, though the china verged on being too hot to hold. "He's very sensitive these days about not having his dad around. Rightly or wrongly, he identified with this little dog having been abandoned, and talked me into keeping her."

Ray nodded. "No idea where the dog came from?"

"No, but after hearing about the incident tonight at the hotel, I'm pretty sure it was no coincidence that she turned up at our door. She was intended for us, and the key lodged in her wound was meant to be discovered."

John Quigley popped the top off the pill bottle and peered more closely at the key. "This the same as the ones that turned up in your cheesecake?"

"I don't know." Dammit, her fingers were trembling. She put her mug down on the coffee table before she managed to slosh the contents on herself. "We just got the call from the hotel minutes before we called you, so I haven't seen those keys. But I presume so. They described them as small, probably to a padlock, which is what that would appear to be." She gestured toward the bottle in his hand. "I did ask them to preserve everything for you guys to examine, although I gather the keys are no longer actually in the cheesecake." She grimaced. "The restaurant manager says his staff hacked it up pretty good, looking for more foreign objects."

"Staff, plural?" the Sergeant asked.

She nodded. "That's the impression I got."

"Well, no need to rush over there to examine a pristine piece of evidence, I guess." John Quigley recapped the pill canister and returned it to Ray. "Any idea how all these events you described might be connected?"

"None." She pressed her hands together between her knees. "I mean, the keys have to be connected. There must be a message for me there, but what about the rabbit? How do you connect that?"

"Mutilation." Tommy shifted on the sofa beside her as though searching for a more comfortable position. "Same as the dog, just a different degree."

Paige shivered.

"Okay, let's talk about this cheesecake of yours again." Ray Morgan was asking the questions again. "There's no way the keys could have found their way into it accidentally, when you were making it?"

She turned her attention back to Ray. "None."

"Could someone have slipped into your house and done it?"

"No." She glanced at Tommy again. "I make a practice of keeping my door locked, a habit I developed from living in a less-than-ideal neighborhood when Dillon was a baby. Dillon carries a key at all times, because he knows the house will be locked, whether I'm home or not."

"Anyone else have a key?"

"No."

"There's no chance your son might have done this?"

Her first impulse was to lash out. Why did everyone think her son was involved with anything bad that happened? No wonder he complained of persecution. Inhaling deeply, she reined in her irritation. They were just doing their jobs.

"No chance," she said evenly. "This is our very *livelihood*. Dillon knows how important my professional reputation is to our continued prosperity, and he's as materially-oriented as the next kid. Not only does my work put food on our table and pay the rent, it provides him with an income so he can pay for the gas and insurance to keep that rattletrap of his on the road."

"He works for you?"

"He does all the computer and graphic design stuff."

"Which means?"

"Well, for instance, he's my webmaster. He built and maintains my website. He produces my promotional material — you know, business cards, flyers, advertisements, whatever I need."

"Okay, what about delivery? Could someone have gained access to the item long enough to tamper with it?"

She shook her head. "No. I baked that particular cheesecake yesterday morning and delivered it myself that afternoon. The hotel is the first stop on my delivery route. It had to have happened after the hotel took delivery."

She saw the two men exchange a glance.

"Look, I'm not trying to escape responsibility, here. Wherever the tampering took place, I know it was a swipe at me. The fact that they used the same kind of key that turned up in the dog's wound pretty much clinches it. Ergo, it's my fault, if only indirectly. I'm just trying to help figure this out."

"Gotcha. We'll check things out at the hotel, figure out how it could have been accessed from that end." Ray flipped the page in his notebook. "In the meantime, we need you to give some thought to who might bear you a grudge, and what this key message might be about."

Unfortunately, on the grudge front — if such a situation could be said to be unfortunate — she knew of no one who might have a hate on for her. She just didn't have relationships, personal or professional, that were close enough or intense enough to spawn that sort of malice. Nevertheless, they spent the next forty minutes or so going over the possibilities, remote as they were.

They even touched on Dillon again. This time, she volunteered her son's arcade alibi. Embarrassing as it was to tell these men that her son had been busy getting himself banned from that establishment for brawling at the time of the rabbit incident, it was preferable to having the police poking into his recent activities.

The other disturbing avenue of inquiry was into her ex-husband. Yes, she'd been married, for just shy of three years. And yes, the divorce had been at her request. No, there were no hard feelings; at least, not anymore. They'd both been too young for marriage and too infatuated to know better. In the end, Steve had been relieved to get out. After the separation, his visits were sporadic, doing more harm than good for Dillon, but it was her ex-husband's spiraling descent into alcohol abuse that clinched it. She'd laid down the law; until he went clean and sober and could be a stable force in Dillon's life, there was no room for him in their lives.

Knowing Tommy was listening, she tried not to squirm as she continued to answer Ray Morgan's questions. No, she didn't know Steve Harmer's whereabouts. In fact, she hadn't heard from him since Dillon's sixth birthday. The last she heard, he was working in the oil sands in Alberta. And no, Steve's relatives were not a factor. He'd been a ward of the Province, like herself, and didn't have any family. Or at least, none who were anxious to claim him, or his offspring, as their own.

She held her head high as she gave her answers, painting the picture of her disastrous domestic history as objectively and unsentimentally as she knew how. She'd done the best she could for Dillon and for herself. Intellectually, she knew it. But it still stung.

Stung? No, dammit, it hurt, to know that the beautiful young man she'd given her heart to couldn't straighten up — couldn't *grow* up — for her and for Dillon. As though they weren't worth the sacrifice.

So she'd had to do enough growing up for both of them. She'd made all the sacrifices. She'd given up her lover, her friend, and her naive picket fence dreams.

Just when she thought the questions couldn't get worse, the detective moved on to quiz her about her love life.

"What about boyfriends? Any unhappy exes out there who might be upset enough to sabotage your business?"

"No." She unclenched her hands, forcing herself to let them lie flat in her lap.

"What about would-be boyfriends who might take exception to being brushed off?"

"No. I don't date at this point in my life, Detective. Ever. Dillon and my business are my priorities. Everyone in my limited social sphere knows that, so no one tries to set me up anymore. Therefore, no need to brush anyone off."

A raised eyebrow from the handsome detective. "But surely men must approach you now and then?"

She smiled. It was impossible not to be flattered by his obvious skepticism. "I've perfected this friendly-but-totally-not-interested persona. Whereas icily-not-interested presents a challenge to a lot of men, a friendly woman who's not interested is about as invisible on a man's sexual radar as his sister." Ray Morgan still looked dubious, for which she could have kissed him. "I also don't slow down long enough for men to hit on me," she added.

The detective moved on, quizzing her about her other connections — friends, neighbors, customers. She answered those questions with considerably more ease.

"So, why keys? Any thoughts as to what that's about?"

"I don't know." She chewed the inside of her lip a moment. "I'm obsessive about locking things — the house, the van — but so are lots of people. But then, it wasn't a house key or a car key; it was a padlock key, so —"

"I think Ray was thinking more in figurative terms."

At Tommy's words, she glanced sideways at him. "You mean, like *key to my heart* or *unlocking my passion*? Something corny like that?"

"I think we can rule those out, given the mode of delivery."

Tommy's tone was dry, but she didn't miss the quick, hard gleam in his eyes. He was thinking about those modes of delivery. Inside a cowering, defenseless dog, and spat out of a horrified restaurant patron's mouth.

She looked away, her hastily averted gaze slamming into Sergeant Quigley's watchful gaze. Yikes! Infinite patience, that's what she saw there. The kind that might eventually make her blurt out her darkest secrets, if she had any. It was a little unnerving.

No, make that a *lot* unnerving.

She focused on Ray Morgan again. "I don't think there's any deep symbolism here, beyond this creep trying to intimidate me." She'd been sick with fear since the hotel had called. Hell, she was still scared, but now, she felt anger stir. "He wants to take away the illusion of safety I get from locking my doors."

Ray frowned. "Sounds plausible. If the perpetrator knows you're compulsive about locking up, they could be saying, 'You can't just turn a key and be safe. I can reach out and touch you in other ways.'"

She noticed he declined to attach a sex-specific pronoun to *the perpetrator*. She found his openness to all possibilities reassuring, yet at the same time, it was a little depressing to think they didn't have enough information to make even that basic assumption.

After a few more questions, Ray leaned back. "Anything else you want to add?"

Again, she looked at Tommy. "Am I forgetting anything?"

"What about the van getting tagged today?"

"Oh, yeah." She pushed her hair back. "I'd completely forgotten."

"Your delivery vehicle was vandalized? Today?" Ray's inquiry was polite enough, but his raised eyebrows communicated the subtext loud and clear. *Your product is sabotaged and your delivery vehicle vandalized on the same freaking day, and you don't connect the two events? Hello?*

To her dismay, she blushed. "I'd hardly call it vandalism. They just wrote on the side panel and the windows with hand soap. Dillon's already scrubbed it off. It happened at the mall, when I stopped to buy some supplies."

"What'd it say?"

"It was just a bit of graffiti. Wait a sec," she said, leaping up. "Let me get my notepad. I made a facsimile of it."

"Gang signature, we figure."

Tommy's voice followed into the kitchen. As she retrieved her pad, she heard Ray's reply.

"A gang? Which one?"

"Don't recognize it," Tommy admitted. Paige felt his gaze on her as she crossed the room and handed the yellow pad to Ray. "Maybe you'll have better luck than I did."

"Nope. Doesn't mean a thing to me." Ray passed it to Sergeant Quigley, who shook his head and handed it back to Paige.

"I figured them for kids," she said. "Washable graffiti scrawled in hand soap? It just doesn't seem to be in the same league as killing or brutalizing animals, or threatening my business."

"I see what you mean," Ray said, but she noticed he sketched a quick outline of the signature before he tucked his notebook away. "I think that'll do it for now. Seeing as the evidence has already been mauled, I'll stop by the hotel tomorrow morning and see what I can learn."

"Thank you. I really appreciate this."

No one made a move to get up, and it occurred to her, belatedly, that they might want to visit with Tommy alone, without subjecting him to the walk next door to his own unit. Maybe if she offered them dessert, then slipped upstairs to give them some privacy . . . .

"So, if we're done, maybe I can offer you a nice raspberry ricotta semifreddo I made today?" She stood, brushing non-existent wrinkles out of her trousers. "I'd feel badly if you won't let me say a premium, high-calorie thank-you."

"Omigod, did you say *semifreddo*?" Ray breathed the word reverently.

She laughed aloud. "At last. Someone who actually knows what it is. Hang on a minute and I'll be right back with it, though I can't join you. I really do have to log onto my computer and check for messages."

***

Oh, perfect, thought Tommy, as he shoveled another bite of the cold dessert — his second of the night — into his mouth. *Just wonderful.*

Not only had Paige found a reason to extend the visit with that offer of dessert, but she planned to abandon him.

Except he couldn't help noticing that for a woman who just had to check her e-mail this very minute, she seemed loathe to leave.

In fact, she was currently looking at the very married Ray Morgan like he was Brad-bloody-Pitt himself, and all because Razor — wouldn't you know it? — happened to know what a stupid semifreddo was. It was *ice cream*, for crying out loud. Any fool could see that. And Ray wasn't helping matters, smiling and being so smarmy.

At least Quigg could be counted on not to — *aw, hell.*

Tommy bit back a sound of disgust as Quigg practically shouldered Ray aside to monopolize Paige.

What the devil was happening here? Had he slipped into an alternate reality? John Quigley was constitutionally incapable of looking at a woman other than Suzannah, let alone *flirting* with one.

Paige had flushed very nicely under Ray's effortless charm, and now looked a little dazzled to find herself caught in the crosshairs of Quigg's intense, openly approving regard.

"Didn't you say you had some e-mail to check?"

It came out sharper than he intended.

"Oh, right. The e-mail." she stammered. "I get orders that way, sometimes. Over the Internet, I mean. You know, from my web-site."

A flush climbed her neck, but not the flattering glow she'd produced under Ray and Quigg's double-barreled onslaught. This was an embarrassed flush. Or possibly an angry one. Guilt pricked him for being such a sonofabitch. She hadn't done anything wrong. Hell, she hadn't done anything, period.

Please let it be an angry flush. He'd rather think she was pissed with him than hurt.

"I've got a ton of work to do," she continued, sounding much smoother now. "So, if you'll excuse me, I'll make myself scarce." Her voice betrayed no trace of internal turmoil he knew she was feeling. "It was a pleasure meeting you, gentlemen."

"The pleasure was ours," said Ray. "But let's hope the circumstances are a little more pleasant next time."

Both men stood as Paige left the room. Tommy did not. The courtesy would be pretty empty after his behaving like such a dickhead.

"Good going, Godsoe." Razor shot him a disgusted look before resuming his seat in the wingback chair. "What'd you have to go and chase her away for?"

"Just trying to save you some grief, old man," he shot back. "You realize after that display, she probably thinks you're gonna give her a call on Friday."

Ray grinned that stupid Hollywood grin. "Maybe I will."

"Like hell you will. Grace'd have your ba —"

"Boys, boys. Can't we all just get along?"

"And you." Tommy rounded on Quigg. "What happened to that leash Suzannah keeps you on? Cripes, if I wanted to set a couple of horn dogs on her, I'da called Sinclair and Mills."

Razor looked at Quigg, extending his hand, palm up. "Told ya."

Sighing, Quigg pulled out his billfold, peeled off a twenty and handed it to Ray, who pushed it carelessly into a pocket.

Tommy shook his head. "Okay, what just went on here?"

Ray's grin widened. "On the way over, I bet Quigg that you had a thing for the neighbor lady, but Quigg here had you figured for more altruistic motives."

Ah, hell. After that display, he was busted. And to deny the physical attraction would only persuade these two that there was something more there, something deeper. Might as well roll with it. "So, you turned the mojo on, did your best to charm that woman, just to get a rise out of me?"

"Pretty much."

"Jerks," he said, without heat.

"Why, thank you."

That from Ray.

"Yeah, laugh about it now, smartass. We'll see if you're still laughing when I give her your address and she turns up on your doorstep to ask why you never called."

Ray snorted. "Like that'd happen with a woman like that. Like you'd *let* it happen."

"I can't believe what a shitheel you are." He turned to Quigg and added, "You, too."

"Always happy to be of service." Quigg leaned back into the cushions of the chair he occupied. "But enough of that. What's this I hear about you getting out?"

He'd started to relax, but Quigg's question sent a jolt through him, setting his nerves to twanging again. "It's no secret. I gave my notice."

"Last I heard, they're holding it in abeyance until you're a little more recovered."

Tommy laughed, a harsh sound. "That's a reliable source you got there, Sarge. Did they also tell you they think I have post-traumatic stress disorder?"

"You got shot, cowboy," put in Ray. "You came pretty damned close to dying. Think anybody'd be shocked to hear you had nightmares about that?"

"I don't have PTSD."

"I heard you declined a consult with Heather."

Tommy turned back to Quigg. "I don't need the staff shrink to tell me what I already know."

"Psychologist," Quigg corrected. "And she knows her stuff. She's helped lots of guys, including me. Civilian victims, too."

"I don't have post-traumatic stress disorder."

"You know, Tommy, it's not a comment on what kind of cop you are. Good cops get it, too. No one's immune."

Tommy felt his gut clench. Despite Quigg's generally accurate information, he'd been wrong about one thing. He *had* been through this with Heather, though he hadn't been too thrilled about the whole process.

"Do I have nightmares about the incident?" He ground the words out. "Yeah. Yeah, I do. Sometimes I wake up in a cold sweat, with my stomach knotted up so tight, I think I'm gonna puke. I'll admit it. But can you tell me you don't have the occasional nightmare when you think about how close that whack-job got to torturing Suzannah last year?" he challenged Quigg. *"With white-hot knives?"*

Before Quigg could reply, Tommy tackled Ray. "And *you*, Mr. Suave and Debonair. You expect me to believe you never wake up in the night with your heart going a million miles an hour 'cuz you dreamed Landis got to Grace before you could stop him?"

"Yeah, but—"

"Am I more irritable than I used to be?" Tommy cut Ray off. "Damn right, I am. But I'm a goddamn invalid; I'm entitled to be cranky. Do I have sleep disturbances? Hell, yes, but you would, too, if you woke up with every nerve in your ass on fire. But be perfectly clear on this point — it's not persistent anxiety, hyper-vigilance or any of that crap keeping me awake."

"I hear you, man, but —"

"Have I turned to alcohol or drugs?" This time it was Quigg Tommy interrupted. "*No*. Do I have waking flashbacks? *No*. Have I experienced psychic numbing? *No*. That's the checklist, guys. I don't have PTSD."

"What about avoidance?"

"Ah, yes, avoidance. Classic symptom." Tommy rolled his shoulders, trying to release the tension there. "I guess turning in the badge could be viewed as the ultimate avoidance behavior, but I sure as hell didn't do it 'cuz I'm scared that a car backfiring in an alley might trigger a flashback."

"Then why *did* you do it?" Quigg's eyes were patient.

Tommy looked away. "Because I'm done as a dog master. I'm done as an active duty cop. All the physiotherapy in the world won't give me that back, and I'm not interested in being a desk jockey."

A short silence.

"Okay," Quigg conceded, "So you don't have PTSD. But think about it — maybe, just maybe, you're not in the best shape to make such an important decision right now."

"Which brings us back to square one, doesn't it? Them sitting on my resignation. But I'm telling you, I won't change my mind. I've worked my last watch."

"Jesus, Tommy."

This from Ray, who for all his ball-breaking had been a good friend. Which was more than Tommy deserved, after that fiasco two years ago when Ray got jammed up between IAD and that Russian wiseguy. If Tommy had kept his mouth shut in the locker room about that wad of cash he'd found in the trunk of Ray's vehicle when he and Max scoured it for explosives, maybe Ray and Grace wouldn't have had to go into hiding. It still made him break out in sweat to think how narrowly they'd escaped Landis's murderous wrath.

Tommy cleared his throat. "It's true. Believe it. Although it seems like I'll have to let some time pass before anyone downtown is going to accept it."

Another pause. Then Ray again: "So … what will you do? I mean, if you're not planning to come back, you must have something in mind?"

"Dunno. My mother left me a little money. Thought I might buy a sailboat, cruise it down south, become a wharf rat."

"Lucky bastard." Ray smiled, but it looked forced. "Travis McGee all over again, huh?"

Tommy's bark of laughter was genuine at the reference to John D. MacDonald's literary character, retriever of lost fortunes, saver of souls, lover of women. "The *Busted Flush* was a houseboat, you landlubber. Besides, I'm more like *Sam* McGee, just aiming to keep my aching bones warm."

Out of the corner of his eye, Tommy spied Paige standing at the base of the stairs, just outside the room. She wore a stunned expression. For a heartbeat or two, he thought she was reacting to overhearing the talk of his buying a boat and sailing away. Then reason reasserted itself. Nothing he'd said could account for that pinched expression.

"Paige, what is it?"

"My web site. Somebody's hacked into my web site and changed all the bullets."

"Bullets? You mean, the little dots —"

"Yes, exactly. But I don't use dots. I used a little graphic of a slice of triple-layer cake on a saucer — something to suggest desserts."

"And someone changed it?"

"Every one of them. At least on the main page." Her eyes hardened. "Three guesses as to what my cake graphic was replaced with."

With a certainty that made his gut spasm, he knew exactly what she'd found. Biting back a curse, he sighed. "A key?"

"A key."

Chapter 7

A N HOUR LATER, PAIGE showed Detective Ray Morgan and Sergeant John Quigley out. Somewhere along the line tiredness had set in, a kind of mental weariness that seeped into her very bones. The moment she closed the door, she turned and sagged against it. What a nightmare. What had happened to her quiet, normal life?

Of course, the detectives' immediate reaction had been to look to Dillon, since he was her webmaster, but she knew they were wrong. She'd shown them the mirror site on her desktop and explained how Dillon had taught her to edit that desktop version, then publish it to the actual live web site using the file transfer protocol thingy. The desktop site was unaltered, indicating the changes had not been made through her computer.

But she'd seen the looks the men had exchanged and known they didn't necessarily concur that that was conclusive evidence of Dillon's innocence. Which, she supposed, it wasn't. He could have done it from any location, just like the hacker had. But Dillon wouldn't do that. He'd never jeopardize the business she'd worked so hard to establish. Never. Which was why she complied readily when John Quigley suggested they remove the computer to have a forensic computer specialist check it out.

Dillon was no angel; she knew that. In fact, she was pretty positive he'd been experimenting with drugs and booze, which, given his father's history, was reason enough for alarm. He'd also been hanging with a less-than-desirable crowd. But he wasn't responsible for this. She'd stake her last nickel on it.

"You look like a stiff breeze would knock you over."

At Tommy's voice, she pushed away from the door.

"It's been a wild day." She walked to where he stood, propped indolently against the living-room door frame. If she didn't know he was using the architecture to hold himself upright, she might have thought it a deliberate pose, chosen to display his lean length to pulse-stirring effect. "And it's not over yet. I still have to call my other customers to tell them about this."

"So you *do* plan to notify them."

She met his gaze, reading approval there. And sympathy. At the latter, unexpected tears stung the back of her eyes. Quickly, she looked away, her gaze falling on the abandoned coffee mugs and dessert dishes.

"I don't have much choice, do I? Until we get to the bottom of this, my customers will have to make a choice between tightening up security in their kitchens and display cases or switching to another supplier."

She walked past him into the living room to gather the dishes. From his post in the doorway, she could feel his gaze following her. Thankfully, he didn't rush to fill the silence with false assurances that her customers would stick it out with her. They both knew that was highly unlikely.

"How's Dillon going to take this?"

Dillon. He'd be so upset. Thank God he hadn't been here. "Not well. He'd like everyone to think this stuff slides off him like water off a duck's back, but he takes things so much to heart."

"Ah, the intensity of youth."

He smiled, and it changed his face, making him look younger and lighter of heart. For the briefest of moments, she had a flash of what he must have been like before the shooting. Before he lost everything that mattered to him. Suddenly she wanted to put the dishes down, cross the room and press her mouth to his. She wanted to touch his chest, feel his strong arms close around her. She wanted to distract herself from her troubles, and maybe him from his.

Would that be so wrong? Dillon wouldn't be home for at least another hour . . . .

Man, what she could do with an hour, a guilt-free dive into lust. A sweet yearning pierced her at the mere thought of a no-strings-attached hour with this man who'd managed to stir her long-dormant libido to life at her first glimpse of him.

"I'm sorry, what'd you say?"

Whoops! She'd must have made some kind of sound. Her face fired. "I was just thinking, I'm not going to tell Dillon until Friday."

His thick black eyebrows drew together. "You think that's wise, keeping him out of the loop?"

"Probably not, but Friday's his birthday, and he's having a bunch of friends from St. Stephen over. I don't want to upset him before then, and I know he'll take this hard."

"But he's gotta know what's going on." Tommy pushed away from the doorjamb, looking anything but indolent now. "With the stuff that's gone down these last few days, you need everybody to be alert."

"Agreed, but if I tell him now, he won't be able to enjoy his birthday."

"Paige . . . ."

"You don't know him like I do, Tommy. There's just me and him. I know he worries, probably too much for a kid his age." She massaged her right forearm, knowing that the self-comforting touch probably betrayed her anxiety but not particularly caring. "But he's always known I was the only thing standing between him and being entirely alone in the world."

Tommy raked a hand through his hair, making it stand out almost boyishly, a sharp contrast to the fierce intensity of his expression. "Remember when that rabbit carcass showed up and I suggested it would be a good idea to call the cops?"

She opened her mouth to protest that this was entirely different, but before she could get anything out, he forged on.

"Well, I'm getting the same sort of vibe about this. You should tell him, Paige. At the very least, he'd be an extra pair of eyes, which you could certainly use right now. But more importantly, he might be sitting on some bit of knowledge that would allow Ray to put this whole puzzle together."

"I *will* tell him. After his party on Friday. I promise."

"Paige —"

"What can happen between now and Friday? It's only a couple of days. My customers will trip over themselves backing away from me, so there'll be no risk to the public. And I'll be able to stick close to home, maybe try out some new recipes."

A pause, during which she felt the weight of his disapproval.

She blew out an exasperated breath. "He didn't have anything to do with this. You know it, Tommy. Besides all the arguments I offered your cop friends, when would he have had time? He's either at your place, outside with the dog, or curled up with Cleo, reading the material you loaned him."

"*Gave* him," he clarified. "I won't need it back."

Again, the sheer lack of expression in his tone gave him away, but she knew better than to call him on it. It didn't take much imagination to know why. A father who'd leave his son to fend for himself in the wilderness probably wasn't big on men showing emotion. He'd probably had that concept drilled into him from a very early age.

"What are you going to tell him about the computer when he sees it's gone?"

Dammit, what *would* she tell him? Then it struck her — she wouldn't have to explain anything!

"I won't have to tell him anything," she said. "He's gone cold turkey on the computer games since Cleo came. Video games, too. No more *Grand Theft Auto* or any of those killing games. He's totally enthralled with that dog."

He leaned back against the door frame again, more evidence of how much his leg bothered him, she suspected, than an indication of his relaxation level.

"You have an answer for everything, don't you?"

An answer for everything? *She wished.*

Unfortunately, there were lots of unanswered questions crowding her brain. For instance, who was doing this to her? Who could possibly hate her enough to sabotage her business?

And why did she feel this relentless, powerful tug of attraction toward a man who'd been dragged so reluctantly into her problems? A man who wanted nothing more than to be left alone. A man who, by his own admission earlier tonight, was ready to abandon the life he knew to literally drift with the tides.

"No," she said at last. "I don't have all the answers. But I have to make the decisions anyway, don't I?"

He sighed. "Okay, Madame Matriarch, have it your way. But if it turns out the kid has the missing piece to the puzzle, I reserve the right to say I told you so. In as many ways as I can think of to say it."

"Sounds fair."

"And if you go anywhere between now and Friday, let me know. I'll ride shotgun."

"Okay. Or should that be *aye-aye, cap'n*?"

One dark eyebrow lifted. "So you did take that in?"

"I guess I did, on some level, upset as I was. Florida, was it?"

"Why not?"

She made an agreeable noise.

"You don't approve."

It was a statement, not a question.

Of course, she didn't approve of his withdrawing from the messy business of life. It would be a perfect waste of a sharp mind and a compassionate nature.

She shrugged. "It's not my place to approve or disapprove."

"That hasn't exactly stopped you before."

For a few seconds, indignation warred with amusement. It was only when she heard her own choked, snorting laugh that she realized the latter won. Tommy laughed, too, the sound as infectious as it was surprising. She found herself laughing again, but this time she couldn't stop. The hilarity kept rising and rising, until suddenly she wasn't laughing anymore.

Oh, damnation.

⁂

Oh, hell. Tears.

Not that he had a particular problem with women crying. He'd seen lots of it on the job. And yes, off the job, too. Though it gave him no pleasure, he knew he'd caused more than his fair share of female tears over the years. But he'd always taken it in stride, offering heart-felt sympathy in the former situation, and no defense in the latter. *Mea culpa.*

But this was different; her tears were different. Though for the life of him, he couldn't imagine why.

Yes, he could.

She was strong, resourceful, and so damnably proud. She wouldn't cry often or easily, and once she mastered herself, she'd probably be mortified that he'd witnessed her breakdown.

But for now, she didn't seem to have any option. Too much fear and worry and responsibility had pushed the water over the dam, and there'd be no stopping it until the tension receded.

"Come here."

He took her arm and guided her to the couch. Careful to position her on his good side, he sank down awkwardly onto the cushions. She went with him, turning blindly into his chest. Sobs tore raggedly at her throat. His heart clenched, and he closed his arms around her, offering her a safe harbor.

"Shush," he murmured. "You're okay, baby. You're okay."

Her response was to burrow closer. And, oh, man, she was crying now like she might never stop. And not prettily, either.

He'd seen plenty of women cry like Hollywood pros, their tears calculated to draw the appropriate response. Not so, Paige. She'd completely soaked his shirt front already. He spared a thought for the dry-clean-only fabric, then pulled her closer.

"It's okay, baby. Come on, let it all out. You'll feel better."

It was over much faster than he imagined possible, like the short, violent storms that sometimes blew through at the height of summer. He'd barely gotten used to the surprisingly solid weight of her small frame in his arms when she pushed away from his chest.

"Oh, God, I'm so sorry. I never do that."

"Don't worry about it." He shifted his weight to pull a clean handkerchief from his pocket, wincing at the white-hot shaft of pain that shot down his leg at the motion. Willing the pain to subside, or at least to not show transparently on his face, he handed the neatly-folded white rectangle to her. "You've had to handle an awful lot in these past few days. You needed to vent, is all."

"Yeah? Looks like I vented all over your shirt." She accepted the handkerchief and blew her nose noisily. "I'll have it cleaned for you."

Her face was puffy, her complexion blotchy, and her eyes bloodshot, and dear God, he wanted to kiss her.

Badly.

Crazy! What was wrong with him? He liked his women fuller and a whole lot faster. Hell, he liked them with bulletproof hearts, if possible. Paige Harmer was the antithesis of those things. And just now, she looked like the wrath of God. So how come he wanted to take her mouth in a kiss that would curl her toes?

She was dabbing at her eyes now, murmuring another apology. "I don't know what happened there."

"Safety valve. You needed to let off some pressure."

She laughed. "Yeah, but I could have done it on the shower where no one would hear me, instead of all over my poor, long-suffering neighbor."

In the shower. What other demands did she answer there? Even as he leapt to censor his thoughts, he felt himself stir, grow hard.

Oh, for pity's sake. When had he become such a lech? The woman was stressed out, vulnerable. He had no business lusting after her.

Man, he needed to get laid, no two ways about it.

Problem was, he was still a pity case, with the mobility of your average octogenarian. Maybe a little physio wasn't such a bad idea . . . .

Face dried, she settled back against him, letting her head rest on his shoulder. It felt good. Too damned good.

"You know, maybe I should leave. Let you get collected before Dillon comes back."

"Dillon won't be back until the stroke of eleven," she said with total assurance. "He's reuniting with his old friends from St. Stephen, and not likely to be back before his weeknight curfew."

He couldn't even pretend to himself he was disappointed that his out had evaporated. "At least he's keeping a curfew. You should be grateful for that."

"Don't I know it. He blew it almost every night when he was hanging with those other thugs." She leaned back to look at him. "I know you think I'm crazy for not cross-examining him about the stuff that's happened, but he's just getting back on track. And you're a big reason why."

"Hey, it's not me," he said, disconcerted once again by the weirdness of the whole role-model thing. "It's Cleo. The dog-training thing. He's found something he has an affinity for."

"What he's found is a passion he can share with *you*," she said. "Do you really think he'd be inspired to borrow library books on dog training if you hadn't put the idea into his head? Do you think he'd be spending hours every day putting the theory he's learned into practice if he couldn't share Cleo's little triumphs with you at the end of the day?"

"You're determined to cast me as a good guy, aren't you?"

"Well, you are."

"No," he said flatly. "I am not."

"Yes, you are."

"Would a good guy do this?" It was a cheap line. A real stinker. But that was the whole point. Leaning into her, he gripped her chin and took possession of those full lips.

Surprise. That's what he tasted there. Then sweetness.

He took it, took every last bit of the welcome he found, and fanned it, deliberately, assiduously, with all the finesse at his command. By the time she pulled back long minutes later, her mouth was attractively kiss-swollen and damp, and the pulse in her throat hammered frantically under the pad of his thumb. Almost as frantically as his own heart pounded against his ribs. But her eyes were serious. A little lust-clouded, maybe, but serious.

"Why'd you do that?"

Oh, Lord, what kind of a question was that? He wasn't sure he knew the answer himself. "Because I wanted to. Because your mouth was made for kissing. Because I'm as opportunistic as the next guy." He shrugged. "Because I thought you could use some distraction." He dropped his hand reluctantly from her throat, missing the warmth immediately. "Hell, I don't know. Take your pick. Any of the above. All of the above."

Her eyes searched his a moment, and he could see her evaluating, weighing. "Okay," she said at last.

"*Okay?*"

"Okay," she repeated. "Distract me some more."

She grabbed him by the shirt and pulled his mouth back to hers. This time, she kissed him. Demandingly, whole-heartedly, single-mindedly. Then, suddenly, kissing didn't seem to be enough for her. Her hands slid under his shirt, streaked over his skin, pulling him closer.

"Whoa." Unbelievably, he found himself pinning her hand against his chest to stop the erotic exploration. Much as he burned to feel her hands on him, she was only seeking an escape from her worries. Ordinarily, he'd be happy to oblige, but he knew she'd regret it afterward. Somehow, that doused the fire. "A little distraction's one thing. Making a brand new, Godzilla-sized regret is another. We'd better cool it, Paige."

"What?" She drew back, green eyes refocusing, widening in disbelief. Or maybe indignation. "You're making the decision for me? Don't you think I should have something to say about it?"

"Sure, you should have something to say about it. And you can have your say in the morning. If you come over to my place in the full light of day and tell me you still want to sleep with me, I'm your man. Of course, with this hip, you might have to do all the work."

"Oh, for the love of Pete!"

"Excuse me?"

"You're doing it again."

It was his turn to draw back. "Doing what?"

"Taking care of me."

He scowled. "Seems like somebody has to."

"You know, it would serve you right if I did."

"If you did what?"

"If I were to go over there in the morning, crawl into your bed and take you up on your incredibly generous offer to have sex with me."

His pulse kicked at the picture she painted with her blunt words. He pushed the images from his mind and willed his blood to slow. "You won't."

She bristled at his tone. "What makes you so sure?"

He leaned a little closer, feeling a certain satisfaction when she pulled back a fraction, just far enough to disclose her unease. "When was the last time you did something completely wild?" he challenged. "Something you regretted? I mean, truly, deeply regretted?"

She looked perplexed by the change of direction. "I don't understand."

"Getting pregnant, right?"

"I've never regretted Dillon's conception."

"Okay, marrying Dillon's dad, then."

Her brow furrowed. "What are you getting at?"

"My point is, you're a smart, careful woman, Paige. A passionate one, but careful. You make major mistakes about, what? Once every couple of decades? You think I'm going to let you rack up another one when you're in this kind of condition?"

"This condition?"

"Yeah, this condition. Scared, worried, vulnerable. What kind of a man would that make me?"

He watched her process that, saw the corners of her lip kick up. Then she laughed. *Laughed*, dammit!

"What's so funny?" he growled.

She wiped new tears from her eyes, these ones tears of mirth. "I guess that makes you the kind of man I accused you of being earlier — a good one."

He compressed his lips. "Don't make me into some kind of hero. I just don't want that kind of responsibility, plain and simple."

"Okay, have it your way." She leaned back, combing a fiery strand of hair back from her face. "But thanks. For the distraction, I mean. It was very ... effective. I'm not sure whether that speaks to my distractibility level, or your talents, or both, but it worked nicely."

"I told you —"

"When someone says thank you, the correct response is *you're welcome*," she said tartly.

"Then you're welcome, I guess, but —"

"But nothing." She stood, smoothing her khakis. "Look, you don't have to stay here and hold my hand any longer. I'm fine now. Besides, I have to call my other customers and let them know what happened."

You're off the hook, Godsoe. Free to go. Dismissed.

"Okay." Slowly — because, dammit, he'd gone too long between pain pills again — he got to his feet. Where'd he leave that blasted cane? Scowling, he turned to scan the room.

"It's right here."

He turned back to see she held the cane out for him.

"Thanks," he said, accepting it. "I'll see you tomorrow."

Tomorrow. Suddenly, his earlier challenge hung between them. *Tell me you still want to sleep with me tomorrow, in the full light of day, and I'm your man.*

For a moment, her eyes blazed with huge, ravenous need. His own pulse took a crazy, jagged leap.

Then she dropped her gaze. "Tomorrow," she agreed. "I'll make supper as usual."

"Oh, and tell Dillon I found a training video he might like to have. He can come over and help himself to it in the morning."

"I will."

❧

Paige closed the door behind him, then turned to lean on it, needing its support. Whew!

For a few seconds there, as Tommy's words had hung so palpably between them, she knew they were both picturing the same thing — getting naked together. Wonderfully, gloriously, forbiddenly naked.

For the first time, she allowed herself to imagine them tangled together on his bed, not as a fantasy, but as something she could translate into reality with a few simple words, uttered in the light of day.

I still want to sleep with you.

Her stomach clenched violently, and her breathing grew ragged in the silence. That's all she had to say, and it could be real.

Dammit, what was she doing to herself? This desire was pointless. Nothing had changed. Dillon was still her number-one priority. She'd long ago promised herself that she'd never saddle him with a stepfather, or even a boyfriend. She'd had too many foster fathers of her own to believe a man could bond with an older child not of his own loins. And it wasn't just because she was a female. She knew lots of boys who'd endured treatment that ranged from the merely hostile to the incomprehensibly brutal.

Not that Tommy would be like that with Dillon. Despite his reservations about being an appropriate role model, she knew he'd never be cruel to Dillon. But anything that might ignite between her and Tommy couldn't possibly last, even if she were comfortable enough to let it happen under her son's nose. What had Tommy said about his approach to dating? *Catch and release?* She wrinkled her nose at the fishing imagery. And just her luck, Dillon would probably decide to take offense on her behalf when Tommy eventually tossed her back, wrecking that relationship, too.

No, nothing had changed.

But, God help her, the man could kiss!

Groaning, she turned and twisted the dead bolt home with more force than was strictly necessary. She'd make her calls, take a cold shower, and generally try to make herself look like she wasn't burning up from the inside when her son came home.

❧

Dillon let his head loll back onto the headrest. Beside him, in the old Toyota's passenger seat, Cleo whined. Automatically, he gave her a reassuring scratch. "Everything'll be all right, girl."

Yeah, right. Fat frickin' chance.

He couldn't go home. And not because the luminous hands on his wristwatch read quarter past twelve. His mother'd get over a blown curfew, if it were that simple.

His heart started pounding again, like it had four hours ago when Derek Weaver had approached him at Killarney Lake. He and his buddies from St. Stephen had spent the day there, paddling kayaks across the tiny lake's glass-smooth surface, playing beach volleyball, flipping a Frisbee around, and generally soaking up the sun. His friends had just fired up the coals for a barbecue, and Dillon had trekked up to the parking lot to retrieve the cooler.

"Yo, nice dog."

Dillon's smile died when he recognized Weaver as the speaker. He put the cooler down and slammed the Toyota's trunk shut. "What do you want?"

Derek bent to pat Cleo's head, but she ducked away from his hand, growling low in her throat with a menacing tone Dillon had never heard from her before.

Derek straightened, the sun gleaming off his shaved head. "Guess she's not the forgiving type."

Dillon's stomach lurched. "What do you mean?"

"Can't say I blame her, I guess. I'd probably hold a grudge, too, if our positions were reversed."

"You bastard! You're the one who hurt her." Dillon launched himself at Derek, but the older man sidestepped easily. Cleo barked wildly.

Barefoot on the hot asphalt, Dillon wheeled and lashed out again, but this time his attempted blow was deflected by a vicious downward chop to the forearm.

Ow, ow, ow!

It was all he could do to stifle a scream. Harder still not to cradle his right arm, which felt worse than useless. Okay, so he wasn't a fighter.

Then Weaver laughed.

Dillon lunged again, this time with his left.

Weaver dodged again, swearing. "Quit it, kid, before I have to really hurt you."

"You sick fuck! You *mutilated* that dog."

"Don't you want to know why I used a key?" he asked, over Cleo's barking, which had grown frantic.

"What I want to know is how I ever got involved with a waste of carbon like you in the first place." Dillon backed up a pace or two. "I told you to stay the hell away from me, and I meant it."

"Or you'll what? Call the cops?" Weaver's face hardened. "Haven't we already had this conversation, little buddy? You go to the cops, I'll be obliged to share the videotape from our little gas-bar job. You were quite the calm, cool, collected wheelman. Hard to believe it was your first stick-up."

Dillon's heart thundered. "I didn't know you assholes were going to rob that store! I *still* didn't know even as I was driving away. There's no way I would have cooperated if I'd known what you were doing."

Weaver snorted. "You think that'll hold up? Especially after all the footage of us partying together at my apartment? Not to mention your little trip to Party Central. How old were those girls, anyway?"

Suddenly and mortifyingly, Dillon wanted to cry.

"How would I know? I was passed out from whatever you slipped me, you *freak*."

"Ah, but were you? Or is it just that you can't remember what you did? See, that's the thing about GHB." Weaver's small eyes narrowed even further. "I guess only the holder of the videotape would know for sure, huh?"

This time, when Dillon lashed out, his left fist made satisfying, if painful, contact with Weaver's chin. His satisfaction was short-lived, however, as Weaver dropped him to the pavement with a well-placed, almost casual blow.

When he stopped seeing stars, Dillon found himself flat on his back, looking at the sun. He also found himself with Derek Weaver's boot pressing firmly on his windpipe. Beside him, Cleo barked and snapped, baring her teeth like a feral wolf.

"I'll make this fast, 'cuz I think we're attracting a little attention. I asked you a question earlier. Have you figured out why I used a key?" Weaver lifted his boot a fraction, but Dillon declined to say anything. "No ideas? Okay, I'll tell you. Remember that little job I asked you to do?"

Dillon spat a curse at his tormentor.

"Ah, I see you have perfect recall. Well, here's the thing — you are the key, my young friend. I need your squeaky-clean rep to make this one little drop for me. All you have to do is smile your way across the border, then take a couple of little packages to the bus station in Bangor and stash them in a locker. Piece of piss. Then you can go back to kindergarten or Sunday school or wherever it is you belong."

"Fuck you."

The pressure on his windpipe increased momentarily, then eased abruptly as Weaver removed his foot. In the distance, Dillon heard the wail of a siren. *Shit. Cops.*

"You're the key," Weaver reiterated. "You *will* cooperate, once you've had a chance to think about it."

With that, Weaver moved off. By the time Dillon struggled to his feet, the other man had fired up his Gold Wing and shot out of the parking lot.

Dillon stood there as the sirens grew closer. Goddammit. He cast a glance toward his friends, who were engaged in a game of volleyball. They wouldn't think much of his cutting out without warning. "Sorry, guys."

He turned to Cleo. "Come on, girl. We gotta run." With a last look at his friends, still engrossed in the volleyball match, he opened the passenger door. Cleo hopped in. Thirty seconds later, as he exited the parking lot, the patrol car rolled in, bar lights flashing.

Now, four hours later, he sat in his car outside Rachel Whitesel's house. Or rather, Rachel's cousin's house. She had no one in Fredericton other than her older cousin, having fled her step-father's house. Maybe that's what had attracted him to her, that sense of aloneness.

Yeah, right. It had absolutely nothing to do with the fact that from the neck down, she looked exactly like Lara Croft from the video game or the movie. But tougher, somehow.

Only she wasn't nearly as tough as she let on.

Beside him, Cleo whined.

"I know, girl. We got no business being here. She doesn't need my trouble any more than Mom does. I don't even know why I came here. Autopilot, I guess."

Another comforting vocalization from Cleo.

God, what he'd give for a little oblivion, an easing of the anxiety constricting his chest. Except that's what had landed him in this mess in the first place, wanting to extinguish his stupid teenage angst in a blaze of alcohol, chased by a little calm-inducing reefer.

No, there'd be no chemical escape. Not ever again. Not if it meant his problems would multiply like this while he was zoned out.

"Okay, girl. Let's get you home. Then I'll figure out where I'm gonna go."

He reached for the ignition, but before he could turn the key, someone rapped on his window. He nearly came out of his skin, and Cleo yipped.

"It's okay. It's me, Rachel."

Shit. Busted. He quieted Cleo, then rolled down his window. "Hi."

"Whatcha doin' here?"

She was wearing pajamas, or what probably passed for pajamas. Gray cotton pants hung low on her hips, displaying abs not often seen among the girls Dillon knew. A cropped black Atticus t-shirt did little to conceal the truly awesome bounty beneath.

He thought about lying, then discarded the idea in favor of the truth. "I don't know."

She bit her full lower lip, then released it. "Room in there for me?"

No, I gotta get outta here.

"Sure."

A minute later, Cleo sat in the back seat and Rachel sat in the passenger seat.

"So, this is Cleo?" Twisting in her seat, she extended a hand for the dog to sniff. Cleo licked Rachel's fingers, then accepted a scratch on the neck.

"Yep, that's her."

"So, you're the female who's been keeping Dillon home at nights, huh?" she asked Cleo.

Dillon blushed, grateful for the dimness of the Toyota's interior. "Sorry."

She swung back to face him. "Don't be. I'm glad you haven't been around."

"Gee, thanks."

She slanted him a reproving look. "You know what I mean. You got way too much going for you to be hanging around Derek and the Dumb-inoes."

Yeah, he knew what she meant, all right. He was way too soft to try to play hard with Derek's crowd. Hell, even with the resentment gnawing at his gut like it'd been doing since they moved to this stupid, stuck-up town, he was still way too straight and law-abiding for that scene. For about the millionth time, he wondered why he'd ever, even briefly, wanted to fit in with them. Clamping down on that perfectly useless thought, he returned her reproving glance with one of his own.

"Seems to me I could say the same about you."

She shrugged, a gesture more felt than seen in the car's ill-lit confines. "I don't hang around Derek. He hangs around me."

And what heterosexual male with a pulse wouldn't? "Point taken."

"So, what brings you here tonight?"

"I dunno." He lifted his shoulder in what he hoped was a casual shrug. "I was driving around with my brain in neutral, and here's where I ended up."

"I guess it's my turn to say, *Gee, thanks.*"

He blushed again at her dryly amused tone. Before he could think of something to say to fill the awkward silence, she spoke again.

"Okay, different approach. What put your brain in neutral tonight?"

At the directness of her question, his throat threatened to close altogether. He cleared it. "I'm leaving home."

Another pause while she appeared to digest that. More soft canine panting from the back seat.

"Why?"

"It's complicated."

"It would be. *You're* complicated." She glanced away, though there was nothing to see from the passenger window but the empty sidewalk and the brick facing of her cousin's low-rent apartment building. Then she turned back to face him. "Where will you stay?"

He shrugged, intending the gesture to be casual, but it felt more like a jerky, defensive huddling. "I don't know." At least his voice sounded half-way normal.

"What are you going to do with the dog? It can be hard to find places that take pets. And you'd need references, a job —"

"I don't know."

"You've said that an awful lot tonight, *I don't know.*" She looked at him squarely. "Tell me, Dillon, what *do* you know?"

What *did* he know?

He knew he was scared. He knew he was ashamed at the way he'd allowed himself to be played by that thug Derek Weaver. He knew his stomach did somersaults when he thought about how his mother was going to react to his leaving home. He knew that before she'd climbed into the car with him, he felt more alone than he'd ever been in his life. But he couldn't say any of that. So he said nothing.

"Do you need a place to stay for a day or two?" she asked softly. "'Cuz if so, you're welcome to crash here."

His throat did close this time. Convenient, because he needed the extra time to stop himself from leaping at her offer. "Nah, that wouldn't be a good idea," he said at last.

Even in the darkened interior of his car, he saw the lift of her brow. "Scared I'm gonna mount an assault on your virginity, Harmer?"

His *supposed* virginity. Before he'd passed out in that wretched, gawd-awful bedroom Derek Weaver had dragged him to, he distinctly remembered two women — or, oh shit, *girls*, if that piece-of-shit Weaver was telling the truth — making a concerted effort to relieve him of that commodity. And what they'd done to him in the car …. Jesus, he could be a walking STD, for all he knew.

He laughed, surprising himself with how adult it sounded. "Rach, babe, I can't even begin to count the things I'm afraid of just at this point in time, but that'd be pretty far down on the list."

She sighed. Dillon couldn't help but notice how her cropped t-shirt lifted and fell.

"I suppose it wouldn't be very gracious of me to say I told you so?"

"Okay, Weaver's a dickwad. You're right. I blew him off a few weeks ago. Or at least I tried to."

"He's not letting you go gracefully?"

God, what was he doing talking about this stuff? He was supposed to leave her out of it. "Okay, Ms. Perfect, why don't we talk about you for a while? Have you dumped that loser biker yet?"

"Seth?" She snorted. "Besides the fact that he was a corporate lawyer, he wasn't mine to dump. He's my cousin's squeeze. Or rather, he was Connie's. Now he's her ex-squeeze. She's moved on to a banker-type."

"Why do I get the feeling if you dated a biker, he'd be real biker, not a lawyer-biker?"

"Hey, cuts both ways. If I dated a lawyer, he'd be a real lawyer, not a biker-lawyer."

Dillon laughed. Damn, but he liked her. "What are you doing out here with me at, what?" — he checked his watch — "quarter to one in the morning?"

"Are you kidding?" Her voice dropped. "Dillon, you're the reason I wasn't sleeping."

His heart jerked painfully in his chest, leaving him breathless. "Don't say that."

"Why not? You know it's true." She planted her hand squarely on his chest, right over his heart. "You know we connected the first time we met. After five weeks, I think it's safe to say it isn't going to go away just because we ignore it."

He clamped a hand down on hers to keep it from roaming. "Don't."

"Why not? Why are you so scared of me?"

He pushed her hand away. "I have to go."

"Kiss me first."

"Rachel—"

"I'm not getting out of this car until you kiss me, Dillon Harmer."

He blew out a breath. "One kiss?"

"Let's start with that."

"Okay, one kiss." He meant it to sound firm, but he feared it rang with more anticipation than finality.

She sighed, a satisfied sound, then leaned into him. Their lips met, and he almost came. They were so cushiony and moist and eager. Then his attention was taken up by how amazingly comforting a kiss could be, even as it inflamed his need. And how easily one kiss slid into another and another.

Finally, when Cleo whined from the back seat, he found the presence of mind to draw away from her mouth, although he still felt dizzy with her sweetness. How long had they been lost in each other? It felt like days, yet it felt like not nearly long enough. He shifted to check his wristwatch, and Rachel groaned at the loss of contact.

"God, do you know it's quarter to two?"

"Who cares? There's nowhere else I want to be."

He swore softly.

She pulled back, her spine straightening. "I take it that means you can't stay?"

"I've got some stuff to sort out before we can take this any further."

"I could help you."

"I don't doubt that for minute. But first, I just have to figure out what it is I need to do. And I think I need some room to do that."

"Okay."

Somehow, he'd expected a fight. *"Okay?"*

"Yeah, okay. As long as you promise to meet me once a day, where we first met."

He rolled his eyes. "At City Hall? In front of the Nude Dude?"

"In front of the *fountain sculpture*, yes."

No way should he agree. He had to get himself out of this jam before he could risk getting closer to her. He opened his mouth to say no, but heard himself say, "What time?"

"Mid-afternoon. I'll bring McDonalds."

Great. *You've done it now, hotshot. You were supposed to keep her out of this, for her own good.* "My mother's a chef. I don't eat McDonalds."

She leaned forward and kissed him again, a quick, hard kiss. "A chef, eh? I'll bring extra fries." On that note, she slipped out of the car, closing the door softly.

Well. That hadn't quite gone as he'd planned, had it?

⁂

Tommy was dreaming, and this time, it was the good one. The one where Paige came to his bed and made love to him.

He'd swallowed two pills the minute he got home, but it seemed like forever before they kicked in. When the pain finally abated enough for him to drift off, he fell immediately into a nightmare of the shooting.

Just like in real life, he saw himself racing along after Max, heart pounding, mainlining adrenalin. One hundred percent dog handler, zero percent cop. Bad recipe. And he damned well knew better, but suddenly there he was, inside the warehouse, blundering right into that fatal funnel like an untrained civilian. Then the two shots.

At first, there was just shock, the stunned realization that he'd been shot. Then everything went wonky, kind of elastic. His hearing … Christ, it came in and out like a bad heavy-metal track. Eerie silence, full-volume mayhem, silence, mayhem, silence … . Or maybe that was just the sound of his own blood in his ears.

Then came the pain, like an afterthought. Hot and excruciating, it blossomed obscenely along his nervous system like the spreading wetness on the concrete floor beneath him. He lay there in a gathering pool of his own blood, sure he was going to die for his stupid lapse, praying that no one else would die for it.

He'd jackknifed up in bed just as he always did when the nightmare reached that point. And like always, the sudden movement sent jagged talons of pain clawing across damned near every nerve ending he owned.

It had taken him forty minutes and another dose of pain killers — *to hell with waiting the full four hours* — to work his way back down to the point where he could fall asleep again.

His reward was Paige. He felt the mattress depress, smelled the sweet soap smell of her skin, heard her call his name. Then, the touch of her hand on his upper arm.

His *arm*? The tentativeness of the touch rang a strange note. Usually, she went for his chest, her touch bold and sure, before those soft hands moved lower, lower .... .

She called his name again, and his momentary confusion evaporated as he caught her urgency. Yes! Urgent was good. Urgent was very good.

He pulled her down with one tug, catching her weight across his chest. He heard her drag in a surprised breath, then sealed her mouth with his. She tensed, as though to draw back, so he closed his hand behind her head and held her there, taking her mouth in the kind of hot, ravenous kisses she always gave him when she came to him like this. Still, she wouldn't relax into it, so he lifted his free hand to cup the side of her breast hotly, possessively.

"Give me your tongue," he commanded. "Come on, baby. You know what I like."

What she gave him was a sharp, two-handed shove to his relaxed mid-section, driving the breath right out of him. He turned her loose instantly.

"Dammit, Tommy! Stop it."

His reply was a choked wheeze.

"I'm trying to tell you Dillon didn't come home."

Omigod, oh no. It wasn't a dream. She was here, *literally here*, in his bedroom. And he'd just treated her like she was some kind of porno chick whose job it was to get him off.

This time he found the breath to curse, pulling himself up to a sitting position on the mattress. "What are you doing here?" He blinked blearily at the clock radio on the night stand, needing to squint to read the glowing digital display. "God, Paige, it's not even five. You might have knocked, or maybe rung the bell."

"I did ring the doorbell."

Of course she would have. He passed a hand over his eyes. "Sorry. I must have been sleeping pretty deeply."

"Dillon's not home."

Right. She'd already said that. He pushed his lengthening hair — longer than it had been since he joined the force seven years ago — back from his face.

"He's done that before, though, right? And you said he was with friends. Solid friends. Maybe he just got carried away. Maybe he had a drink or two, and thought better of driving back. That's not a bad thing."

"No. He came back and left again."

Damn, his brain was still fogged. He really had to work to decipher the meaning in her words. He'd come back and left? "Why'd he leave again?"

"I have no idea."

"Didn't you talk to him?"

"No. I didn't even see him."

Okay, next time he'd definitely wait the full four hours between pills. His brain didn't want to work, tranqed up like this. "So what? He left a note?"

"No."

"Then how do you know he came back?"

"He dropped Cleo off."

Chapter 8

Paige made coffee in Tommy's kitchen as she waited for him to dress and come down. The ritual soothed her. As she spooned the coffee into the filter-lined basket, measured the water and set the machine to brewing, she felt her pulse rate gradually slow.

And Lord knew it had plenty of reasons to be racing. Discovering Dillon had returned Cleo and peeled out again had cranked up her anxiety level. As had entering Tommy's house uninvited when he didn't respond to the doorbell's chime. Technically, wasn't that break and entering? Then he'd grabbed her and laid his mouth and hands on her as though he owned her, controlled her, body and soul.

And what was she doing here, anyway? What could Tommy do about it?

"God, I hope that coffee's ready."

She glanced up to see him standing in the doorway. For a moment, leaning there against the door jamb in his worn jeans and a navy Armani t-shirt, he looked startlingly able-bodied. Then he pushed away, leaning heavily on the cane as he traversed the tiled floor to the table.

"It's ready. Sit down and I'll pour."

He pulled out a chair and parked himself, propping the cane against another chair. "So, what's the deal? What do you know?"

"Not much." She placed a steaming mug in front of him. If he noticed the slight sloshing caused by her trembling hand, he declined to comment on it. "All I know is he came home at some point in the night, dropped Cleo off, packed a few clothes, and left again."

"No note?"

"Nothing." She blinked back tears and turned to fill her own mug.

"Did he take anything else? Anything of value?"

She shot him a narrow-eyed glance. "You mean, like my best silver? The cash from my purse?"

"I mean, anything of value. That might speak to his situation and state of mind," he said, his voice patient.

"How so?"

"If he cleaned out all your valuables, that would suggest a certain level of desperation. If he took very little, you might draw a different conclusion."

She sank down on a chair, putting her mug down with suddenly nerveless fingers. "I didn't check." What if he *had* raided their modest resources? She couldn't even begin to imagine the kind of pressure that would drive Dillon to those lengths.

Surely not drugs. Surely she'd know . . . .

"You said he packed clothes?"

She blinked away a mind-picture of Dillon's father at the front-end-but-escalating stage of his alcohol and drug addictions. "Yes, I did check his room. He took a few clothes, a shaving kit and his Adidas bag, but I didn't really look for anything else."

"So that's where we'll start, right after our coffee. We'll take an inventory of anything that might be missing, assess the situation and make a plan." He leveled a calm, blue gaze at her. "Okay?"

"You think we'll find him?"

"We'll find him."

Reassured by the confidence in his voice, she let out a shaky breath. "Okay."

❧

Forty minutes later, Paige sat down at her own dining room table across from Tommy. A lump rose in her throat as she watched Cleo go back to her self-appointed station, watching out the picture window for Dillon's return. "It doesn't look good, does it?"

"It could look a lot worse. He didn't take anything that wasn't his."

"He's also not planning to come back in a day or two," she said, thinking about the items he'd taken. His boom box, electric guitar, portable amplifier, Xbox. Chilling. But even more chilling was what he'd left behind. Dammit, he loved that dog. "I can't believe he left Cleo."

Tommy made no comment.

She sighed, pushing her still sleep-tousled hair back from her face. "Okay, so what do I do now?"

"Probably the smartest thing is to just sit tight and wait for him to check in."

Her stomach clenched. "I don't think I can do that. What else? I don't suppose there's any use calling the cops?"

"Nothing they can do. He's nearly eighteen, he left of his own accord, and no one can compel his return."

"And he doesn't qualify as a missing person because he's only just gone," she said dully.

"I'm sorry."

Yes, she could see he was. She could hear it in his voice, too. And, oh, God, she was going to lose it if he said something sympathetic. She just couldn't cry all over him again.

Digging her nails into her palms, she sat up straighter. "Okay, what can we do? Besides wait, of course."

He regarded her a moment, as though weighing something. "Couple of things we could try," he said at last.

"Yeah?"

"It's early yet. He will have crashed somewhere. We could just drive around, see if we can find his car parked somewhere."

"Drive around? Fredericton's not that big, but you and me in one vehicle? Where on earth would we start?"

"I know a few places. Boarding houses and whatnot."

Her stomach lurched. "Flop houses, you mean."

"If you prefer. Also, cheap motels. The shelter, even, though it's unlikely he'd go there in this warm weather. Basically, any place we think of he might lay his head down for a rest."

Dillon, her baby, in the men's shelter? The fist gripping her stomach tightened inexorably as she pictured the motley assortment of drunks, addicts and outcasts. And oh, God, even the mentally ill, shunted from institutional care to community care when everyone knew the community infrastructure was still too underdeveloped to handle them.

"You left out the riverbank where the rummies gather." Anxiety sharpened her voice.

"Actually, I left out quite a few of the more unpleasant possibilities, but I'll enumerate them for you, if you like."

His calm offer held no reproach, but she instantly regretted taking her worry out on him. Again.

"I'm sorry. You're right. Why don't you hold those other possibilities until and unless the more pleasant ones fail to pan out?" At his nod, she leapt up. "Okay, there's some stuff on the front seat of the van. Let me move it and push the seat back a bit."

He put a restraining hand on her arm before she could translate her words into action. "My car might be better."

"But he's more likely to recognize the van."

"Exactly."

Again, tears burned the backs of her eyes. "Of course. If he'd wanted me to find him, he wouldn't have slipped away in the middle of the night."

Once again, he knew better than to make sympathetic sounds. His consideration reminded her that he was no stranger to this type of situation.

"You know how to drive a standard?"

His question took a few seconds to penetrate. "A standard? Yes, I do, but shouldn't I be in the passenger seat, keeping an eye peeled —"

"Standard's out of the question for me at the moment."

The statement was flatly voiced, but she knew how hard it was for him to make. Taking a page from his book, she refused to give expression to the sympathy that stirred in her breast.

"Hey, it's your transmission, fella. Just don't yell at me if I grind your gears, okay?"

Forty minutes later, they'd cruised a half-dozen spots on Tommy's list. The only positive thing she could say was she was now used to driving Tommy's car, a meticulously maintained Camaro, the vintage of which she wouldn't even hazard a guess, other than to speculate it must have been hugely popular among the muscle car crowd when he came of age.

"Make a lane change here, and turn left at the next intersection."

Paige obeyed, knowing he'd feed her the next instruction in plenty of time to react. He was a good navigator, and he hadn't yet said anything critical about her driving. She gave him extra points for that.

"The house with the green siding on the right."

She signaled and pulled the Camaro over to the curb. "I had no idea there were so many rooming houses in Fredericton."

"I doubt you'd find them listed as such in the yellow pages," he said dryly.

She shot him a sharp glance. "What are they? Like, crack houses, you mean?"

"Just regular houses with a party reputation, for the most part," came his reply, even as he scanned the street. "There's a certain segment of the population who seem to do little else. They generally keep us . . . the cops hopping with noise and vandalism complaints, so we know where they are." He turned back to her. "Good-looking kid like Dillon could slide right into a place like that, long as he brought beer or weed or cash to help keep the party going."

"You think he could do that? Just move right on in?"

"That's what I'd do if I were in his shoes, looking to become invisible for a while, on a small budget."

She glanced around. "No sign of his car."

"Hey, there's lots more places to check. We'll find him."

"God, I hope so."

Her growing anxiety must have come through in her tone, because he laid a hand on her knee and squeezed briefly. Considering the awareness that always seemed to shimmer between them, she'd have thought such a gesture would smack of sex. It didn't. The brief contact couldn't have been more platonic, or more comforting. She blinked rapidly.

"Okay, move back into traffic and keep going east. There's two more just like this one on this street alone. The first one's about three blocks from here."

Signaling, she eased back into the light traffic.

Tommy spotted Dillon's car first. The ratty old Toyota hunched curbside less than a block from the next party house.

"We found him!" Hands shaking, she pulled into an empty parking spot two cars beyond Dillon's.

"Looks like we did."

She killed the engine and opened her door, but before she could climb out of the low-slung car, he grabbed her arm.

"Have you thought about what you're going to say?"

"Not really." She chewed her lip. "I was mostly just scared we wouldn't find him."

"And now that we have? What will you say?"

"I don't know ... *What the hell were you thinking?* comes to mind."

He loosened his grip on her arm, but didn't release it. Again, the contact was an unexpected comfort.

"You know, if he doesn't want to go home, there's not much you can do about it."

She swallowed with difficulty. "I know. I just have to see him, to know he's all right. I need to understand why he left like this."

He looked away from the naked fear and pain she knew he must see in her eyes.

"Okay, let's go roust him."

Tommy took much longer to climb out of the low-slung car than she did. Nerves jangling, she waited for him. Together, they crossed the concrete walk to the front door, Paige slowing her footsteps to match Tommy's pace.

It took three or four minutes and several jabs of the doorbell to get a response. Eventually, a shirtless young man wearing jeans and a bleary-eyed expression opened the door. From the absence of unlocking noises from the other side of the door, she knew it hadn't been locked.

"Yeah?" The young man, who couldn't have been more than twenty, dragged a hand through his tousled hair.

"I'm looking for my son, Dillon Harmer."

"You're gonna have to do better than that, lady. You know how many people came through here last night?"

"He must be here," she said, feeling the bubble of anxiety in her chest expand again. "That's his car over there. The black Toyota."

The young man craned his neck to get a look at the car. "Never saw it before."

"He's just under six feet tall, blue eyes —"

"Think Toby Maguire," Tommy interrupted, "but darker hair."

The young man's brow smoothed. "Oh, him. Yeah, he crashed here, I think. Lemme check."

The door closed again, only to reopen a minute later.

"Mom?" Dillon emerged, tucking his shirt into his jeans and looking extremely embarrassed. "What are you doin' here?"

"What am *I* doing here? What are *you* doing here, is more to the point. You missed curfew, then I woke up at dawn to find Cleo home, but no sign of you. What was I supposed to think?"

"I'm sorry, I didn't think you'd notice."

"You didn't think I'd *notice*?" She felt her voice rising, but was powerless to stop it.

He had the grace to blush. "I mean, I didn't think you'd notice before I had a chance to call you. I was gonna do that this morning. I figured you'd just think I was in bed."

"I might have," she said, "except for the fact poor Cleo was beside herself. She came and woke me up."

"I'm sorry."

"And well you should be. You can't imagine how worried I was —"

"Look, I've said I'm sorry. I shoulda left a note or something, I guess, or got up early to call. But now that you're here," he aimed a look at Tommy that said he knew he had Tommy to thank for her having found him so quickly, "you might as well know I'm not coming back."

"You can't mean that."

"Oh, yes, I can. I'll be eighteen on Friday. Old enough to leave home. Old enough to get a real job. Old enough to get my own life."

She'd tried to prepare herself for this possibility, but she needn't have bothered. No amount of preparation could have softened the blow of hearing those words.

"Get a job? What about university?"

"Mom —"

"And get a life? Dillon, you *have* a life. A pretty damned good one, if you'd just —"

"Yeah, right. I have the curfew of your average twelve-year-old, but the responsibilities of a grown up. Then there's the weight of your expectations. Christ, sometimes I feel like it's crushing me alive!"

He couldn't have hurt her more if he'd hauled off and back-handed her. "I don't understand … ." She dragged in a breath, hot and searing against her suddenly sore throat. "I know I give you flack about your grades, but school is so important —"

"It's not about school, okay? It's not even about the stupid curfews."

Be calm, Paige. Be reasonable. "Then what is it about?"

"Do you have any idea how it feels to be the man in your mother's life? The *only* man?" He raked a hand through his hair in a way that reminded her immediately and poignantly of his father. "I can't handle that anymore, okay? I need a break from it. I need a break from all of it."

Oh, dear God! What had she done to him? All this time, she'd thought she was doing him a favor by … .

No, don't think about that. Think how you're going to get him home. If he'd just come home, they could work this out.

"But what about Cleo?" she said.

His jaw hardened. "What about her?"

"She misses you."

He shrugged, though the gesture didn't come off as careless as he would have liked. In fact, it looked more like he was trying to get out of his own skin.

"Take her to the SPCA. That's what you were going to do in the first place, right?"

She might have lost it then, burst into tears or started shrieking hysterically, but for the pressure of Tommy's hand at the small of her back steadying her. She took a deep breath. "You don't mean that."

"For chrissakes, would you stop telling me what I mean?"

"You're not coming home to get Cleo?"

"No."

"I don't understand. You wanted her. You begged me to keep her. And I know you enjoyed the training—"

He sighed, a sound that spoke eloquently of his frustration level, but when he addressed her again, his tone was more controlled.

"Look, I tried. I really tried. But it's pretty lame, really. Anyone can condition an animal to give the right response, can't they? I mean, that's what you do with me, right? *I'm sorry, Mom. I'll try harder, Mom.*" His eyes hardened, and once again she was reminded strongly of Steve when he was in one of his alcohol-fueled moods.

"I don't believe you." She felt her fingernails biting into her palms, and unclenched her fists. "You love that dog. And she loves you."

"I gave it my best shot, ma, but in the end, I just don't want to stay home for that mutt all the time."

"Dammit, Dillon, that mutt spends her whole day watching and listening for your car to come home."

His eyes grew harder still. "Hey, I got nothing against Cleo. I just don't want to have to arrange my life around her."

"Or me, it would seem," she said dully.

"Or you," he agreed, looking away.

She swallowed past the growing lump in her throat. "Well, I guess there's no more to say."

"No."

Before the tears could spill, she turned blindly, right into Tommy.

⁕

Tommy swore under his breath as he dug out the coffee maker in Paige's kitchen, spooned coffee into the permanent gold-finished filter of her expensive unit, threw a haphazard amount of water into the reservoir and hit the button.

Jesus, the pain was eating him alive. He'd driven back, and he didn't know which had suffered most, his transmission or his hip.

Paige had been incapable of driving. Hell, she'd been in a complete daze since they'd left Dillon. Tommy'd had to help her into the car, close the door for her, open the door on their return, usher her into the house. She was like a damned poseable Barbie doll.

When the coffee finished brewing, he filled two cups, added a dash of Captain Morgan's dark rum he found in the cupboard by the sink, and carried them through to the dining room where Paige sat stiffly at the table, just where he'd left her.

"Here," he said, placing the mug in front of her. "I put a little of the Captain in it. It'll do you good, put some color in your cheeks."

She picked up the steaming mug and knocked back an imprudent amount of the spiked coffee.

"Whoa, take it easy, Paige. It's not going anywhere."

"God, could he be right?" Her fingers closed so tight on the mug, her knuckles turned white. "Did I really do that to my son?"

He followed her without effort. "No, you didn't."

She carried on as though she hadn't heard him.

"I think he might be right. I expected too much of him. But I didn't realize ... I mean, I know he sort of saw himself as the man of the house, but I didn't realize he thought he had that kind of responsibility to me ... ."

"Un-unh. Forget about it. You're not putting yourself through that guilt trip."

She blinked, as though finally seeing him. "Excuse me?"

"Okay, there might be a glimmer of truth to what he said. A very faint glimmer. But that's it."

"I thought it was for the best. You know, not to get romantically involved with anyone." Her eyes had lost their focus again, and her two-handed grip on the coffee mug tightened as she spoke. He was glad he'd selected an earthenware mug and not one of her more delicate china mugs. "I swore I'd never do that to Dillon," she continued. "You see, I've learned a little something along the way about the difficulties that men have bonding to older children who are not their own natural offspring."

Oh, Jesus. Dread stirred, a cold, reptilian slithering deep in his gut. "You were ... assaulted?"

She laughed, a grim sound in the quiet of her dining room. "Oh, no, nothing that awful. But it was pretty hard to escape the conclusion that most men don't readily accept another man's offspring."

Tommy cursed, pungently.

"No, really. I never had a problem I wasn't able to handle with a threat to expose the creep if he so much as looked at me funny again. But I decided that a step-father wasn't what I wanted for Dillon. I figured I could do a better job on my own."

"You *have* done a good job."

"Not according to Dillon."

"Dillon's got other reasons for running. No matter what else you believe, believe that."

He felt her gaze on him as he tried to settle in the hard-backed chair. Goddamn, but it seemed a long time since he'd had that last pain killer.

"What do you mean, other reasons?"

"That crap about resenting Cleo's claim on his time? That was a total crock. That kid of yours has more tells than a preacher in a whorehouse."

Something flickered in her eyes. "Tells? What do you mean, tells?"

"It means he'd never make a living playing poker. But more importantly, it means he was feeding you a line of bullshit." He lifted his own mug and sipped the hot brew. "His leaving had nothing to do with curfews or having to cart the garbage to the curb or any of that stuff. It also has nothing to do with Cleo. It damned near killed him to tell you to dump her on the SPCA."

This time, the thing that flickered in her eyes was clearly hope. Then just as clearly, she clamped down on it.

"The fact that he doesn't want me to hand Cleo over just proves he doesn't want to see her orphaned again, or euthanized. It doesn't change the fact he doesn't want to be responsible for her. And he damned sure doesn't want to be responsible for me, or to me, or whatever it is he feels. He meant that much, Tommy."

He looked down into his mug, wishing he'd put a smash of rum in his coffee, too. Of course, it wouldn't mix well with the painkillers.

"Maybe there was a grain of truth in some of what he said, but show me a teenager who doesn't chafe at parental authority. Show me a teenager who isn't completely self-absorbed. It's part of the job description, Paige. You know that. You can't take this to heart." He shifted in his chair in an effort to ease the ache in his leg. "But getting back to the point I was trying to make, I think he had his own reasons for moving out, reasons he's not ready to share right now. All that stuff he threw at you was a smokescreen."

A pause. "Do you really think so?"

"I'm rarely wrong about non-verbal cues." He held her gaze so she could read his confidence. This was one thing he was truly good at. "That's why canine work came so easy for me. You need to be able to read the dog."

She stared at him unblinkingly for a few seconds, and he saw the very instant she accepted his reasoning. "You know," she murmured, "I think I believe you."

"I think I'm flattered."

She groaned, but in a good way. A laughing, self-mocking way. "Oh, God, I'm a wreck, aren't I?"

"Yeah, but I think we can salvage you."

She laughed, but her face sobered quickly. "Seriously, I'm sorry about doing this to you again. I know I over-reacted. I know its normal for Dillon to seek out new peer groups, to test the limits at home, to find fault with me. I even understand why he has to withdraw from me emotionally in order to move toward some kind of independence. I read all the parenting books. I know this is necessary."

She looked up at the ceiling and blinked rapidly, a clear signal she was still on shaky emotional ground. "I knew this day was coming. I knew he'd have to leave. But dammit, Tommy, I didn't think it would be today."

"Well, I gotta agree his timing sucks. You had quite enough on your plate."

"Oh, yes, my saboteur." Her hands tightened again around her mug. "Call me an ostrich, but I don't even want to think about that right now."

She looked tired suddenly. Tired, discouraged and defeated, and it gave him a strange, hollow pain in his chest to see it.

Man, he was getting way too involved in her troubles. The last thing he needed was for her to start relying on him. Hell, he could hardly look after himself. She should know that better than anyone.

Still, she needed someone to take charge right now.

"Go back to bed, Paige. You've been up half the night."

"I will. After I walk Cleo."

"I'll walk her."

"But —"

"I am capable of getting down the hill and back up again. Just not as fast as most folks."

"But —"

"Hey, it'll give us plenty of opportunity to practice that heel command." He called Cleo's name, and she came padding in from her post at the living room window, where she'd been watching diligently for Dillon. "Where's her leash?"

Paige retrieved it from a peg by the back door and handed it to him. "Are you sure it's no trouble?"

Are you sure you're up to it? she meant. He refused to bristle. She didn't need any more attitude. "No problem."

He clipped the leash to Cleo's collar, finally seeing a spark of enthusiasm in the dog's demeanor. Poor girl. Soon she'd realize Dillon wasn't coming back, and would look to transfer her affection.

"Look, I was going to take her over to my place while you slept, but I think I'd better bring her back. You'll want her bonding to you, not me."

She smiled, a quick but genuine flash of amusement. "Typical male. You think a single afternoon in your company would clinch it, don't you?"

He grinned. "Sweetheart, ten minutes would clinch it, if I applied myself."

In that split second, as her gaze connected with his, he knew they weren't talking about dogs anymore. His mouth went dry as his mind supplied technicolor images of him *applying himself* to bonding with *her*. And judging by the heat darkening her green eyes and the delicate flush climbing her neck, she was rolling her own mental tape of the same scene.

Bad. Very bad. She didn't need any more drama in her life right now. And he sure as hell didn't need it. He drew back.

"I guess I'll need a key if I'm going to drop Cleo back." He cleared his throat. "I know you'll want to lock the door behind me, especially if you're going to sleep."

"A key? Of course." She crossed to the kitchen counter and dug around for a moment in her purse. By the time she handed him a set of house keys, the flush that suffused her face a moment ago had receded. "The silver key is the one you want for the front door."

"Great. I'll leave them on the counter when I bring Cleo back." He gathered the leash tight and turned toward the door.

"Tommy?"

Oh, Lord, they weren't going to talk about that flash of awareness, were they? He turned back to face her. "Yeah?"

"Thanks."

Thank you, Jesus. "No problem."

A moment later, with Cleo's leash gripped in one hand, his cane in the other, and the mid-morning sun on his face, he headed down the hill.

The unnaturally subdued Cleo came to life at last, wanting to dart off in all directions, but he controlled her easily, without even thinking about it. His mind was otherwise occupied cursing his body for its persistent reaction to Paige Harmer. It didn't seem to be getting the message that getting naked with her was not in the cards.

By the time he'd made it halfway down the hill, he wasn't thinking about Paige anymore. His sole preoccupation was pain.

Realizing he wouldn't be able to manage the whole half-mile trek, he turned back well before the sparsely-populated street intersected with the 105. Fortunately, the uphill climb turned out to be much easier on the hip than his jarring downhill lurch had been. Still, he had to take a break halfway back. Pitiful.

Well, might as well make use of the time. Pulling his cell phone out of his jacket pocket, he called 411 to get the number of a PI friend who owed him a favor. Twenty seconds later, he connected with Del Mulholland.

"Good to hear from you, Tommy. I tried to get in to see you while you were in the rehab center, but they told me you weren't receiving visitors."

The nerves in his hip and back burned like they'd been set on a low flame, and he wished he could sit down.

"Yeah, sorry about that. I guess I wasn't the model patient."

"Hell, don't worry about it. I expect I'da comported myself just about the same, if I were in your shoes."

Tommy thought perhaps the PI meant it. "Look, could you do me a big favor?"

"Name it, my friend, and I'll tell you if it's within my power."

"Do you have a tracking device?"

"You mean, to slap on somebody's car?"

"Exactly."

"I've got a couple of things might do the job. What are you looking for?"

"I'd like you to stick a tracking device on a vehicle driven by my neighbor's son." Tommy glanced down at Cleo, who sat there expectantly. "He's a good kid, but something's got him shaken up. His mother's worried about him, and for good reason, I think. I don't want to dog his steps or spy on him. But for his mother's sake, I'd like to be able to run him to ground in an emergency, if the need should arise."

"How far away you think the kid is likely to get?"

"I don't think he's going to leave town, if that's what you mean."

"Then what you need is a simple RF tracker. It's got a nice, waterproof casing and a short antenna. It'll attach quickly to the undercarriage of the vehicle, and the kid'll be none the wiser."

"RF tracker?"

"Radio frequency. You know, like the radio collars they put on grizzlies to track 'em? It should let you pick up his signal within a radius of a couple of miles. If you lose him, you just have to drive around town until you pick the signal up again."

"What if he does leave town?"

"Then you'd be SOL. Unless, of course, you have access to a small aircraft. You can track one of these RF jobs for about fifty miles from the air."

It seemed pretty primitive to Tommy. "You don't have anything higher tech? I'd have thought this spy stuff would take advantage of the GPS technology."

"Oh, I've got a handy-dandy little tracker like that, all right, but it's designed more for suspicious husbands wanting to track the little woman's travel without the tacky business of actually following her. But you have to remove the unit when the car comes back and upload the information to a PC. It records exactly where your mark went, right down to civic number of the address, but it won't help you find the car while it's out there. It doesn't emit a locator signal."

"It tells you where the car's been, not where it is."

"Exactly." A pause. "So, where do I find this car you want me to collar?"

Tommy gave him the particulars. "And if you could get to it sooner rather than later, it would be much appreciated," he added. "I got the feeling the kid crashed there last night because he could, but today, he might be looking for more permanent digs." Someplace where his mother couldn't find him.

"Consider it done."

"What about the receiver?"

"I'll drop it off for you after I've tagged the car."

"And if you could keep this business just between you and me?"

"Constable, you wound me."

Tommy snorted. Del Mulholland was six-foot-five, minimum, with a hide as tough as a rhinoceros. "Thanks, man. I owe you."

"Happy to help, but it hardly compares to what you did for me."

Del had needed Max's nose and Tommy's discretion. "How is that brother of yours doing?"

"He's back at university, and he's hitting the books hard this time."

"Glad to hear it."

"Well, I hate to rush off like this, but I'd better get a move on before this kid changes his address again."

Tommy agreed and rang off, sticking the slim cell phone back in his pocket.

"Okay, girl, let's finish this safari before your mistress sends out a rescue party."

Cleo quickly attuned herself to his pace. Her attentiveness to his signals was variable, but still pretty impressive in such a green dog. For a guy who claimed to resent Cleo's demands on his time, Dillon clearly must have spent a lot of time working with her.

A pitiful fifteen minutes later, sweat drenched and a little trembly from the exertion, he plucked Paige's mail — a yellow manila envelope and a couple of bills — from her mailbox, tucked it under his arm and inserted the key into the lock of her door. Beside him, Cleo whined softly.

"What is it, girl?" he asked, but as he stepped across the threshold, he realized what the dog was stressing about. From upstairs, he could hear Paige crying out.

With more alacrity than he would have thought himself capable of after that grueling walk up the hill, he dumped the mail on the counter and scrambled awkwardly up the stairs. Cleo bounded past him, disappearing into Paige's bedroom before Tommy reached the top of the landing.

He didn't know what he expected to find. Not an intruder. Cleo's sudden appearance on the scene would have elicited some kind of reaction if there were someone in her bedroom. And thank the Lord for that. There was precious little he could do to ward off an invader besides brandish the business end of his cane. Paige's soft cries continued, punctuated with the occasional anxious whine from Cleo.

Nightmare, he decided, hobbling down the hall.

A few seconds later, he stepped into the room. Yes, nightmare, all right. Paige lay curled under a floral patterned comforter, her head moving restlessly on the pillow. He stepped closer. Her brow was furrowed and the sounds that issued from her mouth were distressed.

"Paige."

When she didn't respond to her name, he laid a hand on her shoulder and squeezed through the blanket. "Paige, wake up. It's just a dream. Come on, honey. Wake up. You can leave it behind."

Her eyes sprang open and she shot up. The blankets fell away, exposing a functional white tank top. A tank top under which she wore no bra, he noticed immediately.

"Tommy?"

He dragged his gaze back to her face to see confusion in her eyes. "You were having a nightmare. I could hear you from downstairs." He stepped back. "Cleo was worried, so I came up to wake you."

"Oh." She dragged her hair back from her face. "I'm sorry to make you come all the way up here. The stairs … ."

Yeah, yeah, yeah, the stairs. He was a goddamn cripple. "What were you dreaming about?" he asked, cutting off her apology.

Her eyes darkened. "It was awful."

He sat down on the edge of the bed before his hip could give out on him, and she scooted over a little to accommodate him.

"Tell me about it," he invited. "It helps to get it out, or so I've been told." Repeatedly. By the staff psychologist.

She shuddered. "You know those Pepsi commercials where you're looking at one celebrity, but then they unzip their skins and step out, and you see they're really someone else? An entirely different celebrity?"

He nodded.

"I dreamed I was talking to Dillon. It started out normal, but the conversation got stranger and stranger, until it seemed like it wasn't Dillon I was talking to at all. Then he did that thing like in the commercials. He reached for this zipper and unzipped his skin, and that scary thug Dillon had been hanging around with stepped out."

His gaze drifted to the pulse throbbing frantically at the base of her throat. "Pretty scary stuff."

"That was just the start of it. This guy, this cold-eyed man with that shaved head of his and the awful tattoos, came after me, so I pulled a knife. I don't know where I got the knife. It was just there in my hand all of a sudden. I warned him to stay back, but he just kept coming at me, so I stabbed him. Except I didn't really try to stick him. I mean, I didn't thrust it at him or anything. It was more like he walked right into the blade."

Jesus. "No wonder you were upset."

"That's *still* not the worst of it."

How could it get worse? "There's more?"

"Once I'd stabbed the guy, he fell down. Dead, I think. Then I realized he was wearing another one of those zippered skins. I don't know how I missed it, it was so obvious. So I very carefully grasped the tab of the zipper right there at his hair line and started unzipping it." Her throat bobbed. "Three guesses as to who was inside it."

Oh, Christ. Tommy felt his own skin crawl. "Dillon."

"Yes." She blinked rapidly.

"Paige, honey, it was just a dream."

"It was horrible. Horrible. I killed my own son." She gripped the comforter in her fists. "What does it mean, Tommy?"

"It was just a dream. It doesn't mean anything," he said, but he could tell by her eyes, wide and dazed, that he wasn't reaching her.

"The minute he tried to grow up, the minute he started to display any kind of rebellious behavior, I killed him. I mean, it, the behavior. Or him. Oh, God, I don't know. What have I done?"

Oh, for pity's sake, she was trying to make sense of her nightmare. If he'd analyzed every dream he'd had since the shooting, he'd be a blithering basket case on the psych ward. Thank God he wasn't prone to that sort of thing. He drew a steadying breath. It wasn't his dreams he was concerned about now. It was hers.

"But in the dream, you said he walked into the knife."

"Exactly. Because he loves me, because he's bound to me. It wasn't in his best interest, but he let me do it. *Helped* me do it."

Okay, enough of that hysterical psycho-analyzing. "Bullshit."

She looked at him, really focusing on him as though she were finally seeing him. "Pardon me?"

"I said, that's a load of crap. The reality is, he got in with a bad crowd, started acting like a jerk, and you called him on it. End of story."

"But—"

"No buts. You acted like a concerned parent. That's it, that's all. How he reacts to that parental concern and loving discipline is his own problem, not yours. Besides which, he doesn't exactly look like he's throwing himself on your figurative blade."

"I'm sorry. You're right. It's just the stuff he said this morning—"

"I told you, he was blowing smoke up your skirt this morning. Sooner or later, he'll get around to telling you what's really wrong." Lord, his leg hurt, and the sweat he'd worked up in the climb back to the house had cooled, leaving him shivering inside his lightweight jacket. He needed to go home, take a couple of pills and fall into his own bed. "Go back to sleep now. The dream won't plague you again. I'm going to go home and crash for a bit, too, but I'll come back at supper time, if you like."

"No, don't go." She shot a hand out to grasp his leg, as though she meant to hold him there on the bed by force. "Stay here with me."

She barely seemed aware that she was touching him, but he was supremely conscious of her strong, warm, capable fingers on his thigh. He was conscious, too, of the curve of her slight breasts under the cotton tank she wore, the crests of her nipples standing out small and dark beneath the thin material.

"I think I'd better go ho—"

She transferred her hand to his shirtfront, hauled him closer, and pressed her lips to his. Her mouth was eager, her lips cool and damp against his. Before he could command it not to, his left hand closed on her right breast.

Oh, yeah. Perfect. It felt just as smooth and firm and flawless under his questing palm as it had looked to his hungry eyes.

At his touch, her breath shuddered against his lips. Then she was shifting against him, using her hands, her body, her mouth. She was like a sleek cat, twining and nudging and purring in frantic demand.

He opened his mouth and kissed her properly, holding her head prisoner while he explored her mouth. Her hands raced over his chest, and when he pulled back to look at her, she came back at him with her luscious mouth. A dozen small kisses, a dozen different angles, different pressures, as though she found his mouth as endlessly fascinating as he found hers. Her hands, quick and light now, found his sweat-damp skin beneath his t-shirt and jacket.

It wasn't until she fell back on the pillows and tried to drag him down with her that any semblance of reason returned. Well, not reason, exactly. It was more like white-hot agony. His damaged hip screamed at the wrenching motion as she dragged him down, the pain blasting away the haze of sensuality that had fogged his brain. He almost hoped his gasp of pain might be mistaken for something else, but no luck. She released him immediately.

"Omigod, Tommy, I'm sorry. I didn't think."

"It's okay."

"Did I hurt you?"

"Just a twinge." He closed his eyes against the liquid flood of pain, tried to exhale it, breathe it away. "It'll be all right in a minute."

"I'm so sorry."

He opened his eyes. "Paige, if you say that one more time, I'm gonna be seriously pissed." He fumbled in the pocket of his jacket, found his pills. "Maybe you could bring me a drink of water so I can swallow a couple of these? Can't have them sticking in my esophagus, can we?"

She leapt off the bed and dashed into her bathroom, returning seconds later with a tumbler full to the brim with water. Her green eyes brimmed, too, with remorse, but she was too smart to apologize again.

He tossed the pills back, took a swig of water and handed the glass back.

"Thanks. I'd better get on back to my place, now."

Which he would do. In just a minute. Just as soon as he could convince his body that it would be a good idea to push himself to his feet.

"Stay here."

He slanted her a wry look. "Didn't we already have this conversation five minutes ago?"

She ducked her head. "I won't jump on you this time, I swear. I just don't want to be alone."

He exhaled, feeling the pain recede a little more. "Did it seem like I minded being jumped on?"

That seemed to help her embarrassment. She met his eyes. "Then why are you intent on going home?"

"Because much as I'd like to, I don't think it's a good idea for us to get naked."

"Why not?"

Even given the pain he was in, the glimpse of remembered heat in her eyes just then was enough to jolt him again.

"Because you're going through a lousy time right now. Because some nutcase is threatening your business and you're scared. Because your kid just left and you feel like hell. Because your life has been turned upside down." He shrugged. "It's just not the right thing to do."

Her chin came up. "What if I said I just needed someone to hold me? The comfort of human touch?"

He inhaled. Did she know what she was asking? Of both of them?

But what kind of a heel would he be to deny her that basic human comfort?

"I'd say I guess we could accomplish that without getting naked."

"You'll stay?"

"For a while."

He shrugged out of his jacket, tossed it on the floor — he really didn't think he could make it to the other side of the room to drape it neatly on the chair — then bent to unlace and remove his runners. Would the day ever come when his leg would be well enough that he could just toe his footwear off like a normal person?

Now that he'd committed to staying, she hovered, reminding him of a hummingbird. An annoying hummingbird. "Just crawl under the covers."

"Do you need anything? Can I do anything?"

"Yes, you can stop fussing."

She crawled under the comforter.

He peeled his socks off, considered removing his jeans, then thought better of it. Not only was it a bad idea, it would hurt like hell right now, anyway. Damned if he'd crawl into bed with his sweaty t-shirt on, though. He'd smell bad enough as it was. Off it came, over the head, and he used the damp, balled-up cotton to swipe the perspiration from his chest and neck and armpits before tossing it on his jacket.

He pushed himself to his feet, glad she couldn't see his grimace. Flipping the covers back, he sat down and gingerly swung his legs into the bed.

"How do you usually sleep?" she asked, flipping the blanket over him.

With great difficulty.

"On my back, mostly. I think you're going to have to scoot over here. I don't scoot very well."

For a woman who'd declared she wanted to be held, she didn't look too anxious to oblige.

"Are you sure I won't hurt you?"

His lips tightened. "Perfectly. You'll be on my good side. Now c'mere."

She moved into his arms gingerly. A moment later, after a little fidgeting and twisting, she settled against him. She felt good, her compact body surprisingly solid against his. Her breath tickled his chest, and the womanly smell of her teased his senses. He closed his eyes and concentrated on his breathing. God, it was going to be one helluva long nap!

Incredibly, her breathing leveled out within five minutes. He felt her body relax against him in increments, completely trusting, until at last he knew she was asleep.

More incredible still, the soft stir of her breath and the sleepy weight of her head on his shoulder lulled him. Even the grinding ache in his hip and lower back seemed to ease much quicker than usual. As he drifted off to sleep himself, it occurred to him to wonder who was comforting whom.

Chapter 9

Tommy woke up to the sense he was being observed. He lifted his lids to find Paige watching him from a distance of maybe a foot, her head propped up on her elbow.

"Hi," he said. *Brilliant.*

"Hi, yourself."

He ran a hand over his face. "Guess I fell asleep."

"Yeah. Me, too."

He lifted his head from the pillow to look for a clock. "What's the time?"

"About four thirty. I was just thinking about grabbing a shower, then making some dinner for us."

"You don't have to do —"

"I know, but I have to cook. It's my therapy. You might as well hang around and help me eat some of it."

"Okay." *Man, what a pushover he was.*

"Can I ask for one more thing?"

"Why not? You're on a roll."

"Could you lie there like that, just *exactly* like that, for a minute, and let me kiss you?"

Jesus. His heart stuttered. "Paige … ."

"I'll take that for a yes."

She leaned in and kissed him, using only her lips. No greedy hands all over him, no frantic urgency, no fear-fueled desperation, just sweetness and an odd kind of lightness and gratitude. It was exquisite, and over too soon.

"What was that for?" he asked, when she lifted her head.

"I don't know. Something about the way the afternoon sun hit your face just now, and the way your eyes look when they're sleepy." She shrugged, or approximated a shrug as best she could do while leaning on her elbow, and laughed like a woman well-pleased with herself. "I guess I just wanted to."

With that, she rolled out of the bed and strode to the bathroom.

He found himself grinning, too, not knowing why any better than she did. It was sorta like the way the sun on his face could make him intensely happy within that particular moment.

In the other room, the shower started. Too easily, he imagined that white tank top coming off over her head and the Mickey Mouse boxers she wore sliding down her legs . . . .

Whoops, time to get out of this bed and go downstairs, unless he wanted Paige to end up back here with him.

Which he did. *Badly.*

Suddenly, getting entangled with her didn't seem like such a bad idea. In fact, it was beginning to feel downright inevitable. But not yet. Not while his mobility was still so limited. Right now, he'd pretty much have to lie there as passively as he had a moment ago.

He swung his legs off the bed and got up, locating his cane. Time to pick up the phone and call the physiotherapist.

He picked up his shirt, smelled it, then quickly rejected the idea of putting it back on. He desperately needed a shower and a change of clothes if he were going to have dinner here. He'd leave a note for Paige telling her what he was up to.

T-shirt and runners in one arm, he descended the steps slowly. Cleo left her post at the window to greet him at the foot of the stairs. Poor thing was still waiting for Dillon to come home.

"Hungry, aren't you, girl? I'd like to feed you, but I think your mistress better do that." He walked past her to the kitchen where he found a pad and pencil by the telephone. "Tell you what — I'll leave her a reminder."

He took a moment to scrawl a note to Paige, leaving the key she'd given him on top of the notepad.

A moment later, he twisted the lock on Paige's front door, stepped out and pulled the door shut behind him. As he turned to cross the lawn to his own unit, a nondescript blue Taurus crested the hill. Before he'd made it to his own door, the car pulled into his driveway. Del Mulholland unfolded his length from behind the wheel and climbed out. Tommy was instantly conscious that both his chest and feet were bare.

Del grinned.

"It's not what you think."

Del lifted an eyebrow. "Too bad. She's a looker."

"How would you know?"

"I Googled her, got a hit on her website. Nice smile."

Googled her? Tommy knew what the PI meant, but the term sounded vaguely obscene. Besides, he didn't want to talk to Del Mulholland about Paige's smile. He didn't want the big, outra-geously-robust man even thinking about her.

"Did you manage to tag the Toyota for me?"

"Sure did." Del passed him a piece of equipment. "That's your receiver. I found it worked for about three miles, which is excellent for one of these babies."

"Thanks, man. I really appreciate this."

"Any time."

"You want to come in for a beer?"

Geez, had he just invited someone in for a beer? Voluntarily? This was all Paige's fault.

"God, that sounds good, but I can't. I got a cheating husband to tail. Can I take a raincheck?"

"Sure. Another time."

As Del drove away, Tommy let himself inside. Immediately, he felt the emptiness of the unit descend on him, resonating like an echo of loneliness. Dismissing the thought, he crossed to the pile of junk mail that had accumulated on his counter and fished out one of the many business cards the physiotherapy company had showered him with. Three minutes later, he had himself an appointment. The physiotherapist would even come to him, to help him outfit his environment for more effective rehabilitation.

Paige's influence, again.

Before he could reflect on whether that was a good thing or a bad thing, he climbed the stairs, showered and dressed in clean jeans and a lightweight, ribbed crew-neck sweater. Eyeing himself critically, he decided he still looked pitifully scrawny, but the freefall of weight from his frame seemed to have been arrested, thanks to Paige's cooking.

From downstairs, he heard the his door open and crash shut.

"Tommy?"

"Up here."

If the tone of her voice had left any uncertainty as to the fact that something was wrong, the speed with which she charged up the stairs would have removed it. She burst into the room, the manila envelope he'd taken from her mailbox clutched in her hand.

"Did you see this on my kitchen counter?"

"Yes. I put it there, actually. It was in your mailbox with a bunch of bills. I brought it all inside when Cleo and I got back from our walk."

"Did you look inside it?"

"That would constitute a federal offence."

"Look." She shook the contents of the envelope out into her hand — a series of Polaroid photos — and thrust them at him. "That's me. Driving in the van, making my deliveries, shopping for supplies. That's a whole day of me!"

Jesus. He pulled his hands back. "No, Paige. Put them back in the envelope."

She froze. "Oh, shit, fingerprints."

"Maybe. Chances are, they used gloves or wiped them clean before delivering them, but if there's one thing I learned in eight years at this job, never rule out stupidity. Just put them back and we'll call Ray Morgan."

She shoved the pictures back into the envelope and dropped the package on his dresser as though it carried some dread contagion.

They'd barely hit the dust-covered mahogany surface before he'd snatched up the phone and dialed the station.

"Hey, Tommy. Wassup?"

"Paige just got some photos of herself, hand-delivered to her mailbox."

"What kind of photos?" Razor's voice changed instantly. "Not the Peeping-Tom variety?"

"No, nothing like that, but still pretty creepy. They pretty much document her daily activity, at least her normal routine before the keys-in-the-cake stunt shut her down."

"Well, that gives us something to work with, at least. I haven't uncovered much from my inquiries at the restaurant."

Tommy glanced at Paige, who was busy worrying a frayed fingernail. "I don't know about that. They're instamatic jobs, so no point canvassing the one-hour places. But you never know, you might find a stray print on the photos or the envelope. I mean, besides mine and Paige's. I'm afraid we handled the envelope a little before we realized what it contained, and Paige rifled through the pictures."

"Anything else for me to see out there?"

"No, I don't think so. Unless you want Ident to dust the mailbox itself. It's a wooden job, one of those tole painted things. But I'm thinking if there's nothing on the envelopes or the prints, there'll be nothing on the box."

"In that case, could you bag 'em and have Paige bring 'em in directly?"

He checked his watch. Traffic would be heavy, but in the other direction. "We'll be there in twenty."

A small pause. Tommy weighed the quality of the silence, waiting for some smart-assed remark from the king of smart-assed remarks. Waiting, at the very least, for some recognition this would be the first time he'd been back to the station since the incident.

"Good idea. She shouldn't be alone."

Tommy let his breath escape. "Right."

"Okay, now get your butts in gear. Grace'll shoot me if I drag my ass tonight. It's our anniversary."

At the mention of Grace's name, Tommy wanted to apologize all over again for the trouble he'd inadvertently helped bring down on them last year. Of course, Morgan would only get that stupid, goofy smile on his face and say that it turned out to be the best thing that could have happened for his marriage. Go figure.

"We're on our way."

Paige searched Tommy's face as soon as he hung up the receiver. "We're going to the station?"

"Yep. Say, you wouldn't have a good-size sealable bag, would you? A freezer bag, something like that? Something clean?"

"Of course."

He picked the envelope up by the very tip of one corner. "Then let's go round one up and get these pics delivered up."

Minutes later, the envelope duly bagged and a wistful looking Cleo secured in the laundry room, they were ready to go.

"Your car or my van?" she asked.

"Your van, I guess, if you want me to drive. Plus, you might not want to leave it here unattended."

She thought about insisting she was okay to drive — she really did feel a lot more composed now. Of course, he might change his mind about accompanying her if she did that. She might have been distraught, but she hadn't missed the tension in him when he told Detective Morgan they were coming in. Going back couldn't help but be good for him. Surely, it would show him his fears about the reception he'd get were unfounded.

"My van, I guess."

He'd told the Detective twenty minutes, but they rolled into the visitor parking lot in just over fifteen. Not that he'd sped. Tommy was a good driver, even more defensive-minded than she was, but traveling north to south, there'd been little traffic to oppose them at this hour.

She climbed out of the van, resisting the urge to move closer to Tommy as they entered the police station, a small two-story brick affair on the corner of Westmorland and Queen. She shivered, knowing the chill that swept over her skin was caused only in part by the sudden cool of the building after the heat of the parking lot.

Walking into the police station was much more intimidating than she would have imagined, like stepping onto some alien shore. A hangover from her childhood, of course, this fear of the authorities. Police, social workers, judges … they'd all held unimaginable sway over her young life.

Except she wasn't a powerless child anymore. God, what a baby she was. She should practice what she preached to Dillon. Only by doing the stuff that scares us a little bit do we learn and grow —

"You okay?"

Realizing her steps had begun to drag to the point that she was slowing *him* down, she laughed. "Just taking it all in."

He seemed satisfied with that, and pressed on, guiding her to the detective's area.

She heard Ray Morgan before she saw him. His voice lowered to a key that would inspire thoughts of endless, languid sex in the mind of Mother Teresa, he was talking into his telephone. Then he swiveled and saw them.

"Whoops, gotta go, babe. Tommy's here."

"Take your time." Tommy wheeled an empty chair from the adjacent desk, gesturing to her to take it while he pulled another up for himself.

"Hah! You didn't think you were getting off that easy, did you? Grace wants to talk to you." Ray thrust the receiver at Tommy, who accepted it with about as much enthusiasm as he'd receive a rattlesnake.

His sexy grin fading, Ray turned to Paige. "So, I hear someone wanted to make a bit of a point with a Polaroid."

"Yes." She pulled the zip-lock bag from her purse and handed it to Ray.

"And these were delivered to your mailbox today?"

"Yes. At least, I think so."

He raised an eyebrow.

"I mean, yes, they were delivered to my mailbox, but I can't say for sure whether it was yesterday or today. I hadn't checked the mail in a while." She resisted the urge to twist the strap of her purse. "These last few days have been, well … ."

"I can imagine."

She watched Ray whip out latex gloves and pull them on with the ease of practice. In the background, she heard Tommy's side of the conversation with the handsome detective's wife, which, she couldn't help noticing, grew more flirtatious by the moment.

In her mind, she formed an image of a younger, more beautiful woman.

She forced her attention back to Ray, who seemed quite oblivious of Tommy's words. "Wow, you look like you've done that more times than Patrick Dempsey on *Grey's Anatomy*," she said, gesturing to the gloves.

He laughed. "I probably have. Now, let's take a quick peek at these, shall we?"

She glanced at Tommy. Despite keeping up his end of the conversation with Ray Morgan's wife, he appeared to be keeping a pretty close eye on Ray as he spread the photos out on his desk.

"They're not close-ups, by any means, are they?" the older man mused. "Of course, I don't suppose your average instamatic comes with a telephoto lens."

"Exactly. If he'd gotten any closer, I'd surely have seen him."

"Or her."

Before she could react to that startling idea, Ray pointed to one of the photos. "I can see that's your delivery van, all right. Are you sure you're the subject in each of these other ones?"

"Positive."

Not only was she sure it was her, she was sure she needed to burn that hideous cardigan the minute she got home. She looked so *old* wearing it. Not matronly — she didn't have the bosom to do matronly. More spinster-like. Neat and prim, but approaching the end of her shelf life. She shuddered. That stupid sweater was history.

"And what day was this? I presume they were all taken the same day?"

She nodded. "Wednesday. The one of my van at the intersection of Brookside and the Ring Road is the first shot."

"Then what?"

She leaned forward to study the sequence of photos as Ray had laid them out. "That's pretty close. If you were to swap number four and number six, you've got a chronological record of my morning. Deliveries, market, and back home."

"Hey, Razor, got a message for your wife before I hang up this phone?"

Ray glanced up, his smile wicked. "Yeah. Don't start without me."

Tommy rolled his eyes. "Grace? He says on this, your anniversary, you deserve the very best, but seeing as I'm currently out of commission, I guess you're going to have to settle for him."

Ray made a half-hearted grab for the receiver.

Tommy pulled the phone out of range, laughing. "I will. Promise. Nice talking to you, Grace."

With that, he hung up the phone. Paige tried not to gape. *Guilty.* Guilty of accepting the grim face he presented to the world as being his natural state. Guilty of believing him to be all but humorless.

As delighted as she was to discover she was wrong, his usual demeanor spoke eloquently to how deeply his injury had crippled him.

"So, what do you think?" Tommy directed the question to Ray, all business again.

Ray leaned back in his chair, equally sober. "Same thing you do. This was intended to crank up the fear factor." He glanced at Paige. "The message essentially is, *I know your routines. If I want to reach out and touch you, I know where to find you.*"

She shivered. That's exactly what she'd felt when she'd shaken the photos out of their envelope onto her tiled counter top.

"It felt more personal," she conceded. "I know the other thing, the tampering with my product, was probably more serious. I mean, it has the potential to completely wreck my business, right? But that's just it — it felt like my *business* was being attacked." She raked her hair back. "Not that I didn't take it personally. I sure as hell did. But this . . . ."

"For what it's worth, that's how I read it, too," Ray said. "This has the feel of a more direct, if somewhat more subtle, menace."

"What have you got on the product tampering?" This from Tommy.

"Not a lot." Ray picked up a pen and rotated it in his hand. "We've made a good start interviewing the staff and delivery people, but I'm not real hopeful. Access to the dessert display case was way too easy. *Was* being the operative word. They've tightened up security considerably as a consequence of this incident."

She licked her lips. "What about the list I made?"

"Well, you were right about one thing; none of the local bakeries wants to disrupt your current business. Believe me, they like it just fine that you're supplying the dining rooms around town. As long as you're doing that, they figure you won't open a *Desserts to Die For* coffee shop and lure all their customers away."

"What about the key shops?" Tommy asked. "Locksmiths? Hardware stores? Anyone buying up padlocks by the dozens, or copying keys en masse?"

"No luck so far, but I left my card with all of them. I'm pretty sure they'd give me a call if someone comes out of the woodwork with a request like that."

"And the dog? Any leads there?"

"Yes, as a matter of fact, I think we did get something there."

Paige leaned forward. "You found something about Cleo?"

Ray reached for a file, flipped it open and pulled out a photo of a yellow dog. "That her?"

She took the photo, examining it carefully. Yes, that was Cleo, all right. Even if she couldn't see the dappled brown splotch on her chest, she'd recognize the haunted look in the dog's eyes. She nodded, handing the photo back. "That's Cleo. Where'd you get it?"

"SPCA. They photograph all their animals, for a sort of before-and-after album, so folks can see how much happier and healthier they look after adoption."

"She was adopted from the shelter?"

"No, she was stolen from the shelter. Someone came to look her over, ostensibly for adoption. They took her out on a leash, and never came back."

"Then you must have a name," Tommy broke in. "A description."

"We got a name — Eric Shrody — but it's false."

Paige frowned. "How do you know that?"

"Doesn't match the address he gave, which is itself fictitious. Plus Eric Shrody happens to be a white rapper of some renown, as the SPCA staff were chagrined to learn."

Her frown deepened. "Never heard of him."

"Sure you have," Tommy said. "You just don't know it."

"Everlast," supplied Ray helpfully. "Or Whitey Ford, if you prefer."

Oh, yeah. "Okay, I know him."

"What about the description?"

Ray grimaced. "These are not folks who are accustomed to being robbed. People drop animals off; they don't generally steal them."

"Conflicting descriptions?" Tommy asked.

"I'll say. He's either five-foot-six, or six-foot-five. Weighs in at anywhere from 160 to 240, and we make his age somewhere between mid-twenties and mid-forties. The only thing they could agree on is he had a shaved head. Bald and white as a cue ball."

Bald ... like the man Dillon had been hanging around with before this all started.

"So, where does that leave us?"

At Tommy's question, she pulled her thoughts back to hear what Ray had to say.

"In a pretty high state of alert. Unfortunately, it also leaves us with not much to go on. Unless we can get something from these photos —"

"Which we both know is highly unlikely."

"Then we've got bupkis. Our best lead is the SPCA folks, with their twenty-or-thirty-or-forty-something bald white guy."

"What about getting them to eyeball the mug shots?"

"We're on top of it. They'll drop in as they're able to, and I'll let you know if anything comes outta that."

Eric Shrody. White rapper. Bald white guy ....

Paige opened her purse, dug through it a moment and pulled out a piece of paper. Praying she wasn't making a mistake, she put it on Ray Morgan's desk. "Remember this?"

"A shopping list?"

"No, the symbol there, near the top."

"Yeah, vaguely. Gang signature, right? You showed it to John Quigley and me when we came out to see you that first night, after the cheesecake thing."

"That's right. My van got tagged with this signature, but it was just hand soap, not spray paint. I didn't think it fit in with the rest of the stuff that was happening."

"But now you think it does?"

"I don't know." She glanced at Tommy, whose expression gave nothing away. "I think I mentioned this, but my son had been hanging around with a pretty nasty crowd. By the time this happened, he'd come around again. He dropped the bad crowd, started hanging around home again. Right after Cleo came, actually. He just seemed to go back to his old self."

"You think there might be a connection?"

"No. I mean, I don't know." She cast another anxious look at Tommy. "I've never met any of them, actually. I just caught a glimpse of this one man. And the way you described the guy from the SPCA ... for some reason, it made me think of him."

"Do you have a name?"

"No."

"Did your son have a falling out with this man?"

"I don't know." God, he was going to think she was the worst parent in the world. How could she explain? "Dillon's always been a really good kid. I mean, *really good*. In elementary school, he was always giving his lunch money away to someone who needed it more. In middle school, he did peer counseling. In high school, he tutored other kids." She leaned forward in her chair until she perched on the very edge. "Back in St. Stephen, he was a hailed as an honest-to-God hero, for a cold-water rescue of two kids in Calais, Maine, after their mentally unstable mother put her Volvo in the river with the kids strapped inside."

"Jesus, the McCready woman?" Ray blinked. "That was your son pulled those kids out?"

"I remember that." Tommy's voice vibrated with excitement. "A toddler and an infant, right? Into the St. Croix River in the springtime? How come you never mentioned that?"

"I don't like to think about it. I know what he did was an incredibly brave thing, but I was so afraid for him, so ... angry. He could have died!" He throat seized up a moment, as it always did when she thought about those heart-stopping minutes with him under the icy water. Then, the second trip . . . . God, he was blue and shivering uncontrollably. I thought he was going to die himself."

She paused to collect herself. Neither man pressed. When she was ready, she resumed. "My point is, he's always been a good kid, with a good heart. But when we moved here . . . I guess I didn't stop to think about how hard the move might be for him. Or maybe it came at just precisely the wrong time. Whatever the reason, I suddenly had an angry young man on my hands. I didn't know what to do besides be patient and trust his fundamental goodness to guide him."

Ray put down the pen he'd been fiddling with. "Sounds like your approach paid off, since he dumped the nasty crowd, eventually."

Another glance at Tommy, who was examining his cuticles now. No cues from that source. It was up to her. "Well, I thought he had. Then two nights ago, he came home well after curfew, packed his bags and left. Tommy and I managed to track him down the next day, but he said he wasn't coming back."

"Does that mean he's back in the bosom of this gang?"

She twisted the strap on her purse. "I don't think so. At least, not yet."

She saw Ray's gaze flick to Tommy, who confirmed her assessment. "Seemed like he was trying to get away from everything. Home, friends, the whole deal. My guess is he's got some thinking to do."

"Think we should be keeping an eye on him?"

Tommy shot her a look, then turned back to Ray. "No, we'll do that. But it might be a good idea to look into that gang signature a little closer. It sounds pretty far-fetched, but maybe Paige's trouble stems from Dillon trying to extract himself from this gang."

Oh, God, no. Please don't let it be true. She covered her mouth to keep the plea from emerging aloud, but a small sound escaped, drawing both men's gazes.

Chapter 10

"**M**S. HARMER?" RAY'S EYES scanned her face. She knew he was taking in every nuance of her reaction. "What do you think of that theory?"

"I think," she said, "that the possibility should have occurred to me earlier. Mostly because it's the only theory I've heard so far that might explain my son's current state of mind." She swiveled to face Tommy, unable to keep accusation from coloring her tone. "I suppose you've been incubating this idea all along?"

He shook his head. "I told you I thought the reasons he gave us for moving out were bogus, but I didn't really put his leaving together with this string of incidents until now. And remember, it's just a theory. It may be way off base."

"Well, having investigated a number of other angles, this one sounds pretty damned promising." Ray held up her shopping list with her hand-drawn facsimile of the swooping signature. "Can I keep this?"

"Of course."

"Anything else you can think of that I should know?"

She shook her head.

"Then I'd best get these photos taken care of so I can go home to my wife."

"Your family, you mean," Tommy said. "That gorgeous daughter of yours can't be much more than a year, year and a half."

"We're temporarily childless tonight." He started gathering up the photos and sliding them carefully back into the envelope. "Much as I love the little sprog, I'm happy to say Aunt Suz and Uncle Quigg have her tonight."

He flashed that sexy grin, and Paige felt a stab of envy, sharp and unexpected. That was all she'd wanted from life, once upon a time. Children and a good man who'd come home to her at night with a look in his eye that said he was glad to be there.

"Your anniversary, and here we are, keeping you." Paige jumped up. Tommy came to his feet beside her, plucking his cane from where he'd hooked it on the edge of the desk.

They said their goodbyes, and Ray headed one way with the envelope of evidence, while she and Tommy headed the other. This time, however, the corridors were not as quiet as they'd been on their arrival.

Three times, they had to stop to talk to people Tommy knew — two patrolmen and a staff sergeant. To Paige's dismay, the greetings seemed overly hearty, and everyone had something they had to rush off to. The patrolmen, especially, couldn't get away fast enough.

Tommy was tight lipped by the time they reached the parking lot.

"Want me to drive?" she offered.

"Why? You think that business back there upset me?" His smile was grim. "I told you, I'm well aware of the psychology in operation here. It's not personal."

"Maybe they just need some time to get used to the idea of . . . ."

"What they need to do is bury me, as deep as they can. The only choice I have in this is where I'm gonna let myself be buried. Frankly, I prefer to it be out here, not in there." He indicated the station they'd just left with a jerk of his head.

He unlocked the van, releasing the passenger door locks with the electronic toggle. By the time she recovered her wits enough to open the door and climb in, he was already behind the wheel.

She reached for her seatbelt, her fingers clumsy on the mechanism. Why was the simple task so hard? She could usually fasten her seatbelt in total darkness and key the ignition at the same time. *Because you're not used to being a passenger, dummy.*

"Okay, so you were right." She jammed the seatbelt home at last and straightened. "So, some people might have a hard time with it. That's hardly your problem."

"No, it's not my problem." He put the van in gear, reversed out of the parking space and exited the lot.

"But you're not going back?"

"I'm not going back."

Not your business, Paige. Leave it alone. She suppressed a sigh.

"So, what now? Should we try to find Dillon, ask him about those friends of his?"

"Why don't we give Ray a chance to see what he can find out first? You know it'll put Dillon on the defensive if we tackle him about this, especially while his blood's still up from before." He eased into traffic, then glanced sideways at her. "You might be better equipped for that talk if you've got the skinny on these yahoos going in."

Relief made her wilt. She hadn't been looking forward to challenging Dillon. Not tonight. Not when he was still so upset about … well, whatever it was he was upset about. Not when he could bolt in earnest. She might never find him if he decided to really lose himself. It was a big country. She shivered.

"Okay, I guess it's home then, James. I've still got a meal to make."

He shot her a quick look. "You don't have to make dinner."

"Hey, I *wanted* to make dinner before. Now I *need* to cook. Don't leave me swinging here, Godsoe. I've got nobody else to feed."

Silence stretched between them for a fraction of a second too long. Was he going to decline?

"Far be it from me to disappoint a lady."

"Remember that."

Smiling, she relaxed back into her seat.

⁂

Damn, but that smile was unnerving.

"Taking the long way, are we?"

Oh, hell, he'd missed the Main Street exit off the bridge.

"Ring Road's quicker this time of the evening," he muttered, then clapped his attention back on the road, lest he find himself headed to Miramichi or some other unintended destination.

Lord, she was transparent. He could feel her sexual interest like an extra passenger between them. Hell, he could practically hear her X-rated thoughts, taste her desire. Was it a purposeful projection, aimed at putting him off balance? Or was she really that guileless?

He pulled up behind a transit bus at the intersection. Didn't matter, he thought grimly. Purposeful or not, her carnal smile had set him off again. It was going to be a damned long evening.

Two hours later, he was ready to concede he must have completely misread her.

Dinner was wonderful — Thai chicken on a bed of angel hair pasta, followed by baked glazed pears. If the luscious, pale fruit put him in mind of female curves, he had no one to blame but his own overactive, abstinence-charged imagination. Paige was circumspection itself.

In fact, over dinner, as she watched him eat, she seemed to genuinely wind down. If this was all it took to help her unbend, he was more than happy to oblige. He pushed his dessert away and picked up his coffee.

"You look good," he remarked. "More relaxed than I think I've ever seen you."

Her lips kicked up in a smile. "Even sleeping?"

"Okay, more relaxed than I've ever seen you while conscious."

She laughed, and the humor reached all the way to her eyes. "Yeah, I feel pretty good."

"So, what's different tonight? I have a hard time believing feeding me was *that* therapeutic."

She shrugged. "I don't know. I guess it's this theory of yours, the idea that Dillon's ex-friends are behind all this trouble. It's the first thing that's really made sense." She caressed her coffee mug — absently, he was sure, but the action drew his gaze. "I feel like we've got a legitimate lead now, something your friend Ray can run to ground. Once I know all the facts, I can figure out a better way to deal with Dillon. I'm sure of it. He really is a good kid."

"I can think of at least one community who'd agree with you. I can't believe he's the kid saved those McCready children."

Pride warred with remembered fear in her eyes. "Yes, he was hailed as quite the hero, on both sides of the border. They had a big ceremony, pinned a medal on him and everything."

"He must have thought that was pretty cool."

"Cool? A little, I guess, after the fact. But at the time, he was mostly just embarrassed by the attention." She traced the rim of her mug with an elegant finger. "Your original reluctant hero."

"Reluctant to be put in the limelight, maybe. But it sounds like he didn't hesitate to cowboy up when he had to, and that's the real measure of a man's character."

"It still scares me silly to think about it." A delicate shudder racked her. "I fully expected to turn gray overnight after that little episode."

"You must be very proud of him."

"I am. I just have to keep reminding myself how brave and smart and resourceful and strong he is. When I think of that, I know he's going to come out of this okay."

"And so will you. Ray'll find this guy. You know that, right?"

"I'm counting on it." She pushed her coffee cup away. "And in the meantime, I'm going to get on with my life."

His brows drew together in a frown. "I like the sentiment, but there's not a lot you can do, is there, until Ray rounds this cracker up? I mean, I shouldn't think the restaurants you supply will be especially anxious to resume deliveries until this is resolved."

"Ah, but there's more to life than work."

She got up and carried her dishes to the sink, but he caught the upward curving of her lips. Yikes! There it was again. The carnal smile. He'd thought he'd side-stepped that particular minefield.

"Like what?"

She smiled at his suspicious tone, and he supposed he should be grateful she hadn't laughed outright. He sounded like a nervous virgin whose virtue was on the line, for pity's sake.

"Like everything I've neglected for the last thirteen years." She moved up behind his chair, and his whole body tensed.

"Paige, we talked about this. Didn't we agree it wasn't it a good idea?"

"No. *You* decided it wasn't a good idea. I didn't express an opinion."

"But—"

Her hands descended on his shoulders, and it was all he could do to keep from jumping.

"You're attracted to me." Her voice poured over him, warm and liquid, even as her fingers kneaded his shoulders. "I may have been celibate a long time, but I know when a guy likes what he sees."

His heart leapt, pounding against his ribs. "Paige —"

"Tell me you haven't thought about it."

He swallowed. "That doesn't mean we should act on it."

"Why not?"

Jesus, he could feel the warmth of her behind him, right through his shirt. He closed his eyes. "For starters, I'm in no shape for it."

Her fingers stilled. "You think I'll hurt you?"

Christ, could he possibly feel more inadequate? Please, God, just let a hole open up in the floor and swallow him. "I think if a woman's waited this long, the experience should be more … memorable than I can make it."

"But there are plenty of ways to make love. I mean, presuming nothing's changed?"

"Paige —"

"Tommy, I think it's time you shut up."

"Huh?"

She leaned around him and kissed him full on the mouth, effectively silencing him.

This is it, buddy. This is where you gotta make your stand. This is where you have to dig deep, be responsible.

Fat chance.

Her tongue was in his mouth, and oh, Jesus, God, she tasted good. Like coffee and brandy and woman. Any thought of resistance fled.

She kissed him endlessly, again and again and again, like she was starving. Like she might never get enough. Like she could eat him alive. It was the sexiest thing he'd ever known.

He pulled her around, trying to position her on his lap, but she protested.

"No." She maneuvered herself up onto the table instead, clearly not wanting to hurt him.

He draped her legs on either side of him. She leaned down and kissed him again, deeply, recklessly, as though she would have his very soul.

He kneaded her thighs, her hips, the outsides of her breasts, delighting in the way she purred in response.

Then, abruptly, she pulled back. "Push your chair back."

"What?"

"Push it back!"

Galvanized by her urgency, he complied.

She slid off the table to kneel at his feet, her fingers going straight for his belt.

"Wait!"

"Why?"

Why indeed?

He forced himself to think. "You may have been celibate for the last decade, but I haven't. What makes you so sure I'm safe?"

Her fingers stilled, but just for a moment. "Ah, come on. You're way too health-conscious to take a chance with the Temple of Tommy. I'll bet you never had unprotected sex in your life."

"You'd lose that bet."

"Yeah? When?"

"My first time. I was fifteen. Got hit and run by a senior. Didn't see it coming and wasn't prepared."

She smiled again, that slow, sexy, incredibly lascivious smile. "I guess that's plenty long enough ago that you should be safe for what I've got in mind."

Any thought of resistance was obliterated by her husky, sex-charged words and the mind pictures they conjured. His heart pounding, his whole body clenched with anticipation, he watched her small hands undo his belt, slide his zipper down, then free his straining arousal.

Weak. Oh, God, he was so weak.

She inhaled sharply, and he looked up to find her regarding him with serious lust. Oh, man. Control, control. Don't lose it.

"May I?"

Her delicate request for permission slew him. "Jesus, Paige."

"Shall I'll take that as a yes?"

"Oh, yeah."

For all that she'd pushed and pushed up until this minute, she didn't rush things. Rather, she skimmed her hands up under his shirt, down his sides, across his abdomen, then up and down his denim-clad legs. Only when she'd explored and stimulated all that territory did she zero in on him.

The first touch of her hands dragged a gasp from him. Then there was nothing but the harsh rasping of his breath, the thundering of his heart, the warmth of her mouth on his bare flesh, and the velvet of her incredibly talented tongue.

Briefly, it struck him as surreal. This was *Paige*, for God's sake! His *nice* neighbor. Martha Stewart in the kitchen, respected businesswoman in the community, devoted mother. Not to mention celibate almost as long as he'd been sexually active.

And oh, sweet Jesus, she was giving him head like he didn't know head could be given. Somehow, he'd equated all that celibacy with virginal, sexless inhibition. Man, was he misguided!

Then he forgot to be concerned about anything but the way his universe was shrinking. All too soon, he felt the edges of his control start to crumble. His body begged him to let her continue, to take the act to its ultimate conclusion, but his mind rebelled at the practicalities. This was *Paige*. He was *not* going to come in her mouth.

"Paige." He touched her shoulders, urging her backward. "You have to stop."

"Why?"

A shudder wracked him. "Because if you do that ten seconds longer, I'm gonna explode."

"That's the general idea, isn't it?"

Oh, Jesus, she was killing him. "Yeah, but not yet. Ladies before gentlemen."

She smiled wickedly. "I would have thought by this juncture, you'd have figured out that I'm no lady."

No, she was a woman. A hot-blooded one. And if there was one thing he'd inherited from the old man, it was how to touch a woman.

"C'mere. It's your turn."

She allowed herself to be pulled to her feet.

"I hate to be a pushover, but I gotta tell you, I don't think this is going to take long." She shivered as he unfastened the button of her jeans. The further he eased her zipper down, the higher her voice got. "The minute you touch me, I'm gonna — ahhh! Oh, my God, Tommy."

Ah, Christ, she was wet. Beneath her panties, his fingers danced over her swollen, sex-drenched flesh. She splayed her legs, covering his hand with hers to increase the pressure as she rocked against him. Unbearably excited by the frankness of the need written on her face, he slid a single finger inside her. She climaxed, fast and hard.

She sagged against him. "Told you it wouldn't take long."

"What? You think you're finished?"

She drew in an uneven breath. "I'm not?"

"Baby, you haven't even started. When I'm finished with you, you won't know where my mouth stops and your body starts."

Two orgasms later, he let her slide off the table. She would have taken him in her mouth again, but he knew he was too far gone for that. So she settled for stroking him with her hands, hands which proved to be just as skilled. But it wasn't her soft hands that blew his mind. It was the thought, *"Omigod, this is Paige"*. And when his orgasm slammed into him, he tried to prolong it, tried to cling to that conscienceless, mindless, boneless release, but inevitably, sanity returned.

Oh, man, what had he done? Dammit, he *liked* this woman. What the *hell* had he done?

⁂

"Okay, how come I'm naked and you're not?" Suddenly self-conscious, she reached for her shirt and pulled it on, noticing that he'd already restored his state of dress.

"Mother nature's little joke, I guess."

"Next time, I want all your clothes off," she said sternly. "The full Monty. Maybe I'll even demand a bed."

He glanced away.

Her stomach muscles, so gloriously relaxed, tightened. "What? You have a problem with getting naked for me?"

He lifted his gaze to meet hers, and her stomach dropped. Omigod, he *did* have a problem. "What?"

"I think this is a bad idea."

"What's a bad idea?"

His face hardened. "You and I are friends, Paige. And God knows right now, I need a friend. And I think you do, too. But if we bring sex into it —"

"What do you mean, *if*?" She pulled her shirt tighter around her. "I hate to break it to you, but we've already had sex. Lots and lots of it, unless we're going to get bogged down in some kind of Clintonesque hair-splitting."

"Okay, we had sex," he conceded. "It was great. Hell, it was *fantastic*. And maybe we both needed the release."

He raked a hand through his hair, making it stand up in wild ways that should have made him look stupid, but only made him look sexier.

"But?"

"But you don't want to get mixed up with me that way. Successful romances aren't the Godsoe men's long suit. Much as I hated the old man for stepping out on my mother, it turns out that I am my father's son. Except I'm smart enough not to try to do relationships. Nobody gets hurt that way. I get off, then I get out. I'm not proud of it, but that's pretty much my *modus operandi*."

"But —"

"Look, I like you, okay? I like you a *lot*. Too much to want to drive you away, which, unfortunately, is also one of my specialties."

She felt the blood suffusing her throat, her face, but was powerless to stop it. "So, what are you saying? That I have to choose between my lover and my friend?"

He looked away again. "Pretty much, yes. And I think I can safely guarantee the friendship would last a helluva lot longer than the other."

"Well, isn't that a bitch?"

"I'm sorry."

"Me, too." Damn, but her throat hurt. She had to push the words out. "Because, you know, I could sure use both right now."

"I'm —"

"Sorry. Yeah, yeah, I know." She folded her arms across her breasts. "Well, I guess it's a no-brainer, isn't it? I need a friend right now more than I need a lover."

He seemed to sag, but she couldn't say whether it was relief or disappointment.

"Good decision."

Was it? It sure as hell didn't feel good.

But, dammit, he was probably right. She'd seen it with her own eyes, time and time again. You couldn't spend ten years as a ward of the state without encountering a fair number of emotionally stunted kids. Sometimes it was sexual abuse, sometimes it was alcoholism. The parental misconduct always found a way to imprint itself on the child. Chronic infidelity on the part of a parent was probably no different. His father must have been a real prince.

And, oh, boy, didn't that explain a lot. No wonder he was so hard on himself, so damned unforgiving of his failures. He must struggle every day to believe there was something — *anything* — good inside.

And there was. So much good. Anyone could see it, except maybe for Tommy himself.

But maybe he could be made to see it . . . .

"Okay, here's the deal," she said.

He lifted a dark eyebrow. "The deal?"

"Yeah. Tonight we're lovers. That's a *fait accompli*, right? So I say we enjoy it for one night, and tomorrow, we can revert to friends."

"What's that mean, exactly?"

"It means, we go over to your place, dig out the stash of condoms I know you must have over there, and make love for the rest of the night. Then I'll vacate in the morning, and we won't ever have to talk about it. Scout's honor." Surely that prospect of conscience-free sex would appeal to him. She was banking on it.

"Jesus, Paige."

"Come on, Tommy. I've been celibate for thirteen years. And as you may have deduced, it doesn't exactly come naturally to me. Can you blame me for wanting to get some mileage out of this before we have to nix it?"

"Oh, baby, you deserve so much better … ."

"You're right about that," she agreed, "but tonight, I intend to take what I want."

"Okay." His Adam's apple bobbed. "Okay."

⁂

Eight hours later, with the dull grey of dawn creeping into his Spartan bedroom, she lay there quietly, just watching him. His head rested on the pristine white pillow, his face slack and slightly soft with sleep. He also sported the most amazing case of bed head she'd ever seen. Of course, she'd contributed to the wild disarray of his luxurious hair, having spent most of the night with her fingers tangled in it. No doubt hers probably didn't look any better.

The images flooded her mind. *Would it ever be that good again, with anyone else?*

No. Never.

They'd both thrown themselves into it, wanting to make the very best of the hours they had available. The first time, she'd climbed on top, carefully riding him to their mutual fulfillment. The next time, he'd insinuated himself under her, bringing her to a shuddering climax with his mouth, a favor which she'd returned. The final time, she'd faced him on the firm mattress, hooking one leg over his hip, carefully rocking them to a long, slow, rolling climax.

Now, the hour of reckoning was upon her.

She'd taken what she wanted, all right, wringing every last drop of pleasure out of the experience. She'd drunk in his extraordinary physical beauty with her eyes, memorized his shape with the tips of her fingers. She'd gloried in the touch of his hands, his mouth, been scorched again and again by that blazing blue gaze. But somehow, everything had changed.

Somehow, while he'd slept with his body curled around hers, she'd gotten closer to that guarded part he kept so well protected during the waking hours.

Yeah, she'd do this friend thing. She'd do it because she didn't have a choice. But she wasn't giving up. Because, dammit, while he'd slept, he'd gotten closer to her, too. She'd stake her line-of-credit on it.

She pressed two fingers to her lips, kissed them, then applied her fingers to his mouth, gentle as the brush of a butterfly. He stirred, but didn't wake.

Come on, Paige, keep your promise. Don't weaken now.

Throat aching, she slid out of bed, collected her clothes and left.

⁂

"Paige?"

Tommy lifted his head from the pillow and scanned the room, his eyes gritty from lack of sleep.

She was gone, but not more than a minute or two. He still felt her presence in the room like an echo. Worse, he felt it like an ache inside, a void.

Oh, shit.

Generally, at this point, all he felt was relief if the woman in his bed got up and left. And if the woman in question was still in his bed and presumed to lay hands on him, all he felt was revulsion. What he wanted come morning was solitude, and making that point, as tactfully but plainly as possible, usually earned him a pass from any future engagements.

But right now, God help him, all he wanted was to have her back in his arms. He wanted to hold the warm solidity of her body against his, inhale the shampoo smell of her hair, listen to her breathing . . . .

Something had happened last night.

It was supposed to be just sex, gratifying and uncomplicated, by mutual agreement. Glorious, hot sex, but without the strings and the phony sentiment the act so often entailed.

It had been hot, all right. But it had been so much more. And the surprises just kept coming.

After that first explosive climax, he waited for the usual hollow feeling to invade his gut, the feeling that said *What the hell are you doing here, Godsoe?*, but it hadn't. And when she'd collapsed on him, he welcomed her weight, her body heat, the slide of her sweat-slicked skin against his, without once flinching.

Even more remarkable, he'd wanted her again, right away, with a single-mindedness that silenced the dull, grinding ache in his hip. Oh, Christ, it felt like too much of her could never be enough. Even now, he hardened as he remembered loving her, intimately, enthusiastically, endlessly, with his mouth. And she'd insisted on returning the favor.

Afterward, she'd tried hard to look like the kind of woman who'd be able to walk away from this in the morning, but in fact, she'd looked fragile, vulnerable. With an ache in his heart worse than any pain his hip had ever given him, he'd wrapped her in his arms and lulled her to sleep with whispered, unintelligible assurances. Assurances he had no business making.

Then she'd woken him near morning. There'd been a soft quality to her loving that final time. Liquid, sad, exquisite.

Final.

"Oh, man," he breathed into the silence. "I think I mighta made a mistake."

Problem was, what was his mistake? Sleeping with her in the first place, or telling her it couldn't happen again?

Chapter 11

PAIGE WALKED CLEO ALL the way down to the 105, crossed the highway, then continued on up the walking trail on the other side. She'd hoped to chew up an hour or two in this fashion, but it eventually occurred to her that such an ambitious walk might be too much for the little dog's healing leg. On that thought, about twenty minutes into it, she turned Cleo around and headed back.

Once home, she spent some time grooming Cleo. As comforting as it was to stroke the warm, appreciative little creature, her mind cried out for busy work. So she put down fresh food and water, gave the dog a last pat and left it to its meal. Then she took on the kitchen.

Climbing onto a chair, she dug out the contents of her upper cupboards and scrubbed the dark interiors. Then she replaced everything and repeated the exercise with the lower cupboards. Her commercial refrigerator, the regular refrigerator, the range, the convection oven, the dishwasher, nothing escaped her one-woman war on microbes. When all that was done, she waxed the floor. Finally, exhausted, she flopped on the couch with a glass of ice water.

Of course, the minute she stopped moving, thoughts of last night crashed in on her. Too tired to fight it anymore, she lay back in the cushions and allowed herself to feel all the conflicting, chaotic emotions she'd been trying to tamp down.

Amazement at her own aggressiveness.

Wonder at her responsiveness, which had clearly been honed by her long abstinence.

Awe at Tommy's physical beauty, despite his impaired mobility.

Joy in the memory of the way he'd loved her, with all the skill and finesse she'd expected, but also with a single-minded, focused thoroughness she really hadn't been prepared for.

But for each of those wondrous things, there was a painful or frightening parallel.

Did he feel he'd been pushed into something against his better judgment? She really hadn't given him much wiggle room ....

And would he now find it too weird for words to resume their friendship, after the intimacies of last night?

Was he appalled at her conduct?

Oh, yes, she'd felt his surprise, his initial struggle to make the mental adjustment to her degree of sexual sophistication. She knew beyond the shadow of a doubt that he'd enjoyed the fruits of her experience, but was it too much for his male ego to handle? Some men preferred innocence, or at least the pretense of it.

And beyond *his* reaction, how was she supposed to manage her own? How was she supposed to pretend it never happened? How would she contain her anguish — and yes, *anger* — at being obliged to choose between lover and friend? How could he give her a taste of heaven and then yank it back?

And underlying it all was a sneaking but powerful sense of guilt about spending the afternoon, evening and night indulging in what could only be described as wild sexual abandon, while her son sat in some strange house struggling with a problem so overwhelming that he couldn't share it with her.

But even considering the guilt, did she regret it? Would she take it back, if she could?

Not a chance.

The answer came immediately, and with conviction. Maybe she'd eventually come to regret it, but not yet.

And if she did come to rue the day she seduced him, so be it. She tipped her glass up and drained it, leaving only the ice cubes. As Tommy had once pointed out, she hadn't done anything worth repenting since marrying Dillon's father. It was damned well time she made room for some new regrets.

Past time.

And maybe it was time Tommy made some new ones, too. He was altogether too mired in the old ones.

Feeling lighter of heart and filled with purpose, she climbed the stairs to the bathroom. She had a lot of work to do before dinner tonight. Beginning with a soak in the tub to ease the pleasant ache in all-but-forgotten places, followed by a quick trip to the mall.

The next time Tommy Godsoe laid eyes on her, she was *not* going to look like anybody's mother. With any luck, he might not find it as easy as he seemed to think it would be to revert to their old roles.

⚬❧⚬

Rachel leaned back on the park bench in the public square in front of City Hall, the better to expose her legs, bared by a pair of cutoffs, to the sun's rays. Working night shifts at a 24-hour coffee shop and sleeping a good part of the day didn't leave much time for working on a tan.

A passing suit — a civil servant on his way back from lunch, no doubt — slowed to give her bared legs and full breasts a closer look, gawking so long he almost collided with a parking meter.

What a tool. She resisted the urge to hurry him along with a few well-chosen words, mainly because she felt too good to let anything bother her today.

Stupid to feel so good over the idea of just hanging out with a guy.

Guy? Guys were men, weren't they? And Dillon was practically a boy.

Well, strictly speaking, he was only younger than her by maybe a year, if that, but somehow she felt much older.

Boy, man … . Whatever. The point was, it was incredibly stupid to let him matter so much. Unfortunately, it was way too late to worry about that now. With those serious blue eyes and that impossibly clean-cut wholesomeness, he'd somehow gotten inside her barbed wire. He just flat-out sidestepped her defenses.

A transit bus chugged by, expelling a black plume of diesel exhaust. The cloud hung in the humid air for a few seconds before slowly drifting away. *Ugh.* She waved a hand in front of her face.

Then she spotted him on the sidewalk, about a half a block away, weaving through the thinning post-lunch hour crowd. Her heart took a joyful little leap. The kind of leap she used to roll her eyes at when other girls described it. God, was she regressing to a simpering thirteen-year-old?

So she wouldn't look too eager, she pushed her sunglasses back up on her nose, closed her eyes and lounged back even further on the bench, the picture of an oblivious sunbather.

"Rach?"

She pulled her sunglasses down and peered at him over their lenses, then promptly forgot about acting cool.

He looked awful.

Well, as awful as he was capable of looking without someone physically messing his face up. The muscles of his jaw bulged with tension, and his eyes looked flat and curiously shiny. She sat up abruptly.

"Dillon? What's the matter?"

His brows drew together in a scowl. "Nothing. And hello to you."

Nothing? Yeah, right.

"Sit," she commanded, scooting over to give him room. He sat, but made no move to touch her. Unable to stop herself, she took his hand. When it tightened around hers, she relaxed a fraction. "There, now," she soothed. "Tell mama what's wrong."

He yanked his hand away. "You're not my mother!"

She drew back, her stomach lurching with alarm. "Jesus, Dillon, it was just a joke. You know, funny ha-ha? 'Cuz I'm older than you."

He slumped back on the bench, but she could tell he was forcing the relaxed posture. "Sorry. I'm a little grouchy today."

"That's allowed, I guess," she murmured, watching him lift a hand to rub the back of his neck.

Suddenly, in that moment, with that one gesture, he looked like a man, with a man's problems. And she didn't know how to help, especially if he wouldn't tell her what was wrong.

"Do you need money?" The question was out before she could stop herself. Criminey. She had a rule about men and money. *Never give them any.* Which was pretty much the same rule she had about sex, though no one was likely to believe it.

"What?" He swung around to look at her.

Too late to pull back, she held his incredulous gaze, ignoring the curious looks their exchange was drawing from some of the other users of the public square. "Yeah, money." She kept her voice down. "I've been in a few tight spots that would have been easier to get out of if I'd had some cash."

He averted his eyes. "I don't need money."

She chewed her lip. "Trouble at home?"

He turned to face her, wearing that flat-eyed look again, but she'd already seen the way his shoulders drew together at her question.

"Home? Why would I have trouble at home? I haven't been back since I left."

"Doesn't mean there can't be trouble there."

He looked away again, the line of his lips thinning even further. "Look, I only came because I promised to meet you here once a day. I didn't want you to think I'd screwed off on you, is all."

So he didn't like the third degree? Too bad. 'Cuz sure as they were sitting here, there was something eating at him, and he needed to let it out.

"Is something up with Derek? Is he still giving you a hard time?"

He leapt to his feet, startling a small flock of pigeons into flight. "Quit it with the twenty questions, already. Dammit, this is why I left home!"

So his mother had asked him a few questions. Big freakin' deal. He was a boy after all, she decided. A spoiled child who had no idea what he'd thrown away.

"At least your mother cares enough to try to protect you, look out for you. That's more than some people ever had. That's considerably more than I had." Her temper slipped another notch. "You really don't have the first idea how damned lucky you are, do you?"

She had every intent to let him have it with both barrels, but suddenly his face contorted, as though her words had slid into him like knives.

"Oh, God, Dillon, I'm sorry," she found herself saying.

"I gotta go."

"Wait!"

Ignoring her plea, he turned and loped off down the sidewalk, back in the direction from which he'd come.

Way to go, Rach. Man comes to you needing to talk and you go and unload on him. That damned big mouth of yours again.

She thought about giving chase — unless a man was a trained runner, which Dillon wasn't, she could usually keep pace — but discarded the idea. It wouldn't do any harm to let him cool off. He wasn't in any mood to listen right now, that much was for sure.

She looked down at her lap where her hands had squeezed into fists, as though to do physical battle with her frustration. Too bad it wasn't that easy.

Suddenly conscious of her audience of tourists and office workers brown-bagging it, she forced her fingers to unclench and her posture to relax. From behind lowered lashes, she watched Dillon thread his way through pedestrian traffic, telling herself she'd made the right decision to let him go.

Then he disappeared from view.

A cloud slid over the sun, and she shivered.

Oh, shit.

Something was wrong. *Really* wrong. She felt it in her bones. She should have gone after him.

She leapt up and scanned the crowd, but he'd disappeared.

⋘⋙

Tommy glanced at his watch for about the tenth time in the last hour. Twenty to three. Where the devil was Paige?

He'd been listening for her all afternoon. Despite some serious apprehension about seeing her for the first time after last night, he couldn't stem the flood of anticipation. He just wanted to see her, hear her voice, eat dinner with her.

Okay, he wanted a lot more than that, but after his speech of last night, *more* was going to have to wait. He groaned at the memory. What a self-involved, arrogant sonofabitch he must have sounded, laying down the ground rules like that.

No, what a self-involved, arrogant sonofabitch he *was*. Not to mention emotionally arrested and a number of other unflattering things.

He just hadn't known, had never once suspected, that he could feel like this the morning after.

All day long, even as the physiotherapist worked with him, his subconscious struggled with why it should be so different with Paige. It wasn't until Michelle, the physio, had left that he let himself confront the answer — he *liked* Paige.

He really, really liked her.

And to his shame, he realized he couldn't remember the last time he'd made love with a woman he actively, whole-heartedly liked. Maybe never. In fact, he'd actively avoided women who might threaten his shallow existence. What that said about his character, he didn't even want to contemplate.

Not that he hadn't had long-term relationships — okay, *medium-term* relationships — but at their core, they'd been essentially sexual. He'd used Max and the job, he realized, as an excuse to bail out whenever things threatened to move beyond his comfort level.

What a pitiful excuse for an adult he was.

Next door, he heard Cleo's nails clicking on the hardwood floor as she roamed. She'd been getting more and more restless as the afternoon wore on. No doubt she needed to empty her bladder. He checked his watch.

He supposed he had to cut Paige some slack. She clearly wasn't used to having a pet whose needs she needed to worry about. He'd talk to her when she got back.

For another twenty minutes, he tried to ignore the increasing sounds of canine distress from next door. When three o'clock rolled around, he decided to take matters into his own hands.

It took him almost six long, awkward minutes to finesse the lock on her front door. Fifteen years ago, he could probably have done it inside a minute, probably less. But he'd had actual lock-picking tools back then, and more practice. Fortunately, he'd grown out of his delinquent stage before that particular talent could come to the attention of the authorities. Or rather, he abandoned his illicit activities when his father died. After all, what was the point of raising hell if the old man wasn't around to be antagonized by it?

Cleo was very glad to see him. He located the leash, left Paige a note and took the dog for a walk. Again, he was only able to walk halfway down to the highway and back up the hill again. His leg ached fiercely when he'd finished, and he almost wished he'd left the bindings in place that the physiotherapist had put on. Wrapping his hips in all those yards of elastic bandaging had stabilized his coccyx sufficiently to make locomotion much easier and much less painful, but it felt, and looked, like a goddamned girdle. As he'd told the physio, he was prepared to wait until the exercises she'd prescribed strengthened his muscles enough to compensate.

Back at the house, he fed Cleo and changed her water. He was just about to leave when the phone rang. Instinct urged him to answer it, but he curbed it. He'd already invaded her house, albeit on a mission of mercy. He wouldn't invade her privacy further by fielding her personal phone calls.

Turning, he headed for the door. He'd almost reached it when he heard the answering machine click on.

"Mrs. Harmer? Are you there?"

Ray Morgan.

In four lurching steps, Tommy picked up the receiver. "Ray?"

"That you, Tommy?"

"Yeah, it's me. I just came over to let the dog out for a whiz."

"Dammit."

"Huh?"

"Paige isn't there, I gather?"

"Haven't seen her since this morning." Very early this morning. And he hadn't seen nearly enough of her .... .

"Do you know what her plans were for the day, by any chance?"

"Not a clue." He kept his voice casual, but felt his stomach clutch at the tightness in Ray's voice. "Any reason for concern?"

"Her van was found idling outside the mall. Customer noticed it running with no one in it when he entered the mall, but figured the owner must have accidentally started it with an auto starter.

But when our shopper went back out an hour later, he noticed the van was still idling."

The fist around his gut clenched harder. "Then she couldn't have started it by accident with her remote starter. It woulda shut down in ten or fifteen minutes."

"Exactly. We paged her in the mall, repeatedly, with no result."

Tommy swore. "Somebody grabbed her."

"That's the assumption we're operating on, given all the other stuff that's happened."

Tommy fought down a surge of terror the like of which he'd never experienced.

Not that he was a stranger to fear. He'd felt its clammy touch when he'd lain on the concrete floor of that warehouse, expecting to take another bullet, if he didn't bleed out first. He'd felt it to a lesser degree every time he and Max went out on a track, but in that situation, it was a positive thing, an edge that kept him sharp and alert.

But this was so vastly, horribly different. This was *Paige*. She'd been grabbed by the lunatic who'd stalked her and photographed her and hacked into her web site and sabotaged her business. What kind of whack-job were they dealing with? He swallowed to try to wet his mouth gone suddenly dry.

"Any witnesses?"

"We're still canvassing, and Jake's looking into the security-camera angle."

Tommy resisted the urge to blister the air with more invective. Paige had disappeared, and they had nothing. *Nothing.* If someone had witnessed her being snatched from her vehicle, they'd have called the cops. Fredericton had its share of crime, all right, but citizens hadn't become anywhere near inured enough that they'd turn their heads at something like this. No, if no one had come forward by now, it was because there were no witnesses.

"What do you expect to learn from the security cameras?" he asked. "Sounds like she was grabbed right out of the vehicle, and I doubt if there's anything trained on the parking lot."

"No, there's no footage from the parking lot, but there were a couple of shopping bags inside the van, suggesting she got snatched after she'd finishing her shopping. If we reconstruct her path through the mall, maybe we'll get lucky and pick up on someone following her."

"This is all my fault."

A pause. "How do you figure?"

"I'm the one who suggested this was about Dillon, and she totally bought into the idea. If I hadn't planted that suggestion, she might have been more vigilant. And all the time, it was really about her —"

"Hold up, there, friend," Ray said. "Before you flagellate yourself any further, let me just say I think you were right. I think this is about the kid."

"What do you mean? What's Dillon up to?"

"It's not so much Dillon as the company he's been keeping. Or rather, *had* been keeping. I gather he's distanced himself from these guys in the past few weeks."

Tommy realized his nails were biting into the unyielding plastic of the receiver and relaxed his grip. "You cracked the gang signature?"

"Not much of a gang. Bunch of losers, like to hang out at the pool hall, drink beer and smoke dope. Every one of 'em has had at least one brush with the law, but nothing real hard-core. Possession, small-time trafficking, an assortment of B&Es. The usual doper-lifestyle stuff."

Cleo came over to sit beside him, watching him with concerned eyes. Tommy glanced away. "They don't exactly sound like criminal masterminds. What makes you think they're involved in this?"

"Does the name Derek Weaver mean anything to you?"

Tommy searched his memory. No hits. "No. Should it?"

"Well, it apparently means something to the folks who's job it is to worry about our national security."

Tommy's stomach lurched violently. The guy who most likely snatched Paige was wanted by the *Canadian Security Intelligence Service*? "Oh, man, are you saying what I think you're saying? CSIS?"

"I'm saying my inquiries caused more consternation than a toxic spill at a daycare center. CSIS, RCMP, and Lord knows who else."

"Christ, Razor. What kind of connections do these jerk-offs have that would attract that kind of attention?"

"Not all the jerk-offs. Just one of them."

"Our friend Derek What's-His-Name. Weaver?"

"Yes, Weaver. And so far, no one's been real forthcoming about what that connection is, but I'm hearing off-the-record hints that it's big. As in Syrian-based big."

Oh, sweet Jesus. "Al-Qaeda?"

"That would certainly account for the attention my little inquiry stimulated."

Tommy clenched the receiver so hard, his fingers hurt. "We gotta talk to Dillon."

"Agreed, but that's easier said than done at the moment. He's no longer at that George Street address you gave me."

Tommy blinked, his mind racing. "Wow, you got on that pretty quick."

"I wish I could say I was that efficient, but I can't. This was before we knew anything about this mall incident. I just wanted to have a word with the kid about the company he'd been keeping, see if we could make a tie to the threats against his mother. Unfortunately, he'd already bailed out of that address, not long before my visit. His girlfriend was there looking for him and seemed quite upset about his change of address."

Girlfriend? "I don't know how much weight I'd attach to what this alleged girlfriend said." Tommy shifted his weight to ease the throbbing in his hip. "Paige says he doesn't have a regular girlfriend, and he's only been at that George Street address a couple of days. If this chick is calling herself his girlfriend, that might be *why* he bailed."

"I dunno," came Ray's reply. "You'd have to see her, I guess. She doesn't look like anybody's cling-on, if you ask me. And I got the distinct impression they go back further than the last few days. Anyway, that's neither here not there, since she didn't seem to know where he mighta gone, so we went ahead and BOLO'd young Dillon and his vehicle."

Tommy's heart took another leap, this one positive. "I can do you one better than a BOLO."

"Oh, yeah? How's that?"

"Can you get up in a chopper up in the air in short order?"

"I'm sorry … can I what?"

"Paige was worried about Dillon, so I got a PI friend to tag his car with a radio-frequency tracker, so I could track him down if the need arose. If we can get up in the air soon enough with the receiver, we should be able to locate him. Thing's got a range of around fifty miles from the air, or so I'm told."

A pause. "So, it's like that, is it?"

With you and Paige, Ray meant. *You procured a tracking device to ease her anxiety about her son's coming and goings. You got involved.* Tommy didn't need to hear the words to know what Ray meant. He rubbed vigorously at his forehead.

"Look, I don't know how it is. Christ, I don't know *what* it is. But I do know I care about this woman, Ray. And I care about the kid. I wanna see them both home safe."

"That's the general plan, my friend."

Tommy knew Ray's tone was ingrained, an unconscious projection of confidence designed to reassure. Suddenly he wished he could suspend everything he knew and just trust Ray's tone with a civilian's unquestioning faith. He swallowed once, twice. "So, what do you say? Can you get up in the sky with this receiver before he potentially gets out of range?"

"Rounding up a helicopter won't be a problem. Just get that receiver over here, pronto."

No problem to round up a helicopter in less than a half hour? That alone spoke volumes about the tenor of the *interest* Ray must have garnered on his inquiries. The fist squeezing Tommy's stomach clenched a little harder, but his voice was steady.

"I'm on my way."

Chapter 12

Tommy crossed the lawn to his own unit with a gait he knew probably resembled a crazed crab. His hip screamed, but he didn't slow up. It took him less than two minutes to get into his house, retrieve the RF receiver, find his car keys, and get out again.

As he unlocked the Camaro, it struck him that he was going to have a bitch of a time driving. Muttering an advance apology to his standard transmission, he wrenched the driver's door open. Before he could lever himself into the seat, a female voice stopped him.

"Hey!"

Dammit. He'd been so focused on getting to the car, he hadn't even noticed the woman on Paige's doorstep. A young woman, and, judging by the tattooed forearm and shoulder exposed by the rolled up sleeves of her t-shirt, safe bet she wasn't calling for Paige.

"Are you Tommy?"

"If you're looking for Dillon, you won't find him here. He's moved out," he called. "And I gotta go."

"Wait!" She hurried toward him, laying a hand on his arm as though to prevent him getting in the car. "I know Dillon's not here anymore. I was looking for his mother. Can you help me locate her? It's important."

He inhaled sharply. Could this be the girlfriend Ray talked about? "You talked to Dillon recently?"

"Today, shortly after noon."

"Did he seem all right?"

Her hazel eyes darkened. "No. As a matter of fact, he didn't seem all right. And when I tried to track him down at the place he was staying, they said he'd moved on. That's why I'm here looking for Mrs. Harmer."

"Do you have a driver's license?"

She blinked at the change of subject, but answered quickly. "Yes."

"Can you drive stick?"

Her gaze flicked to his cane and back up again. "Piece of cake."

"Great." He handed her the keys. "You're elected."

By the time he hobbled around the car and folded himself into the passenger seat, she'd climbed behind the wheel, adjusted the seat and mirrors and belted herself in.

"Where to?"

"Police station." He reached for his own seat belt. "Can you talk and drive at the same time?"

"I can talk and do *anything* at the same time." She reversed out of the drive, then turned to him. "How much of a hurry are we in? Push the speed limit but obey the traffic lights?"

At his nod, she accelerated strongly, shifting gears as they shot down the hill toward the highway.

"I'm liking you more and more," he said, flicking on the RF tracker. Nothing. No surprise there. Dillon was unlikely to be on the North side. He left it on, though, just in case, and turned his attention back to the young woman at the wheel.

Worried as he was, he couldn't help but notice — and appreciate — the generosity of her curves. He forgave himself instantly. A man would have to have been clinically dead for a full week not to notice a body like that.

"You have a name?"

"Rachel Whitesel." She shot him a quick look. "And I take it you *are* Tommy, the guy Dillon talked about?"

"Yep. That's me." He shut up to allow her to make the left-hand turn onto the highway undistracted. Her arms were lightly muscled and highly toned, he noticed. She could probably handle herself very well, maybe even knew some martial arts. Which would explain her almost palpable air of self-assurance.

Again, she accelerated quickly, overtaking a slow-moving Neon. "So, why are we racing to the police station?"

"Looks like Paige — Dillon's mother," he clarified, "has been abducted. Cops think somebody grabbed her out of her van in the mall parking lot."

"*Fuck.*"

"My reaction exactly."

She sucked in an audible breath. "Poor Dillon."

Tommy shifted his weight in the bucket seat to ease the shooting pain in his leg. "I'm gonna have to reserve judgment on *poor Dillon* for the moment, since it looks like his buddy might be implicated in Paige's disappearance."

"That little rat-bastard! I knew it!"

"What little rat-bastard?"

Beside him, Rachel thumped the steering wheel with the palm of her hand hard enough to jar the steering column, and Tommy flinched. Maybe quizzing her while she was at the wheel wasn't the best idea. Except he didn't have time to waste.

"Rachel, who are you talking about?"

"That miserable little prick, Derek Weaver. He's gotta be behind this. Dillon's been trying to shake him for weeks now, but for some reason, Derek doesn't want to let him go."

His pulse jumped, this time with hope. "So, you know this Weaver guy?"

"Unfortunately, yes."

Tommy smiled grimly, his fingers tightening on the handle of his cane. "Rachel, honey, there's nothing unfortunate about it. I'd say it was downright lucky you came knocking."

"You think I can help?" She shot him a quick look, then turned her eyes back to the road.

"Do you know where to find him?"

"Derek, you mean?"

"Yeah, Derek."

"If you're asking do I know where he is right now, this minute, then the answer's no."

She moved into the passing lane to overtake slower moving traffic, her maneuvers reassuringly smooth.

"But you know some of his hangouts, places where he's likely to turn up?"

"I know where he lives, and some of his haunts, I guess, but I wouldn't say I know his routines inside and out. I don't really like the guy any better than Dillon does."

"What about his associates?"

She pulled up at the red light at the intersection leading onto the Westmorland Street Bridge, and slanted him a glance. "You mean, the Dumb-inoes?"

"The *whats*?"

"Sorry. That's what we — Dillon and I — call Derek's little group of followers. Derek and the Dumb-inoes."

Dumb-inoes? That invisible fist in his gut squeezed a little harder. Smart criminals were dangerous. Stupid ones were infinitely more so.

"So, where do you want me to start?" The light changed, and she accelerated through the intersection. "Names or places?"

"We're just a minute away from the station now. Might as well save it for Detective Morgan."

She started to say something, then appeared to change her mind.

"What?" Tommy prompted.

She shot him a surprised look, which quickly turned to resignation. "I was just thinking ... this could get Dillon in a lot of trouble, couldn't it?"

"Not nearly as much trouble as he's likely to find himself in if we don't catch up to him. Trust me, you're doing the right thing, Rachel."

"I hope so," she muttered. "I really hope so."

❧

Paige woke up sick.

Not a gradual awakening to the realization that she had a headache and a queasy stomach. Rather, it was quick, a full-on, sit-up-and-vomit kind of wakening.

When she finished retching, a process that felt like it was going to make the top of her head come off, she sank back on the overly-soft double bed, wiped her mouth with the back of her hand and looked around.

Okay, what was going on, and where the hell was she?

The mall parking lot!

Memory came in a jagged flash. A man in a floppy-brimmed Tilley hat approaching her with a map to ask for directions, but when she rolled her window down, he'd pulled her door lock up, yanked the door open and hauled her out of the vehicle. Her scream had been choked off by a hand clamped over her mouth. A hand containing a solvent-soaked rag . . . .

Abruptly, she leaned over and vomited again. The jackhammer pounding in her head revved up another notch. Oh, God, the solvent! It had smelled like some unholy cross between household bleach and floor stripper, and it had taken what seemed like forever to knock her out. She could taste it still. Please, God, let it have been chloroform and not some homemade concoction cooked up from disinfectant or pesticide.

Of course, she had more immediate problems to worry about than potential liver damage. Like, who had grabbed her? And how was she going to get out of here?

Another memory flashed through her mind — a picture of her struggling with her captor before the knock-out compound did its work. To her sluggish mind, it felt more like she was watching a trailer for a low-budget thriller than remembering something that had actually happened to her.

But it had happened. Hadn't it?

She lifted her trembling hands and examined her unpainted fingernails. Yep. It definitely happened. Beneath each pale oval was a grayish material she knew was skin. Her assailant's skin.

Her stomach squeezed again, and she leaned over to retch, but there was nothing left to come up. After an unproductive minute, she was able to sit back again, her face sheened with sweat. Thank God he hadn't gagged her, or duct-taped her mouth shut.

Her head banged with every beat of her pulse. Her stomach ached from its convulsive gymnastics and the smell of vomit assaulted her nostrils. Briefly, she wished she could escape back into unconsciousness, but thrust the thought away. She couldn't afford that luxury.

She took a deep breath. *Okay, Paige, you're smart. You're resourceful. You're organized. Just take it one step at a time. Now, what's priority number one?*

Getting this bastard out from under my fingernails!

She clenched her hands into fists and counted to ten. As much as her mind screamed for a tool to scrape her nails clean, she knew the DNA trapped there might turn out to be the evidence by which the police nailed this guy.

And nail him they would. She couldn't afford to think otherwise.

But who was he? Her memory was a blur, a distorted impression of a Tilley hat and an unfolded map. Blue eyes, maybe? Strong hands she couldn't pry loose even in her desperation, and the acrid smell of fear-sweat. His, she was sure.

With a jolt that actually dizzied her, she realized her captor must be the same person who'd followed her, photographed her, sabotaged her business. To think she'd convinced herself this was about Dillon when all the while . . . .

Enough! What she needed to do is find a way out of here. Now.

She forced her attention to assessing her situation. She was in a small bedroom, maybe eight feet by ten feet, most of which was occupied by the double bed she perched on. What served as a bedspread was one of those plush, black-and-white blanket/wall-hanging thingies, this one with a picture of a cheetah on it, white on black. She didn't have to flip the corner of the blanket to know it was reversible, the same cat's image rendered on the other side, black on white. It looked reasonably clean, but then again, the black side was up.

The carpet beneath her feet looked irretrievably soiled. She'd managed — mostly — to hit a small area rug when she'd vomited, but somehow she suspected the carpet itself had seen its share of bodily fluids. A night stand stood beside the bed, on the other side, but no telephone, clock radio or reading lamp graced it. The walls were covered in what looked like the world's most unattractive textured wallpaper. Briefly, she thought she might have caught a break when she eyed the odd foam tiles on the ceiling. She scrambled onto the bed and pushed upward on a tile, expecting it to give. *Shit, shit, shit.* Fixed ceiling.

She climbed down from the bed again and crossed the room, finding herself steadier on her feet than she figured she'd be. She only wobbled once, just as she reached the room's only window, which was shrouded by blue curtains. She pushed the heavy velvet-like material back, only to discover the hidden window was much smaller than the curtains had led her to expect. She also discovered a number of other things.

Like it was still daylight, shading toward late afternoon or early evening, maybe. She'd either been lights-out for a long time or a short time.

Like the window unquestionably belonged to a mobile home. She'd seen enough of the inside of trailers in her teenage years to know what she was looking at.

Like the trailer's window looked out on a thick, spreading spruce tree that obscured the view so completely that she couldn't say whether her prison was urban or rural, let alone where the nearest neighbor might be.

And oh, God, the mechanism to crank open the window had been removed!

Reflexively, she tried to force it outward. It refused to budge.

Dropping the curtain, she moved quickly to the door, her feet quiet on the carpet. The doorknob turned a few millimeters, just enough to send her hopes soaring, then it stopped. Locked.

She'd expected as much, but it didn't stop the wave of claustrophobia that swept over her like a monster wave swamping a struggling swimmer. For the second time inside a minute, she battled herself. *She must not panic.* Like the figurative swimmer, she had to hold on, keep her head.

Two steps carried her back to the bed. Sitting on the edge, she put her head between her knees, breathing deeply. The dizzy, panicky sensation passed within a minute and she was able to sit up again.

Okay, Paige, let's do this one more time, but without the histrionics.

She got up to inspect the door again. It opened into the room, so the hinges were on her side, but they were inset into the trim. If she had some kind of a tool, she could probably chisel or scrape away enough of the trim to expose the hinges and pop out the pins. Or maybe pry the trim right off so she could get at the pins. Of course, there was no chance she could do that surreptitiously in this tin can of a trailer, and her captor would be on her in a second.

Okay, maybe the lock itself. Once more, the knob moved clockwise just enough to give her hope before catching. She bent to inspect it. It didn't look like much of a lock. Maybe she could pick it quietly, if she could improvise a tool. She pressed her eye to the crack between the door and the jamb and her heart sank. A narrow band obscured the light at eye level, and another about a foot lower. Dammit! Bolted from the outside. No point trying to pick the lock.

She moved back to the window. It was small, and high off the ground, and it looked to be double-glazed. But she might be able to wriggle through it if she could knock the panes out. Maybe she could fold the blanket and drape it in such a way to protect her from any jagged bits she couldn't knock out. Again, it would be noisy, and time consuming to break through both panes, but it was worth thinking about.

She thought about it for all of about forty seconds, which was how long it took to determine there was nothing in the room solid enough to batter out the panes. She even thought about wrapping her arm in the blanket and trying to break the window with her elbow, but the pane was so small, it was bound to be strong, and there were two of them to get through.

Clutching her head, she sat down to think. After several moments, the only thing that seemed clear was she wasn't going to learn anything stuck in this room alone.

"Okay, asshole, let's see what you want."

She stood, strode to the door and pounded on it.

At her summons, footsteps approached. She could feel his tread, heavy but unhurried, vibrate through the trailer's floor, and her mind painted a picture of a mountainous man. All muscle with small, mean eyes. Her small spurt of courage drained away.

She stepped back automatically as the bolts were thrown. Then the door was thrust inward. Her first reaction — a momentary flash — was relief. He didn't look brawny enough to be a bar-room bouncer let alone the Mike Tyson-sized heavyweight she'd pictured from his tread. Then she fixed on his eyes. Pale blue, flat and emotionless. Dread, cold then hot, singed her nerve endings. She knew those eyes.

"Good timing, Mrs. Harmer." Dillon's shaven-headed thug friend held out an oversized wireless phone. "I've got your son on the line."

⁂

Dillon gripped the payphone receiver grimly as he waited for his mother to come on the line. His stomach churned from too much stress and too little food.

"Dillon?"

Her voice was high and scared. He felt another geyser of acid erupt in his stomach. "Mom? Mom, are you okay?"

"What's going on, Dillon? What does this guy —"

Her voice faded as though the phone was taken away, then the sound of a door closing and muffled pounding.

"Mom? *Mom!*"

"Relax, kid. She's fine."

"If you hurt her, I'll kill you."

"I'm telling you, she's fine. Just a little chloroform hangover, is all." Derek's voice hardened. "You said you wanted to hear her voice and you just heard it. Now I suggest you get on with the job."

The background noise had faded, but he wasn't sure that meant his mother had stopped pounding the door or whether Derek had just moved far enough away that the phone no longer picked up the sound. "How do I know she's all right?"

"Guess you'll just have to trust me."

"Like I'd trust a goddamn scorpion."

Laughter. "Seems like you don't have a lot of choice, kid. Now, are you going to get on with it, or do you want to hear more from your mama, along the lines of the noises she made earlier?"

Dillon gripped the receiver so hard the bones of his fingers ached. When Derek had called the first time with his unorthodox ransom demand, Dillon had insisted on hearing his mother's voice. All he heard over the telephone line that time was a low moan. The best she could do in her unconscious state, Derek said, and Dillon had literally seen red imagining what Derek must have done to elicit that sound. But he'd dug his heels in. Anyone could have made that sound. He needed to hear his mother's voice, so Derek had agreed to a second phone call.

"You'll burn in hell for this, Weaver."

A pause. "No doubt, my little friend, but I'm between a rock and a hard place, here. I don't have any choice."

"You always have a choice." Even as he spoke the words, Dillon heard his own mother's voice. How many times had she told him that?

"Choices!" Derek laughed uproariously, but to Dillon's ear, he sounded closer to tears than hilarity. "That's right, Boy Wonder, we all have choices. Like the choice I'm giving you. Make the goddamned run or say goodbye to your mother. I mean it, Harmer. I'm a desperate man."

Another spurt of stomach acid seared Dillon's gut. "Okay, okay. I'll do it. But you'd better keep your word."

"Hey, make the delivery and you'll get your mother back, safe and sound. Unless I smell cops." Derek's voice rose again. "That happens and I'll shoot her in the goddamn head, I swear to God."

"Jesus, Derek, I said I'd do it."

"You pick up the packages like I told you?"

"Yes." As soon as he'd hung up the phone after Derek's first call, he'd gone straight to the bus station as instructed. His head buzzing like he was drunk, he'd used the key Derek had planted for him in the Toyota's wheel well Lord knows how many weeks ago to open one of the bus station's rented lockers. He'd taken the contents from the locker — what appeared to be six cartridges for a particular brand of inkjet printer — and placed them in his backpack. Then he'd gone to meet Rachel.

Rachel. Oh, Christ. He shouldn't have stopped to meet her, but their rendezvous spot was just up the street from the bus depot, less than a minute away, and he'd needed so badly to see her. What a mistake that was. He'd almost fallen apart in the face of her concern. He'd held it together, though. Sort of. And he'd made it back to this payphone outside the donut shop, as instructed, with time to spare. And now he was preparing to act as Derek's mule to smuggle God knew what kind of drugs across an international border, exploiting his status as a local hero to get away with it.

Some goddamn hero.

"You listening to me, frat boy?"

Jesus, he'd tuned Derek right out. "What's that?"

"I said, do you remember the number of the locker you're gonna put the stuff into?"

"Yeah, yeah. I got all that. Number 135. I'll open the locker, which'll be empty. I put the knapsack containing the stuff in the locker, lock it up and stroll out. Then I get in my car and drive back to Fredericton, where I'm gonna wait by this payphone until you call to tell me where I can pick up my mother, who won't have so much as a scratch or a bruise on her."

"That's it. So, got your passport?"

"Of course."

"Perfect. Eighteen years old and free to cross the border without Mommy's consent. Old enough to be tried as an adult if you fuck this up. Of course, that'll be the least of your troubles, won't it?"

Dillon's hand tightened on the phone, but he said nothing.

"Make sure to chat up those border guards," he said. "Make sure they know who you are."

"Don't worry. I understand perfectly why you picked me." Because even if he was the random car they were supposed to search, there wasn't a guard at the tiny border crossing who'd do it. Not after he'd saved that border guard's kids after his mentally unstable wife tried to drown them by letting her car roll into the river. All he'd have to say is, *"How are the McCready kids? Better than last time I saw them, I hope."*

"Better get going, kid. Clock's tickin'. You fall behind schedule, I might get nervous, if you know what I mean."

At least the time frame Derek had allowed was reasonable, so he wouldn't have to risk getting stopped for speeding. But what if there was a longer than usual lineup at the border? Acid surged up into his esophagus, liquid fire in his chest. No, he couldn't think about that.

"I'll be on schedule. You just worry about keeping up your end."

"Here's a tip for you, kid. Don't bust the balls of the guy holding your mother hostage."

Dillon's found himself listening to a dial tone. Feeling strangely disembodied, he hung up the phone, shouldered the knapsack and headed for his car.

⁂

Derek closed the connection on the satellite phone but didn't power it down. That made him nervous, leaving it on like that, in case the cops could locate it. He'd read about the technology they use to locate cell phones, but he was pretty sure it only worked if the phones were turned on.

But the big guy said this was satellite technology, not cellular. He said everything was encrypted. He said there was nothing to worry about.

Of course, he'd noticed the Big Guy was also careful how he phrased things when he gave instructions. Maybe he wasn't too sure about how secure it was after all, encryption or not.

Fuck it, he decided. No point worrying about it. The odds had to be pretty small that they'd crack the satellite phone, and there was nothing else to lead them here, to the lonesomest corner of this crappy, half-empty trailer park.

Frankly, he'd had his doubts about the suitability of this place, but he had to admit the Big Guy was right. In this corner of the park, nobody gave a shit who came or went, as long as you were prepared to turn an equally blind eye to your neighbor's activities. Plus, it was the last place anyone would look, right? Who in their right mind would guess someone would stash a hostage in a mobile home in a trailer park?

Dillon Harmer, maybe.

Nah.

Well, okay, Harmer'd been here that one time, but that was nothin' to worry about. Even if the little punkass got it into his head to rat him out, he'd never be able to locate this place again. He didn't know his way around town even when he was stone-cold sober, and he sure as hell hadn't been sober that night. Yes, ol' Derek had made sure of that. The little puke was shitfaced on a single beer, thanks to the surreptitious addition of a little GHB.

Not that the little chickenshit would risk calling the cops anyway. He was a mama's boy, through and through.

Cops. Jesus. How'd he ever get in this deep?

Because you couldn't make money like this in fifty liquor-store holdups. Never earn it in a lifetime of dead-end jobs or small-time smash-and-grabs.

He picked up the vodka cooler he'd cracked a few minutes ago and drained it. Then he carefully wiped the sweat from his forehead, dried his hands on his camouflage pants and picked up the satellite phone.

He punched in the one speed-dial number programmed on the phone and waited. Two rings later, a male voice answered, identifying the place as a laundromat.

Derek rolled his eyes. If the phone was safe, it was safe. Why jump through these retarded hoops? But if nothing else, he knew how to follow orders.

"Whoops, sorry, partner," he drawled. "Guess I got the wrong number. Thought this was a Chinese joint. I was looking for a couple of combination plates."

"No problem, sir."

Weaver closed the line and wiped fresh sweat from his head. Wouldn't be long now. The phone shrilled in his hand, making him jump even though he'd been expecting it.

"Hello, sir."

"You have news for me?"

"Yes, sir. The courier's on his way."

"Excellent work. I'll be in touch again when delivery is confirmed."

Sensing the big guy was going to hang up, Derek said, "Wait!"

A pause.

"Yes?"

The chill in the one word made his cojones shrivel. Furious with himself, he forged on, "I was thinking you could pay me half now and half on delivery."

In case things went south.

In case they got ... wet.

In case he had to split in a hurry.

A silence. "Sorry, my young friend, but the deal is C.O.D. I must insist on our original terms."

Piece-of-shit, sand-kissing .... Derek reined himself in. Taking a deep breath, he made a deliberate attempt to expel his rage. Another breath, another expiration. *There. Calm again.* "But sir, how can I be sure you'll ... complete the transaction?"

Another shriveling pause.

"Have I ever failed to deliver in the past? Have I been less than generous in support of your ... endeavors?"

Derek wanted to roar like a stuck bull. That was different! Everything until now was chump change compared to the plum that had been promised, compared with what he was about to deliver. With difficulty, he reined in his temper. "Of course not, sir, but once the package is delivered—"

"Once the package has been delivered, you will have completed your contract and you will be paid accordingly. Goodbye, sir."

Goddammit! The line went dead. Derek closed the phone, then he started to shake. He'd been counting on being able to persuade the Big Guy to advance partial payment. Even half of it woulda been plenty to keep him in Tequila and whores in Mexico for the rest of his life, and he could have gotten a head start. Hell with the fact Dillon or his mama could ID him. He could have been long gone before the shit hit the fan, and no one would have to get hurt. Now, things were going to get a lot more complicated.

He caught himself reaching for his stash, actually had the Ziploc bag in his hands before he came to his senses. Jesus, that was the last thing he needed, to mellow out on weed. He remembered the dog, then. Remembered the three-quarters of a quart of Absolut he'd had to pour down his throat before he got mean enough to cut that cowering mongrel and shove the key in the wound. If ever he needed to find *mean* again, it was now.

He tossed the weed back on the coffee table and went to the kitchen cupboard for the vodka.

·❖·

You didn't get through a childhood and adolescence like Rachel's without having seen the inside of one or two police stations. She supposed this one wasn't much different than any other she'd seen. Intimidating in its very design. Not that she had a lot of time to absorb the ambiance, such as it was.

A detective — a pretty boy by the name of Ray Morgan — met them in the parking lot. Quickly recognizing her from the George Street dump where he'd talked to her earlier today, he virtually leapt on her.

She answered a half dozen rapid-fire questions before they even got inside the building. When they reached what she supposed must be the detectives' area — they probably had a disgustingly macho-sounding name for it — she was greeted by more introductions. Sergeant John Quigley, in charge of the unit. Three more plainclothes detectives. Then the questions intensified.

What made her think Derek Weaver was behind Paige's abduction? It couldn't be about money; a prospective kidnapper would recognize Paige's small, home-based business made her a poor target. What then did he want? Whatever he wanted, clearly he must want it from Dillon, since Mrs. Harmer had no other family here and since Dillon was known to associate with Mr. Weaver. How long had Derek Weaver been cultivating Dillon's friendship? Was it true Dillon had been trying to break away? How long had he been trying to get out? Did Dillon ever confide what Mr. Weaver was doing to try to keep him within his sphere? Could she name Mr. Weaver's closest friends? Associates? Partners in crime? If Weaver went to ground, did she have any ideas about where he was likely to go?

Rachel answered each question as fully but quickly as she could, appreciating the need for speed. One of the detectives — Munroe? Mulroney? something like that — wrote key answers on a dry-erase board. She found that whole thing, the recording of her answers, distracting at first, but with Ray Morgan in her face she quickly forgot about it.

Just when she thought he was done, he shifted his line of inquiry from Derek to Dillon. When had she last talked to him? What had he said to make her think he was in trouble? Did he say anything about his mother? About Derek Weaver? Who would he turn to if he needed to share his burden?

At this last question, she dragged a hand through her hair, lifting it off her temples. It was so damned hot in here! Too many bodies in too small a room.

"He doesn't really have anyone here besides his mother. And me. Or maybe him." She nodded her head toward Tommy, who shifted uncomfortably, as though she'd IDed him as the perp in a lineup, for chrissakes. Whatever.

She turned back to Detective Morgan, or Brooks Brothers Suit, as she'd mentally dubbed him. "I think he wanted to tell me, but I screwed up. When I saw he was upset, I made some stupid, flip comment like, 'come to mama' or 'let mama kiss it better', something like that, and he wigged out. I couldn't reach him after that."

"You think he might reach out to Tommy?"

"I think he might, yes." She glanced at Tommy, lifting her chin in a silent challenge. "He talks about you all the time, you know. About how the two of you worked together with Cleo and all the stuff you're teaching him."

"Cleo?"

This from the Brooks Brothers suit, but instead of swiveling to look at him, Rachel kept her gaze trained on Tommy.

"His dog," Tommy clarified, holding her gaze for a beat before shifting his attention back to his buddy, the pretty suit. "The one that got dumped on the doorstep. Remember the key I showed you and Quigg? The one the vet extracted from the dog's hip?"

"Like I could forget something like that."

"Whoa, back up a step!" Rachel interjected. "What's this about a key *in* the goddamn dog?"

"Part of Weaver's escalating campaign." The clipped words came from a stone-faced Tommy. "Preceded by the gift of a skinned rabbit carcass, and followed by the sabotage of Paige's business and a handful of other threatening acts. Except we didn't know who the perpetrator was."

Rachel took in the bleak mask of Tommy's face and revised her opinion of him. She'd known immediately that Detective Morgan's polished image cloaked a certain ruthlessness. Okay, maybe not ruthlessness, exactly. But definitely a core of toughness and that announced he'd do whatever he had to do to win. But that wasn't a quality she'd have necessarily associated with Tommy. Until now.

The phone on the head honcho's desk rang and he grabbed it. "Good work. Thanks." He hung up the phone. "We got a chopper, courtesy of J Division. This is now officially a JFO."

"J Division?" Rachel said. "What's that?"

"RCMP headquarters for New Brunswick," Ray said.

"And JFO?"

"Joint forces operation," he replied, but his gaze was fixed on Tommy, who looked white enough to faint. "You all right, Tommy?"

"I'm fine. Just relieved it's all coming together so quick." His voice cracked. Clearly embarrassed by the show of emotion, he fumbled in the pocket of his jacket, producing the gadget he'd fiddled with in the car. He handed it to Brooks Brothers. "Here's the RF tracker. My guy says it's good for fifty miles, presuming Dillon hasn't discovered it and ditched it."

"Hey, Godsoe, there's probably room on the bird, if you want to be there," Sergeant Quigley said. "Though you'd have to rescind that resignation and grab your gun and a vest if you want a seat."

Resignation? Rachel thought Tommy was just on the DL, so to speak, with his bum leg and all. And she was pretty positive she wasn't imagining the sudden shift of energy in the room.

Tommy shook his head. "Thanks, but I think I'll stay on the ground. There's always the chance that Dillon will call. In fact, I should check my messages right now, then get the phone company to forward my home line to my mobile." He held up his cell phone to demonstrate he had it on him.

"Plus you wanna be here in case something breaks with Paige," Morgan said.

"Yeah," Tommy allowed heavily. "Yeah, I do."

Rachel's gaze had been jumping back and forth between the two men like she was watching a tennis match, and she knew she wasn't the only spectator. She flicked back to Tommy in time to see his Adam's apple bob, but his tone earlier had already told her all she needed to know. Tommy had it bad for Dillon's mother! Dillon had hoped something would happen there, and it sure looked like it had.

Ray Morgan raised the little tracking device Tommy had given him in a kind of salute, then turned and trotted off. After that, the room seemed to dissolve in a kind of organized chaos, with the Sergeant directing activity.

In the midst of the chaos, a thought hit Rachel. A thought so unexpected, so outlandish, she immediately schooled her face to make sure it didn't show.

What she thought was, *I could do this. I'd be good at it. I'm strong, mentally and physically. I'm smart, I'm organized. I could so do this.*

She shook her head, as though to dislodge the weird idea — hell, the *granddaddy* of all weird ideas — then noticed the room had emptied out. Just she and Tommy remained.

"So, what now?" she asked. "What are you going to do?"

Tommy exhaled. "First, I'm going to make those calls, get my phone forwarded like I said."

"And then what?"

For a brief second, the look that flashed in those pinup-caliber baby blues revealed his desire more clearly than any words could — he wanted to get armed and dangerous. He wanted it so bad it hurt. Then the look was gone, replaced by the carefully noncommittal one he usually wore, but he answered her question.

"Then we're going to find some coffee, sit down in one of the interview rooms, and you're going to tell me everything Dillon ever said to you, and I'll tell you everything I know. Maybe between the two of us, we can come up with something to help the boys break this case."

And to make him feel less like a cheerleader on the sidelines while other people took action. Man, did she know how that felt.

"Okay, handsome. Let's get ourselves a room."

Chapter 13

PAIGE SAT ON THE bed, her body still, finally, except for the occasional involuntary tremor. But her mind raced.

Dillon.

What could they want from her son? What could he possibly give them that would warrant her abduction? And they definitely wanted something. She might be a little slow on the uptake sometimes, but that had been a ransom call!

Oh, Dillon. Her poor baby. He'd sounded so close on the telephone line, like he might be right next door. Except she knew he wasn't. He was out there somewhere, scared and alone. She probably hadn't helped things. Cue Ball Head had wrenched the phone away from her after a mere few seconds, shoved her back into the room and thrown the bolts before she could regain her feet. In a fury of maternal protectiveness, she'd pounded on the door and shouted until her voice grew hoarse, but it didn't bring her abductor back.

Clearly, he wasn't too concerned about her shouts carrying to the neighboring trailers. Either they were in a rural setting, or the adjacent trailers were unoccupied this time of day, if at all. Or maybe the neighbors were inured to all manner of noise from this trailer. Or this particular trailer was more soundproof than most.

She shivered. None of those scenarios boded well for attracting help from the outside world.

Dillon. He must be so scared. Tears blurred her vision. She had to get out of this safely, if for no other reason than to fix things with him. She wanted to make sure he knew she loved him, that she'd always be proud of him. She wanted to tell him that he should stop thinking about her and start making his decisions based on what his heart told him was right. She should have trusted him more, held on to him less desperately. Maybe things would have been different .... .

Oh, please, God, let him turn to Tommy. Tommy would know what to do.

Tommy.

Fresh tears stung her eyes. Would he notice she wasn't home? Would he eventually grow worried? Or would he be counting each hour that passed as a reprieve? Would he be thinking about last night?

Last night .... .

She closed her eyes and saw him again as he'd looked when she sat astride him in his bed, his disheveled hair impossibly black on the pillow, blue eyes blazing with raw sexual need. Again she drank in the striking contrast of dark beard stubble against his pale complexion, and those full, sensual lips, swollen and slightly reddened from their kisses. Oh, God, his mouth! She could spend hours kissing it —

She snapped her eyes open. *No.* Tempting as it was to curl up and escape into her head, to crawl back into Tommy's arms, she couldn't afford the luxury. She needed to get out of this room. She needed to interact with her captor, to see what she could learn, to assess his weaknesses.

She licked her lips, ran a hand over her hair, straightened her clothes. Then she went to the door and knocked on it twice, politely, like she would a neighbor's door.

"Hello? Hello, out there! I need to use the washroom."

※

Dillon checked his rear-view for about the millionth time, but there was nothing behind him. He didn't know which he expected to see, cops or thugs, but was relieved to find the lane behind him empty. His gaze flicked to the speedometer. Dammit, speeding again. He eased off. Last thing he needed was to blunder into a speed trap.

In his mind, he heard his mother's voice again, high and scared, asking what was going on. *I screwed up, that's what's going on. I brought that animal into our lives.* A painful, now familiar, spasm

in his mid-section persuaded him he needed to think about something else.

He lifted his t-shirt away from his chest where it was once again
plastered to his skin, and pumped the material a couple of times.
Both the driver's window and the passenger window were wide
open, but the evaporation factor couldn't seem to keep up with
his sweat production. The border guard was going to think he'd
been swimming, for God's sake. How in hell was he supposed to
pull this off?

Another spurt of liquid pain. Jesus. At this rate, he'd have no
stomach lining left.

He twisted the knob on the stereo, and The White Stripes latest
number filled the car, the deep bass notes resonating in his chest.
There. That's what he needed. Music so loud he couldn't think.

We all have choices.

His mother's voice rang in his ears even as The White Stripes
segued into Papa Roach. He cranked the volume higher.

We all have choices.

Papa Roach faded. He gave the volume knob another twist, and
the Queens of the Stone Age urged him to *Go With The Flow*.

We all have —

"Okay, goddammit." He snapped the radio off. "What do you
want me to do?"

No answer came, as he well knew it wouldn't. It was up to him.
Every neuron he owned screamed at him to keep going, to just do
it, to make the goddamned delivery and collect his mother.

But would that really work?

He'd clear the border, all right. Apprehensive as he was about
what he was doing, he knew he'd have no real difficulty. Who better
to carry contraband across the border but a clean-cut, sandy-haired,
blue-eyed kid? A local freakin' hero, no less. He'd trade jokes with
the border guard, and the guard would ask after his mother. It
would be too damned easy.

But would Derek let his mother walk away after he made the
delivery? How could he afford to? Derek was a dipshit, but he
wasn't completely stupid. He had to know she'd go to the cops the
minute she was free.

For that matter, how could Derek let Dillon go free? And what was to stop him from having someone set up at the Bangor end, ready to quietly whack him once they'd taken delivery of the goods?

And what exactly was his payload? Jesus, the reservoirs on those cartridges had to be filled with the world's purest, uncut heroin for the street value to come anywhere close to justifying these measures.

Or maybe Derek owed a debt to someone else, the kind of debt you couldn't walk away from ... . He'd said he was a desperate man, and Dillon believed him. Worse than desperate. He had to be over-the-edge, hopped-up crazy to do this.

Dillon's foot eased on the gas pedal.

Maybe Derek *was* crazy. Christ, he'd killed and skinned his own pet to send a message. He'd rounded up Cleo, the gentlest, most timid little dog he could find at the pound and mutilated her for the same reason. And this was the man he was trusting to release his mother once the demands were fulfilled?

Yes, by God, he had choices. And suddenly he knew which one he had to make. Which one his mother would have him make. Stepping on the accelerator, he picked up his speed again. He needed to find a phone.

⁂

Tommy shifted in his chair, silently cursing his short-sightedness in not bringing his pain pills with him. The nerves along his hip were on fire, jumping in an excruciatingly regular counterpoint to the ever-present, steady ache.

They'd been over and over and over again all the conversations Rachel had had with Dillon. Tommy was even able to fill in some information blanks from what he knew from hanging around Paige's place. Now, he just had to tumble all that information around in his head for a bit, see if anything floated to the top.

"More coffee?"

He glanced up from the notes he'd been studying to see Rachel holding up the insulated carafe they'd confiscated.

"Why not?" He pushed his chipped mug across the table. "I wasn't planning on sleeping for another week or two anyway."

She poured the coffee and pushed his mug back within easy reach. "You okay?"

"I'm fine."

She nodded to his leg as she refilled her own mug. "Looks like the leg might be giving you a little trouble."

"Nothing I can't live with."

"I've got some Ibuprofen in my purse. Want me to dig out a couple?"

"Make it three."

She did. Then she sat down again, directly across from him. "What's it like?"

He'd taken a sip of lukewarm coffee to wash the pills down, and almost choked. He lowered his mug. "What's it like to be *shot*?"

"No." She colored for the first time. Interesting. He'd have put money on her being too hip to blush. "What's it like to be a cop?"

He shrugged. "I worked patrol for the first four years. It's okay. Shift work, though. You don't realize how hard it is on you until you stop." Of course, there were a bunch of other things you realized when you stopped, but there was no point going into that.

"But you're a dog master, right?"

"*Was* a dog master. Now I'm retired."

She sipped her coffee. "Retired? What's this — Freedom 30? And where do I sign up?"

"Just lucky, I guess."

She didn't look convinced but seemed to accept that the topic was closed. "So tell me about police work. What's it like? Boring? Exciting? A little of both?"

"Mostly boring. And I mean ninety percent or better. Traffic enforcement, barking dogs, vandalism, kids partying. But the other ten percent is pure adrenaline."

"Ah, but the exciting part could come at any time, couldn't it? You'd never know when you were gonna have a situation, right?"

"Yeah, and that's both the good and the bad of it. It's a different kind of stress, not knowing."

"Ever have to do things you didn't want to?"

He lifted an eyebrow. "Like what?"

"I dunno. Like arrest somebody when you didn't really want to?"

"Sometimes," he conceded. "But we have a lot of discretion. Unless it's real flagrant, we can deal with it pretty much as we see fit. Besides," he added, "any job's going to have aspects to it you don't like."

"Ever go home feeling good about what you did?"

God, where did the girl come up with these questions? "I was dog master, Rachel. We got called in to track down people who'd robbed seven-elevens or raped women at knife point. So yeah, I went home some nights feeling pretty good about what we'd done when we found the guy." He narrowed his eyes. "Why does this feel like career days? You interested?"

"Just askin'."

Tommy thought her shrug was just a little too casual, but he let it go.

"Okay, tell me again about this hero thing," she said. "I can't believe Dillon never mentioned it. We spent hours on that bench in front of City Hall, telling each other bits and pieces about ourselves, and he never let on. Which is in itself pretty amazing. Most guys I know would have worked that for all it was worth, trying to impress me."

Tommy agreed. If he were in Dillon's shoes, he definitely would have used it to get laid, especially with a bombshell like Rachel. Not that he'd ever actually had to resort to boasting or lying. Playing all cool and remote had generally done the trick for him, and hadn't required the outlay of much energy.

"Paige told me he was embarrassed by all the media attention he got back then. Maybe he just wants to stay out of the limelight. Or maybe he wants to be judged for who he is now, not for some moment of glory in his past."

Rachel's eyes were fixed on his face, but he got the idea she didn't really see him. Rather, she seemed to be looking inward. "Or maybe he doesn't feel he's been living up to that moment of glory lately."

Wow. Tommy sat back to consider her theory. It seemed to resonate with a certain amount of—

His cell phone rang, its tone hollow on the hard wooden desk. He snatched it up and flipped it open. "Godsoe."

"Tommy?"

"Dillon?" *Oh, thank God.* "Dillon, are you all right? Where are you?"

Rachel leapt up and rounded the table to stand closer to the phone.

"Mom's in trouble, Tommy."

"We know, son."

"We?" The kid's voice cracked on the single syllable. "Define we."

"I'm at the police station right now. The cops called me when they found your mother's van abandoned in the mall parking lot with its engine running. In light of everything else that's happened, we figure she must have been grabbed up. Can you confirm that?"

"Yes. I got a call just after twelve noon."

"From Derek Weaver?"

A pause. "How'd you know that?"

Tommy's eyes flicked to Rachel, who nodded almost imperceptibly. "Rachel Whitesel's here with me, Dillon. She was concerned about you and came around the house this afternoon looking for your mother. I'd just been alerted to your mother's abduction, and when I told Rachel about it, she put the finger on Weaver. But I gotta tell you, Dillon, we were already looking at him."

"He wants me to make a delivery to a bus depot in Bangor. But I'm scared, Tommy. Not because I think they'll nail me at the border. I know I can slide through. But my mother ... I just don't see how Derek can let her go like he said he would. It doesn't make sense. She can ID him. Hell, I can ID him."

Tommy felt the adrenalin surge rip along his nerve endings, leaving a metallic taste in his mouth. "You did exactly right calling me, Dillon. But this package ... you didn't open it, did you?"

"The package? No."

"Good. Don't touch it. Given Weaver's contacts, it could be extremely hazardous."

"Whaddya mean, Weaver's contacts?"

"Seems like he's acting as the local agent for a terrorist group."

"Terrorists? What kind of terrorists? You mean, like the animal protection people?"

"More like the extremist Islamic kind of terrorist."

A muffled sound that could have been a curse or a moan. "Jesus, it's not drugs, is it?"

"I don't think so, no."

A pause. "Then what am I carrying? What have I got in my trunk, Tommy?"

"That's what we have to find out, son. Where are you? You haven't crossed the border yet, have you?"

"No. I was going to. I mean, if I'd put the pedal to the metal, I could be nearly there by now, but the more I thought about it, the more I knew it wasn't going to work the way Derek said."

Tommy felt like someone had buried a fist in his gut and was twisting his innards. "And what was the arrangement to get your mother back?"

"I'm supposed to leave this package in a locker at the bus depot, then drive back to Fredericton, where I'm supposed to stand by the payphone at the mall and wait for Derek's call. He says he'll tell me where I can pick up Mom. Except once I stopped freaking out, I finally figured out there's no way he could let Mom go. So I stopped at this gas station to call — Oh, shit!"

"Dillon? Dillon, what is it?"

Tommy pressed the phone closer to his ear and heard Dillon open the phone booth door. The unmistakable sound of a helicopter's rotors pulsed in his ear.

"Omigod, Tommy, there's a helicopter landing in the field right behind the gas bar! I mean, it's right behind me. I can feel the wind inside this telephone booth."

"It's okay, Dillon." He shouted to make himself heard over the growing throb of the helicopter. "It's the cops. My friend Ray Morgan is there, and some Mounties."

"Jesus. How'd they find me?"

Tommy grimaced. "There's a good reason, son. I'll explain it later."

"They're out of the helicopter now, running toward the parking lot. What should I do?"

"Do they see you?"

A pause. "Yes. Someone just pointed at me."

"You're gonna need to put your hands up and step out of the booth, but don't hang up. Understand? Leave the receiver dangling from its cord. I want to talk to Detective Morgan as soon as this next bit's through, okay?"

"Okay."

"These are good people, son. You can trust them. Do whatever they tell you, all right?"

"All right," he echoed, his voice tense and high.

"Now, big breath and step out there."

"Okay. I'm stepping out now."

Tommy winced as a loud clunk sounded in his ear. The receiver hitting the side of the phone booth, no doubt. Poor Dillon. He must be scared shitless. Tommy ran a hand over the back of his neck, picturing a tactical team swooping down on the kid . . . .

Rachel surged to her feet. "What's going on? Is the helicopter there already?"

He glanced at Rachel. Her skin had taken on a definite greenish hue, as though she might be sick. "Yes."

"Will he be okay?"

"Absolutely," he said in his most reassuring voice, and watched her relax a little.

The wait seemed interminable. He heard the shouted commands for Dillon to put his hands behind his head, kneel, then lie down on the parking lot. He pictured Dillon spread-eagled on the pavement, his heart pounding in fear. All too easily, he imagined the rush the officers would be feeling, felt it course through his own system.

More noise, voices. Finally, Ray's voice on the phone. "Tommy?"

At last. "Hey, Ray. Guess that tracking device performed okay."

"Like a charm. Kid called you, is that what I understand?"

"Yes, just minutes before your bird set down, looking for my help." He turned away from Rachel's gaze. "You guys'll give him credit for doing the right thing, right?"

A pause. "You mean, is he in bracelets right now?"

"Yeah."

"Jesus, gimme a break, Tommy. We know who the bad guy is here."

Tommy lifted a hand to his neck again, trying to rub away the tension there. "Sorry, Razor. It's just that it's a JFO, and with blood running high over something of this magnitude .... Well, sorry."

"Forget it. I shouldn't have jumped down your throat. Once we heard he'd called you and got his assurance that we'll have his full cooperation, the tension dropped."

"Did he tell you what Weaver wants him to do?"

"Yes. We have the package in hand. I think ... just a minute."

More dialogue in the background. A few minutes passed, then Ray's voice came back on the phone. "You still there, Tommy?"

"Yep."

"Can you hang on a few minutes longer. We're working out the next move."

"I'm not about to hang up."

The line went quiet this time, as though they'd taken the discussion out of range.

"What's going on? Is he okay?"

Tommy glanced at Rachel, who was doing a pretty number on her lower lip. "He's fine. They're working out what to do next." He neglected to mention it could well involve sending Dillon on to complete the drop. Otherwise, the timeline they had to recover Paige would shrink. That fist in his gut clenched again, hard.

"I wish they'd hurry."

So did Tommy. Every minute that ticked by was another minute Paige was at that thug's mercy.

Finally, Ray came back on the line. "Okay, we have a plan. I'm gonna need to hang up quick, but here's the bones of it. The package is going straight to DRDC Suffield for analysis."

"Whoa, what's that?"

"Defence R&D Canada. Part of the military. They run a Counter-Terrorism Technology Center out of Canadian Forces Base Suffield in Ralston, Alberta, complete with a top-notch chem/bio forensic lab."

Tommy sucked in his breath. "They really think it's a CB threat?"

"They do."

He swore. "Okay, what about Dillon and the delivery? Will that go ahead."

"Yes, they're gonna have him continue on. His vehicle will be waved into a particular inspection bay and will appear to get waved through with only a cursory look, giving authorities there a chance to slip an identical dummy package into his car."

"You got all this worked out already?"

"Trust me, it will be by the time he reaches the border. Man, you should see this parking lot. Every one of these guys is on a phone, calling authorities at every level on both sides of the border. Canadian Armed Forces, RCMP J Division, CSIS, FBI, Integrated Border Enforcement Teams, Sheriff's Office, you name it."

"Then what happens? He carries on to the bus station and makes the drop?"

"Yes."

"How do we know he'll . . . ." He turned away from Rachel's big hazel eyes. "How do we know he'll be able to leave safely?"

"There'll be a team on him, from the minute he pulls into the bus station. Anything looks the least bit hinky, they'll grab him up. Ideally, he'll make the drop, walk away, get into his car and drive home, which will allow the authorities there to watch the locker and wait for something to develop. They really want to scoop up whoever comes to clean out the locker with a minimum of fuss. Chances are, it'll be a Derek Weaver-equivalent who probably doesn't know what he's into, but he might just be able to lead them to the next contact. That's how these cells work. Even the terrorists within a particular cell often don't know the other members so they can't give them away. It's a bitch to root them out."

Yeah, yeah, yeah. Right now, at this specific moment in time, Tommy hardly cared whether or not they nailed the tangos on the other end. His concern was focused on Dillon, and Paige. If they won Paige's freedom at the cost of Dillon's life or his well-being . . . well, it didn't bear thinking about. He knew Paige would gladly lay down her own life to spare Dillon, and she'd be out for the blood of anyone who allowed the kid to endanger himself.

Tommy cleared his throat. "Will he get a discreet escort back, to make sure nothing happens on the road?"

"Absolutely. Both sides of the border. Where the Maine authorities lay off, the RCMP will pick up."

"He knows he doesn't have to do this?"

"He insists on doing it. We'd have to arrest him at this point to keep him from carrying through."

"He knows the risks?"

"No question. If there were any doubts in his mind, I think they were erased when they asked him to model the latest in bullet-resistant fashions."

A vest. Tommy relaxed a little. "That's good."

"And if he were still a little foggy on the dangers, Descharmes, the RCMP point man here, took care of that. He doesn't mince words. He also strongly recommended substituting for him, but the kid wouldn't hear of it. Said nobody'd mistake a poised 25-year-old Feeb for a scared 18-year-old kid whose mother's life hangs in the balance."

"Kid's got a point."

"He does. Look, I gotta go. I'll call back again as soon as I can. Ten, fifteen minutes, maybe."

"Wait!"

"What?"

"Can you put a cell phone in Dillon's car? I'd like to talk to him while he drives, if you think he's up to it. We need to get a jump on finding Paige. If this thing goes south, you know Weaver's gonna get the word to deal with Paige. Maybe Dillon can offer us some clues. Maybe we can find her before the US authorities move on the bus depot."

"Good idea. I'll make sure it happens, though I expect the Feds'll want to be on the other end of any phone we put in his hands. Of

course, that doesn't mean they won't share. Everybody wants the
... Paige back safely."

Hostage. He was going to say the *hostage.*

"I'll make sure they keep in touch with Quigg," Ray continued.
"Sound good?"

Tommy raked the back of his neck. "Thanks, buddy."

"Gotta go. Later."

Tommy flipped the phone closed. "Come on, Rachel. We have
to find Sergeant Quigley, fast."

⚜

Paige heard the footsteps approaching the door and took a step
back. It had taken ten minutes of intermittent pleading, but it
sounded like he was finally going to open the door. Five minutes
earlier, she'd thought he was coming, only to hear his footsteps stop
some distance down the hall, followed by banging and thumping
noises. But this time, the footsteps came all the way to her door.
She heard the bolts being thrown, one after another, then saw the
doorknob turn. The door opened far enough for her captor to
glare at her.

"What do you want?"

His breath reeked of liquor, even from several feet away, and
those eerily pale eyes looked flat and hard. It took all her courage not
to take another step backward. "I need to use the bathroom."

"I suggest you hold it."

"Please! The stuff you knocked me out with made me throw up,
and now I think I'm going to have diarrhea. It'll be bad enough
cleaning up the vomit ...."

"Oh, Jesus." His nose wrinkled as though he'd just smelled
something foul. "Okay, but make it quick." He pulled something
out of the front of his pants, and pushed the door wide.

Shit! It was a *gun* he'd pulled out of his waistband! Once she
clapped eyes on it, she couldn't look away. The pistol's barrel was
enormously long, completely out of proportion to the rest of it.
Then she realized why — it was fitted with a silencer. *Oh, God.*

"Yeah, it's a gun, and I'll use it if I have to. Now come on." He
gestured with the pistol. "Bathroom's the next door on your right.

And don't bother thinking about the window in the shower. It's permanently closed, just like the rest. It's made of laminated glass, too, so don't bother hurting yourself trying to break it."

Laminated glass? Guess she wasn't getting out the bedroom window.

She moved out into the hall, lifting her gaze from the gun long enough to find the door he'd indicated. Or rather, the door frame. The door itself had been removed. That's what all the thumping and banging was about.

She turned back to him. "You expect me to use the bathroom without privacy?"

Something shifted in those icy eyes. "Look, I couldn't give a rat's ass for your finer feelings, Mrs. Harmer. Like I said, I won't hesitate to shoot you, if I have to. But I'm no pervert. I'm not gonna stand here and watch. I just didn't wanna have to bust the door down, if you decided you was gonna lock yourself in there. Now use the damned toilet or not. Don't matter to me."

With that he moved off down the hall. Relief dizzied her head, making her stomach churn anew. She heard a refrigerator door open and close and the tinkle of ice cubes hitting a glass.

Pulling herself together, she moved quickly into the bathroom. A quick look at the window and her heart sank. She'd hoped to get a different view of the trailer's location, but the small window was too heavily frosted to make out anything through its opaque panes.

She moved quickly to the mirrored medicine chest, intending to open it and rifle through it quickly, but her own reflection shocked her into immobility.

God, she looked awful! Her lips were drained of color, her skin so pallid every freckle stood out. For a macabre few seconds, she saw a flash of herself as the corpse she was likely to become if she couldn't extract herself from this situation. Fear tightened her stomach muscles, and for a moment she thought the fictitious diarrhea she'd invented might translate into reality.

Closing her eyes against her own reflection, she breathed deeply, forcing the fear back down below the panic line. When she felt relatively steady again, she opened her eyes and reached for the medicine cabinet. The door opened silently, but the contents were disappointing. If this was her captor's principle residence, you'd never know it from the staples he kept in the cabinet. No prescription drugs, for one thing. She'd hoped to find a label with a name or maybe even an address so she could orient herself.

Quickly, she took inventory of what was there. Condoms, disposable razors, Alka-Seltzer, Aspirin, and a tube of something.... Hoping it was prescription, she picked it up and rotated the tube so she could read the label. Yuck. A lubricant, the purpose for which had her replacing it hastily on the shelf.

From the kitchen, she heard the squeak of a chair as he settled into it. Biting her lip, she closed the medicine chest silently, then knelt and opened the grime-encrusted door to the vanity. This time, the door squeaked on its hinges. She froze.

"Whatcha doin' in there?"

"Just looking for more toilet paper," she improvised. Thankfully, there was some under there. "Found it," she called.

"There's some paper towel under there, too," he called. "When you're finished, you can use it to clean up the puke in that bedroom."

An angry retort rose automatically to her lips, but she bit it back. She couldn't afford to aggravate him. And besides, she really did want to clean up the *puke*, as he so delicately put it. With a gritted "Thanks," she resumed her exploration. Nothing helpful. No prescription drugs with identifying information, no wrench she could stow on her person to clunk him on the head with if the chance arose, no chemicals she could improvise a weapon from.

Leaving the vanity's door ajar, she quickly used the toilet, then flushed it to cover the sound of the door's closing. After washing her hands, and with nothing else to learn from the bathroom's contents, she poked her head out into the hall.

"I'm ready to clean up the mess in the bedroom," she called. "Do you think I could have a bucket of water, some disinfectant and a scrub brush?"

"Don't have nothing like that here." He was on his feet again, coming down the hall, gun held loosely in one hand, drink in the other. "You'll have to make do with the paper towel."

His choice of words confirmed what she'd concluded from her examination of the bathroom; he might use this place occasionally, but he didn't live here. Probably no one lived here. She hoped the same couldn't be said about the neighboring trailers, presuming there were any.

"Okay." Paper towel in one hand and the unlined flimsy plastic wastebasket from the bathroom in the other, she headed back to the bedroom. Her stomach churned, but she got the job done. Moments later, she emerged with the wastebasket.

Her captor now slouched in a chair at the kitchen table. His gun, she noticed, lay in the center of the woven place mat in front of him like the next course of a bizarre meal. She had a sudden flash of that old Warren Zevon album with the Smith and Wesson lying on a bed of glistening vegetables. *Willy on the Plate.* She swallowed, held out the garbage can. "What should I do with this?"

He nodded toward a huge plastic garbage can, the kind most people kept outside and carried to the curb on garbage day. That unit was lined with a heavy duty orange garbage bag. Was that how he planned for her to leave this place, in a plastic Rubbermaid garbage can?

"Go on," he jerked his head toward the garbage can. "Dump it in there, and get back to the bedroom."

Woodenly, she complied, then turned to face him. Her mouth had gone so dry, she had to work up some spit just to get the words out. "What do you want with my son?"

"Relax. I'm not asking for anything that's not easily within his power to deliver."

"Obviously, he didn't want to do it, or I wouldn't be here, right? So it must be dangerous or illegal —"

"Nothin' dangerous about it. He's just delivering a little package for me, is all."

Not dangerous, but he hadn't said anything about not illegal. She swallowed again. "And after that, after he does this *not*-dangerous thing for you, you're going to let me go? You'll let Dillon go?"

He picked up the full shot glass that stood by his elbow, tossed the clear contents back and thumped it down on the table. "That's the deal."

"So you'll—"

"Jesus Christ, enough already!"

He surged to his feet and picked up the pistol. Though he didn't point it at her, her heart jumped, thudding so hard in her chest she figured he could probably see it. How hard could a heart beat and not explode?

He gestured to the hall with the barrel of the gun. "Now move that nice ass of yours back to the bedroom 'fore I start getting ideas about how to pass the time."

Mentally she shrank away from his anger and his ugly words, but physically she held her ground. She couldn't let him lock her up in there again. She already knew escape from that particular room was wildly improbable. Though she might be marginally safer there, it would be a very short term safety. When Dillon did whatever they wanted him to do, they were both going to die. She had to think longer term.

Somehow, she had to keep him talking. She had to make him see her — and Dillon — as people. She had to make him empathize.

"No! Please! Not the bedroom. Don't put me back in there."

He looked more amazed than annoyed at her protest. "You think I'm just gonna let you wander around? Maybe look for a knife to stick me with, or hair spray to blind me with? Or maybe you were hopin' I'd fall asleep?" He shook his head. "Man, you must think I'm stupider than that hayseed son of yours."

She let the slight against Dillon slide by, her mind fixing on his comment about hoping he'd falling asleep. They must be in for a bit of a wait. Hours, at least. Hours in which she could use the only weapons she had. Her brain. Her humanity.

She lifted her chin. "Tie me up, then."

"'Scuse me?" His eyebrows soared. Had his head not been shaved, they'd have disappeared right into his hairline. "Is that an offer, Mrs. Harmer?"

Tears pricked the back of her eyes and she felt a painful flush climb her throat, but she didn't blink, and she didn't release his gaze.

"It's whatever it has to be so that I don't have to go back into that bedroom alone and think about my only son out there somewhere doing God knows what, and how scared he must be —"

"Oh, for chrissakes. Shut up and sit, then." He indicated one of the kitchen chairs with the barrel of his pistol. "I'm sure I can find something here to tie you with."

Chapter 14

TOMMY FELT THE CONSIDERABLE weight of Rachel's gaze on him as he wrapped up his latest progress report from Ray and hung up the phone.

"Is Dillon all right?"

"He's fine," he said, turning to look at her. Her hazel eyes burned like someone suffering from a fever. "He's holding up great, according to the FBI. Everything's going as planned. The agents came through with the look-alike package. Dillon was waved into a Customs inspection bay just long enough for them to put the stuff in his car, then sent on his way."

"So if anyone was watching the border, they'd think he sailed through pretty easy."

"Exactly. He's now on his way to Bangor."

"That's a long drive."

Tommy massaged the back of his neck, but it did nothing to ease the tension accumulating there. "Thank God for that. We're going to need every minute."

She picked up her coffee mug, holding it both hands as though for warmth. "She'll be all right until Dillon gets back, won't she? I mean, what if Dillon demands to talk to her? They gotta figure if he thinks they've already whack … well, they gotta know he'd go to the cops. Right?"

Oh, Jesus. A blast of adrenaline electrified his system, leaving his skin tight and tingling, but he did his level best to keep it from showing on his face. "Unless the plan was to make sure he doesn't make it home, in which case they won't have to wait for his return to move on Paige."

She made a small, distressed sound and he kicked himself for being an idiot.

216

"Not that anything's going to happen to Dillon. Believe me, Rachel, there's no way they can get to him." He took the mug from her trembling hands before she could slosh the hot liquid on herself. "The place is gonna be positively crawling with undercover agents. He'll have a ghost car escort in and out. They even got him to put a Kevlar vest on under his shirt, as a precaution. He'll be all right, I promise. But you do see what I mean about Paige? If our friend Derek has been cued to move as soon as he gets confirmation of the drop …."

She slumped back in her chair. "I wish there was something I could do."

"You already have. We've got detectives going through Derek's apartment for clues as to where he might have taken her. Patrol will be checking out some of the hangouts you mentioned, and the last of the Dumb-inoes will be rounded up shortly for interrogation, if they're not already in custody. We'd be in a lot worse shape without your information."

She smiled, a tight, fleeting thing. "Thanks. But I still feel like I'm missing something …."

"Well, keep thinking about it. In the meantime, I should tell you that they gave Dillon a mobile phone when he stopped in that inspection bay. He'll use it to communicate with the FBI, who'll relay any ideas he might have about where Derek might have taken his mother."

"Good. That's good. He might know something."

"And so might we. Are you up for going over what we know, or think we know, again?"

She lifted her chin. "However many times it takes."

Twenty minutes later, after going over it all once more, they fell silent again. Tommy closed his eyes. There had to be something here. There just *had* to be.

The troops were out checking the obvious places — motels, cabins and the like — but he didn't hold out a whole lot of hope for that to pan out. No point looking for Weaver's trashed-up pick-up; it was in the parking lot of his Union Street apartment building. Chances were he'd borrowed — or stolen — a vehicle for the grab.

And if they didn't come up with something to lead them to Paige soon, his gut told him she was as good as dead.

Dead.

For the first time since he'd learned of her abduction, he allowed himself to think about the very real possibility as more of a probability. What if they couldn't extract her in time? What if that piece of shit, that failed genetic experiment that was Derek Weaver, had already gotten the execution order?

Suddenly, he felt as though a black, bottomless void had opened beneath him. Emptiness. That's what was in the hole. And if he lost Paige now, that's where he'd wind up, falling into that endless, cold, utterly empty vacuum. Which ironically was where he thought he'd been before she blazed into his kitchen. He'd thought he'd bottomed out, that he couldn't feel any worse, couldn't lose any more . . . .

Oh, Jesus.

"You okay?"

He opened his eyes to find Rachel watching him. Shit, he must have made a noise or something. He blinked. "Just a little vertigo."

"Vertigo?" Her brow creased. "Isn't that what you get from heights?"

"I'm fine. Just thinking."

Rachel shrugged and went back to massaging her temples, which she'd been doing for the past ten minutes, as though she might somehow tease the missing piece out manually.

Tommy went back to the thought that had dragged the gasp out of him. He loved her. He *loved* Paige Harmer, with her smart mouth and her sassy smile, her selfless love for her son and her ability to see what mattered. He loved the way she cut to the chase. He loved her sweet tooth, her easy laugh and her boundless passion for life.

Meanwhile, he'd been sleepwalking through his own life, and not just since his injury. He'd long ago insulated himself from his own emotions to the point where he didn't even know how the hell he felt most of the time. To the point that it didn't even much matter how he felt. To the point where someone as wonderful as

Paige had given herself to him with a mind-blowing generosity and he'd been busy throwing up barriers and setting boundaries and planning how to repel her.

The door to the interview room opened and Ray Morgan strode in.

"You're back." Rachel, who'd been leaning back precariously in her chair, brought all four legs back into contact with the floor.

"Marvels of modern air travel."

Tommy came to his feet. "How's Dillon holding up?"

"Good."

Ray's gaze took in Rachel's wan face then settled back on Tommy's. From Ray's expression, Tommy could only assume he looked as shaken as Rachel.

"In fact, all things considered, I'd say he was holding up real good. Kid's a tougher customer than he looks."

Tommy swallowed. Christ, after all the coffee he'd drunk, how could his mouth still be so goddamn dry?

Fear. That's how.

"Was he able to give you anything that might help us locate his mother?"

"That's why I'm here." Ray pulled up a chair, flipped it around and sat astride it. "He says Weaver's got a party pad somewhere. Seems our boy was Derek's guest for a night of debauchery."

"Debauchery?" Didn't sound much like Dillon.

"His expression, by the way, not mine. Anyway, he thinks that might be where Weaver is holding his mother."

"You check it out already?"

"That's gonna prove a little problematic."

Ray dragged a hand through his hair, and for the first time, Tommy noticed how tired and strained he looked.

"How come?"

"Kid was stoned out of his gourd when they took him into the dump, and unconscious, he figures, when they carried him out. He doesn't have a clue where it was, nothing about the neighborhood, couldn't even guess urban or rural, let alone north side or south side. No freakin' idea."

Tommy glanced at Rachel, who looked a little stunned by this development. "Any of this ringing a bell? Dillon ever talk about that night?"

"No." She shook her head. "No, he never mentioned anything even remotely like that."

"The depravity factor," Ray said. "Not the kind of thing you'd be inclined to tell your girlfriend about."

"Hold it right there!" Rachel surged to her feet. "I don't know what he told you and I really don't care, but they don't come any straighter than Dillon. Believe me, I do know the difference, and there's nothing … *bent* about that boy."

Ray held up both hands in a gesture of self-defense. "Hey, I'm not casting aspersions on the kid. In fact, I think he could probably make a case for sexual assault, if he wanted to make an issue of it. He wasn't in any kind of shape to consent to anything, let alone initiate anything."

"Not to diminish the trauma Dillon might have suffered, can we just think about how we're gonna find this party house?" Tommy interrupted. "Think we should lean on the Dumb-inoes?"

"They're already sweating blood under RCMP interrogation. I promise you, if they know something about this place, we'll know it in very short order."

"I wouldn't put a whole lot of faith in that line of inquiry."

Both men turned their gazes on Rachel. She flushed, as though realizing she'd chimed in like a regular member of the team.

"Why not?" This from Ray.

She subsided back on her chair. "If the Dumbinoes know about it, no way Derek is going to stash Mrs. H there."

Tommy's gut clenched again. Jesus, she was right.

"Rule number one, Ms. Whitesel," said Ray, "never underestimate the potential stupidity of criminals. Most of 'em are criminals for a reason, to wit, they're too dumb to hold a real job."

She shook her head vigorously. "No. Derek may be a criminal, but he's not criminally stupid. If there is such a party pad, and if Derek's holding Mrs. Harmer there, his little posse of punks don't know about it. You can take that to the bank."

Ray swore in a fashion that told Tommy he conceded Rachel's point. For a moment, they all just sat there, silent.

"Okay," Ray said at last. "One way or another, we should know soon. I can't see these kids holding up too long."

Hardly did Ray get the words out when his cell phone rang. He flipped it open. "Morgan."

Ray met Tommy's gaze as he listened to the party on the other end, but Tommy read nothing there. "Okay, thanks. Keep me posted if they get anything else, okay?"

"What?" Tommy and Rachel spoke in unison when Ray closed his phone.

"Derek's associates say they know nothing about a party house. Said they did all their partying at Derek's Union Street dive, and we've got disgruntled neighbors up the wazoo to bear that story out. Also, they liked to congregate at the pool hall a few blocks away, and sometimes frequented a sports bar to watch the peelers. That's it."

"And the Mounties believe them?"

"They'll keep the pressure on them, but yeah, they think it's the truth."

Tommy swore. Viciously.

Rachel swore too, but her epithet had an entirely different kind of ring. A *duh! why didn't I think of this before* kind of ring.

"What?"

She turned to Ray. "Did Dillon say what happened that night?"

Ray looked like he was working hard to suppress an eye roll. "I already told you —"

"Couple of girls work him over in the back seat of the car?"

Tommy blinked. "Work him over?"

"Yeah, work him over." She flicked him a glance, then zeroed in on Ray again. "Did they go down on him in the back seat of the car? Perform the flag salute?"

Ray coughed. "Uh, yeah. Yeah, I guess that's the general gist. Does that mean something to you?"

"Bitch!" The word emerged on a hiss. "That had to be Dillon she was talking about."

"Huh?" Tommy's head was starting to throb about as bad as his hip. "Who was talking about Dillon?"

"There's a girl I know — she comes in to the coffee shop sometimes when business is slow."

Ray's eyes narrowed. "Hooker?"

"She wouldn't call herself that, but yeah, she turns the occasional trick. Anyway, she was telling me about this one night she and another girl were paid to keep a young guy occupied in the back of a car, then get it on with him when they got to their destination. But she said he passed out when he hit the bed. Easiest money she ever made."

"Doesn't sound too easy to me," Ray observed.

"Guess it's all relative. Anyway, this woman figured the guy who paid them might want a partial refund because, like, they didn't have to do him and all."

Ray snorted. "Sounds like he got *done* to me."

Rachel rolled her eyes. "There's doing and there's *doing*."

Tommy held up his hand. "You mean, nothing happened once they got to the house?"

"Nothing of consequence. He was too wasted, she said."

"Kid'll be relieved to hear that," Ray put in. "He's been sweating it pretty hard. Seems our friend Weaver told him he got it on with both of them, on camera."

Rachel shot to her feet again. "That weasel-faced little rat-bastard!"

"Weaver also told him they were pretty seriously under-aged."

"No. No way! Not this gal. She's twenty if she's a day, probably older, and I'm betting her friend is, too."

"Think you could find her?"

"Shouldn't be too hard. She takes night classes at one of the business colleges here in town."

Ray grunted. "Business? How appropriate."

Rachel lifted an eyebrow. "What? She's taking business so she's gotta be the next Heidi Fleiss? Just so you know, I've seen law students and science majors get into the escort business."

Tommy's frustration boiled over. "Come on, you guys. Think we could leave the tricks-for-tuition discussion for later and focus on actually *finding* this woman?"

"Sorry." Rachel turned contrite eyes on him. "I can take you there right now."

"A name and the class location are good enough." Ray took his pager out and looked at it. "You should stay here with Tommy."

Yeah. Stay here with the gimp. Tommy controlled the surge of impotence with difficulty.

"Yeah, that'd work," agreed Rachel. "That is, if I knew her name, which I don't. But I do know her face. I'll ID her for you."

Ray frowned, clearly not thrilled. "Guess we don't have much of a choice, do we? Let's go."

"I'm coming too."

Ray gave him a considering look. "Sure you don't want to stay here and help quarterback things from this end?"

Stay here, where you won't be in the way. Problem was, he couldn't *not* go. If this woman knew something that could help them locate Paige . . . .

"That's Quigg's job, and he's got it under control. And I don't really feel like haunting the halls until you get back."

"Okay, Hop-Along. Let's shake a leg."

❧

Maybe this wasn't such a hot idea after all.

Paige rolled her shoulders to the best of her ability to ease the strain on them. She sat now on a chair in the middle of the kitchen, her hands tied behind her back with a length of pantyhose. Another pair of pantyhose anchored her elbows to the spindles of the chair. Lord, but her shoulder sockets hurt. Not to mention her ankles, where her captor had used a less forgiving binding to lash her legs to the chair. It felt like piano wire, the way it dug into her flesh, but from the brief glimpse she got of it, she'd have guessed clothesline cable. Except not the right color. It was black instead of bright blue. Coaxial cable, maybe. Whatever it was, it hurt like hell.

On the upside, the pain kept her from reflecting too much on where the pantyhose might have come from.

The important thing was she'd escaped banishment to the bed-room. If she was going to get out of this alive, she needed to work on her captor. Twice she'd tried to initiate a conversation with him. The first time, he'd told her to shut her 'cake hole'. The second time, he'd gotten up without comment and left the trailer.

She used his absence to test her bonds, which proved discour-agingly strong. And why, oh why, did the spindles on this ancient chair have to be as rock-solid as though they'd been glued last week? Everything else in this dump looked ready to collapse on itself, including the cheap chrome table and mismatched, splay-legged chairs.

After rubbing her wrists raw and setting the ball sockets of her shoulders on fire, she was ready to concede she wasn't going to get free without a knife to saw at her bonds.

Okay, goddammit, so she'd find a blade.

Desperately, she scanned the room, looking for something — *any-thing* — that she could improvise a cutting edge from. In under a minute, hope shriveled. There wasn't a God-blessed thing that might serve as a blade, even if she could somehow rabbit-hop the chair over to it and pick it up with her increasingly numbed fingers through the dowels forming the chair's back. Still, she couldn't help scanning and evaluating every object in the room, again and again and again ....

Oh, God, she was never getting out of here.

The sound of the trailer's door opening and closing pulled her back from the edge of panic. *Come on, Paige. Keep it together. Stay calm. Think.*

Seconds later, Derek Weaver stepped into the room. His gait had a distinct unsteadiness to it, she noted.

"Still here, I see," he said, and laughed.

He crossed to the table, plunked down his quart of vodka and took his seat on the same chair he'd occupied earlier. The legs of the old chrome chair seemed to splay even further under his weight. Her gaze went to the vodka bottle.

Yikes! The level of clear liquid had declined a good two inches, maybe three, since he'd left. Had he shared a drink with someone else, or had he consumed it all himself? She shuddered, not knowing which scenario she preferred.

If he'd shared it, that must mean there was someone else posted outside. A guard. Another level to get past to win her freedom.

If he'd drunk it himself, he could well turn out to be a mean drunk. She didn't need him any meaner than he already was.

Of course, if he drank enough to actually pass out, she might be able to hop her chair over to the table, knock that satellite phone to the floor and maybe dial 911 with her toes.

But then what? She didn't even know where she was. Could the 911 system get a fix on a satellite phone?

"Thirsty?"

Her mouth was dryer than old parchment, but she knew it was fear, not dehydration, that stole the moisture from her mouth. "I could use some water."

"How 'bout a drink of this?" He tipped the neck of the vodka bottle in her direction.

Jesus. He wanted her to share a *drink* with him? How incredibly screwed-up was that?

On the other hand, he might loosen her bonds, maybe free one hand so she could hold a drink . . . .

"Yes," she managed through dry lips. "Yes, I would like a drink of that."

He dragged his chair closer, proffering the bottle. "Open up, sweetheart. Here it comes."

"But can't I —"

Her words were cut off when he thrust the mouth of the bottle against her mouth. Automatically, she pursed her lips, more as an automatic reflex to protect her teeth than any desire to imbibe the spirit. He tipped the bottle and she found herself with a liberal mouthful of straight vodka. An equal volume dribbled down her chin and onto her t-shirt.

"Swallow," he commanded, his alcohol-tainted breath fanning her face from a distance of just a few inches.

Short of spitting it out, she didn't have much choice. She swallowed.

Oh God, oh God, oh God. Her esophagus flamed. She dissolved into a fit of coughing, each spasm wrenching her shoulder sockets. Every breath she dragged in felt like it was super-heated. Then the liquor hit her churning stomach. As she fought to control the nausea, she heard her captor laughing and hooting. *Laughing*, the sonofabitch.

She blinked away the tears the alcohol had brought to her eyes, fixing on her captor who now lolled back in his chair.

He waggled the bottle at her. "'Nother holler?"

Rotten little pissant. She held his gaze with a challenging one of her own. "Why not?"

This time, she was ready, controlling the amount of alcohol she took in by partially blocking the bottle's mouth with her tongue. When he pulled the bottle away, she swallowed, gasping and coughing as though she'd imbibed much more.

He sat back and laughed again, apparently entertained by her reaction to the straight liquor. Then he tipped the bottle up and drew deeply from it himself. Unlike her, he tossed it back with only the slightest of grimaces. Then, thankfully, he put the bottle back on the table.

Okay, Paige, start talking. That's why you're here with your shoulders ready to dislocate themselves instead of curled up on that bed. She licked her lips. "You seem to be pretty good at that."

"Good at what?"

"Drinking that stuff." She nodded at the bottle. "Did you put that all back by yourself?"

"Hey, I ain't wet behind the ears like that kid of yours. I can handle my liquor."

She controlled her expression carefully as she watched him sit up straighter and sort of puff his chest out. God, what was she dealing with? In some ways, he seemed much more immature than Dillon, despite the years and experience he clearly had on her son.

Well, at least that answered one question. He hadn't shared the bottle with a guard outside. Unless of course he was lying .... .

"Look, I hate to be a pain, but my arms are going to break right off at the shoulder if I can't rotate them soon. Isn't there some other way we can do this?"

He scowled. "You think I'm stupid? You think I'm just gonna untie your hands?"

"No, I don't think you're stupid." She didn't even cross her fingers behind her back at the lie. "I figure a smart guy like you can find a way to tie them in front of me, while still binding me to the chair."

He scowled and ran a hand over his bald head. God, why did he keep doing that? Did he just like the feel of it? Was it a comfort thing? Or was he just checking for stubble? She wished she'd asked Tommy about some of that body language stuff.

"Anybody ever tell you you're a mouthy broad?"

She lowered her lashes, trying to approximate an air of sub-servience. "I'm sorry. It's just … ." She stifled a convincing sob. "I had a frozen shoulder once, and it doesn't stand up to this kind of hyper-extension very well. I don't know how much longer I can take it." She sucked in another sobbing breath. "And when I lose it, I just fall apart. I mean, I just totally lose it. Crying and stuff."

"Okay, dammit, I'll tie 'em in front." He lurched toward her and she smelled his breath on her face again. "Just don't start blubber-ing on me. That happens, you're back in the bedroom. And if you really piss me off, I might just have to join you, give you a reason to cry."

She dropped her gaze. "I'll be quiet. I promise."

⚜

Dillon nosed the Toyota into a vacant parking space between two newer-model sedans and turned off the ignition. In the ensuing quiet, he heard the tick-tick-tick of the engine cooling in the early evening quiet outside the bus station. And damned if he couldn't hear his own breathing, shallow and ragged and scared.

Jesus. How was he supposed to get this done with his heart slamming in his chest like a freaked-out budgie battering itself inside its cage?

He looked around the parking lot, searching for evidence of the backup he'd been promised. He saw nothing that looked like police or FBI or National Guard or whatever the hell they were.

Of course, they'd said that was the whole point. No one would be able to pick them out.

Unless maybe they weren't here yet. Or maybe they'd gone to some other bus depot. Could there be more than one in Bangor? Maybe they really didn't have the manpower to cover him, but they told him they would just so he wouldn't spaz out when he walked in there. I mean, how would he even *know* if they were here or not, unless something went wrong? Like Agent Illsley said, they couldn't wink at him or give him a hand signal or anything because they didn't want to tip off anyone who might be watching.

He yanked at his shirt to ease the constriction around his throat and his fingers came in contact with the unfamiliar bulk of the Kevlar vest.

His friggin' eighteenth birthday — *yeah, yeah, Happy Birthday to me* — and here he sat in a bus station in a foreign country. And in a minute he was going to go inside and deposit two packages in a locker. The area might or might not be swarming with undercover agents, and was almost certainly being watched by terrorists. And back home, his mother was in Derek's clutches. Derek, who couldn't possibly let her go no matter what he said.

For a few seconds, he teetered on the very edge of his sanity, close enough to the brink to glimpse the other side. Close enough to be tempted. It would be so much easier if he could let go, stop fighting this terror .....

Then he heard Tommy's voice in his head. *These are good people, son. You can trust them.* Dillon latched onto that voice like a drowning swimmer might latch onto a life preserver. Closing his eyes, he pictured Tommy as clearly as though the other man were sitting right here, his face serious, eyes kind but with a little of that no-bullshit edge a man couldn't help but respect.

"Okay." He blew out his breath, took another deep lungful of diesel-tainted bus stop air, expelled it slowly. There. He could do this.

Dillon got out of the car and walked around to open the trunk and retrieve the knapsack. *Don't look around. You're just a kid, stowing a beat-up old book bag in a locker. No one's gonna look at you twice.*

He crossed the parking lot as casually as he could with the hair on the back of his back prickling. He told himself the watching eyes he felt were the good guys.

These are good people, son. You can trust them.

When he reached the door, he had to sidestep to allow a man with a heavy bag to exit. Holding the door open, he slipped in.

The place was fairly full. A dozen people waited, either to board a bus or meet a bus. Some sat, some paced, some leaned against walls. Some sat reading magazines and sipping coffee from Styrofoam cups. Others stood in line for tickets. He stood there, feeling the sweat sheet down his back beneath the Kevlar vest, and felt the loneliness that inhabits bus depots everywhere.

He shivered. Gathering himself, he forced his feet to carry him past the ticket counter. He kept his eyes on the bank of lockers at the end of the room, as he strode toward them. There it was, 135. He stopped in front of it, finding the key in his hand with no recollection of having dug it out of his pocket. He inserted it in the padlock and it turned effortlessly. Thank God! A flick of the wrist, and the padlock came off in his hands. He wadded the knapsack up and pushed it into the locker, closed the door and fumbled to get the padlock back on.

Whether it was nerves or just the sheer amount of sweat dampening his palms, the padlock slipped and hit the tiled floor with a crash that seemed to echo around the cavernous room.

Stupid. Clumsy, stupid idiot.

Everyone was looking at him now, or so it seemed. Quickly, he bent to retrieve the lock. This time, he managed to secure it without further catastrophe.

A flush still burning his overheated face, he turned and strode out. *Don't run, don't run, don't run.* Only by repeating the words like a mantra was he able to keep his steps slow and unhurried. Out the door, across the parking lot. He climbed into his car and just sat there for a few seconds, his hands clamping the steering wheel in a death grip.

Move. Go! Get out of here.

It took two tries to get the keys into the ignition, but the engine fired on the first try. He took another moment to master himself — it wouldn't do to lose it now and go peeling out. When his hands no longer shook so violently, he put the car in reverse and eased out of the parking space. Seconds later he was out of the lot. Another few minutes, and he was back on the highway, headed north again. He checked his rearview mirror, then grimaced. Like he'd recognize a tail in all this traffic.

The cell phone on the seat beside him rang, startling him into poking the accelerator. His car shot forward. He eased his foot back and grabbed the phone. "Hello."

"You okay, son?"

Agent Illsley.

"Okay?" He tried to laugh, but it came out more as a sob. "I'm shitting myself."

"You did great, kid. And you're safe now. Two cars behind you, there's a dark blue Taurus. He's FBI. He'll pass you in a minute. You follow him all the way to the border, you hear?"

"I hear."

"And just for good measure, there's a marked patrol car behind you, a state trooper. He'll be with you for the duration, too, but he'll hang back five or six cars, just to discourage any ideas our friends might have about trying to stage something."

"Thank you, sir."

"No, thank *you*. You did good, son."

"Any word about my mother?"

"Hang on a second. I'm gonna check with Fredericton."

Dillon chewed the inside of his lip, waiting for Agent Illsley to come back on. He almost didn't notice the blue Taurus overtake him and move back into the right hand lane about thirty yards ahead. *FBI*. Good. He checked his rearview, but couldn't see far enough back in the line of traffic behind him to say whether the patrol car was in place yet.

They're good people. Trust them.

Tommy's voice in his head, again.

Now that his heart no longer threatened to smash itself to a pulp against his ribs, he thought about the significance of that. Unable to think of his mother without completely losing it, he'd focused on Tommy and the core of strength that ran through the man.

Despite his injury, despite his limp, Dillon could sense his strength. It was like a piece of rebar buried deep in concrete, unseen but undeniably present. Back there in that bus station, he'd borrowed that strength, used it to glue his shredded sanity back together. If it was the last thing he did, he'd thank Tommy for that.

"Dillon?"

He pressed the cell phone closer to his ear. "Yeah, I'm here. You got anything on my mom?"

"They're still looking into that house you described."

"*Described* is a little generous, considering the only thing I remember is the stains on the bedroom ceiling." Bile rose in his throat. How could he have been so freakin' oblivious?

"Seems like your girlfriend might have a lead on the young ladies who … um … accompanied you that night. Sounded pretty encouraging to me."

Oh, God. Rachel knew about that night?

His mouth went dry at the wobbly memory of what had transpired in the back seat of Derek's car. How was he ever going to be able to look Rachel in the eye again? Would she believe he'd been powerless to stop it?

His stomach did another flip. Why should she? Christ, he hardly believed it himself. Yeah, Derek had slipped him something, for sure, but even without the drugs, would he really have resisted very strongly?

He burned with shame when he thought about it, no question. But his shame had a flip side. He'd gotten hard a dozen times remembering what they'd done to him with their hands, their mouths. God only knew what happened in that godforsaken bedroom. If only he could remember … .

"Dillon?"

"Sorry. I'm still here. You say Rachel might have a line on those girls?"

"That's the latest. Also, Mr. Weaver's associates claim to have no knowledge of the place."

"How solid do they think that is?"

"The interrogation was done by the RCMP, who leaned on 'em pretty hard. Sergeant at your local PD says he believes them. He figures they'd have spilled it inside the first minute if they knew anything about this place, just to alleviate the pressure."

"Makes sense." Dillon's hands flexed on the steering wheel. "Derek always made sure the other guys weren't around when he talked about this job. And they definitely didn't ride along that night."

"I'll relay that."

"What about Derek's sister in Moncton? Did they follow up on that?"

"She's in the regional hospital there, recovering from an appendectomy. According to the neighbors, nobody's been in or around her place for days, and phone company records disclose nothing to get excited about."

"And they checked Derek's place? The other guys' places?"

"Yes and yes, but they found nothing, beyond a small quantity of hashish. They've also taken a real hard look at motels, tourist cabins and the like."

"And no luck?"

"No luck. Which makes this other idea of yours sound pretty plausible. Could be that it's a safe house."

Safe house. Except it wasn't very safe right now for his mother, if she was there. What was to stop Derek from killing her now that the job was done? Would he really wait until Dillon called him from that payphone in Fredericton? Or would he move the minute he got confirmation the drop had been made?

"Agent Illsley, can I ask you a question?"

"Of course you can, son. That's what I'm here for."

"And you'll tell me the truth?"

A pause. "Yes, I'll tell you the truth."

"Do kidnappers usually release their hostages when the ransom demand is met?"

Silence.

"There's nothing *usual* about a kidnapping situation, Dillon."

"Okay, let me rephrase that. Do kidnappers often release their hostages when the ransom demand is met?"

"I don't know about often. Depends on the situation."

"How about *ever*? Would you say they ever release them?"

"Oh, yes, definitely. I've seen 'em released."

"What about when the parties involved can ID the kidnapper? What happens then?"

"I guess that depends on whether or not your man thinks he can make an exit before the authorities come down on him."

Dillon clenched the cell phone too hard, hitting a key and making it beep loudly in his ear. "Sorry. I'm just thinking that now that I've made the drop, what's to stop this *al-Qaeda* boss man from calling Derek and giving him the thumbs up?"

"I see what you mean, but I doubt if they'll be able to confirm the delivery immediately."

"Why not? It's there. I just dropped it off. They must have been watching for it."

"These guys are careful. I doubt they'll send someone in there right away. They'll want to watch the place, try to determine if the locker's being watched, if there's a police presence, and all that stuff."

Dillon blanched. "Jesus! Then they'll call Derek for sure and tell him they've been double-crossed."

"They'd only do that if they picked up our people, which they won't."

Dillon braked as the traffic in front of him slowed for a few seconds, then picked up again. "You sound pretty sure."

"We're good at this, son. Our guys won't stride in there dressed in black suits and sporting clip-on IDs. They'll be dressed like any other traveler. They'll be old, young, male, female. They'll be waiting for buses, helping load buses, cleaning buses. Someone'll probably be washing windows, and maybe another agent'll be dispatching packages at the freight desk."

"So they'll blend in?"

"They'll be invisible."

"Okay." Dillon felt the tension banding his chest relax a fraction. "So, how long you think they'll watch it for?"

"Hard to say. Couple hours. Couple days. Depends on what their plans are, how urgent their need to get their hands on the stuff."

The *stuff*. He squeezed his hands tightly around the steering wheel to suppress a shudder. "Do we know what it is yet?"

"That'll be another few hours, I'm told. They put it on a military flight, to a forensic lab that can handle a Level Three chem-bio threat. But I'm told we won't be long getting a report, once it gets there."

Dillon didn't even know what a Level Three chem-bio threat was. Anthrax? Old-fashioned mustard gas? Maybe that nerve agent Saddam Hussein used against the Kurds. Surin? Sarin? Starin? Something like that. Or the stuff used in that Tokyo subway attack .... Whatever the hell it meant, it had sweat beading on his forehead.

He swallowed. "Can I ask one more thing from you, sir?"

"Sure. What can I do, kid?"

"Can you get a message to Tommy Godsoe?"

"Godsoe? He's the ex-cop neighbor been working the case from that end?"

Ex-cop neighbor? God, Tommy was so much more than that. Though how that happened in so short a time, Dillon didn't exactly know. But sometime between the long talks about dog training, the mini non-lectures on responsibility, and the laughs over supper, they'd sorta gotten close. And at the risk of straying into the *ick* zone, he thought Tommy and his mother had gotten pretty close, too. But he wasn't about to get into any of that with Agent Illsley.

"Yeah, that guy. Could you give him a message, please?"

"Sure, as long as you don't mind if it's relayed through his Sergeant."

"I don't care how he gets it as long as he gets it."

"Okay, shoot. I'm all ears."

"Tell him thanks." Noticing the distance between him and the blue Taurus sedan in front of him had lengthened more than he liked, Dillon accelerated to close the gap. "Tell him he saved my ass back there at that bus station. Tell him it was thinking about him and the way he just goes about doing whatever needs doing that got me through that drop without freezing up or running."

"Why not tell him yourself?" Agent Illsley's voice dropped an octave, into what Dillon would call the reassurance register. "Nothing's gonna happen to you now, son. You're safe as houses with the escort you have. You'll be back home in a few hours and you can tell it to him face to face."

Dillon didn't doubt the man's assurances, but he still couldn't shake the feeling that his message shouldn't wait. Problem was, he didn't know if it was his own safety he was worried about or Tommy's.

"Just humor me, okay? Get the message to him."

"You got it. Whatever you want."

He released a relieved breath. "Thanks."

"Anything else?"

Yeah, find my mother. Except there was no point saying that. Even though he couldn't get out there himself, Tommy would no doubt be riding herd in Fredericton, making sure no avenue went unexplored. "Can I keep this phone all the way home? I mean, if something breaks, I'd like to be in contact."

"Absolutely. That's the plan. Once you cross the border, you'll get a call from the RCMP operatives who'll escort you from there."

"Okay. I guess that's it, sir. Thanks for everything."

"No, thank *you*. You did something very brave today, son. Something with international ramifications. God bless you."

Dillon's throat tightened. "I'd rather He blessed my mother."

"That too, son. That too."

Chapter 15

Tommy sat in the principal's office wishing like hell that his hip would allow him to take some of his anxiety out by pacing.

Finding the girl — a twenty-two year old business major, who went by the name of Danni Robertson, turned out to be easy. Upon learning that one of his students might be a material witness in a serious crime, the principal had been very cooperative. Ray was all for walking into the classroom, flashing his badge and dragging her out, but Rachel talked him into letting her extract the girl, to minimize potential repercussions for Ms. Robertson. Which is why Tommy sat here like a useless tool while Paige remained at the mercy of —

The door opened to admit Rachel, followed by an astonishingly wholesome-looking young woman, with Ray bringing up the rear.

Tommy's gaze locked on Danni Robertson. Her dark hair was drawn back into a ponytail, and her face had that fresh-scrubbed Ivory-girl look. Or it would have if it hadn't been pinched with fear.

Her panicked gaze flew to Tommy, then jerked back to Ray. "Oh, man, I can't afford to get busted. If the College finds out ... ." Her words ended on a sob, but she swallowed and tried again. "Do I need a lawyer?

"Relax," said Ray, gesturing for her to take a seat. "We don't care about your extra-curricular activities, although you might give some thought to a more conventional occupation."

Her face firing, she took a seat. Tommy didn't have to be an expert on body language to read her agitation, her vulnerability and her defensiveness. "So, if this isn't a bust, what is it? What do you want from me?"

Ray took a photo of Dillon from his pocket — Christ, where had he gotten that so fast? — and plunked it down on the coffee table between them.

"Recognize this young man?"

She turned the photo around to examine it more closely, her forehead knitting into a frown.

"Take your time," Ray said. "I understand you're more familiar with the terrain south of the neckline, but this was all I could scare up."

"That's enough." Rachel's voice rang with a command that had Razor and Tommy gawking at her. But she ignored them, turning to the witness.

"Danni, you don't need a lawyer. No one's gonna try to make trouble for you. We just need to find the place Derek Weaver took you and your friend and this guy Dillon. It was this guy, right?"

Danni studied the photo again. "Yes, that's him." She looked up at Rachel again. "You're just looking for the place?"

"That's all, I swear. And it's important. Really important. Otherwise, I wouldn't have brought these people here." She indicated Tommy and Ray with a shrug of her shoulder, but didn't break eye contact with the witness.

Danni's gaze slid to Tommy, stuck on Ray a few seconds, then went back to Rachel. "I don't know how much I can help you."

"Just start by telling us what happened. Derek hired you to show Dillon a good time, right?"

Ms. Robertson dropped her gaze to her knees. "Yes, that's right. Me and another girl. Ashley something-or-other. I don't know her last name. Derek wanted us to keep the young guy —"

"Dillon," Rachel said, her voice cracking a little. "His name is Dillon."

Danni glanced up, then back at her knees again. "Okay, Dillon. Derek paid us to keep Dillon completely preoccupied on the car ride. He was wasted … I mean, totally intoxicated, but even so, he didn't really seem too eager. Kind of inhibited, you know what I mean?"

Ray snorted. "And that didn't give you cause for pause?"

Danni's chin came up at last.

"Derek said that was the whole problem with the kid. He told us he suffered from social shyness to the point that it prevented him from interacting with girls. He said the idea was to cure him. You know, give him a little confidence with the ladies."

"Which you were somehow supposed to instill by blowing him in the back seat of a car while he was blind drunk?"

This time it was Rachel who turned and glared at Ray. "Could you just let her talk, already?"

The girl shot Rachel a grateful look, then her gaze slid back to Ray's. "We were supposed to do more, when we got to the trailer."

"Trailer?" Tommy leaned forward.

Danni flicked him a glance. "Yeah, it was definitely a trailer."

"As in mobile home?

"Yes."

"Where?"

"I don't know."

Tommy's heart banged against his ribs. "What do you mean, you don't know? North side? South side? Inside the city limits or beyond? You must have some idea."

Danni's face fired again. "I think I already explained, I was otherwise occupied at the time. All I know is the car rolled for about twenty minutes before it stopped. I can't say where we went."

"What happened when you got there?" The question came from Rachel, and Danni turned her attention back to her.

"We were supposed to do him, you know? But he passed out as soon as we got him inside. I thought Derek would be pissed, but he said it didn't matter. He got us to pose for a couple of pictures to make it look like we'd ... well, you know."

Tommy's stomach clenched. "Polaroids?"

"Yes. He figured that would work just as well to boost his confidence, since he wouldn't know the difference. Derek said he'd just tell him what a stud he was and let the kid fill in the blanks."

The questions began in earnest then. Danni fielded them, making eye contact with each of them by turns. Yes, it was definitely a trailer, and yes it was in a trailer park, but maybe in a back corner. It had seemed a little removed from the rest, or maybe some of them were vacant. She didn't remember too many lights from other buildings. No, she didn't remember crossing the river to the North side, but she couldn't rule it out, for obvious reasons.

"Wait a minute," Tommy said, as the obvious occurred to him. "I can understand you didn't notice where you were going en route to the trailer, but what about the return trip? Surely you noted a few basic landmarks, like whether or not you crossed the Saint John River?"

He hadn't thought the young woman could slide any lower in her seat, but he was wrong. "Oh, crap. I was hoping you weren't gonna ask me that."

"Why not?"

"I was kinda busy on the way back, too," she admitted, her face reddening.

Tommy frowned. "I thought you said Dillon was passed out?"

"He was, but Derek wasn't." She grimaced. "I guess he got a little hot and bothered by the action in the back seat and wanted a little for himself."

"Chrissakes," exploded Ray. "Did anyone *not* get blown on this trip?"

Danni's gaze came up then, her eyes glinting with tears and suppressed anger. "Yeah. Those of us without dicks."

Tommy held up a hand. "Okay, who was driving?"

"The other chick. Ashley."

"Know where we can find her?"

She shook her head. "I only saw her once before, at a frosh party. I only noticed her at that party because I suspected she was working the crowd. Kept disappearing and reappearing. You get to recognize the pattern."

"Where was the party, when, and who was there?" This time, the question came from Ray.

After extracting the answers, he called to get someone over to the Graham Avenue address where the party had taken place, to see if anyone could ID this Ashley girl or otherwise help them locate her.

As he listened to Ray's end of the telephone conversation, the heavy feeling in Tommy's gut worsened. It could take hours — hell, it could take *days* — to find this Ashley person. Or she might have left town weeks ago. Yes, it was a damned good lead, the best they had, but they might not have that kind of time. His chest tightened to the point where he had to work to draw breath.

When Ray finally hung up the phone, Tommy jumped in. "We gotta do something now, Razor. We can't just wait around and hope this woman turns up."

Ray raked a hand through his hair. Of course, his hair fell right back into place, but the gesture itself spoke volumes about his anxiety level. "You got a better idea?"

"Yeah, I do. Call out the search and rescue dogs."

"Can't our K9 teams handle it, between us and J Division?"

"General-purpose police dogs are tracking trained. You need a trailing-trained search dog to track something scent-specific when the trail is cold like this. Local ground search and rescue has two dogs."

"Great. I'll call right now. If we can get them to mobilize both teams right away, we could probably cover the most likely trailer parks inside two or three hours."

"If you can get Max's new handler to lend him to me, you could have a third team."

Ray frowned. "I thought you said police K9s can't do this kind of work."

Tommy grimaced. "I was kinda teaching Max trailing on the side. I think he can be effective."

"On the side? As in not department approved?"

Tommy nodded his head at the girls and hobbled outside the principal's office. With an exasperated sigh, Ray followed.

"I guess that's a 'yes' on the lack of departmental approval?" he said.

"Hey, it doesn't interfere with his work. Max can still do a straight track, and his work still stands up in court. He doesn't go into trailing mode unless I present him with a scent article and give him the specific command."

"Oh, Jesus. If that got out, the defense could have a field day with this, Tommy. What's to stop you giving some skell's scent to the dog and prejudicing the outcome by having Max find him, whether the actual track leads to him or not?"

"*Me*, Ray. *I'm* what stops me. Or what used to stop me. You might have noticed I don't do this anymore."

"So what? You just neglected to mention this other work you've been doing with him when you testify about training?"

"It's not material. It's not the same as mixing bomb sniffing with drug sniffing or with general-purpose police work. The experts say as long as a dog is trained solidly in tracking first, it doesn't do any harm to teach trailing. Besides, you can tell whether a dog is tracking or trailing. On a police track, I can see he's tracking, so I can testify in good conscience."

"Jesus, Tommy."

"I just thought it might be good to have that capacity. Like *now*."

"And you're the only one who can work with Max on this, I suppose."

"Yes."

Ray leveled a glance at him. "You really think you're up to it?"

"I'm up to it, Ray. Even supposing I have to *crawl* behind the goddamn dog, I can get the job done."

Ray measured him with a hard look, then nodded. "Fair enough. You're deputized. I'll arrange to get Max brought in. What else do we need?"

"Scent articles. Three of them, one for each team. Ideally a piece of Paige's recently worn clothing."

"There was a jacket in the van. Would that work?"

"Already logged by Ident?"

"Yep."

"Then it's contaminated, for this purpose anyway. Ideally, it'll come out of the laundry, picked up with stainless steel tongs and deposited in a bag to prevent contamination from other sources. If you can mobilize the search and rescue teams, I can whip back to Paige's and get the scent articles bagged."

"Sounds good. We'll cover the south side first," Ray said. "Then the north side, then outlying areas last. We'll need tactical backup with each team."

"You'll tap J Division for tactical help, so we can do the sweeps concurrently?"

Ray nodded. "I'll get Quigg on it right now. We'll need to stay on the hunt for this Ashley too. With any luck, we'll find the girl and her information will let us focus all the dog teams on the right park."

"Good thinking."

The girls emerged from the principal's office.

"Hey, do you think I could go back to class?"

Ray, his hands already busy on his cell phone, turned to Danni Robertson as though he'd forgotten she was still there. "Yeah, we're done here for the moment. But leave your contact information with this guy." He jerked a thumb towards Tommy before turning his attention back to the phone.

Tommy pulled a pen and notepad out of his pocket and handed them to Danni.

"You guys aren't going to come looking for me again, are you?" Her voice broke, and Tommy almost feel sorry for her. She swallowed and started again. "I mean, am I going to have to testify? Is all this going to come out in court? Because if it does, I'll be finished here."

"I don't know," he answered honestly. "But if you really can't afford to take a hit like this, I'd recommend you take up waitressing. I understand the tips can be good."

Ducking her head, she scribbled her contact information on the pad and handed it to him. "Can I go now?"

He looked at what she'd written to make sure it was legible. "This your real address?"

"Yes."

"Yeah, you can go."

Shoulders hunched, she turned to leave but stopped when Rachel called her name.

Rachel glided over to the other woman and laid a restraining hand on her arm. When she spoke, her voice was low and steady, but Tommy had no trouble hearing her message.

"I know you were just doing a job, Danni, and Lord knows I hate to judge another woman for her choices, but I'm telling you right now, you will never lay a hand on that boy again. Not to shake hands. Not to brush a piece of lint off his shoulder. Not to goddamn put him out if he's on fire. Am I making myself clear?"

"Perfectly."

The moment Rachel released Danni's arm, the other woman fled. Rachel turned back to Tommy. The fire had died out of her eyes and she looked as scared as Tommy felt. "What now?"

"Now we're going back to the station where I'm going to grab a uniform to drive me to Paige's place to get those articles, and then I'll go back to the station to hook up with Max and the tactical team to get this underway."

"Hey, what about me?"

The two men looked back at Rachel, who stood uncertainly in the hall.

"You can't just leave me here."

Tommy and Ray exchanged a glance.

She tipped her chin. "I'm not going home until this over."

"She's been helpful," Tommy said. "Maybe she'll have more to offer."

Ray inclined his head in agreement. "Come on, then. You can hang with me until we get the K9 units deployed. Then we'll figure it out from there."

"I'm going to need a radio car to get me to Paige's as quickly as possible," Tommy said.

"Already handled. A.J. is waiting on you."

"Great. Can you do one more thing for me?"

"What's that?"

"Get me a first aid kit. A real one, not one of those things with two Bandaids and a pair of nail scissors."

"You got it."

                        ⚜

Paige needed to use the washroom again, but she wasn't going to ask. Because Derek Weaver — yes, the dumb-ass had told her his name, dispelling any doubt she might have been nursing that he'd let her go after the ransom demand was met — appeared to be getting sleepy.

The level in the vodka bottle had declined steadily, with minimal help from her. She glanced down at her drink, a Diet Pepsi and vodka mixed in a plastic pop bottle, which she clutched against her belly with her bound hands. He'd plunked a straw in the bottle so she could dip her head and take a sip whenever she wanted. Or rather, whenever he demanded she drink.

Her stomach gurgled loudly, reminding her how long it had been since she'd eaten breakfast this morning. Not that she needed reminding how empty her stomach was. The few mouthfuls of straight vodka she'd choked on before the amusement factor wore off for her captor, had gone straight to her head. Fortunately, he'd agreed to her request to retie her hands in front of her. Not so fortunately, he hadn't left her hands free so she could handle a glass, as she'd suggested. Rather, both hands were firmly bound together and her elbows were also secured to the chair. Still, she was in a better position than she'd been before, with her arms lashed behind her back. Her shoulder sockets still throbbed from the stretching.

So here she sat, lashed to a chair, an impromptu, unwanted highball clutched against her mid-section, while Derek Weaver's head seemed to grow heavier on his shoulders.

His chin took another dip toward his chest, and Paige held her breath. Yes. His eyes were closed! If he'd just slump forward a few inches and let his head rest on the table . . . .

Suddenly, he lurched upright again with a surprised cry.

Shit, shit, shit.

The hand holding the vodka bottle had relaxed until some of the liquid spilled on his thigh, waking him from his stupor.

Dipping her head to hide the tears of disappointment she knew he'd see glittering in her eyes, she squeezed the pop bottle tighter. *Relax, Paige. Take it easy. He'll drift off again. Just give him time.*

Except she didn't know how much time they had before the telephone rang . . . .

"Whoa, I almost nodded off there."

"Really?"

"It's too goddamn hot in here, that's why."

Hoping her poker face was back in place, she lifted her gaze. "Maybe you should open a window. It must be cooling off out there now."

"Yeah, right. Open a window so you can scream your head off. Why don't I just untie you and let you wander outside?"

She held his gaze. "You didn't seem too worried about me yelling before."

"Wasn't." He laughed. "This whole trailer has been soundproofed. Soundproof wall sheeting inside the walls, laminated glass on the windows, acoustic foam tiles on the ceiling, the whole shebang. We could have ourselves a party in here and no one would know."

She swallowed, thinking of any number of sinister reasons why someone might do that to a mobile home. Maybe this wasn't the first time it had been used in a kidnap. Recalling some of the stains she'd seen on the bedroom carpet, her fear level, which she thought had already maxed out, took another hike. Maybe it was used for all manner of crimes — rape, torture, snuff movies —

"Used to belong to a guy played in a band." Weaver's careless explanation arrested her terrifying thoughts in their tracks. "And I'm talkin' heavy metal, not that boy-band shit. Him and the boys liked to practice here. It was either do somethin' about the noise or take it somewhere else, so his buddies pitched in and they soundproofed it."

"Fascinating."

Weaver cocked his head and looked at her through eyes that were not nearly as bleary looking as they'd been just minutes ago. Dammit, he was coming around. And he must have sensed her palpable relief at learning why the house had been so thoroughly sound-proofed.

"What, you thought it was like some kind of torture chamber? A regular prison?"

She decided not to lie about it. He only *looked* stupid. As she'd discovered in these past hours, he had a certain sly intelligence. "The thought crossed my mind. I'm glad to hear I was wrong."

"Didn't say you were wrong." He lifted the bottle and took a long pull from it. Then he used the bottle neck to gesture around the room. "These walls have seen plenty of action, some of it at the hands of that son of yours."

"Dillon was *here*?" She blanched. Oh, God, what had this pervert done to her son in this house of horrors? "What did you do to him?"

Derek snorted. "Wasn't me did the doing, but your lily-white boy got done, sure 'nuff."

Oh, Dillon. Not like that.

"No need to look at me like that. I just laid the table; I didn't force him to eat." Derek grinned, obviously pleased with his analogy.

"Stop it!"

He regarded her through narrowed eyes, eyes that looked just a little meaner than they had a few minutes ago. "What? You think your son is some kind of freakin' saint or something? I hate to break the news, but his prick gets stiff same as the next guy's."

She dug her fingernails into the plastic Pepsi bottle, causing a small spurt of fluid to overflow the cap. *Careful, Paige. Don't let him get you going.*

Except Dillon would hate that it happened that way. She knew her son. He was such a romantic at heart.

Don't think about it.

She straightened her spine, at least as much as her restraints would allow. "Did you know Dillon saved two children from drowning when he was just fifteen? Did you know he jumped into an icy river in the middle of January to pull those kids out of a submerged car? Did you know their mother had strapped them in there before pointing her car toward the river and putting it in gear?"

"The hero thing?" Derek flipped a hand dismissively. "Hell, yeah, I know all about it. That's why the Big Guy picked him for this little cross-border courier job, after all."

Cross-border courier? Oh, God, they were using her son as a mule! But who was behind it? She wet her dry lips. "The Big Guy? Who's he?"

Derek smiled slyly. "Don't you worry about the Big Guy."

"*Worry* about him? If that bastard's behind this, I hope he burns in hell."

Derek slapped his thigh and laughed. He laughed until the tears came, and still he laughed.

"What's so funny?" she asked when he regained control.

Derek wiped away tears. "The Big Guy — he thinks he's earning a ticket to paradise with this gig. Meanwhile, you think he's going straight to hell." He paused to take another swig of the vodka, then wiped his mouth with the back of his hand. "You know what'd be funny? It'd be funny if it was one and the same place. I mean, the place he wants to go and the place you wanna send him. Heaven and hell —"

A ticket to Paradise? Derek's voice faded out as her mind processed the import of what he'd said. The Big Guy, the boss, the man who selected Dillon as the perfect mule to smuggle something across the border, thought he had a ticket to Paradise? The pieces of the puzzle realigned themselves in her mind until they all fit together.

Sweet merciful God in heaven. The puppeteer pulling Derek Weaver's strings was a terrorist, and he'd dragged Dillon into his demented scheme.

Oh, dear God. *Terrorism.* It all made sense now. Fear and dread and despair met, merged.

Oh, God, it would be bad, whatever they were planning. Very bad. It had to be. 9-11 changed everything, upped the ante. It would be daring. Probably bloody. Definitely high-casualty. And they were making her son an instrument.

She sagged in the chair, barely noticing the way her bindings cut into her flesh.

"Ah, there we go. I see you finally twigged to it."

His words barely registered. Her brain had flipped the switch, shut itself off. Numb, that's what she was. Blessedly, blankly numb.

⁂

What the hell? Derek cocked his head and looked at her. Why wasn't she goin' off on him?

He'd seen awareness explode in her eyes. She'd figured it out, all right, just like he wanted her to. And now she was supposed to whimper and cry and annoy the livin' shit out of him so it'd be easier to do what he was gonna have to do. Man, nothing pissed him off like a sniveling woman. Unless it was a woman who acted like a goddamn doormat. He'd seen enough of that growing up, thank you. His old man could lay a beating on his shadow of a mother until she whimpered for mercy, but the stupid cow still rushed to wait on him. To *defend* the prick.

Idiot. He gave himself a mental whack upside the head. Don't think about those losers. It's not like they ever spared a thought for him, unless it was to hope the devil took him.

Schooling his expression into that flat stare he knew gave her the heebie-jeebies, he forced his attention back to his captive. Unfortunately, the effort was wasted. She was gone. Not *gone* gone. Zombie gone. And, Christ, it was creepy.

He moved closer until he stood right beside her chair. "Hey, what's your problem?"

She made no response. Bitch didn't even lift her eyes. Did she think he'd tolerate that lack of respect? He gripped her chin hard enough that she should have flinched and forced her head up.

"Hey, you hear me?"

She met his gaze, and suddenly he wished he hadn't forced the issue. That look in those eerie green eyes ... *Jesus.* He wanted to snatch his hand back, but then he'd look like a pussy. He tightened his grip on her chin until it had to hurt like a sonofabitch.

"Hey, Deaf One, I asked you what's your problem?"

"What did they do to you?"

His fingers flexed again at her softly-voiced question. "The fuck you talking about, lady?"

"Your parents. Your teachers. The bully down the street. What'd they do to you to bring you to this point, where you'd betray your country for —"

He yanked his hand away from her face.

Pity.

Holy Christ, that's what he saw there in her eyes, that other thing he couldn't identify. Pity. For him.

"Screw you. You can just take that psycho-babble and shove it."

"I'm so sorry."

Again with the eyes. *Jesus Christ.*

He lashed out, smashing the near-empty vodka bottle off the table. It slammed into the kitchen cabinet in an explosion of glass and liquid that made her jump satisfyingly.

"Don't you goddamn feel sorry for me. There's nothing wrong with me. My old man didn't beat on me. My momma didn't abandon me. The world didn't fuck me over. I'm just in it for the money, you hear?"

"Your thirty pieces of silver?"

The fuck did that mean? Some hoity-toity literary reference, probably, intended to make him feel stupid. "Look, that crap's wasted on me. I'm just doin' what I have to do to get out of this shit hole. Once I collect my paycheck, I'll get out of this armpit of a city in this armpit of a province and go somewhere better. Somewhere they'll call me *Mr. Weaver* and carry my bags and open doors for me."

Somewhere where they gave him more respect that she was giving him right now, he might have said. Jesus, she was still lookin' at him with those eyes, almost like she knew something he didn't.

"But what kind of life will it be if you can't look at yourself in the mirror when you get up in the morning? Is that really what you want?"

He snorted. What kind of a pansy did she think he was? The same kind as her son, obviously. "Let me worry about that."

"Well, while you're worrying about that," she said, her voice taking on a bit of a bite, "you might also worry about where on the planet you're going to hide. You might find yourself living in caves, scurrying from one hole to another, like some other fugitive who comes to mind."

"Shut up!" God, Weaver, why'd you have to go and smash the vodka bottle? He could do with a stiff belt. "I'll be able to go anywhere I want, 'cuz this isn't gonna follow me. Nobody's gonna know, 'cuz nobody'll be around to tell, if you take my meaning."

A shadow moved in the depths of her eyes, but dammit, she still wasn't sniveling. What was it going to take? Chrissakes, he'd as much as told her he was gonna whack her and her stupid son, too.

"What's wrong with you, lady? Don't you know enough to be scared?"

She stared back at him calmly. "He won't do it."

Derek's blood ran cold. "Whaddya mean?"

Her gaze locked onto his. "Dillon won't cooperate."

Don't panic, don't panic. You're still in control. She's yanking your chain.

He bared his teeth in a menacing smile. "Are you kidding? Your precious Dillon was pissing his pants on the telephone earlier. He'll do it, all right."

"No, he won't. I taught him better than that."

Her voice rang with a confidence that infuriated him.

"Yeah? Well, I guess I underestimated the little fucker, then. Any man who'd sacrifice his own mother rather than smuggle a few drugs across the border is one nasty piece of work. I could use a man like that on my team."

She blinked. "But he's not smuggling drugs. He's smuggling—"

"Ah, but he *thinks* it's drugs."

"He'll figure it out."

His gut cramped. "For your sake, you'd better hope he doesn't."

She lifted an eyebrow. "Why on earth should I hope that? You as much as told me you were going to kill us both, no matter what. You're the one who better be praying he doesn't figure it out."

Bitch. She wasn't supposed to stand up to him like this. She wasn't supposed to undermine his confidence in the plan. It was a good plan, dammit.

"Didn't I tell you to shut up?" he said softly.

"He'll figure it out, and when he does, he'll call the police and—"

Before she could say another word, he hauled back and belted her across the face, hard enough to rock the chair she sat on. Her head snapped back, then lolled forward. And she was quiet.

Chapter 16

Rachel stayed out of the way, but close enough to be of use if anyone had questions. They didn't. So she just stood back and watched the organized chaos as the search and rescue K9 teams and the tactical teams assembled in the parking lot. The very air was charged with urgency.

Max must have felt it, too, because he started whining softly from the back of the Expedition where he'd been stashed again after his reunion with Tommy. She glanced at the vehicle to see Max watching Tommy with a fierce intensity, anticipation making the animal's gorgeous hair coat seem to quiver.

Yeah, it had been quite a reunion. Tommy'd had tears in his eyes and his voice as he greeted the leaping, delirious dog. And if she didn't know better, she'd think Brooks Brothers here had fogged up a little bit, too.

Not that she could blame him. Man, if anyone or anything ever loved her as much as that dog loved Tommy, they could stick a fork in her, 'cuz she'd be done.

"Ready to roll?"

At Ray's question, she dragged her attention back to Tommy.

"Almost." He limped closer, leaning heavily on his cane. "Did you manage to get the bona fide first aid kit I asked?"

"Yep." Ray produced it. "Though I still haven't figured out what you wanted it for, unless you're figuring on getting shot again."

"Not if I can help it."

Tommy put his equipment on the hood of the Expedition, then flipped the huge first aid kit open. After digging around for a few seconds, he came up with something. Rachel peered around Ray to see that Tommy held a sizeable roll of elastic bandage, the kind of stuff athletes used to wrap sprains and shit. He handed it to Ray, who took it automatically.

"Whoa! What's this for?"

"Razor, buddy, I'm gonna say something to you I never imagined I'd ever say to another man."

Ray swore. "Okay, what?"

Tommy opened the SUV's door. There in the darkened parking lot, from behind the relative privacy of the vehicle's door, he unzipped his jeans and dropped them. "Strap me up."

✦

Tommy's brain screamed at him to quit. No, it S-C-R-E-A-M-E-D, in great big upper case letters. Flashing neon letters.

He and Max had searched most of the south-east corner of the Hutchins Trailer Park. The seediest and most sparsely-populated section of the park, they'd pegged it as the most promising. Just two streets remained of this section, but that still left about seventy percent of the park to cover. Just the thought of all that ground, putting one foot in front of another about four thousand more times, made him falter.

Oh, come on, Godsoe, suck it up. And for Chrissakes, don't fall.

Max gave an anxious whine. Tommy realized he'd stopped. Poor Max. He must be confused as hell. He was used to the two of them running on a track. They both liked it that way, and it helped keep Max pumped up and motivated. The snail's pace they'd been moving at would be confusing enough for the dog. The full stop would really throw another curve at him. Not to mention the shorter lead they were using — twenty feet instead of thirty — and the absence of the bullet-resistant vest. Toss in that he'd been asked to find a scent-specific trail and ignore the other things he would normally alert on, and it was a wonder poor Max hadn't quit.

"Find him!" he called, using his standard, if not quite gender-appropriate, search command, and Max started off again. Tommy lurched back into motion, giving copious thanks for the tensor bandages he'd convinced Ray to wrap his pelvis with. If it weren't for that extra stability from that tight binding, he'd have never made it this far. Even so, his legs trembled. Despite the coolness of the evening, sweat drenched the back of his shirt, his hair line, the palms of his hands.

And the damned dark glasses weren't helping. The sparse street lights had begun to taper off toward the edge of the park, and he could barely see Max well enough to read his signals. He now had to tip his head and look over the shades' rims.

Max cornered at the next street and started down it. Tommy followed, closing his mind to the hot shriek of excited nerve endings. The pain now radiated down to the soles of his feet and halfway up his back. Belatedly, he realized he'd forgotten to keep his white cane moving back and forth in a convincing, slow arc in front of him for the benefit of anyone who might be watching.

Okay, it wasn't a cane, exactly. It was one of those skinny white curtain wands plucked from a set of mini-blinds back at the shop, by a quick-thinking Rachel.

The other K9 teams could rely on speed and stealth to get in and get out of their assigned search areas without arousing too much excitement, especially with darkness falling. But with Tommy's poor mobility, he had no hope of ghosting through. He'd said as much to Ray, who'd suggested he just pretend he was a lame guy out for a walk. It was Rachel who'd come up with the idea that he impersonate a blind man. Even Ray had had to concede it was brilliant. The only thing less threatening than a gimp was a blind gimp.

Tommy heard a car door slam, followed by an engine starting. Two houses away, headlights leapt to life in a driveway. Dipping his head so he could see over the dark glasses, he reeled Max in, continuing to swing the cane in a rhythmic arc. With a curse, he realized that even that motion — the swinging of the cane — was starting to hurt. Blind people, he concluded, must have incredible forearms.

The vehicle, an early-model Toyota 4Runner, reversed onto the street, then drove past without incident. A sideways look confirmed it was a woman at the wheel, and the backseat window sported one of those sun shades emblazoned with a 'Baby on Board' message. Max didn't give the 4x4 a second look, either.

"That anybody we should be worried about?"

Ray's voice was low and clear in Tommy's ear. He dipped his chin closer to the mic taped to his chest. "No. Just a mom on a grocery run or something. And Max has just cleared this street. We're going to cut across the last lot to Carmichael. No fencing, and it sure would be easier than tramping back down this street."

"You covering both sides as you go?"

"Yeah, we're weaving back and forth checking out each driveway. I was counting on be able to scoot through at the end of this cul-de-sac to save some wear and tear."

He'd been casting the dog deep into each driveway — chances were if Paige had been brought here, her feet would have touched the ground for only a few steps, if at all, from the back seat or — oh, Christ, the *trunk* of a car — to the trailer. Not much of a scent trail.

On the plus side, he knew how skin rafts billowed off of everyone, an invisible cloud of dead skin cells showering to the ground. Even if Paige had been carried, there would still be skin rafts. And it hadn't rained.

Max would find her if she was here.

Probably.

Maybe.

"Speaking of wear and tear, how you holding up?"

Tommy lifted his cane arm to swipe sweat from his forehead. Much as he wanted to say he was doing fine, he couldn't. "I think I'll need a lift to the next starting point once I clear Carmichael."

"Copy that."

Reaching the end of the street, Tommy crossed the unkempt lawn of the last trailer, which gave every appearance of being unoccupied. The terrain was rough, churned up by the tires of vehicles that had taken this same shortcut. The result made the going horrifically hard. Shit. Maybe he should have gone the long way after all.

At last he reached Carmichael Street, where he reined Max in, gave him the scent again, followed by the search command. Once again, Max took off. Tommy barely had time to fall back into his cane swinging routine when Max picked something up. The dog veered sharply to the left and into the driveway of the trailer directly opposite the vacant one, then alerted by lying down.

"Holy shit!" Max had found her! He'd found Paige. Or at least, he'd found where she'd been.

"Hey, Tommy, you got something?"

Ray's voice in his ear again. Before he could answer, a pair of bright lights winked on over the trailer's front door. Dammit. Motion sensor jobs. Max hadn't triggered it, but as soon as Tommy stepped toward the dog, his added height must have put him within the sensors' range.

"Tommy, you okay?"

Again, Tommy ignored Ray's voice in his ear, principally because the trailer's door had swung open. A man, mid-to-late twenties with a shaved head, stepped out.

Bingo. Derek Weaver.

"The fuck you want, buddy?"

Max who'd surged to his feet the minute the door opened, growled deep in his throat.

Think quick, Godsoe.

"Sorry. I'm new to the park." Tommy swung his cane as though trying to find the curb again, grateful he'd automatically taken up the slack in Max's lead. It'd look pretty suspicious for a guide dog to be on anything but a short harness handle. Tommy prayed Weaver was half as dumb as people seemed to think. "New to this dog, too, I'm afraid." He grimaced. "Guess he musta led me astray somewhere back there."

In his earpiece, Tommy heard Ray relaying the situation to Gabriel Cormier, the Emergency Response Team leader. Could Weaver pick up the buzz of Ray's voice from where he stood? Probably not, with Max growling. And hopefully, the light wasn't illuminating the incriminating wire running up to the earpiece. He should have yanked it out.

"If they gave that nasty-assed animal to you for a seeing-eye dog, I'd take it back," said Weaver, eyeing Max's bristling stance. "Trailer park's rough, but it ain't *that* rough."

Tommy glanced a little off to the right as though he couldn't quite get a fix on Weaver's voice, using his peripheral vision to scan the other man without the impediment of the dark glasses.

Despite his words, Weaver looked less than convinced on the blind man/guide dog situation. Deliberately, the younger man drew back his shirt, exposing the butt of a pistol shoved down the front of his pants. Against the white of his t-shirt, it stood out like a beacon.

"Can you tell me which way to go? Max here musta picked up a rabbit or a squirrel or something. He's got me all turned around."

Weaver's hand went to the pistol's grip, and he drew the weapon out. Jesus, it was a big motherfucker. Bigger than the 9mm that had nearly killed him in that warehouse. Probably a .40 or .45, from the look of it. Tommy forced himself not to react, playing blind for all he was worth. Unfortunately, he couldn't communicate the same restraint to Max, who went ape-shit at the sight of the firearm.

He could have silenced Max with a sufficiently forceful command, but he knew it wouldn't come off right for a blind guy taking a stroll. Instead, he pretended to try to calm the dog.

"Some fuckin' guide dog. What the hell's wrong with him?"

"I'm sorry. He's never done anything like this before. This is so embarrassing. I think the rabbit or whatever it was he got wind of back there must have got his blood up."

Even as he kept up the prattle, he reeled Max in closer. He had to kill the barking for real and get the hell out of here. If Weaver'd had Paige's place under surveillance, which he had to assume from the Polaroids he'd seen, chances were he'd seen Tommy, too. Tommy didn't want to risk the little prick recognizing him now. But the trick was to quiet Max without coming off like a cop.

"Just tell me which way to turn and we'll be out of your hair." By now, he'd hauled the still barking Max in close enough to catch his harness.

A pause. "Do a one-eighty, then turn right and you're back on your way."

"Thanks, man."

Weaver pushed the long-barreled pistol — oh, man, that had to be a flash suppressor extending that mile-long barrel — back into his pants.

"Just get that psycho dog offa my property."

"No problem." Thank God. Tommy almost folded to the ground in sheer relief. Now he could retreat and let the ERT guys move in and do what they trained so hard to do. They'd glide in here like shadows and take the trailer before Weaver knew what was happening. Nobody was going to get shot. Not this time. Not today.

Weaver started to turn back toward the trailer when a crash sounded and the door burst outward. Max barked wildly and lunged hard against the lead, almost dragging Tommy off his feet. A wave of pain arced through him, darkening his vision and setting stars to sparking and shooting in his peripheral vision.

Come on, Godsoe, don't faint, don't faint.

It felt like an eternity, but probably took no more than a couple of seconds to drag himself back from the edge. Vision clearing, he focused on the partially open door.

Oh Jesus oh God oh no.

Sprawled on the floor was Paige, and oh, Christ, she was lashed to a chair. The top of the high-backed chair was actually holding the door open. Tommy zeroed in on her face. Her mouth was sealed with duct tape and her face looked swollen, but she was alive. Dear Lord, she must have launched herself, chair and all, at the door.

Weaver swore. "You stupid, stupid woman. You just fucked the gimp, and his guide dog flunk-out, too."

Tommy's eyes leapt back to Derek, who was going for that cannon again. "Police!" he shouted. "Drop your weapon or I'll send the dog!" In his earpiece, he heard Ray shouting a Code 10-33.

Weaver's arm faltered at the word "police", but then he resumed lifting the gun. Without hesitation, Tommy released the clip on Max's harness and set him loose. Max needed no command to do exactly what he was trained to do in this situation.

Tommy heard the *phut, phut* of the silenced automatic as Weaver unleashed two frantic, hurried shots at the charging dog. Time seemed to slow, stretching itself out to the point that Tommy found himself marveling at how minimal the muzzle flashes were and how efficiently the silencer/suppressor did its job. Max, God bless him, didn't flinch from the gun fire, and not just because the report was so well muffled. He'd always been fearless in his master's defense.

Then Max was on Weaver, catching his right arm in a deep, grinding bite. Weaver screamed and dropped the gun, which hit the chip-sealed driveway with an audible thunk.

"Get him off me! Get him off! Jesus Christ, make him *stop*!"

Sirens rent the night air as radio cars responded to the Code 10-33, but Tommy could already see the ERT team filing quickly across the chewed-up ground that he and Max had crossed not five minutes ago, moving quickly in a standard stack formation to present the smallest target to potential hostiles.

Tommy drew his own weapon, its weight familiar even after all these months, then lurched forward, Frankenstein-like, to kick Weaver's fallen gun into the shadows of the trailer. The kicking motion sent a million more stars sparking at the edges of his vision, but once more he fought them off.

Weaver stumbled and went down, flailing ineffectually at Max, who wasn't about to release his bite over a few blows.

"Get him off!"

Tommy shot a look at Paige, who was craning her neck awkwardly to see what was happening. Her eyes were huge and scared, and the duct tape covering her mouth made him want to let Max chew a little longer on Weaver.

"Anyone else in there?"

She shook her head no.

He rephrased the question to make absolutely sure she understood what he was asking. "The house is empty?"

A nod this time.

Another cry from Weaver. "Call him off! Oh, Jesus, please!"

Tommy looked down at Weaver. "When the dog releases you, you need to roll on your belly, face to the ground, and link your hands behind your head. If you don't do as you've been instructed, I'll let Max here have another piece of you. Do you understand?"

"I got it! I got it!"

"Out!"

At Tommy's command, Max immediately released Weaver, who wasted no time assuming the position. Tommy was wondering how in the hell his hip was gonna let him get down there to cuff Weaver when the ERT team arrived. Thank God.

"Hey," he called, "Can somebody cuff this mope for me?"

"The hostage?"

Tommy's gaze went to Paige's. Her eyes seemed to shine like emeralds, at least until his vision started to flicker like a TV set whose vertical hold was shot. "She's all right. She says the house is clear. Now, if you'll excuse me, I think I'll just throw up."

He turned away, but he didn't throw up.

He fainted.

⁂

Paige saw Tommy go down, saw one of the black-clad SWAT guys rush to his aid.

Oh, God, he'd been shot! That bastard Derek Weaver shot Tommy. And it was her fault. If she hadn't dragged him into their lives, if he hadn't tracked her down here, if she hadn't recognized his voice and panicked, afraid he'd walk away not knowing she was inside . . . .

A keening noise rose in her throat but all that escaped the gag was a nasal whimper.

Then another of the SWAT team members was there, asking her the same questions Tommy had. Was there anyone else in the house? Anyone else cooperating with Weaver? She shook her head emphatically from side to side, anxious for him to get on with it. He produced a knife and dealt with her bonds quickly, pushing the chair back out of their way. The moment her hands were free, she sat up and tore the duct tape from her mouth herself.

"Tommy! What happened? Is he hit?"

"I don't know, ma'am, but he's being seen to. My job is to make sure you're all right and to get you out of here."

The man turned and gave a hand signal. Two heavily-armed men stepped past them and into the trailer. Evidently, they wanted to satisfy themselves there was no one else lurking inside.

"Let me up! I have to go see."

"Whoa, whoa." His hands restrained her when she would have scrambled to her feet. "Let's just make sure you're okay first."

"But Tommy —"

"Look, there's the ambulance. See it?" He leaned to the right so she could see past him and out the open doorway. "It was standing by the whole time. Could be another one en route, too, what with shots being fired."

The fact that paramedics were on the scene helped her ratchet back the fear level, but she still needed to see for herself. "I'm fine, officer. I just really need to see how Tommy's doing."

"You're sure there are no injuries? You didn't hurt your back or your neck when you went down?"

Her neck hurt all right, but she thought it had more to do with the minutes she'd spent on the floor trying to elevate her head enough to see what was happening outside. Her head also throbbed horribly, but she was sure it was the KO blow Derek Weaver had delivered earlier, not the door-ramming incident.

"No, everything's fine." Her feet tingled painfully from restored circulation, but she wasn't about to mention that.

The two officers returned, confirming her assertion that no one else was in the structure.

"Okay. Let's get you out of here." The officer stood and offered her a hand.

She grasped his large hand, amazed at how badly she needed the assistance. The fact that he practically had to lift her to her feet probably didn't bode well for his letting her rush off to see Tommy.

"Paige?"

Suddenly Ray Morgan was standing there, blocking her already limited view of the activity outside. He looked, she realized with a jolt, about as close to disheveled as she imagined he got.

"Ray! Thank God! What's going on out there? Was he hit again? Will he be all right?"

"Nothing like that. But they did load him in an ambulance."

"Ambulance? Why? I mean, if he wasn't shot . . . ."

"His hip."

The young SWAT guy backed off a little to give Ray better access. He knelt beside her. "He just overdid it by about a thousand percent, is all. He'll be okay."

"And Dillon? Where's Dillon? I want to talk to him."

"Dillon's fine. He's just about half an hour away, under police escort."

The relief was exquisite. It took enormous concentration not to just fold up like a house of cards. He was all right. Dillon was all right. She took a deep breath and expelled it slowly. Then she remembered Tommy. What was he even doing here? He could barely walk.

"Tommy … ."

"Is gonna be fine," Ray filled in. "Honest."

"The dog … he was handling it, wasn't he?"

"Yeah. Police dogs don't usually do search and rescue work, but it turns out Tommy had taught Max some extracurricular tricks. The dog's never done anything like that with his new handler, so Tommy was our only choice. Not that he'd have let anyone else do it anyway."

Oh, dear Lord, he must be in agony. She'd seen how shaky and pale he was after a leisurely walk with Cleo. "But he can't … I mean, he said he'd never be fit enough to do that again."

Ray bared his teeth, but she wasn't sure it could be characterized as a smile.

"He's not, but he wasn't about to let that stop him. Not with you and Dillon on the line. I'm thinking he's going to need some serious pain control and maybe some medical management of that bum leg." As though to punctuate his statement, the ambulance's siren wailed to life and the vehicle pulled away. The flashing of its lights bounced crazily off the walls. "Which is why they're carting him off to hospital right now."

"They've taken him already? But I need to talk to him!"

"Well, I think you're going to get your wish, but you'll have to do your dialoguing at the hospital. If I'm not mistaken, that's your ride arriving now."

Another ambulance pulled into the spot vacated just moments ago by the other ambulance.

"But I don't need to see a doctor," she insisted. "I'm okay."

"You need to be checked out, Paige." Ray's words were gentle but they brooked no argument. "You were abducted against your will and confined. At this point, a medical doctor is going to have to make the determination that you're okay. Standard operating procedure. Plus," he added, "it'll put you in the ER right beside Tommy-Boy, and you can see for yourself that he's going to be all right."

"What about my son? He's on his way back, you said?"

"Less than half an hour away."

"And he's all right?"

Ray nodded. "Fine."

"Did he make the delivery? Oh, God, please tell me he didn't."

Ray moved aside so the EMTs could get in. "Not to worry. Your son called the authorities and we arranged for him to deliver a dummy package."

The paramedic addressed a couple of questions to her, which she answered tersely, then directed her attention back to Ray.

"A dummy package? My son delivered it?"

"Yes, ma'am."

"You let my son walk into danger?"

Ray held up both hands. "Hey, we tried to talk him out of it. The FBI would have supplied an agent to impersonate Dillon and make the drop, but Dillon wouldn't hear of it. He didn't think an agent could look the part of a scared kid."

"But—"

"I know. I'd be mad as hell, too. But he had solid coverage, Paige, every step of the way. I promise you. And we kitted him out with a Kevlar vest in the event of a worst-case scenario."

She leaned around the EMT, who was fitting a blood pressure cuff around her arm. "A Kevlar vest? Omigod, Ray. Is he really okay?"

"He's fine, he's fine," Ray hastened to assure. "It was just a precaution. There were FBI agents crawling all over that bus depot. It went smooth as butter. And Dillon had an escort all the way home. He's safe. I swear to God, he's safe."

"Detective, I'm going to have to ask you to stop interacting with my patient. I'll never get an accurate BP if you don't stop giving her new information."

"No problem. I'm about done, anyway. I'll see you at the hospital, Paige."

A second EMT moved in, effectively removing Ray Morgan from her line of sight. "Ray?" she called.

He leaned around the paramedic. "Yeah?"

"Do you like hazelnuts and raspberries?"

"Do I *what*?"

"Hazelnuts and raspberries. Do you like 'em?"

"Yes. I sure do."

"Good. Because when I get home, I'm going to make you the most fantastic Linzer torte flan you've ever laid eyes on."

He drew his breath in on a reverent hiss. *"European style?"*

"Absolutely."

A pause while the EMTs helped her onto the gurney.

Ray stepped close again, eyes narrowed: "Are we talkin' genuine hazelnut pastry?"

She smiled. "From scratch. A nice latticework job on top, too."

He groaned. "Oh, man, that sounds great. But I didn't do anything to warrant your —"

"Hey, Dillon's safe, I'm safe, Tommy's going to be okay. I'm a happy woman. Let me cook, okay?"

He smiled. Despite herself, she was a little dazzled. But she lifted her arm obediently for the paramedic to take her blood pressure.

"Okay, Paige Harmer. You got yourself a deal."

"And bring your wife."

His smile broadened. "Are you sure about that? You do realize Grace is a reporter for the local paper? Which means she'll probably try to pin you down to an exclusive on this little adventure of yours."

She grinned back at him, feeling incredibly light. Everyone she loved was alive and well. *Safe.* What more could she ask for? "I'm sure," she affirmed. "And invite your Sergeant, too, along with his wife."

The EMT unwrapped the blood pressure cuff, took the stethoscope out of his ears and sent a look toward Ray. "Sorry to interrupt, but we're just about ready to roll," he said, as the other EMT covered her with a blanket and secured the straps for transport.

Ray stood back while they elevated the gurney. Then he touched her on the arm. "Hey, take care of Tommy, will you? He's a really good guy. He just hasn't figured that out yet."

She was too surprised to respond. Fortunately, he didn't seem to expect an answer, since he'd already moved to get the door for the ambulance attendants.

As the two white-shirted EMTs manipulated the gurney out of the house and across the drive to the waiting ambulance, she wondered just what Tommy had told Ray about their relationship.

More importantly, what was their relationship?

Chapter 17

O H, FOR CRYING OUT loud! He was lying in a hospital emergency room because he'd fainted.

Fainted, for chrissakes.

The physician covering the ER turned out to be Ketan Patel, one of Tommy's poker buddies. Patel, the jerk, had gravely presented his diagnosis — *syncope resulting from an exaggerated respiratory response, leading to ventilation exceeding metabolic demands, resulting in hemodynamic and chemical changes*. When Tommy'd looked at him blankly, he'd laughed and said, "Relax, Tommy. You hyperventilated and fainted. At least we're pretty sure that's what happened. But we'd like to watch you for a while to rule out cardiogenic causes."

And now, here he lay, confronting the fact that in layman's terms, he'd been scared shitless.

Which, he supposed, was fair to say. He'd never been so scared in his life, including the day in that warehouse when he'd thought he might bleed out on the concrete floor. And except for the embarrassment of being carted here stone cold on a stretcher, he didn't mind admitting it.

Because Holy Mother of God, it had been close. Another twenty minutes, maybe a half hour, and the outcome could have been very different for Paige.

Beep, beep, beep, beep, beep!

Ah, hell. There he went again with the exaggerated respiratory response. Even with the help of the Demerol they'd given him to get the pain under control, he couldn't seem to let go of the fear.

Come on, Godsoe. Relax.

He concentrated on regulating his breathing, willed his heart rate to slow down. The rapid beeping from the monitor beside him slowed. Better. Last thing he needed was another visit from the rather frightening ER nurse.

He'd already been through that drill. Twice.

Quigg had visited earlier, and the picture he'd painted of what they'd found inside that double-wide on Carmichael had sent Tommy's pulse rate jack-hammering, which triggered an audible alarm at the nurse's station. The stern-faced nurse had descended on him. It had taken some talking to persuade her that everything was cool and that Quigg could stay.

The minute she disappeared, Tommy demanded Quigg continue. Quigg obliged, grimly. The place was completely sound-proofed, he reported. Ceilings insulated with acoustical tiles, too, and the laminated glass windows for extra sound insulation. But the most hideous discovery was the plastic drop sheets laid out in the kitchen, right where the chair to which Paige had been tied must have sat.

Despite his best efforts to stay calm, despite repeating the mantra that Paige was safe and beyond Weaver's reach, the monitor betrayed him again, bringing the nurse back to his bedside looking like a thunder cloud. Quigg had had to leave anyway, which was good, because she'd been about to chase him off. Sergeant or no Sergeant, it was clear who held rank here.

The nurse had fussed around him for a few minutes after Quigg left, adjusting this and that. But eventually she left, too, leaving him alone with a head full of disturbing images.

And around and around those images went. That fuck-wad Weaver had been planning to kill her. No doubt about it. Probably a point-blank shot to the back of the head. And dear God, Paige had to have known it was coming. Had Weaver been planning to shoot her where she sat, tied to that goddamn chair? Or would he have made her lie down on the plastic? Was he planning to use that big .45 on her, or did he have something smaller? Maybe a .22 for the execution-style head shot. He must have thought about the mess, tried to figure the best way to keep her blood and grey matter from—

Beep, beep, beep, beep, beep!

Damn, enough was enough. He found the call button suspended on the bed rail, pressed it and held it down until someone answered.

"Can I help you?" came a female voice from the speaker beside his bed.

He released the button. "Tom Godsoe. I'd like to check out, now."

A pause. "I believe the doctor wanted to monitor your vitals a while longer before we let you go, Mr. Godsoe, and your imaging ...."

"That's *Constable* Godsoe. And I'm only here because I fainted, okay? I fainted because I hyperventilated after the woman I love was kidnapped and nearly died. But she didn't die. She's okay, and now I'd like to go see her before we both grow another year older. So if you'd just —"

The movement drew his gaze, and suddenly he forgot what he'd been going to say. Paige!

She stood there, holding the beige privacy curtain of the exam cubicle open. Beside him, that blasted monitor started beeping crazily. And the expression on her face — she looked ... stunned. Oh, Lord, had she overheard his exchange with the nurses' station? Or did he just look that bad, hooked up to all this stuff?

Cursing under his breath, he swept his hand over his chest, tearing away the electrodes, then yanked the oversized clothespin-like contraption off his finger. The monitor alarmed again, but that was infinitely preferable to having the damned thing bleep an audible announcement of his every emotion, with Paige standing right there to hear it.

"Mr. Godsoe? What's going on?" The nurse's voice, sharp and no-nonsense, emanated from the intercom above his bed.

"I'm fine," he said, not taking his eyes off Paige. "I just untethered myself, so you might as well shut that monitor off."

The monitor stopped bleating.

"Thank you."

"Don't rush away just yet," the voice said. "Your x-rays are back, but the doctor still has to look at them. It shouldn't take much longer."

"Okay," he called. "I'll wait for the doc."

Paige moved into the cubicle. "X-rays?"

"Yeah." He found the lever at the side of the bed and elevated the head of it a little so he wouldn't feel so ... prostrate. "I told them not to bother. Nothing wrong with me that a little rest won't fix." With the help, in the meantime, of some narcotics.

"I just talked to Sergeant Quigley in the hall. He said you fainted back there. I'm so sorry. Your leg ... all that walking ... the pain must have been excruciating."

He opened his mouth to say his leg felt better than it had in months, thanks to the Demerol, but he caught sight of the bruise darkening the right side of her face. He dragged his breath in on a hiss. That sonofabitch!

"Come here," he commanded gruffly.

She put a hand to her face self-consciously. "Oh, yeah. That. Pretty impressive, huh?"

"Come here, Paige."

She moved to his bedside almost shyly. When she came within range, he pulled her still closer. Covering her hand with his own, he said, "Let me see, baby."

She let him pull her hand away to expose her face, but dropped her gaze.

Bastard. He should have let Max have another bite. Or ten.

No, he should have dropped that fake white cane, drawn his weapon and shot the motherfucker dead when he'd first lifted his t-shirt to reveal his weapon.

But he didn't say any of that. Instead, he smiled and agreed with her assessment.

"Very impressive." He ran his fingers over the soft, freckle-dusted skin of her face. So translucent. So soft. So completely ... Paige. "I think you're gonna have one helluva shiner."

"That's what the doctor said. But no concussion or anything like that."

He caught her left arm and brought her wrist up for inspection. It was encircled with gauze and tape. Thank God the monitor was turned off. "What's this?"

"It's nothing." She shrugged. "A little chafing from where I tried to wriggle free of the bindings."

"I can imagine." He summoned up the satisfying picture of Derek Weaver writhing and screaming under Max's deep, sawing, tenacious bite. Again, he kept the violence out of his voice. "Anywhere else?" he asked softly.

"I banged my right knee and elbow when I rushed the door, but they're fine. Just a little bruising. They gave me some Ibuprofen. It feels better already."

He ran a hand down her arm, needing to assure himself of her physical soundness. "You're really okay?"

She smiled into his eyes. "Yes, I'm really okay."

"And Dillon's safely back." It was a statement, not a question. Quigg had already filled him in.

She nodded, tears springing to her eyes. She blinked rapidly. "He's got a girlfriend, you know. Rachel. Rachel Whitesel."

His smile broadened. "I know. I've had the pleasure. She's a big reason we found you, by the way. Maybe the *only* reason."

She lifted a hand to wipe moisture from her cheek. "I like her. She'll be good for Dillon." Her voice was huskier than he'd ever heard it, except maybe in the bedroom. "They're out in the waiting room now."

He lifted an eyebrow. "Are you cleared to go already?"

"Yes."

"And the police are finished with you?"

She nodded. "For now. We all gave statements. I'm told there will be more questions tomorrow, but they're through with us for tonight."

"Then why don't you join Dillon and Rachel, let Dillon take you home? You must be anxious to get back there, crash in your own bed in your own house, with those great locks and Cleo on patrol."

The fleeting fear on her face told him how much she longed to do just that, retreat behind the security of her locks, but she said, "I'll wait for you."

He glanced away, knowing his own eyes would be sheened with moisture. "You heard the nurse. It could be a while. Doc's got to look at those x-rays."

"I've got a while. Thanks to you."

Oh, Lord. She was thanking him. If he'd been less self-absorbed, less preoccupied with his own little soap opera, if he'd *really* been paying attention, it would never have happened at all. "Don't thank me. I should have seen this coming, should have figured it out —"

She laughed, sounding like the old Paige. "Isn't that just like you? Tommy, you couldn't possibly have figured it out because Dillon wasn't talking. He chose to try to handle this by himself."

"He thought he was protecting you, you know, by moving out. If he'd known what the real stakes were, if he'd thought something like this could happen ... ."

She blinked rapidly. "I know."

"You should be proud of him, Paige. Once he thought it through, he stopped at a pay phone and called me. And he insisted on making the drop himself, over our reservations, because he knew it had to look right."

"I am proud of him. But it's like that time he went into that icy river for those kids. I'm incredibly proud, but I don't know if I'll ever get over the fear."

"That makes two of us." He lifted her hand to his lips and kissed her fingers. "God, I thought I was going to lose my mind when we figured out you'd been grabbed up."

Her fingers flexed in his hand.

"I had a few tense moments there, myself."

He laughed, but it emerged on a strange choking sound.

"Seriously, thank you, Tommy. If you hadn't put the radio transmitter on Dillon's car —"

"He called in anyway. We didn't need it to locate him after all."

"Yeah, but you saved twenty minutes or more."

"On that end, not on this end. It was this end that mattered."

She shook her head. "That's twenty minutes sooner that Dillon relayed his story about being drugged and taken to that place by those girls. If you hadn't had that bit of information, and if you hadn't pulled Rachel into the investigation, she wouldn't have put it together." She paused to swallow. "No, I think you know what a difference those twenty minutes could have made."

He made no attempt to disguise the shudder that went through him. "Oh, God, Paige."

Whether he pulled her into his arms or whether she moved into them of her own volition, he couldn't have said. But she was finally in his arms. And he didn't plan to let her go any time soon.

⁖

Safe. At last, she felt safe. Paige burrowed closer, clung harder. Oh, Lord, it was good. He smelled of anxiety and stale sweat and exertion and pure, sweet sanctuary.

It didn't make any sense. Hell, she was probably in better shape right now than he was to fend off a threat if one presented itself, but her heart wasn't having any part of logic. At least, not for the next few minutes. For the immediate future, she just wanted to soak up this feeling of safety, let it permeate through her until it thawed the last lingering chunk of fear in her chest.

He made a noise deep in his throat and she tilted her face upward, knowing what he sought. His lips closed on hers urgently, and she met him with equal fervor, answering demand with demand. It was all she could do not to crawl onto the bed with him and press her body to his. She was alive and he was alive and they were both on fire.

He broke the kiss. "Oh, baby, get up here!"

Seconds later, she was on the bed, specifically because he dragged her across his torso to deposit her on the other side of him.

"Whoa, careful!" She shifted to avoid his hip. "I don't want to hurt you."

"Like this," he said, helping her shift her position and settle her against him. Then his hands were all over her, kneading her breasts, biting into her waist, gliding over her hip . . . .

She reciprocated, finding his chest gloriously available. And everywhere her hands traveled, she felt compelled to follow with her mouth. And whoops! Everything was pretty much available, thanks to that hospital gown .... .

The brisk drawing of the privacy curtain was the only warning they had.

"Tommy? I've got your radiographs here and — oh, I'm sorry. Pardon me."

Paige clambered off the bed in record time, turning to face the same handsome East Indian physician who'd cleared her to go home less then twenty minutes ago.

"Ah, Ms. Harmer," he said dryly. "Nice to see you again."

She murmured an acknowledgment, feeling her face flush.

"Sorry 'bout that, Doc." Tommy's voice was husky, but he didn't sound in the least embarrassed. "We were just kinda celebrating surviving the day."

He laughed. "Can't say I blame you."

"So, those x-rays ... same old, same old, right? No new damage?"

"Essentially, yes. I'm sure you're in a great deal of pain right now, but it will subside. You have painkillers at home?"

Tommy nodded.

"What are you taking?"

Tommy supplied the drug's name.

"Good. You'll want to take a couple in about ... ." He shot his sleeve back to check his watch. "An hour and a half. I'd give that leg a little rest." The doctor's gaze strayed toward Paige, who blushed anew. "I would think you should be able to resume physiotherapy within a few days, but your PT could probably advise you better on that than I can."

"Thanks, Doc."

"As for your syncope, we're pretty sure it's not cardiogenic." He shot Tommy a reproving look. "I'd have liked to monitor you a while longer, but I guess I'll have to make do with what we've got."

"It's definitely not my heart."

"Well, if it happens again, I want you to get yourself back here, pronto."

"Deal," Tommy agreed.

"Any questions?"

"No."

The doctor scribbled something on his chart. "Well, okay, then. I guess you can go. I'll get someone out there to see about a wheel-chair."

Tommy looked like he wished he could decline the offer, but he clearly wasn't up to it, particularly without his cane, which Ray had told her he'd left in the K9 unit vehicle.

"Thanks, Ketan," he said.

Paige murmured her own goodbye, then moved back to Tom-my's bedside the moment the doctor left. "Wow, caught necking in the emergency room. That's a first."

"By my poker-buddy, no less." He lifted an eyebrow. "Does that bother you?"

She thought about it a few seconds, then laughed. "No. Maybe it should, but I can't say it does."

"Good. Because if I have anything to say about it, it's not the last time you're gonna be caught necking somewhere."

Her breath stalled in her chest. "Is that a fact?" she managed to breathe.

"You better believe it." He sat up and swung his legs gingerly over the edge of the bed. "Guess I'd better get dressed if you're gonna wheel me out of here. Can you hand me my clothes?" He gestured to the pile of clothing stacked on the chair beside the bed.

Ignoring the way her heart pounded against her ribs, she reached for the clothes. Jeans. Hmmm. "Need some help getting these on?"

He grinned wickedly, sending her heart into overdrive.

"Is that an offer?"

Lust swamped her all over again. Dear God, he was gorgeous. Objectively, inarguably, movie-star gorgeous. But mere beauty could not have made that face as dear to her as it had somehow become. No, that had taken a good, long look at the man behind the face. It had taken seeing his firm but gentle approach with Dillon, his compassion for Cleo, his strong protective streak. It had taken a glimpse of that vulnerability he tried so hard to hide, as well as the strength of character he seemed to try even harder to conceal.

"Yeah, that's an offer, handsome," she replied. "And it's likely to be the best one you'll get tonight, so I'd advise you to take it."

His laughing eyes sobered. "Then let me make you an offer, Paige Harmer."

She grinned. "Okay. Shoot."

"Marry me."

⁂

Dillon sat slouched in a hard, uncomfortable chair in the Emergency Department's crowded waiting room. His back ached from all those hours behind the wheel of his car and another couple of hours spent with the police, telling them everything he knew or thought he knew. But sore back and all, he'd happily spend the rest of the night right here, as long as he got to keep holding Rachel's hand.

God he was lucky, in so many ways.

Incredibly, she wasn't pissed at him.

Well, okay, yes, she had been pissed, mainly because he hadn't confided in her. But she totally got that he'd been trying to protect her. She didn't *agree* with his decision, which she'd made clear in her usual blunt manner, but at least she appreciated his motivation.

And thank the Lord, those girls hadn't been *girls* after all. They were women. Pros, in fact. And apparently he *had* passed out, just as he'd thought/hoped/prayed. Derek, the prick, had photographs — they'd found them in the search of his apartment — but the one woman, Danni What's-Her-Name, the one Rachel had helped the cops track down, swore they were staged. Faked.

Oh, Jesus, it made his face burn with humiliation to think about them stripping his clothes off and posing his unconscious body. Thank God the cops hadn't offered to show him the pictures, and he sure as hell wasn't gonna ask. He'd just as soon see them destroyed, but he supposed they'd have to be preserved for evidence. Maybe he'd even have to look at them, eventually. There'd be a trial . . . .

He realized his fingers had tightened on Rachel's when she squeezed back.

"You okay?" she asked.

He rolled his head sideways to look at her. She was similarly sprawled, her own head lolled on the back of the poorly padded chair, her face just inches from his.

His breath caught in his throat. Again.

Oh, man, this woman had saved his mother.

Well, Tommy and the SWAT team had done the literal saving, but according to Detective Morgan, it was Rachel's information that led them to focus their attention on the trailer parks in the first place.

As he looked into those bottomless hazel eyes, his heart felt like it was swelling, getting too big for his chest, constricting his breathing.

"Dillon?" she prompted again. "Is everything okay?"

"I didn't know if I'd ever see you again."

Her throat bobbed, but she said nothing, waiting for him to continue.

He dropped his gaze to their linked hands. "I figured if I made the delivery, they'd just whack me the first chance they got. I still can hardly believe we're all right, that Mom —"

"But they didn't get you and they didn't get your Mom. You got *them*, and where those sons-of-bitches are going, there's no coming back from. It's over, Dillon."

He couldn't stop the shudder that worked its way through him. Four men arrested so far, two in Maine, one in New York state, and another in Montreal, with the fervent hope of more arrests to come. And all in connection with a plot to unleash some kind of nerve agent. If Detective Morgan knew what the intended target was, he wasn't saying, or maybe he couldn't say. Dillon wasn't sure he wanted to know, anyway. It made him sick enough as it was, just thinking about how close he came to aiding and abetting those people.

"Yeah, you're right. It's over."

She kind of turned on her hip so she was facing him, and brought her other hand up to cover his. "You sure it's okay for me to spend the night at your Mom's house? 'Cuz I could go home."

"Are you kidding? My mother's not going to let you out of her sight until she's had a chance to cook about fifty different things and make you eat all of it." He angled his own body toward her, resting his weight on his nearly numb right butt cheek. "That's her way of dealing. And saying thank you."

She smiled into his eyes. "Well in that case, she can thank me as many times as she likes. I can't remember the last time I had a home-cooked meal that I didn't make myself."

God, he wanted her so much, it hurt to breathe. It hurt to think about how rotten he was going to feel if she didn't want him right back just as fiercely.

Her eyes sobered as she picked up on his intensity. "What?"

"I made myself a promise on the drive back here."

She hiked herself up the chair a little. "You did."

"Yeah."

She smiled again, lifting that pretty pierced eyebrow. "So, is it a secret, or are you planning to share it?"

"I promised myself if I got out of that mess, I was going to ask if I could court you."

Her face went blank. Not a good sign.

"*Court* me?"

"Yeah. You know, dinner, movies, long talks in cafes."

"Dillon, people don't court anymore. They date, maybe, but they don't —"

"Sure they do," he interjected. "When a guy feels like this."

She sat up abruptly, pulling her hand away. "Okay, maybe *some* women get courted, but honestly, Dillon, do I look like one of them?"

She crossed her arms, as though to make sure he got a good look at the thorny roses tattooed on her upper arm. In fact, from their petting session in his car, he already knew that particular tattoo extended to cover her shoulder, at the very least. And he was betting there were more.

"Yes." He smiled. "Rachel, you look perfect to me."

She wilted back into her chair. "Oh, Dillon."

"Is that a yes?"

"I'm scared, and frankly a little bit sick to my stomach."

"You, too? Oh, thank God." Dillon cast a glance around the waiting room, then brought his gaze back to her face. "I'd like to kiss you, but I'm not going to do it here."

A gratifying flame leapt in her eyes and a smile curved her lips. "Maybe tonight, at your place."

He let her see the heat in his own eyes. "Definitely tonight."

Too quickly, her face sobered again. "Before we get too carried away, maybe I should tell you I made a decision of my own today."

"Yeah?" He did his best to ignore the clenching of his gut. "What's that?"

"I'm thinking about going to college, if they'll accept me. I actually had pretty good grades in school."

"College?" He laughed. Was that all? "That's great."

"Holland College."

He recognized the name of the community college on Prince Edward Island. That would mean a separation; he still planned to go into UNB's computer science program this fall, here in Fredericton. But P.E.I. wasn't that far away. Piece of cake. Except her eyes were so somber.

"What's the matter? You don't think we can handle a few hundred miles separation?"

"I want to go to the Police Academy there."

"Great."

"Great?" She blinked at him. "Dillon, it's an idea that wouldn't have entered my head in like … a *million* years … if today hadn't happened. Aren't you surprised?"

"Maybe a little," he conceded. "But I can totally see it."

She blushed. "I don't know about that. Brooks Brothers tells me they screen for the right psych profile. They'll probably bounce my application faster than you can say *anti-establishment, cartilage-piercing freak*."

He just looked at her. "Brooks Brothers?"

"Detective Morgan."

Ah. "He talked to you about police academy?"

"Yeah, a little."

"And did *he* think they'd bounce your application?"

She rolled her eyes. "He said I wouldn't have made the cut in his day, but that things are different now. He figured I'd have to take the facial piercing out."

Dillon lifted a hand to touch the silver barbell gracing her left eyebrow. "You could still wear it for me."

"Yes," she agreed. "I could still wear it for you."

⁂

Paige felt her whole world wobble. This couldn't be happening. "*Marry* you?"

Tommy's face colored, but his voice was ruefully amused. "I have to say that's not exactly the expression I hoped to see on the face of the woman I proposed to, when I finally got around to it."

She shook her head as though the crazy suggestion could be dislodged that easily. "But you can't mean it."

"Oh, but I do."

"We hardly know each other."

"Paige, honey, you know more about me than anyone alive, the good, the bad and the downright ugly. And still, you haven't run away screaming. That's gotta be worth something."

"But I only moved in less than a month ago —"

"And we've spent hours together every day, with and without Dillon, for most of that time."

"But you don't really know me, Tommy."

"I know enough. I know you're brave and strong and resourceful. I know you raised a great son all by yourself. I know you'd die to protect him. I know you haven't had nearly enough support."

She fisted her hands at her sides, trying to quell the violent upsurge of emotion inside. "You've just described a mother, Tommy. Any mother. That's what I am."

"Oh, you're more than that. You're a beautiful woman. You're a creative, generous lover, which you'd pretty much have to be with me in this condition, granted."

"You were pretty generous yourself," honesty compelled her to say, but he held up a hand to stop her.

"I'm not finished. You're a good friend and a concerned citizen."

"And a damned fine cook and entrepreneur," she added.

"I was getting to that."

"Okay, so you know a little about me. And I know a little about you. You think that's a good reason to get *married*?"

"It helps, but no. The fact that I love you is the reason I'm proposing marriage. I swore if I got you back safe, I'd tie you up, tie you down, do whatever the hell I had to do to keep you safe, keep you with me."

The other shoe dropped. Of course. Guilt. Responsibility. That over-developed protective streak.

"Ah."

He frowned. "What does that mean, *ah*?"

It meant that he just needed a period of adjustment, time to come to terms with what had happened, time to reassure himself that she was fine, that she'd continue to be fine, without his sacrificing himself at the matrimonial alter. And in the meantime, she could have him on the no-strings-attached basis she'd already prepared herself for.

No need to expose those embarrassingly naive teenage dreams about marriage, kids and picket fences. God, it scared the hell out of her just to think about resuscitating that particular dream, especially with a man as intimacy-challenged as Tommy. A *younger* man. A more beautiful man.

She smiled. "It means I hadn't thought that far ahead yet." Still clutching his jeans, she approached the bed, where he stood half leaning, half sitting on its edge. "I'm still back here in the 'let's have a torrid affair' stage. Can we do that for a while?"

His frown deepened, and he was silent for a moment. A long, long moment. Finally, he said, "How long?"

She smiled tremulously. "Oh, I think we'll know when it's time to move on from there."

Except they wouldn't be moving to the next level of intimacy and commitment. He'd be moving on alone, his guilt and fear having subsided. Her heart ached at the thought, but she had no intention of letting the inevitable parting rob her of the joy she could have today.

He searched her eyes a moment, but seemed satisfied with what he saw there. "Okay," he agreed. "We'll do it your way. *For now.*"

The way he said those last two words made her heart quake again with possibilities, but she brought it under control quickly.

"Come on, then. Let's get you dressed."

⚜

Tommy allowed her to help him dress and help him into the wheel-chair. He allowed her to push his chair out into the ER waiting room, where they picked up Dillon and Rachel. He allowed her to help him into the car, then out again at his place. After Dillon and Rachel disappeared into Paige's apartment — no doubt to do some serious necking — he let her help him into his unit and up the stairs to his bedroom.

The drugs they'd given him had started to wear off, and he could already tell he was going to feel like dog meat in about forty minutes. Still, when he sank onto his bed, nothing could have stopped him from pulling her down with him. This time, there was no talking. No sultry torment, no playfulness, no laughter. Just pure, burning need, coupled with an acute, painful joy at being alive.

In the aftermath of their lovemaking, he held her shuddering body next to his and knew with complete certainty that she loved him. With every sobbing breath, with every gliding touch of her small, white hands, every heavy thud of her heart, she'd told him so.

But she wasn't ready to say it. She didn't believe in him, didn't think he could be constant. And who could blame her? He'd done nothing but embody the antithesis of husband material. She'd be crazy not to have reservations.

But goddamn it, he wasn't his father.

Even as the thought flashed through his brain, the truth of it reverberated inside him.

No, he wasn't his father. He wasn't *anything* like that old bastard. He was more like his mother. Just as Mama had been a one-man woman — God help her, there'd been no one for her but his faithless, lying father — he was very much afraid he was a one-woman man. Maybe he'd always known it. Maybe that was why intimacy had always scared the bejesus out of him. On some level, he'd known it was game over if he committed his heart.

Well, he could forget about *if*. The worst was done. He'd committed the damn thing. Rusty and untried as it was, his heart was effectively hers. Now, all he had to do was convince Paige of that.

He grinned at the thought. Yeah, she might be skeptical, but she had no idea how single-minded he could be when he wanted something. All she'd ever seen was the apathetic Tommy. The self-defined invalid. The pity-party guest of honor who just wanted to be left alone so he could go back to licking his wounds.

But he wanted something now. He wanted *her*. Hell, he wanted it all — marriage, kids, the whole shooting match.

She nestled closer, settling herself against him softly in a way that spared his injury. And damned if his leg didn't feel better.

"That was .... God, I don't even know if there's a word for it. It was ... exquisite."

He smiled into her hair, thinking about the days that stretched out ahead of them. "Paige, honey, you ain't seen nothin' yet."

Chapter 18

P AIGE WATCHED TOMMY CONVERSING with Grace Morgan, Ray's beautiful wife. If she didn't know he was giving the newspaperwoman an interview for a feature article on his new German Shepherd breeding kennel and K9 training facility he'd established on this sprawling property just outside of town, she'd be seriously jealous.

No. No, she wouldn't.

Her lips curved into a smile as he glanced up and caught her eye. As always, it gave her a jolt to see him looking at her with those eyes, as though she were the only woman he could see. She thought it would run its course, this attraction between them, but nearly eight months later, he could still make her blood leap with one look. Hard as she found it to believe, she clearly did the same for him.

Oh, Lord, he was killing her! How was she supposed to keep her expectations under control when he looked at her like that?

She'd known from the outset that Tommy Godsoe was a veritable roller coaster ride. Indeed, a number of women had actually seen fit to warn her. He was a midway ride, exhilarating as hell, but he took you nowhere. He'd thrill you, steal your breath away, then spit you out at the end of the ride, right back where you'd started from. And there you'd be, wondering if you had enough emotional capital to stand in line for another ticket.

Except *that* Tommy had never materialized. He'd been nothing but focused, on her and on rebuilding his life.

"Hey, Mrs. H."

Paige turned to greet Rachel, who looked fantastic on Dillon's arm.

"You made it."

"You think I'd miss Tommy's big day?"

"Of course not." She hugged Rachel and gave Dillon a peck on the cheek.

"Omigod, look how well he's getting around!"

Paige turned to see Tommy leading a group of off-duty patrol officers toward the indoor kennels where two females nursed new litters. She turned back to Rachel. "It has been a while since you were home, hasn't it?"

"Three weeks and four days," Dillon supplied.

Rachel laughed. "No, *you* came to *me* that time. It's been almost eight weeks since I've been back here."

Both of them had committed to focusing on their studies, making do with electronic communications between the monthly visits. Paige was so proud of them.

"He's done so well," Paige said. "His physiotherapist can hardly believe the progress he's made."

"Guess he just needed a little motivation, huh?" Rachel said.

"He needed an anchor."

At his quiet words, both Paige and Rachel turned surprised eyes on Dillon, who blushed.

"Hey, come on. I think I know a little something about losing your direction and needing some help getting it back."

Tommy and his friends emerged from the barn that served as a kennel, and Paige's gaze went to him automatically. He still walked with a noticeable limp, but he no longer needed the cane. And when he worked particularly hard laying a scent trail or working a dog, he still had pain at night. She knew he always would. But he never complained about his discomfort. He just took a couple of Ibuprofen and tried to talk her into the whirlpool bath he'd had installed in the old farmhouse.

He'd also asked her to marry him at least once a month since that first time. And he never complained when she stalled him yet again.

She knew he was disappointed each time; she could see it in his eyes. But what she also saw in those baby blues was patience. He was wearing her down with his slow smile, his easy way with Dillon, his quiet assumption of some of the weight she carried without trying to take control. She'd successfully rebuilt her business in the months since the sabotage, but it had been a lot easier with Tommy at her side.

Oh, man, how could she hold out against that?

More to the point, why was she even trying?

Tommy broke away from the knot of men, who looked like they were deeply embroiled in shop talk.

"Dillon, go show Rachel the new puppies."

"Huh? Shouldn't we say hi to Tommy first?"

Rachel must have caught something in Paige's voice, or maybe seen the way she was looking at Tommy, because she tugged Dillon's arm, rolling her eyes at his obtuseness. "Come on, Einstein, show me the puppies."

Tommy reached her a moment later, sliding an arm around her in an easy display of affection she once would have thought was completely beyond him, at least in a public environment. She returned his hug, tipping he face up for a quick kiss.

"Hey, didn't I see Dillon and Rachel?"

"I sent them off to the barn to see the pups."

He pulled back, cocking an eyebrow. "You *sent* them? As in, wanting to get rid of them?"

"Yeah, I didn't want any wisecracks from the peanut gallery when I asked you to marry me."

His face went blank. "*You're* asking *me* to marry you?"

She blinked back tears. "Hey, if you're tempted to turn me down eight or nine times before you accept, I'll totally understand. I mean, it would only be fair. Just so you know I'm not going to stop ask—"

Her words were cut off by his kiss, fierce and triumphant.

When he let her breathe again, she said, "Was that a yes?"

His laugh rang out, clear and joyous. "Baby, that's a *hell*, yes."

⁂

Message from the Author

Thank you for investing your time — that most precious of commodities — in my book! If you enjoyed *Protecting Paige*, I would be thrilled if you could help me buzz it. You can do this by:

Recommending it. Help other readers find this book by recommending it to friends, readers' groups and discussion boards.

Reviewing it. Please share with other readers what you liked about this book by reviewing it wherever you purchased it, or at readers' sites such as Goodreads. If you do choose to review it, I would be delighted to gift you with an electronic copy of your choice of any of my other titles. Simply email me to alert me to your review and let me know which one of my books you would like to have and in what electronic format. My email address is norahwilsonwrites@gmail.com.

Again, thank you for choosing to read my book!

Read on for an exclusive excerpt from *The Merzetti Effect: a Vampire Romance.*

Also available from Norah Wilson:

Sensual Romantic Suspense
GUARDING SUZANNAH, Book 1 in the Serve and Protect Series
SAVING GRACE, Book 2 in the Serve and Protect Series
NEEDING NITA, a novella in the Serve and Protect Series

Sensual Romantic Suspense w/ Paranormal Element
EVERY BREATH SHE TAKES
(coming 6/19/12 from Montlake Romance)

Sensual Paranormal Romance
THE MERZETTI EFFECT: A Vampire Romance
NIGHTFALL: A Vampire Romance

As N.L. Wilson
(writing partnership of Norah Wilson and Heather Doherty)
Dix Dodd mysteries (humorous)
THE CASE OF THE FLASHING FASHION QUEEN
FAMILY JEWELS
DEATH BY CUDDLE CLUB (coming soon)

As Wilson Doherty
(writing partnership of Norah Wilson and Heather Doherty)
YA Paranormal
THE SUMMONING: Book 1 in the Gatekeepers Series
ASHLYN'S RADIO

About the Author

Norah Wilson lives in Fredericton, New Brunswick with her husband, two adult children, her beloved Rotti-Lab mix Chloe, and numerous rats (the pet kind). Norah has had three of her romantic suspense stories final in the Romance Writers of America's Golden Heart® contest until she sold her first story in 2004. She was also the winner of Dorchester Publishing's New Voice in Romance contest in 2003.

Norah loves to hear from readers!

Connect with Her Online:

Twitter: http://twitter.com/norah_wilson
Facebook: http://www.facebook.com/#!/profile.php?id=1053773212
Goodreads:
http://www.goodreads.com/author/show/1361508.Norah_Wilson
Norah's Website: http://www.norahwilsonwrites.com
Wilson Doherty's Website: http://www.writersgrimoire.com

Excerpt from The Merzetti Effect
(A Vampire Romance)
Copyright © 2011 by Norah Wilson

Delano Bowen has been a medical doctor for a very long time. More than 170 years, in fact. For much of that time, he's been searching for a way to reverse the curse foisted on him by a vampress who sought to own him. With the emergence of medical technology, he now also aims to develop a vaccine to protect the vulnerable from predation by rogue vampires. After a century of searching, he thinks he's found the key to his vaccine – a surviving descendent of the Merzetti family. The Merzettis were virtually hunted to extinction over the years by rogue vampires who feared the anti-vampirism properties in their blood.

A foundling, nurse Ainsley Crawford has no idea that she carries a genetic gift, and Delano aims to keep it that way. He must keep her close, and ignorant, for he can leave nothing to chance. He manipulates events to ensure her unwitting cooperation. But when Delano's arch enemy Radak Janecek mounts an all-out assault to destroy Delano and the fruits of his research, Delano is forced to draw Ainsley even closer to protect her. Inevitably, the attraction that has sparked between them from the first flares hot and urgent. Ainsley sees no reason why that attraction shouldn't be consummated, but Delano knows succumbing to it is not just ill-advised; it could literally be the death of him.

The Merzetti Effect

AINSLEY CRAWFORD STEERED HER 1993 Crown Vic to the empty curb, wincing at the ugly crunching sounds her power steering made as she cranked the wheel. Great. Fluid must be leaking again. She needed another repair bill like she needed a bladder infection.

What she should do is dump the old boat and get something smaller, something easier on gas and maybe with a bit of warranty left so she wouldn't have to pour money into it so regularly. Of course, if she ever wanted a new car, she was going to have to learn to keep her mouth shut.

Right. Like *that* was gonna happen. She'd pretty much sabotaged her prospects when she'd reported that handsome anesthetist who was dipping into the anesthetic agent, shortchanging patients in the process. Although the situation was dealt with promptly and appropriately, it turned out no one liked a whistle-blower.

Well, at least she had a lead on a new job. A better-paying one, even, and God knew she needed the money. Lucy and Devon were depending on her, maybe for their very lives.

Which was why she was here. Except *here* looked pretty creepy. She glanced around, reluctant to kill her engine or release her door locks.

Okay, not *creepy*, exactly. It was a respectable enough commercial zone; not a slum by any stretch of the imagination. And she'd lived here in St. Cloud, New Brunswick long enough to know she was less than three or four blocks from the club district, which would be hopping even on a Wednesday night, so it wasn't like she was in the middle of nowhere. But the quiet buildings gave off a different vibe once they were abandoned for the night.

Beneath the streetlights, the empty avenue shone after the warm August rain.

Ainsley turned off the ignition and the engine stuttered and coughed to a stop. The *tic-tic-tic* of her cooling motor sounded overly loud in the ensuing silence. Then the rain started up again, drowning out other sounds. Raindrops pattered on the car's roof and smeared her view of the urban landscape, intensifying her sense of isolation.

Before the cast of her thoughts could get gloomier, she grabbed her umbrella from the passenger seat and shouldered her door open. She fumbled with the umbrella a moment to get it open, then stepped out into the night. Closing the Crown Vic's door, she peered around. Not a soul moved on the street. Though lights burned in the office building windows, she knew they were deserted.

Well, mostly deserted. Her prospective employer, Dr. Delano Bowen, waited for her in one of them.

She'd balked when he'd asked for an evening interview, and his warm-whiskey voice had cooled over the telephone line. He had a conference to attend in San Francisco, he'd informed her, and he intended to fill the position before he left, one way or another. Desperate as she was for the job, she'd agreed to the nighttime interview.

Of course, that hadn't stopped her from checking him out. If the research sponsor, a major bio-medical company, hadn't confirmed his claims, she'd have cancelled. But he had checked out. According to Bio-Sys Genomix, he was analyzing the DNA of individuals afflicted with a particular blood disorder in the hopes of unlocking a cure.

What he needed, he'd said, was a cross between a phlebotomist to draw blood, a research assistant to help with his investigations, and a secretary to deal with the paperwork.

She stood there a moment, rain spattering up on her legs as she contemplated her utter lack of experience in the foregoing areas. But dammit, eight years as an OR nurse in a Level One trauma center had to count for something.

She pulled the folded piece of paper out of her purse and checked the address again – 420 St-Laurent Street – compared it with the number on the closest building, then headed west. Shouldn't be more than a half a block.

As it turned out, it was more like a block and a half, which carried her closer to the club district than she'd expected. The rain fell harder and she picked up her pace, cursing. Her low-heeled leather pumps were going to be ruined. She dashed up the walkway to the building's front door and tried to yank it open, but it didn't give. Another tug. Locked.

Great. She glanced around for a buzzer, but instead found a note taped to the glass door from the inside.

Ms. Crawford. My apologies. Please use the entrance at the back of the building.

Freaking wonderful.

She backtracked to the sidewalk and dashed westward, stopping at the alley running between Dr. Bowen's building and the next building. The lane was narrow, barely wide enough for a single vehicle to pass. It was also liberally spotted with puddles. Her shoes would be ruined for sure if she slogged through that.

Maybe she'd be risking more than her shoes.

The thought sent a jitter of uneasiness through her. She glanced around quickly. Nothing moved on St-Laurent. She looked back down the alley. At the midway point, a single security light mounted on the brick facing of the adjacent building cast enough light to show the alley was empty. No nooks or crannies for an assailant to jump out of; no doorways, no garbage bins for them to hide behind.

So why were the hairs on the back of her neck lifting?

She chewed her lip a moment, then made her decision. She had Dr. Bowen's phone number on the paper in her purse. She'd dash to the nearest bar and use a payphone to call him. If he still wanted to do the interview, he could damned well meet her at the mouth of the alley to escort her into the building. Or better still, in whatever warm, dry pub she found from which to make the call.

She turned to continue up St-Laurent, but a blur of motion caught her eye. She swiveled toward it.

A man, black clothing and a white blur for a face. Where had he come from? Before she could so much as gasp her surprise he was on her, pushing her into the alley.

She brought the umbrella down, intending to defend herself with it, but he was too fast. He squeezed her wrist in a grip that shot paralyzing pain up to her elbow. She dropped the umbrella. And then he was driving her deeper into the alley, bearing her along as though her resistance presented no more challenge than a feather.

Crackhead. Had to be. No ordinary man had that kind of strength. Fear surged as she remembered the one she'd seen in the ER last month. Out of his mind on a dose of crystal meth that should have killed him, he'd shaken off three cops like they weighed no more than dandruff on his shoulders.

She gathered her breath to scream, but again he was too quick. He clamped a hand over her mouth and slammed her against the unyielding brick wall. Tears leapt to her eyes, blurring her vision.

Think.

Resistance was likely to get her killed.

Reasoning was out of the question.

Cooperation … . He probably just wanted money. For these guys, it was all about feeding the habit, buying more gack to snort up his nose or shoot into his veins.

Her right hand dropped to her purse, which was still slung over her shoulder. She pushed it toward him. "Take it." She mumbled the words out against his palm, hoping he'd understand. "Money. Take it."

His lips curved with real amusement, which stirred a far deeper fear than had his physical attack. For the first time, she looked closely at his face. His eyes gleamed an eerie yellow-gold under the security light. They were most definitely not the eyes of a hopped-up junkie.

"It's not your money I want."

Oh, God. She was going to be raped in a rainy alley while everyone huddled indoors where it was warm and dry. Where they wouldn't hear her cries.

"No, sweetheart, I don't want that, either."

His lips parted on a smile and her gaze dropped to his bared teeth. As soon as she saw his incisors, she knew what he did want. Her rational mind rebelled against the truth, but her blood knew. Her pulse leapt into overdrive.

"No!"

The word was smothered against his hand. He angled her neck and sank his teeth deep into her throat. She felt the pierce of his grossly elongated incisors like the hot stab of IV needles. Adrenaline arced through her, lending her strength as she fought him, but she might as well have tried to knock down the brick wall at her back.

On and on she struggled, but he clung to her, oblivious of her efforts. But he didn't seem to be doing much more than just hanging on. Why wasn't he sucking or otherwise working the wound? Wasn't that what vampires did? Or did they tear throats out and lap the blood?

She shivered. God, she was so cold . . . .

Cold. Blood loss. Shock!

Oh, shit, she was going into *shock*.

Goddammit, he'd pierced her carotid artery. He was letting her own thundering heart pump the lifeblood out of her. A bubble of hysterical laughter rose in her chest at the irony.

Seconds later, she sagged against the building, mirth – and strength – gone. Only his weight against her held her upright.

A violent tremor shook her. *Cold.* She was going to die here in this alley.

And her shoes were ruined.

Then, miraculously, he released her. She crumpled to the wet asphalt. Dear God, she was so cold. Was she dead?

No, not yet. If she were dead, she wouldn't feel the cold rain or the hot abrasion of the asphalt on her hands and knees.

So why had he left her?

She managed to lift her head to peer through the driving rain, searching for her assailant. There, deeper in the alley. And dear God, he was locked in combat with another man! A man who must have pulled the creature off her.

She wanted to shout, to warn her would-be savior that he wasn't dealing with your average thug, but her vision wobbled. Feeling oddly detached, she put a hand to her throat and it came away red. The rain quickly washed her hand clean, but a downward glance confirmed she was still bleeding. Her tan trench coat was streaked with red.

Oh, man, she was tired. More than anything, she wanted to lie down. She wanted to just curl into herself and let the hovering blackness take her. But the man who'd tried to save her … the Good Samaritan … if she didn't get help, he'd die.

She pushed herself to her feet and stumbled toward the mouth of the alley, one hand pressed to her neck to try to stem her bleeding and the other pressed against the building's wall to keep herself upright. She'd lost one shoe, so she kicked the other one off. Almost there.

Then the world started to swim. She blinked and blinked, but the blurriness refused to clear. She found herself on the ground again, felt the asphalt burn her already scraped knees. Then the same abrasive surface kissed her cheek as she pitched face-first onto the street.

Too late, Ainsley. As usual. You're nobody's savior.

⁂

Delano Bowen watched the beaten vampire's retreat long enough to be certain the creature was really leaving. He expelled his breath. *Thank God.* It had been close. For a moment, he'd thought he was going to have to destroy it. Black-hearted devil hadn't wanted to give up his kill.

Well, they'd soon see who killed whom.

And speaking of dying, he'd better see to the woman before she succumbed to shock. He strode to the mouth of the alley where she lay crumpled on the wet asphalt. Kneeling, he rolled her over, bent close and deftly arrested her bleeding. He drew away from her to find that her eyes had fluttered open.

"It's okay," he said. "I've got you. You're going to be all right."

The assurance seemed good enough for her, for she slipped back into unconsciousness. He gathered her into his arms and stood.

"Come on, Ainsley Crawford. We have work to do."

⚜

Hot sex.

No, not just *hot* sex. Incredibly erotic, deliciously forbidden *stranger* sex.

Ainsley knew it was a dream. Knew it wasn't really happening. But dear God, it was good. And it felt so damned real. She could almost smell him, musky and male and incredibly arousing . . . .

A small sound tugged at her awareness, but she clung to sleep. She wanted to stay in the dream, wanted the stranger to keep on stroking and licking and sucking her as her hands clenched in his hair. She wanted him to keep his mouth on her intimate flesh, his hands on her body. Just a few minutes more . . . .

Then the sound came again. A beeping. Familiar but wrong. Out of place in the dream. What the hell was it? It sounded like a . . . oh, hell, a monitor alarm!

She came awake with a start.

The first thing she saw was the bedrail on the left side. Then the IV pole with the suspended bag of deep-red fluid. She glanced down to see an IV line disappearing into her arm.

Holy shit. She was in hospital. And the beeping *was* a monitor. It blinked at her from its position right beside the IV pole.

Glancing at her hand, she saw the pulse oximeter had slipped off her finger. She slid the clothespin-like device back on and the beeping stopped. A quick glance at the monitor showed her oxygen saturation was okay.

Oh, man, she was really in hospital? Being *transfused*?

She pressed her legs together beneath the blankets, and the last traces of arousal from her sex dream withered. Urinary catheter. *Ugh*. She was definitely being transfused. But why?

Omigod, the alley! Heart suddenly hammering, she struggled to sit up.

"Ah, you're awake. That's good."

She yelped, more at the unexpected hand on her shoulder urging her back against the pillows than at the masculine voice from the right side of her bed.

"Easy. You're safe now. I'm a doctor."

Her gaze locked on him and she let out a gasp.

It was *him*. The man she'd been imagining, the stranger/lover.

Okay, she was still dreaming. She must be. How else could she have conjured him to look exactly like the man in her dream?

Then another thought struck her: *maybe she was dead*.

Maybe she never escaped the alley after all. Maybe her lifeless body lay there still in a blood-darkened puddle, and this vision, this whole hospital-room encounter, was just the result of her oxygen-starved brain dying.

She closed her eyes for a second and reopened them. The man beside her remained unchanged. Shoulder length black hair, glossy under the lights, sprang back from a widow's peak. Behind the lenses of Italian designer frames, dark brown eyes glowed like banked coals under heavy, slashing eyebrows. Dark, intense, sexy.

She started to lift a hand, thinking to touch his face to test if he were flesh and bone, but – *ow, ow, ow* – was quickly reminded that her arm had been harpooned with an IV catheter.

Okay, so it looked like she hadn't dreamed him, she wasn't dead, and she really was being transfused. So she had to be in hospital. But oh, baby, if this was the ER, this guy was new to the rotation.

"Where am I?"

"You're under my care, and you're currently being treated for blood loss and shock."

Blood loss.

She shivered convulsively. The alley. A creature straight out of her nightmares had attacked her, driven his teeth deep into her neck and –

No!

Her mind shied away from the memory. Better to stick with the rational, the world she knew. Medicine.

Her gaze flicked back to the IV pole. "Whole blood?"

"Yes."

"How much have I had?"

"We're coming up on 2000 mls."

She felt her face go slack. "So much?"

"By my estimate, you'd lost almost forty percent of your blood, Miss Crawford."

Holy Hannah. Her gaze leapt back to the unit of blood suspended from the IV pole, her brain ticking at a hundred miles an hour. "Then you wouldn't have had time to crossmatch the blood …."

"It's perfectly crossmatched."

She blinked. How'd he manage that feat? With this kind of blood loss, they usually started pushing the O-neg while they waited for typing and crossmatching, switching to the precise match as soon as they had the info. In any case, if they'd pushed that much blood, her coagulation factors would almost certainly be out of whack ….

She lifted her right hand – carefully this time – to her neck, only to find her puncture wounds covered by a dressing. She clapped her gaze back on the hunky doctor who sat so quietly at her bedside. The doctor who in her dreams had blazed a trail of kisses down her body ….

She blinked the image away, cleared her throat and asked, "What about the possibility of a bleed?"

He lifted a dark eyebrow. "You know your transfusion medicine."

"I should. I'm an OR nurse."

"Indeed." The corner of his mouth lifted in what might have been a smile, but he obligingly ran down the numbers – hemoglobin, platelet count and the rest. "Based on what I'm seeing, I don't think we'll have to worry, but we'll keep monitoring the situation."

Okay, so she seemed to be out of immediate peril. Time to tackle the hard stuff.

"How'd I get here?"

One beat, two, three, as though he were weighing how much to tell her.

"I brought you."

"*You* brought me?"

"Yes. I was there, in the alley. I saw the attack."

"No." The denial emerged on an exhalation. She wasn't even sure what she was denying.

"Yes. I witnessed it. I saw that creature attack you."

Her heart started banging again. A man fiercely grappling with her attacker. A black-haired man.

"You were there." A statement, not a question. She remembered now. And she remembered something else.

His was the face she'd seen when she'd surfaced from that cold hell she thought was death. Then she remembered what had wakened her from that icy place – his mouth, hot on her bare throat, like a lover's.

No. No way. It hadn't happened. It couldn't have. Just a dream, like the other one.

She wet her lips. "Where are we?" Lifting her head, she scanned the room. No nurses came and went. Nothing fit her experience with various wards at the hospital. "This isn't the Regional."

"You are in my home. But I assure you it is as well equipped as your hospital to deal with your particular emergency. Better equipped, in fact."

This was his *home*? It looked more like a trauma treatment room. And how freaky was it that he'd brought her here to treat her? *Scary*-freaky. Fear warred with anger. By the slimmest margin, the latter won.

"I can see for myself that you're well equipped. My question would be, *why*? And while we're at it, why didn't you call an ambulance to take me to the emergency room? That would be the logical response."

Those glowing eyes narrowed to dark slits. "And what would you have told them at your ER, Nurse Crawford?"

She lifted her chin. "That I'd been attacked by . . . ."

"A vampire?" he finished.

"Yes! You know I'm telling the truth. You were there. You saw it."

He didn't move so much as a muscle, but for all his stillness, he emitted an odd leashed energy. It poured off him in waves so potent, she could almost imagine she saw an aura of energy surrounding him.

"Indeed I did witness it. But the ER staff who would have attended you weren't there. They didn't see it."

"You could have hung around and explained."

His lips turned up at the corners in a flash of amusement that was gone so quickly she wondered if she imagined it. "Yes, I suppose I could have given them the *Readers' Digest* version of events, but I rather value my professional reputation."

"Okay, yes, they'd be skeptical in the extreme, until they'd seen *this*." She lifted a hand to her throat, where she could still feel the pain of her wounds beneath the bandage.

"Remove the dressing."

She blinked. "What?"

He opened the drawer on her bedside table and extracted a hand mirror, which he offered to her. "Remove the dressing and have a look."

Panic flared. Did she really want to view those puncture marks? She knew the attack had happened. She remembered it in horrifying detail. But to look on her wounds would make the proof of it incontrovertible. If she looked in the mirror, she couldn't then decide she'd dreamed it. She couldn't then conclude, for the sake of preserving her own sanity, that she'd had some kind of psychotic break.

"Not up to it? I see." He started to return the mirror to the drawer.

"Give it to me."

"Are you sure?"

Her answer was to peel the adhesive dressing away with one swift motion.

"So be it."

She accepted the mirror from him, angling it to get a look at the puncture marks. Once again, her pulse skyrocketed. The skin of her throat was smooth and unbroken, with nothing but some faint bruising and some redness from the adhesive removal to suggest any kind of trauma.

Impossible.

She put a hand to her throat, running her fingers over the area to confirm what her eyes had already told her. Sweet Jesus.

"You see why the medical staff at the hospital might question your story?"

"But how? I was bitten .... I can still feel the burn. Where did the puncture marks go?"

Behind the lenses of his glasses, his eyes seemed to blaze even stronger than before. "These creatures cover their tracks by infusing their victims with a substance that promotes coagulation. It's similar to the MPH beads you might use in surgery to stem a bad bleed, but it also promotes ultra-rapid healing of the wound."

She laughed, a choked sound that bordered on weeping, which God knew was closer to what she felt like doing.

"You're telling me vampires walk around with Bleed-X in their pockets, ready to sprinkle it on their victims' wounds afterward?"

"They secrete the substance at will." He pried the mirror out of her hand and put it back in the drawer. "Of course, the victim of an attack like this typically expires from shock shortly after the evidence fades."

"Well, that must give the Coroner's Office fits on cause of death." She heard her own words and marveled at how reassuringly sarcastic they sounded. Was she really having this conversation with this stranger about *vampires*?

He shrugged. "Occasionally. Though many victims are street people – drug addicts, prostitutes, vagrants, runaways. No one investigates too closely when one of them turns up dead."

The truth of the latter statement was undeniable. She'd seen for herself the ease with which street deaths were accepted. She'd even protested it. Until the business with Lucy. Until she decided she couldn't afford to make waves over something she wasn't going to be able to change anyway.

She forced her numb mind to work. "I still don't understand why you brought me here. Why not call an ambulance and let someone else worry about it?"

"Because, as you must be coming to appreciate, I have a special expertise in these matters that conventional medicine lacks. Indeed, I think it's safe to say I'm alone in my field."

Well, there was something she had no trouble believing.

"Besides," he added, "had you not been coming to meet with me, you would not have suffered the attack. For that, I feel a burden of guilt."

Going to meet him? Then he must be .... "My God."

A smile ghosted over his lips. "No, not God, Ms. Crawford. Though on occasion, I have been accused of harboring a God complex." He offered his hand. "Dr. Delano Bowen."

Printed in Great Britain
by Amazon

19074643R00174